CINDER X BELLA

DAMSELS OF DISTRESS

DAKOTA KROUT

MOUNTAINDALE
PRESS

This book is dedicated to my sister Amber, a star on the rise who won't let others put a limit on her ambition.

PROLOGUE

"How truly *marvelous*," Master Merchant Alaric Vigatori lamented dramatically, slapping his left palm to his forehead while gesticulating wildly with his right. "There go my hopes of returning home after buying fruit in bulk. By the time we make our return trip, all that will be left is overripe *remnants*. Who was in charge of this wagon? You! How do you expect me to pay your wages if I can't even turn a profit!"

Rubbing both hands through his hair, he shook his head and scoped out the land around him. "I bet you all think we're going to make camp here? Two days in a *row*? Well... you might be right. Sometimes these things can't be helped. On the other hand, perhaps they could, if my wife didn't adopt every creature we came across! Look how that turned out... my newest apprentice has burns bad enough that I will need to pay a Healer to mend his flesh. Yet another expense, and even less profit to be made!"

Alaric looked over to Elara, wondering if his complaints would get through to her this time. Unfortunately, she was ignoring him and casually scratching the chin of the ascended beast in the wagon... right *beside* him? The merchant scrambled away, even as Elara skeptically stared at him. "Aw, Boo-

boo, there's always at least *one* issue on every trip. You can't judge everything only by the profit to be made."

"*What* profit?" Alaric snorted derisively while keeping an eye on the smoldering beast. "It's not just an issue. That one is going to be more trouble than he's worth, my sweet Bappy."

"*Boppity*, Alaric! How long have you known my nickname?" Elara gently teased, rolling her eyes at the familiar joke.

"I wish you hadn't brought that *thing* along with us. No matter how you treat them, monsters and beasts start as wild animals. You can never be sure how they will act. Not to mention, who they will hurt."

Just as Alaric was a Merchant by his system-granted class, Elara was an Exotic Beast Enchanter—a highly specialized version of a Beast Tamer. Both of them viewed the world through the lens of their class and skills, which often caused them to disagree on how any given subject should be covered.

Even as Alaric glared, Elara distractedly rubbed the smug little head of the smoldering beast then offered a flattened palm holding a small sweet pepper to the salamander. Complying with her unspoken request, the flaming lizard leaned forward and increased the intensity of its body heat, roasting the vegetable so Elara could pop it in her mouth.

With a winning grin, she looked up at her husband and offered him the next treat. "Want to try? I think I've got this trick fully formed in its mind."

She shifted toward Alaric, and even though he was annoyed, the man couldn't help but let his scowl fade. Elara was dressed comfortably, wearing cloth pants and a loose-fitting tan blouse to hide the dust of the road. As she waited with her hand outstretched, her head slightly tilted as she tried to catch his eye. The sun hit her golden curls, and the merchant forgot what they were arguing about for a moment.

He took the offered pepper and tossed it in his mouth, grumpily conceding the fact it was rather tasty. "A hot meal is always nice, but training a new beast on the road and not in a secure environment is basically asking for accidents to happen. Even if you're planning to train this one to help some noble's kitchen, right now you are merely cooking with disaster."

"He's just a *baby*. You can't blame little Sigismondo for that accident." Elara's eyes went wide, her mouth pursing into a pout as she tried to convince her money-driven man. "That's his name, by the way."

"Sigismondo the salamander? Bit of a mouthful. Wait, how can you be certain it's a 'he'?" Alaric let out a rueful chuckle despite his resolution to be firmly against this interloper singeing his lace-trimmed seat cushions.

Elara placed another pepper in front of her new pet, a victorious smile pulling at her lips—she knew she'd won the argument, even if her husband wouldn't admit it. "Just a part of my class. I felt his distress, and you know I can't just leave some small creature to suffer, once I know they are there. Besides, he's an extremely *rare* ascended beast. As you said, I'm certain we could sell him to some noble house, or perhaps even gift him to the palace directly, once he's trained. Rumors are that the young Prince has quite a bit of talent with fire, so this would be a well-received pet…"

She trailed off at that moment, knowing Alaric would be trapped in his own mind for a few minutes as he worked out the best profit incentive. A direct sale was always good; he could earn his money and move on. However, such an appropriate gift to the Crown Prince could earn him not just the favor of the crown but *favors* from the crown. Perhaps even tax breaks… or the outright removal of certain tariffs as he moved through the kingdom.

"As for his long name, I'm certain Bella will find him a proper nickname. She seems to have a knack for giving beasts names that stick." Elara chuckled for a moment before her eyes went wide, and she grit her teeth. Exactly as she'd feared, her husband's nostrils flared, and his mind snapped back to the present.

"You keep that *thing* away from our daughter!" Alaric shoved his finger at the small red lizard, who was now curled up and napping on Elara's lap, as if it *hadn't* burned someone's flesh badly enough to require a magical Healer in the last half hour. "I have no intention of allowing you to bring it all the way to our home after this trip. There is a reason we have a small menagerie off-site for training and *safety* purposes. Besides, you don't see me storing all my goods in our house. Why would we continue paying for a proper stone training area if-"

"Boo, you say the same thing every time we come across any new beast!" Elara's frustration seeped into her voice. "Bella loves small creatures! Don't you remember the snake? The griffons, I admit, were a bit large. But she *loves* the goose-"

"You *know* my history with geese."

Elara paused, lips twitching, before finally giving in and tipping her head back to laugh heartily. She reached her hand over and placed it on her husband's lap, trying to comfort and calm him. "You can't hold her back, if this is her path. She's already showing signs of being a Beast Tamer, exactly how I started out. She's not going to have the terrible experiences you used to have before I came around. Think of how much profit properly trained horses have brought you, able to pull your wagons thirty percent farther than your competitors each day. How many caravans do you have going at once now?"

"While I admit there are benefits," Alaric stiffly stated, "Bella has already begun acting in a way not fitting with her station in life. The servants tell me how she goes to the barn, singing and dancing for our beasts of burden. Her maid tells me she refuses to sleep without at least two kittens in bed with her… and on the subject of nicknaming your beasts? They are always childish nicknames, and the creatures tend to answer her call, even when we are trying to get them to listen to us using their *proper* names! While I love what you have been able to do for our family, she is not *you*. We've been able to buy a noble title, land, and have been teaching her etiquette since she could sit upright."

"Where are you going with this?" Elara questioned her husband in a dangerous tone.

"Do you really think a noble child should be practically living the same life as our servants?" Alaric finally spit out the thought that had been on his mind for far too long. "There is an order to these things, and frankly, *any* beast is dangerous. Look at how tiny this creature is, then look at what it did to Jaxon. What if that had been Bella? What if it had burned her face and left behind scars which would preclude her marrying up into higher nobility?"

"You can't judge everything by the profit to be made, Alaric!" The Beast Enchanter shook her head in exasperation as she repeated herself once more. "If the system says this is what she will be best at, if this is the path it gives her in life, we need to respect that! Plus, marrying into *higher* nobility? It's been less than a decade since we were able to purchase a title from the crown. The peerage would never allow it, let alone the King and Queen. Don't let your dreams get too disconnected from reality."

The merchant sucked in a breath, only to let it out in a great puff of air. As the breath left his lungs, his mounting anger seeped out of him. After thinking for a moment, he plaintively shrugged and spoke in a softer tone. "I want more for her than we had."

"We've had it pretty good though, haven't we?" Elara grasped his hand, pulling on him gently until her husband scooted closer and wrapped an arm around her. "Would this be such a bad life for our daughter?"

"I suppose not." Alaric finally admitted, settling into his ruined cushion. "Perhaps what happened with Jaxon has a silver lining. He's all elbows and knees, crashing, bumbling, and fumbling. Perhaps, were he not as green, he would have moved away from the salamander in time for you to intervene."

"He overestimated his abilities and underestimated mine," Elara firmly stated. "Jaxon will heal, and he will have learned a lesson which will stick with him forever. It may well be that he makes a better apprentice going forward, due to this incident. It will be as the system wills."

"You have too much faith in the system." Alaric started the familiar argument between them, though he course-corrected as his wife stiffened next to him. "No matter, no matter. I understand your point. I trust you, and if you find value in the beast... I suppose it can stay."

Recognizing the peace offering for what it was, Elara leaned in and kissed him on the cheek. Then, looking around at the assortment of caravan workers who were waiting for orders, she took a deep breath and stood. "I suppose we should tell them to make camp? By the time the wheel is repaired, our daylight will be gone. I'm sure the Duca wouldn't appreciate us fixing it, only to need to park outside his walls for the whole night. The way some of these people snore, the guard might think they're trying to blow the walls down."

As she spoke, Elara nudged her husband's shoulder and finally got a laugh out of the man. He arched an eyebrow at her, flashing a cocky smile before leaning over and waving at his second-in-command to begin making camp. "I feel it's odd that you waited more than a decade to voice a complaint about my sleeping habits."

"Couldn't risk this cushy life and noble title," she quipped back at him, earning an eye roll from her husband—both of them fully understood she would be perfectly happy sleeping in the woods, not to mention perfectly safe. In fact, the beasts there would likely build her a home and act as impromptu servants, if she so desired.

For the final exchange of gentle squeezing and murmurs, the two separated, and Alaric stepped out to look over the eight wagons in his caravan. As per usual, his own led the way, as it was only half-filled with wares, the rest filled with adequately comfortable sleeping materials.

In his early years, he'd stuffed the wagon to the brim and slept under it. But with his increased status, it wouldn't give the proper indication of his wealth and position if he were to do something so copper-pinching. At any rate, his business had been flourishing over the years, in no small part thanks to his wife's ability to keep their animals well-trained and in excellent condition.

The third, fourth, and fifth wagons were filled with trade goods, but the second was currently housing the two griffons he'd finally convinced his wife to sell off to the Duca's menagerie. They were so close to his own conveyance to ensure Elara could keep an eye on the terrifying things and soothe them as needed with her skills.

Alaric shook his head and gave the second wagon a wide berth as he moved to help with preparations for the evening. "Nasty things, those. Vicious to anyone other than their bond, and they act like seagulls—constant squawking and a disgusting amount of feces to clean each day. Can't get rid of them soon enough for my liking."

The sixth wagon was essentially a small kitchen and currently housed the grown daughter of their main house chef. Giada had taken after her mother and was working on her to become a highly-trained cook, though she would never be as magically gifted at the craft as a proper system-gifted *Chef.* She'd joined the caravan to get some experience cooking in a different environment, as well as making connections on the road for when she set out to seek her own fortune.

Alaric appreciated the better-quality food, but more than

that, was pleased she came at a reduced rate, compared to her highly-skilled mother. "Can't believe she charges twice as much if she has to travel... I'd have to point her out to the guards and warn them there was a bandit on the road if she came with us. Yes, this is better for everyone."

The final wagon didn't belong to the Vigatori merchant house, and this one captivated his attention for a few moments longer. Alaric wasn't certain how he felt about the situation, but only a few days before this trip, Elara's oldest friend, Bibbidy La Fata, had unexpectedly arrived at their home. Bibbidy was practically an enigma to the merchant, being neither young nor old, oddly plain, yet captivating to the eye. She was sharp, both mentally and with her wit, and she refused to hear any argument when she'd made her mind up about something.

Without asking, she had simply *announced* at the last moment that she would be joining them on their journey. All he could do was throw up his hands and loudly question why competing merchants would travel together, and now he could only grumble her response before shaking his head and walking back to look at the wagon undergoing repairs: "'We're not competing. You have multiple caravans; I have one little wagon'. Sure, Bibbidy, *sure*. I swear, if a single customer purchases from her instead of me..."

He let the threat hang in the air unfinished, knowing it was an absurd thing to worry about. Still, as far as the merchant knew, Bibbidy had never been married and had no staff or workers. How she traveled the back roads of the kingdom without being robbed had long been a mystery to him, especially as she made no attempt to hide the fact that she drove a wealthy wagon. The duo of stallions pulling it along were black as midnight and absolutely majestic, trained even better than those in his own caravan. Not only that, she sat sideways on the driver's seat, singing at the top of her lungs the entire day, wearing clothes dyed *royal purple*, of all colors!

"Perhaps they think she is actually some royal, and bandits don't want to call that kind of attention to themselves?" Alaric could only grunt in dissatisfaction at not knowing and drop the subject. The merchant moved over to help hoist his damaged wagon, double checking the placement of the wheel after the original, broken one had been fully removed and the axle re-greased.

Nearly an hour later, just as the sun began to dip below the horizon, the wagon was gently set down, earning a cheer from those who'd been working at it. Alaric looked up, a bright smile on his face, finding his wife walking toward him from their wagon and waving at her as she came closer.

Just then, the new apprentice, Jaxon, came through the gap between wagons two and three, coming face-to-face with Elara. Specifically, his gaze landed on the salamander in her hands, and he hastily lept backward away from the creature that had burned him earlier that day.

Craw-k!

Out of nowhere, a raven swooped at the young man, and the boy twisted away and rolled his ankle on something in the road. The pot of soup he'd been carrying flew from his hands and splashed over the griffons in the second wagon's cage. The near-boiling liquid earned a screech of pain and fury from the proud creatures who had just been doused, and they lunged at the fallen boy, their talons reaching through the cage and swiping at him.

The air filled with shouting as everyone noticed what was going on, but Elara moved fastest, rushing forward to grab at Jaxon—only for him to jerk away as the salamander came close to him once more. The startled lizard let out a splash of flame, burning the extended leg of the larger male griffon, Gregario.

Now absolutely furious, the ascended beast slammed itself against the cage, managing to bend then *break* the bolt holding it closed. The griffon screeched and jumped at Jaxon, but

Elara jumped in the way and activated her skills, doing her best to calm the monstrous cross between a lion and an eagle. Confused, Gregario reared back as its instincts warred with the magic coursing off his trainer.

"Shh, it'll be alright. It's going to be fine…!"

The griffon settled down at the intonation, dropping to all fours and staring at her with an aggrieved expression. It let out a sigh, then started turning as if to return to its wagon. Just then, Gregorio's mate, Gabriella, furious at being covered in soup, leaped out of the wagon over the larger monster, extending both talons to slash at Jaxon.

Instead, the black claws came directly down onto Elara, rending her from neck to navel.

As Alaric's howl of grief tore the night, one person who had been watching from a distance slunk back into the shadows.

"Yes, *yes*. The mission is complete. The stage is set. Yes, *yes*… the daughter will be a perfect fuel. The plan is in *motion!*" the figure cackled as a raven dropped to her shoulder, hunching and staring at her intently before nodding a single time, opening its wings, and flapping away.

CHAPTER
ONE

IsABELLA VIGATORI, known simply as Bella by her father and the servants of the household, had been having a rough time since just before her tenth birthday, when her mother had died. Now, being just shy of *fourteen* years old, her father had increased his expectations of her, putting the young woman in charge of tracking all commitments and deadlines for the household. Yet, to her great frustration, no matter where she looked, she simply couldn't remember where she'd placed her notebook—the only copy she had of the tasks and schedule for the manor.

"There's going to be a visitor two hours after midday, but who is it? If we serve them incorrectly, Father is going to have a *conniption*." Bella frantically opened cupboards and drawers, quickly searching through them and coming up with nothing time and time again. "If it's Sir Pertanlona, he'll be a bit easier. He's over often enough that I know he likes tea cakes, but if it's Matteo Corretto... the Duca's butler likes finger sandwiches and would likely need a room to be made up. Ugh, where *is* it?"

Each of the potential guests had notes written about them, such as Sir Pertanlona's wife becoming sick if she ate certain nuts, and fresh pecan shortbread was on the plan to be served today. Bella moved into the parlor, quickly searching among the many shelves and drawers as she hummed a tune to help calm herself. Moments later, something tickled against her ankle, and she glanced down in annoyance, nearly choking on her song when she saw the adorable mouse who'd run up to listen to her melody.

Sweeping the creature to the side, she quickly shooed him away. As it scurried off, she whispered after it, "Apologies, I didn't mean to call you, little one. Be happy Father didn't see you. I'd hate to have to teach you to avoid the poisons he would put out. It would be disrespectful and unfilial. At least… that's what he would tell me."

Bella continued on her task, grumbling softly under her voice about how strict and severe her father had become over the last few years. "I don't need another lecture about purposefully calling creatures or the dangers of my 'cursed' tamer skills. Seriously, where *is* my notebook?"

As she continued her sweep of the room, her eyes landed on a faded portrait of her mother—a woman who had been known far and wide as a powerful Beast Tamer. Bella couldn't tear her eyes away, studying the perfectly captured, carefree way her mother had held herself. She could practically hear the unbridled, *common-style* laughter the lady had always let fly, and for a long moment, she allowed herself to mourn her.

Then she took a sharp breath and got back to searching. "What an ill match she and Father must have been. She was laughter and excitement, possibility and fun… and he's cold and hard, just like the coins he's always so determined to gather."

As much as she didn't want to admit it, the memory she had of their time together had greatly dimmed over the last several years. Even then, when they'd all been together, her father had always been in the background, setting up plans for what they would be doing through the day. Conversely, her mother would be enchanting animals to do tricks for their entertainment, calling small fish to tickle their feet as they swam or even practicing different roaring cries with Bella as her father watched on with his mouth dropping in horror. In almost all the memories she had, Bella remembered her father hissing at them to act as stuffy as the ladies at court and her mother simply laughing him off.

Just then, the clock struck ten o'clock, and Bella let out a squeal of sheer nerves as she turned and rushed up the stairs. "Only four hours to spare? How am I supposed to figure out this social conundrum if I can't find my abyssal *notebook*! Please be in my bedroom! I know that's unlikely, since I always keep it in the parlor, but perhaps-

"Bella? Is that you?" her father called from his study.

The girl froze on the stairs then whirled around and slowly descended the steps, calling toward the immaculately ordered room. "Yes, Father. Sorry to disturb-"

"Enough of that, come here. I won't be yelling through the house like some... banshee. What's all the ruckus?" Bella could tell by her father's tone that he was stressed, and an excuse would only cause him to take his frustrations out on her with a long-winded lecture. So she made her way to the bottom of the stairs and stepped into the room with him. The master of the house, Alaric, sat at his desk with his papers strewn before him and a frown deeply creasing his brow. "*Well?*"

"I don't know how it happened, Father, but I simply cannot find my..." Bella's voice trailed off as her father slapped his paper to the desk and pulled her notebook out of his drawer. Sputtering in indignation, the teen glared at the notebook, though she got control of her expression a moment later. "What? *Why?*"

"Why do I have this? Come now, you can't expect that this is the first time I've checked up on you. It's merely the first time I forgot to put it back after I finished." Alaric tossed the notebook to her, then he gestured for her to take a seat. He waited for her to reluctantly sit before laying into her with a clipped tone. "As you've clearly *forgotten*, tonight we will be hosting Matteo Corretto. The Duca's butler... if you've forgotten that, as well. Frankly, you should have informed me of his visit a *week* ago, as you have nothing proper to wear for his stay."

"There's still time; I could repurpose some of my old-"

Bella's offer was cut off before she could go any further. "There's no need for you to wear old clothes like some scullery maid. I checked the schedule two weeks ago and made arrangements while waiting for you to catch your mistake and inform me of it. But here we are, the day of, and you have to rely on *my* forethought when I am supposed to be able to rely on yours. That's the whole purpose of giving you responsibilities, Bella. So *you* can be responsible for them. Now, Signor Tobias should be here within the hour with at least two new dresses in the current fashion."

Bella felt no thrill at the new garments, as the gift was coldly offset by the disappointment burrowing into her. She clenched the arms of her chair, head low, as she was unable to meet his gaze. There was a second reason as well, so she could mouth the words of the lecture she'd heard time and again without her father seeing and realizing he was being mocked.

"You're turning into a lovely young woman, and even with all your faults, I'll make sure you will make a fine wife for some young lordling one day. But, for this to happen, you need to focus. You need to look ahead. Living day-to-day is not the noble's way. If you had planned ahead, as I've taught you to do, your ducks would be in a row, and I wouldn't need to be looking over your shoulder to fix your mistakes all the time. Failing to plan is planning to *fail*."

Her father leaned forward, waiting for her reply, but between the frustration of the morning and the invasion of her notes, she sounded off with something that was *absolutely* the wrong thing to say: "Ducks wouldn't exactly be lining up on my command anyway, would they?"

"What. Did. You. Just. Say?" Her father had gone as still as stone, and the words escaping his lips had a sharp chill which made Bella shiver. Still, she straightened in her seat and let her eyes drift to her left arm. A single swipe of her fingers would reveal her class and skills, but she didn't dare to showcase them here. Still, she'd started this argument, and she was going to see it through.

"You heard me. You want me to have my ducks in a row? I could have them jumping into the cooking pot for you! I could herd *cats*. I could be an asset to the family business, but you've refused to let me train or learn from someone who knows what they're doing! Sienna is only eleven years old, and she's already able to heal burns with merely a touch! The kitchen staff loves her, as does anyone who works with fire. But you know what? Yesterday *she* made fun of *me*, because everyone *knows* she has higher level skills than I do. I could be like her, *better* than her, but my talents are going to waste, and I'm stuck-"

"*Enough.*"

Bella's tirade cut off instantly, her teeth **clicking** together, even as she locked glares with her father.

"Be like her? You want to be like *her*? The very thought makes me sick. I'm protecting you, keeping you ladylike and marriageable. You think someone in high society wants to wed a willful Beast Tamer?"

Her father slowly rose to his feet, red-faced and furious, "That curse on your arm won't keep food on the table and a shelter over your head. As soon as I'm convinced you have high enough acumen with other, *proper* skills, we will unlock your Advanced Class at the Class Shrine. So long as the system knows you want to pursue a different path, at least your secondary class will be better suited to you."

"*You* wanted a willful Beast Tamer." Bella was on her feet, all but shouting in his face. "Food on the table? From what I remember, we had meat every day when my *mother* was here. We didn't need to send out for dresses when an important guest was arriving; we were able to simply purchase a new dress whenever we wanted! You weren't so angry all the time, because the horses pulling your wagons worked better, harder, and you earned more money-"

"Then she *died* for it, Isabella," Alaric stated with forced calmness. "Never again will a mindless beast cross my threshold. I will not let there be a chance for a repeat of the incident which cost me my wife. Get out of my office. Go on a walk, and be presentable for the Duca's butler when the time comes."

She didn't move, so he stormed around her desk, gripping her arm and shoving her out of his study, slamming the door behind her. Bella slowly stumbled away, then she raced up the stairs, taking them two at a time before slamming the door of her own room and allowing furious sobbing to burst out of her.

Looking around her well-maintained room, Bella found herself glaring at the closet for being a reminder that she had gotten herself nothing suitable to wear for the guests coming for dinner. With great frustration, she admitted that, without her father planning ahead on her behalf, she would be spending the rest of the time before their guests' arrival cutting up a dress and adding lengths and frills to another, just so she wouldn't embarrass the family.

Glancing down at her current attire, she let out an aggravated sigh. It was suitable for tea, perhaps a lawn game such as croquet. But, as always, dinner attire had higher expectations.

"It's even worse that he's *right*." Even that small concession filled her with nearly overwhelming emotion, so Bella thumped her head against the windowsill and closed her eyes, singing a few broken lines of the lullaby her mother used to sing to her.

"*Sing, sweet nightingale, and someday I'll fly. Fly away with you… free and light and high.*" All of her anger had drained away at this point, leaving only an empty pit in her gut. "Fly away is what I actually want to do. Fly to the Class Shrine to advance my class, to not be trapped in this monotony, always pressured to be a proper lady. If I could fly away, I'd finally be able to do the amazing things Mother did…"

Her thoughts faltered as a clatter of wings made her yelp and jump back, her eyes locking on four birds flapping just outside her window and looking at her quizzically. "Oh, not *now!*"

Opening her window, Bella waved her hand at the birds, who flew away without looking back. She watched them go, angry with herself for wishing she could go with them.

CHAPTER

TWO

WISHING that she were a more dutiful daughter—but only out of fear of being chastised—Bella ensured she took the time to be cleaned up and properly prepared for Signor Tobias' arrival. As he arrived, the young lady kept a smile on her face when selecting her new dress to wear that evening, as she would never purposely embarrass her father, especially in front of company.

While they yelled at each other loud enough for the servants to hear, that was no excuse to do so in front of outsiders. Profusely thanking the tailor for his assistance as well as for personally delivering the dresses, Bella sent Signor Tobias on his way, only then allowing her smile to melt away.

Staring at the gowns now laid out on her bed, Bella ever so slowly began changing and getting ready for the evening, her eyes constantly drifting over to the notebook now placed squarely in the center of her writing table. "It seems my task of running the household has just been a charade this entire time. So… all the duties and tasks I've been assigning would've happened either way?"

She scoffed and pulled the dress on roughly. "No *wonder*

Sienna was making fun of me. Most likely, the *entire* household staff has been laughing at my instructions. When I handed them out, they were merely humoring me on my father's orders, as he gave them those same instructions, or likely, even better ones the night before. He's made me a laughingstock."

Bella tried to tell herself she didn't care, as in truth she loathed the chore in the first place. Frankly, she detested the stately manner, delegating household tasks, and having to be prim and proper. Halfway through getting dressed, she was flushed and sweating from anger, needing to shed the clothing and clean her face before trying again.

"Lo, the house!"

Freezing in surprise for a moment, Bella quickly turned and started dressing as hastily as possible. "The carriage is already here? They're nearly half an hour early! How am I supposed to be pleasant before sitting down for tea?"

As soon as her clothing was in place, and her hair was properly ordered, Bella rushed down the stairs, only to be stopped by the icy glare of her father just before the butler pulled the door open. Slowly, as gracefully as possible, she finished her descent. "I can be nice. Maybe we can just talk about the weather?"

As it turned out, she needn't have worried so much. The Duca's butler was perfectly comfortable allowing her to be seen and not heard. In fact, he barely looked at her his entire visit, addressing all questions and conversation topics solely to her father.

Given how the day had gone, it was a snub that rubbed Isabella the wrong way, and she couldn't help but be sullen over tea. Obviously, this went unnoticed by Matteo, but it greatly distressed her father, who responded by being noticeably tense and over-proper. "Maestro Corretto, perhaps you would favor me with a walk about the grounds whilst my daughter checks on the arrangements for dinner?"

"*Nobile* Alaric, I am a guest in your home! I insist you call me Matteo, or we shall be drawing out conversation for no reason the entire night!" The tall, proper man chuckled as he swirled a glass of wine in one hand. "I'd be more than happy to stroll to erase some of the aches of the day's travel, but perhaps we could circle round to... the cellar at the end of the tour?"

A great amount of relief showing on his face, Alaric gestured Bella away and stood up to direct the tour. "I'd be more than happy to show you our fine vintages... Matteo. Let us away."

Instead of going down to the kitchens, as would likely be expected of her, Bella sulked her way up to the bedroom, pausing only to look in the mirror at the sage green dress she was wearing. With a huff and shake of her head, she tried to move on and ignore the fact that the fabric was doing her skin tone no favors. Smoothing her dress, the young lady sat on the side of her bed and slowly slid until she was prone so she wouldn't wrinkle her new dress.

More out of annoyance than anything else, she whispered a fighting song to give her enough mental energy to tackle the rest of the evening.

"*Rise, rise, warrior! And I will tell the tale of valor, this time of glory and pride!*"

Mice came running from all corners of the house, as she knew they would, as they always did. The sight would infuriate her father for more reasons than one: first of all, because it would show how many vermin had actually infiltrated his domain. Second, she'd been banned from singing ever since she had gained her very first skill upon turning ten and unlocking her Basic Class—known generally as a *child* class.

Even so, it had never stopped her from singing, which had led to her lying to her father and the entire staff for *years*. She claimed that her levels had been stifled, but they'd been steadily increasing in preparation of turning fourteen, when a simple trip a few hours down the road to a Class Shrine would unlock her Advanced Class and the more powerful skills that came with it. Then... when she was eighteen... unlocking her Full Class would give her the final skills the system had determined she earned.

With all the mice watching on, Bella gently trailed her fingers across her arm, willing the system to show how she'd grown. As her skin traced along her forearm, golden words—swirling tattoos placed by the system—appeared and faded as she read, only to be replaced by more until she had finally gone over the entirety of her class and skill details.

Basic Class: Beast Singer
Basic Skill: Animal Communication: Level 10/10.
When vocalizing in a melodic manner, animals can [Perfectly] understand your intentions. Unless you do something to enrage them, non-magical creatures will go out of their way to protect you.

Advanced Skill: Minor Creature Control: Level 3/10.
When communing with non-magical minor creatures—size limit: the tips of your fingers to your elbow in body length, maximum of five pounds—you are able to exert [Rudimentary] control over their actions.

Requirement to advance to level 4: Chain together a series of at least ten commands for an animal under 1 pound in weight, making it successfully learn and complete the desired action smoothly and in the correct order.

Breakthrough Skill: Locked.
Reach Skill level 10 with [Basic Skill] and [Advanced Skill] to unlock!

"You know what? Maybe tonight's the night I finally push to level four-" Footsteps along the wooden hallway just outside her room caused Bella's eyes to flare wide with terror, and she sucked in a sharp breath, waving at all the gathered rodents to scatter and hide. The last of them ducked into the folds of the curtains just before the door flung open, revealing Bella's favorite maid, Mia.

"Signorina Bella? Are you in—oh, there you are! I thought you might need help with your evening dress, but I see you're already prepared." The maid swept a critical eye over her attire, reminding the young lady that, favorite or not, Mia would always be loyal to the person who paid her. If she knew what Bella was up to with singing to her creatures, she would immediately inform her father. "I know you've had a hard day, so I brought a cloth to wash your face and thought I could perhaps redo your hair? There's enough time for it."

Feeling completely spent, Bella reached over and gave Mia's hand a grateful squeeze, then she turned so the maid could begin braiding. After enjoying the relaxing, glorious feeling of someone else preparing her hair, she thanked Mia and descended the stairs in much better spirits.

"You look lovely, Isabella." Her father was waiting at the landing, a slight flush in his cheeks showing that the walk had invigorated him—that, and perhaps a bit too much pre-dinner wine. His formality had mostly vanished, though he escorted her to the dining room and personally pulled her chair out. Both Alaric and Matteo waited until she sat to seat themselves, as was only proper.

Dinner was quickly served. The men immediately began discussing hunting, allowing Bella to focus on her first meal since breakfast. She had nothing to add to the conversation, having never been on a hunt, which she rather appreciated. Her close ties to animals had made the idea of eating meat less appealing, and she'd even tried not eating meat—only for her father to ruthlessly stomp that idea out of her. A week with only meat on her plate had taught her to appreciate a good balance, so she ate with gusto.

Still, the cook knew her habits and liked her. Her plate

always had plenty of vegetables, and there was fish for at least three dinners each week. As she tiredly contemplated her meal, Bella's ears perked up as her father finally asked a question which interested her.

"Matteo, how very rude of me. I never did ask why, exactly, you were headed to the Barony in the first place." Alaric blinked rapidly, clearly having consumed a fair amount of wine, going by how red and splotchy his cheeks were. It was rare for guests to stay for dinner, and the merchant allowed himself to drink even less often. When he did, oftentimes he needed to head to bed earlier than usual.

"No offense taken, none at all, Alaric!" The Duca's butler waved off the question. "You know the Baron's wife is with child, yes? She's due at any moment."

"Are you off to play midwife, then? What a fine set of skills you have." Alaric chuckled, smiling to the side as Bella giggled along at the thought of the overly proper man playing doctor.

"No, no. Nothing nearly so shocking. You see, the Baron's son is also turning ten." Matteo raised an eyebrow and nodded knowingly, "He wants all his staff in attendance, on hand for his wife, but wants to balance this with a celebration of the boy unlocking his Basic Class and first skill. Apparently, the young man already has a way with plants, and the Duchess has been looking for someone of high enough birth to tend her exotic garden. I'm to report back if he has a proper skillset, after offering the young man a sponsorship under the Duca's tutelage."

"Can I come with you, too?" Bella blurted out, feeling nearly as shocked as the others appeared. She backpedaled furiously, but it was too late. "I'm so sorry, I don't-"

"Ahem. Young mistress, that certainly wouldn't be... frankly, it would be unheard of for a butler, a young master, and a young mistress to be traveling without a proper entourage," the butler sputtered, quite put off by her boldness and not seeming to hear her attempt at an apology.

Bella glanced to the side, noting the thunderous expression on her father's face, and decided she had already come this far. "I'm certain there will be guards for the Baron's son, and I'm sure I can secure a proper chaperone? Perhaps our cook wouldn't mind?"

"You expect me to make my own meals, then?" Her father tried to question lightly, though it came off with a slightly too-dangerous tone. "That doesn't seem very polite of you. Her place is here, as is *yours*."

Matteo squinted at Bella, "How old are you, girl?"

Bella blushed, opening her mouth to answer, though her father took control of the conversation with a low voice, "Just shy of fourteen."

The waves of anger roiling off her father caused Bella to slink down in her seat, lowering her eyes. Completely unaware of the by-play, the butler let out a polite chuckle, "Well, see, what reason would you have to come along to the Barony? Oh, you wanted to meet the new baby? Completely understandable. However... I do not think it is in the cards, this time around."

"No, I was hoping to gain the tutelage of-"

"That's *quite* enough, Bella. There is such a thing as pushing too far," Alaric stated without looking at her. "You were neither invited, nor would it be right for you to use your position to force the issue. You seem rather tired, so *perhaps* you should retire for the evening?"

"Don't worry, young miss! If you're just about to reach the important age of fourteen, you should be unlocking your Advanced Class soon. I'll make sure to swing by and see if you have some skills the Duchess would appreciate. Perhaps you could even become a lady-in-waiting someday!" Matteo kindly stated as Bella stood and gave a dispirited curtsy. Seeing her reaction, the butler glanced over at Alaric. "You will be off to the Class Shrine fairly soon, won't you?"

"At some point." Her father calmly tried to avoid the

conversation. "Currently, we are working on building up her managerial skills so as to help her run a household in the future. I've been planning to put it off until she's shown not only interest, but aptitude."

"Oh, I see. I'd worried for a moment you were a follower of the Sect of Scoprire. I'm glad to hear you aren't setting this poor young lady up for failure. I'm certain there aren't many awakening artifacts left undiscovered in our kingdom." At Matteo's words, Bella paused and glanced over, just so happening to meet the butler's eyes, causing him to uncomfortably explain his words. "Apologies, I am referring to a small but unfortunately rapidly growing group of people who believe unlocking their classes at a Class Shrine is too simple. At the ages of fourteen and eighteen, they embark on a quest to find an awakening artifact."

"I didn't even know it was possible to increase your class outside of a Class Shrine." Bella's words caused her father's face to flush red, and he slowly began to stand to shoo her out of the room.

"Ah, I hadn't realized that wasn't common knowledge." The butler took a swig of his wine, noticing the glare being directed from father to daughter and continuing to speak so as to hold off the incumbent awkward silence. "There are three ways, in fact. A Class Shrine is the most common and easy. Finding an awakening artifact is another, though as I mentioned, quite difficult. Other than that, any ruler of a nation can make a direct request to the system to grant you access. Often, the third option is offered by the crown as a mark of favor."

"Thank you for your teachings, Signore. And... goodnight." Bella curtsied once more, this time with much more happiness behind the action. Quickly, she stepped out of the room before anything else happened, though she waited just on the other side to try and calm her rapidly beating heart.

"I know you have *ambition*, Alaric. Though... I certainly

hope you are not holding out in hopes of seeing her blessed by the King? No? The Queen, then? I hope you know how unlikely-"

Bella raced up to her room, a new plan forming in her mind.

THREE

THE NIGHT WAS FILLED with fitful sleep, both from her sudden, shining hope as well as dread filling the pit of her stomach. She knew there would be ramifications for causing her father to be humiliated, but Bella hoped the remainder of the evening had gone well and smoothly after she left. "Perhaps he won't be all *that* angry."

She woke up too early to leave her room and hummed a funeral dirge for herself as she dressed and made herself ready for the day. Letting out a satisfied sigh at the same time her stomach wambled to inform her she'd been awake too long without eating, Bella turned toward the door... and paused. An extremely fluffy mouse was staring at her, trying to understand what she was trying to communicate with her song.

"Hello, Mert. I wasn't calling you, I was only feeling sorry for myself." The mouse scurried a few feet closer, then he sat down and stared up at her, waiting for more. After a moment of contemplation, Bella shrugged and decided now was as good a time as any to practice her skills. Matteo had been planning to leave early this morning, so she decided to give her father another half an hour to decompress before leaving her room and going down. "Let's see if I can teach you to waltz, Mert. Step forward with your left foot, right foot sideways to the right. Left foot to the right foot…"

She began to hum, performing the steps herself to show the rodent how it was done. Watching the tiny creature attempt to follow along was quite comical, and it continuously fell over itself as it tried to complete the orders she was sending into its mind, thanks to her Perfected Animal Communication Basic Skill. "Don't worry, I know you understand what I want you to do. Maybe go and practice those for a while on your own, as I'm quite certain I'll be busy for the entire day."

Mert nodded frantically and scampered away, vanishing in an instant. Bella watched him with amusement before walking to the door and stepping out. "I suppose it's time to face the music. Might as well get it over with."

She glanced down at the faded blue dress she had chosen to wear that morning, once more humming the gallows tune as she descended the stairs, though this time, she specifically imbued the music with the desire for all small creatures to remain hidden. Even so, dozens of tiny pairs of eyes peeked out at her from their hiding spots, which she'd become familiar with over the years. Reaching the landing, Bella rolled her shoulders back, raised her chin slightly, and knocked gently on the door of her father's study.

With her myriad chores, she knew it was possible for her to avoid him for the better part of the morning, but with how dinner had ended, how she had acted, Bella knew she would rather get this over with than spend the day sick to her stomach wondering what her punishment would be. Her father's solemn voice came through the sturdy door immediately.

"Enter."

Trying not to show her fear, Bella twisted the handle and smoothly stepped into the room. It was only as she glimpsed out his window that Bella realized it was a dark, gloomy day outside. The study was even darker, with the fireplace having not yet been lit. Then her father's visage caught her attention, and she couldn't look away. Unlike his usual mannerisms, right now he wasn't finishing his work or fiddling with paper. Instead, he was staring at her, chin over his steepled fingers, as though he were trying to decide what to say.

"Father, I wanted to apologize for my behavior-"

"Not now, Bella. Sit." As she slowly slid into the seat, her father began without further preamble. "As of this morning, I have released both Mia and Henry from our service. They took their daughter with them to find work at the Baron's estate, so you won't need to worry about Sienna's taunts any longer. Signor Corretto generously offered to allow them to travel with him. I'm hopeful this change will allow you to better focus on the tasks I assign you. Now, please *promptly* inform me in the future if any of the servants are speaking above their station, instead of allowing for a repeat offense."

"Father, *please* give me a chance to speak." Bella barely got started before Alaric held up a hand to silence her, though he paused upon realizing she was being polite and motioned for her to continue. "You know I respect your decisions for the household. I *also* believe that, if we do not guide our decisions with compassion, we could find ourselves in a situation which could have been resolved much more easily. Dismissing our servants so abruptly disrupts their lives, but it may impact us even harder."

"That child *mocked* you. For following *my* orders." The lord of the house growled into the gloomy room. "This was a direct attack on my authority, and I'll not stand for insubordination. Not in my house. I have no doubt her words were what led you to lash out at dinner, and now I'm certain it won't happen again. *Will it?*"

"But... that wasn't-"

"*Will. It?*" Her father's hand slapped down on the desk,

and Bella clenched her mouth and shook her head. "Good. Now, do not interrupt me again. I will think on what you've said. You've grown much, Bella... perhaps more than I've realized. You can certainly *argue* eloquently."

Silence stretched between them for a moment, and she looked on with hopeful eyes as his words hung in the air like a dense fog.

"Yet... I don't know if that is a good thing or not. So, until I know for *certain*, there will be some further changes in the house. First, we are now three servants down and would have been four, if Cook hadn't threatened to leave if I sent Giada with them as well. Even so, I've reassigned Giada the younger to tend to the chores outside of the household—Henry's previous responsibilities—and have ordered her not to speak with you. I am done having your head filled with unnecessary children's stories. You are growing into a fine young lady, and it is time you start acting as an adult would."

After waiting a moment to ensure he'd finished speaking, Bella, reeling from the consequences of arguing with her father, finally found a way to ask, "How are we supposed to manage the manor without-"

"You. I noticed your displeasure with me yesterday and how you ignored the rest of your tasks for the day under the assumption that someone else would take care of them for you." Alaric pulled out a paper then a small pen knife, and began sharpening a quill. "It has come to my attention that you have too much time on your hands. Perhaps you have been fixating on things you've been ordered not to? Skills which are beneath your station, perhaps? Well... since you seem to insist upon forging your own path, I will make sure you have very busy hands."

"I *haven't* been..." Bella trailed off, the ring of falsehood in her words clear to even her own ears. Her hands balled up into fists, and she went silent while glaring at him.

"As I thought," Alaric growled without bothering to meet

her eyes. "There are plenty of things around the estate which are beneath your station yet will not bring shame to our household, if you try your hand at them. So long as you are not seen by your peers, that is. To start with, you will complete the dusting, sweeping, and mopping each day. Twice a week, you will clean and press the laundry."

"You *can't* be serious-"

Alaric barreled onward, speaking slightly louder to drown her out. "Each weekday, you will report to the kitchen after dinner and assist Cook in cleaning the dishes. On Saturdays, you will learn to cook. If I find you still have idle hands, we will increase that workload, as needed. Don't forget to keep up with your standard household management tasks in your notebook, or you will have additional duties added on."

Bella stared at her father, jaw having dropped well before he finished speaking. He saw this and shook his head, motioning toward the door. "I hear there is great pride in completing hard work. Perhaps, by the time I return, you will have decided following my orders is a far lesser burden than the tedium of tasks *below your station*."

"You're leaving? How... how long do I have to do this for?"

"I'll be leaving upon the morrow," Alaric stated lightly. "I spoke with Matteo late into the night, and he impressed upon me the need for you to have a maternal guide in these vital years before you reach marriageable age. He blatantly *shilled* the information of a suitable widow a month's ride from here who may be amenable to a union."

"You're leaving to get *married?*" Bella nearly sank to the floor, only her pride refusing to allow her to swoon like some of her peers were known to do. "Father, I'll... I'll listen. Please, don't change our whole lives just because I-"

"*Certainly*. All I need from you is a binding oath to the system that you will renounce your class as a Beast Singer. Perhaps, if I know you no longer have access to the skills I've forbidden, we can put an end to this, instead of disrupting our lives further."

Alaric stared at her, and several minutes passed as Bella's mind furiously worked.

"No? I guess we both have our answer, then. Perhaps the issue we've been having is the fact that there have not been proper consequences for your failings. That ends today. You are dismissed, and I would recommend breaking your fast and getting to work. Sleep will not be allowed until your new duties are completed."

The young woman stepped out of the study, her gaze hollow as she walked toward the kitchen as if marching to the gallows. "No Mia to do my hair, no Sienna or Giada to speak my mind with. I'm meant to do the chores? When am I supposed to find the time to read, sew, paint? If I don't manage those as well, Father will tell me I won't be able to marry well and make my burden even heavier."

Another thought struck her just then. Her father would be gone for at least two months. If she simply ran for it, making her way to a Class Shrine on her own, perhaps she could unlock a powerful skill which would allow her to make her own way in life or gain an apprenticeship under some Meister. "Could I leave it all behind? Or... would one of the servants come after me and drag me back here, kicking and screaming?"

They lived well into the countryside, and a journey to a Class Shrine meant at least a multi-hour ride just to get to a city with a shrine, not to mention getting inside. "Where would I get enough money to pay for access? Maybe they'd just let me sneak in?"

Every Class Shrine was heavily guarded to ensure people with darker bents—such as thieves and the like, who'd twisted the gifts from the system into something villainous—couldn't become even more dangerous and powerful by increasing their class. Anyone who wanted to gain access needed to allow a guard to inspect the status on their arm, as well as offering them a donation so they would take the time to do so. Until now, Bella had always thought this was perfectly acceptable, but now it was working against her.

"Maybe… maybe having a new mother wouldn't be so bad? A *stepmother*, not my mother," she hastily amended as she walked by her mother's portrait, which seemed to be staring at her. "Perhaps Father will be happier? Maybe I don't *need* Mia, in order to have someone who would braid my hair and buy me dresses which work with my skin tone? What if she insists on letting me upgrade my class? If both of us are working together, maybe Father won't be able to say no!"

The happy daydream caused her to hum as she walked along, her steps growing stronger as she approached the kitchen. A few mice ran alongside her, and a bird *smacked* into the window as she passed it. Bella winced at that, but there was nothing she could do about it now. "I suppose I might as well use the time he's gone to put full effort into increasing my skills. I'll *never* renounce my class, no matter how much work I need to do, so I might as well make it as powerful as possible before he figures out what I'm doing."

She had two months before her father would be returning. So much could change in that amount of time, and hopefully it would be more than enough for him to forget his anger. "Even if I'm only a servant in this house for now, I have my room and my own space. Not as many servants means fewer people to report on what I'm doing."

Her mind was made up, so Bella burst into the kitchen with powerful strides, barely remembering in time to send the mice scurrying away. The servants looked over at the noise, startled at the abrupt entrance.

"Aria, I'm here for breakfast, then to learn whatever you have to teach me."

FOUR

THE NEXT TWO and a half months passed without incident, Bella's fourteenth birthday coming and going at the end of summer without being remarked upon—though Cook did make sure to prepare her a special meal. As the master of the house was away, everyone else seemed more at ease, doing their work briskly and quickly so as to be able to find time to relax in the evenings. For Bella, every passing week meant a loosening of the noose she'd felt tightening around her throat.

Aria, now the head maid, was a cold, if pretty woman. She went about her tasks joylessly, rushing Bella to perfect her assigned tasks so she could be rid of the young nuisance. On her first day of her punishment, Bella had apologized to the cook for getting Sienna sent away, only to receive a stern order in reply:

"Apologize to me once you've burned yourself."

As the first Saturday of the week came along, Bella nearly immediately burned herself trying to pull a pan of bread out of the oven, having her wrist brush across the open door. As she held the injury in a pot of cold water, the cook, whose name was *also* Giada, just like her daughter—hence everyone only ever calling her 'Cook'—clucked her tongue and shook her head. "Now you know why you needn't apologize for this, young mistress. Your father has very... shall we say, *intense* feelings, when it comes to the gifts of the system."

The cook paused for a moment, placing a flour-coated finger on Bella's chin and lifting it so their eyes would meet. "Between you and me, your father is very unreasonable about this. We've all seen you trying to follow his demands, but I knew your mother. You have her heart. You should be out in the woods, learning by doing. But, Signore Alaric only knows one way forward. His way. Do your best; it's all any of us *can* do.

For her part, Bella quickly found that she actually enjoyed spending time in the kitchen, at least, after Cook finally decided that losing her young burn-healing apprentice wasn't her fault. As the weeks went by, she had longer and more in-depth conversations with the matronly woman, at least when she wasn't busy preparing food for the staff. Finally, Bella became comfortable enough with her to even be slightly rude.

"Cook?" the young woman ventured nervously as the older woman sat down for the first time all morning. "I know it's terribly impolite to ask this, but... what's your class?"

The woman looked up from her work with a quizzical expression on her face. After a moment, she replied in a tone which made it clear Bella's question had been a foolish one. "Child, I'm a *Cook*."

"Well... I know it's your *job*, but what do the glowing words on your arm say your class is?" Bella spoke haltingly, her face blazing with heat from her embarrassment. "I know it's not something we're supposed to ask, but... I just have no idea what to expect."

"Well, you're about that age, aren't you?" Cook let out a long sigh, tapping her own left arm hesitantly before speaking once more. "Bella, these gifts are just tools to help us be better on our path in life. I'm a Cook, just as my mother was, and her great aunt. My daughter's gift is to be a Storyteller, which is why she was so willing to travel with your father when she was younger. I taught her to cook, but she'll never have the ability to create masterpieces such as I can. Still, being a Storyteller doesn't exactly earn enough for her to make a proper living, which just goes to show that having talents outside of what's given to you by the system is at *least* as important as what it does give you."

Cook paused for a long moment before hesitantly offering an opinion, "I think that's what your father has been trying to teach you all along, in his own way. On that note, I'll thank you very much *not* to use our conversation in an argument with him. He likes the food I make, but not enough that he wouldn't throw me out on my rear if he thought I was turning you against him. Understood?"

"I think I've learned my lesson about fighting with Father." Bella ruefully gestured to her overall disheveled appearance, earning a chuckle from the cook. "So... what does it mean, to have the class of a Cook? Why can't Giada do what you do?"

"Very well, come here and take a look. I hope you understand not to ask someone to do this for you in the future, as some people are secretive enough to immediately start a fight if you ask to know their strengths and weaknesses." Cook held up her index and middle fingers, then ran them along the inside of her left arm.

Basic Class: Joyful Meal-maker
Basic Skill: Meal Assemblage: Level 10/10.
You find joy and fulfillment in creating and preparing a meal. Any kitchen you enter will allow you to locate all tools of your trade [Perfectly].

Advanced Skill: Herbs and Fungi: Level 10/10.
When viewing any herb growing from the ground, you are able to [Perfectly] tell which one is the freshest and most flavorful. On sight, you can [Perfectly] determine what fungi are dangerous or delicious to eat.

Breakthrough Skill: Permanently Locked.

Advanced Class: Rotisseur
Basic Skill: Dairy Determination: Level 10/10.
When viewing dairy products, you can [Perfectly] determine how fresh it is, as well as how long until it will spoil. You are also able to Perfectly determine the best dish to use the dairy in to complement the unique and subtle flavors it provides.

Advanced Skill: Carnitarian Chef: Level 9/10.
When viewing animal flesh, butchered or otherwise, you are able to [Masterfully] determine what is fresh, healthy, and unlikely to make those who consume it sick. Based on the cut, you are able to [Masterfully] determine the best method of preparing the meat to create the best version of the intended meal.

Breakthrough Skill: Permanently Locked.

Full Class: Chef de Partie
Basic Skill: Breads and Pastries: Level 6/10.
If present when items are placed in the oven through the duration of the baking process, breads and pastries will have a [Considerable] likelihood to neither burn, fail to rise, nor fall. The taste will increase [Considerably] from the base taste of the item, matching no matter the personal preference of the person eating them.

Advanced Skill: Locked.
Reach Skill level 10 with Breads and Pastries to unlock!

"Three classes…" Bella jealously murmured as she traced over the golden lines, accidentally tickling the cook. "Why do some of your skills have multiple modifiers? Your breads and pastries one has two, but all of my skills only have one."

"Ah." The slight grin on Cook's face faded, shifting into a wince. "There's no real *proof* of it, but it's said that the more modifiers in any given skill, the higher rarity the skill is for that class. There are many employers who'll only hire people with multiple modifiers, though they will never admit that's the reason for it."

"Oh." Bella swallowed hard, her throat suddenly feeling very dry. "So, if someone wanted to get an apprenticeship…?"

"Multiple modifiers would help, though anyone could get one, if they paid enough. It's just, the more modifiers you have, the more nuanced control you have over your skills. A single modifier is considered the mark of a *common*, low-class skill." The cook turned away, not wanting to see the stricken expression on the young woman's face. "Everything and everyone has their price, as your father well knows. Anyway, now you know what a cook with a Full Class looks like."

"T-thank you, Giada." Bella turned away, holding back tears as she thought of her *common* skill. As she rushed out of the kitchen, she whispered to herself, "No wonder Father never had faith I'd be able to turn it into something worthwhile. All these years, he's been hinting at wanting something more *high class* than I have to offer. He actually meant my *skill*? Not the fact that it's all about working with animals? No… it had to be both."

The days of the long two and a half months passed uneventfully, with her slowly learning to do the chores well enough to escape the cold scrutiny of Aria, eventually even progressing well enough in the kitchen to not burn every meal. Each night, she retreated to her room, singing to the birds and the bats, teaching Mert how to waltz as she practiced her courtly skills of dancing, sewing, and painting.

As the date her father was due back came and went, Bella found herself kneeling on the cool, stone floor of her room, humming her song as she worked with the fluffiest mouse in the house. Though she'd been feeling quite burdened recently, as Bella sang and watched Mert put serious effort behind following her instructions, a gentle warmth began to spread through her chest.

"Good work, little friend!" Bella's voice was soft yet clear as she let the final notes of her song hang in the air. "Let's try this again, just like we practiced. Step forward with your left— exactly like that! Good."

Mert's paws continued to shift back and forth, moving faster as Bella gently corrected him, humming the waltz in a soothing pattern. As her mind drifted away slightly, she found herself thinking over the nature of her Basic Skills. "Why was it so easy for me to reach Perfection with Animal Communication but so hard to improve Minor Creature Control?"

Bella lunged forward, barely managing to catch Mert as he managed a clumsy yet spirited turn. "There you go, keep at it! What was I…? Oh right! What's the real difference, I wonder?"

Juxtaposing the skills allowed her to think through them more clearly, and she started to notice a pattern she hadn't thought of before. "Now that I think about it, Animal Communication isn't about giving commands. It's only about forming connections, trying to understand creatures and making them understand me. Is that why the Advanced skill is so clunky for me? I've never enjoyed giving orders. On that note, I'm not a huge fan of being ordered around, myself."

Bella chuckled softly to herself, her eyes drifting back to the small mouse, who was quivering with what she hoped was effort and not exhaustion. "Thanks for sticking with it, Mert. It's hard not to admire your spirit; in fact, it helps me get through the day. Don't worry, soon you'll be the best dancer at the mouse-querade ball."

For the next few minutes, she continued humming, even as she stepped back and continued getting ready. As she brushed her hair, she danced along to her own melody, imagining the fluffy mouse being as tall as she was, so she could have a proper dance partner. Though the mental image made her giggle, Bella could imagine herself twirling around a ballroom, her fluffy mouse leading her through the steps.

The gentle warmth in her chest, which she'd assumed was just feeling happy for a short while, collected and spread to her arm, a soft light shining off of her limb for a moment. Caught completely off guard by the sudden skill advancement, Bella lifted her hand and swiped her fingers along her arm, reading the message the system had sent.

Skill increase! Minor Creature Control [Level 3 (Rudimentary) → Level 4 (Basic)]!

Requirement to advance to level 5: Control more than one creature under three pounds at a single time, giving each a series of separate tasks each must complete simultaneously.

Slowly lifting her eyes from her arm, she turned and watched with genuine delight as Mert the mouse stepped around a two-inch space, following the pattern of a ballroom waltz better than most young men she'd been forced to dance with. Eyes sparkling, she scooped the mouse into the air as his sides heaved with exertion, beginning to swing him around in happiness, even as he squeaked in alarm. "You *did* it, Mert! You're *fantastic!*"

Setting the mouse down, she allowed him to scamper off as she thought over the amount of effort and practice she'd needed to put into this, and Bella's happiness faded slightly as she analyzed the situation. "Was it so difficult because I haven't been able to spend much focused time doing this, or is it the fact that I don't have a high skill rarity?"

She lifted her chin, a spark of resolve igniting in her eyes as she clenched her jaw. "No! I did this, I *earned* it, and no one can belittle my efforts by calling them *common*. Not even me! My skill might not be exotic, but it's wonderful. Mother had a skill similar to this, and I've never heard anyone *hint* that it was anything out of the ordinary. You know what? I bet she had the exact same rarity I did, and look what she was able to accomplish with it. I'll do even *better*. I'll push it even further, and *no* one is going to stop me."

At that moment, Bella swore a vow to herself that she would push her skills to the utmost, no matter who or what tried to stand in her way. Making sure not to step on any of her friends, she returned to her tasks, feeling lighter and happier than she had in weeks. Just as she settled into her seat and began mixing some of her paints together, a knock came at the door. Without waiting for an answer, Aria poked her head in and motioned for Bella to follow her.

"Signorina Bella, I need you to come downstairs." The strict formality in the maid's voice caused Bella's heart to sink. There was only one reason for such a shift in conversation: her father must be returning. Checking her appearance in the mirror, Bella quickly followed Aria down the stairs, pausing in surprise when she saw a man waiting in the foyer.

"Signore?" she called out questioningly, deciding against closing the distance with the unknown person. "What can House Vigatori do for you, this fine day?"

"Signorina Bella, I presume?" The strange man turned, failing to hide his sneer as he stared down at her. "I am Luca, First Footman of Matringa Treesbane. She and your father have sent me ahead of their retinue to prepare the household for their arrival in three days' time."

Without waiting for a reply, the man marched into the house as if he owned it, vanishing around a corner in moments. Bella and Aria exchanged glances, neither wanting to be the first to break the silence.

Eventually, the younger lady caved. "I hope his attitude isn't what we can expect from the rest of the group?

FIVE

"A DAY'S rest after travel? I'd say that's fair. But *three*? I don't know what sort of effort he's had to put in with his previous employer, but around here, that's downright *lavish*," Aria muttered, not quite under her breath, as she used a rag to angrily buff the family's silver so it would gleam properly. Though she was speaking to Bella, all of her displeasure was aimed at Luca, as the intrusive presence in their household had dominated their one-way conversations since the man's arrival.

Bella glanced askance at the head maid, keeping her mouth firmly closed. She knew the lady didn't truly want an answer. Aria had spoken more to the Beast Singer in the last two days than she had in the nearly three months since Alaric's departure. But whenever Bella tried to weigh in on the subject, she was chastised for speaking negatively about a 'guest'. So, the young woman merely focused on her tasks as Aria vented her frustrations.

"He just... *swans* in and decrees that every chamber must be 'spruced up'? *All* of the rooms? Why? First of all, there's only the two of us to mind the manor after the other servants were dismissed, and Giada began traipsing around the countryside. How are we supposed to air out the rooms, prepare them while also taking care of our normal tasks, and bringing a *peer* his meals on a covered tray?"

The last sentence was nearly snarled as Aria recalled that dinner would soon be prepared. "I'm not going to do it again, I tell you! He calls himself a first footman? More like a layabout! If he's going to be one of us, this falls directly within his duties."

She punctuated the statement by practically *hurling* the silverware back into its drawer. Bella simply bobbed her head, knowing a reply wasn't necessary. At this point, she was a warm body for Aria to focus on as she spoke to herself, nothing more. To be fair, Bella was just as annoyed with the man who had arrived, announced her life would be changing permanently, then sequestered himself in the grandest room he could claim as his own.

They'd been left to their own devices since then, the duo frantically attending to the household, which had fallen into disarray. They had needed to begin their days before dawn, working late into the night to repair, clean, and prepare the five rooms which had been mostly neglected since her mother's passing.

After seeing how much work had been laid out for them, there was only one thought on Bella's mind: she needed to find a way to cheat.

Whenever she could take a task and stay away from Aria, she quickly and quietly would begin singing, weaving her melodies and intent through the air to create a gentle summoning for as many tiny helpers as would answer her call. As per usual, the mice were the easiest to convince, and they rushed to her aid.

Climbing through the walls, they scurried to the top of the chimneys, into, and down them, while clawing loose soot and debris which had collected along the stone; saving her from either having to clamor onto the roof and put herself in a precarious position or getting showered with filth while cleaning it from the inside. Sparrows and other small birds responded as well, fluttering through the windows, which had been tossed open to air out the rooms. They would fly up the chimney or brush through the leavings to remove twigs and chunks of old nests, as their beaks were literally designed for the task.

Seeing how well her first attempt had gone, Bella had become slightly more brazen in her efforts. Instead of carrying the heavy linens down, she tossed them out the window, where dozens of squirrels would catch the sheets or blankets and bring them over to the wash basins for her. If the linen simply needed to have the dust beat out of it, she would toss a corner over the line, then have birds or squirrels grab onto it and pull it down from the other side. As Bella completed task after task faster than the seasoned maid, she found Aria giving her strange looks, though the maid never once commented or asked questions.

"So long as the work is getting done, she won't say a word?" Bella had scoffed at the drastic shift in their relationship—only a few months ago, Aria had been all but openly reporting on Bella to her father. Still, even with the woman clearly being willing to benefit off her efforts, she made sure not to show Aria even a *hint* of disrespect, knowing how fragile the silent truce between them was.

Once everything was cleaned, she still needed to carry everything up by hand, as she didn't have the level of skill required to coordinate the complicated task of returning everything to the rooms. From there, the short remainder of the time was spent sweeping, mopping, dusting, and now, finally, polishing the silver.

"I bet I'll need to reach *Proficient* at the minimum before I could coordinate a dozen birds grabbing onto a blanket and flying it through a second floor window," Bella murmured to herself as Aria continued her spiel about Luca. "Throwing it out the window and having it moved from one spot to another? Sure. Hold on, wouldn't they tear holes in the fabric? I'd need to account for that. Mmm... maybe *Extensive*, when I frame it in that way."

Bella broke from her thoughts, taking a moment to look down at herself and contemplate how things had changed over the last few weeks. The hard work, especially over the last three days, had taken its toll on her body and clothes. Her daily wear gown was filthy and stained with soot, grease, and dirt. Then there were the unmistakable traces of tiny paw prints where small animals had been holding on to her as she walked from room to room. Birds had also been landing on her shoulders, and not all of them had been able to... get outside when needed.

Beyond the filth, her hands were red and raw, several of her nails broken in various spots. A glance at the clock caused Bella to realize her father would be expected within the next hour or so, and she stood to go and make herself presentable. "I'm sorry to need to leave you to do these chores by yourself, but if I don't go prepare, I'm sure my father would be quite displeased."

"At the very least, Luca could've ridden along with another maid, and *she* could have helped out if housework is *beneath* him." The normally icy woman was flushed, and dark circles were evident under her eyes. She reached for a silver platter, clearly having not heard Bella. The young lady coughed loudly into her hand, and Aria paused to blink at her owlishly. "*Excuse* me?"

"I can't meet my father looking like this, certainly not my new stepmother." Bella held up her hands to show how ragged she looked. "If I don't get into the bath, and a new dress, I'll-"

"Oh, *certainly* not. The young mistress *mustn't* look like someone who *works* upon her first impression." Though what she said was accurate, Aria's words held a deep, underlying sarcasm. Then she seemed to realize who she was speaking with: not another servant, no matter how the last few weeks may have felt. "That is… it's good you're working to meet your father's requirements. I'm sorry there's no time for us to heat your bath; you'll just have to hop in."

Bella stepped closer, reaching out a hesitant hand and placing it on the older lady's shoulder. "I know you're tired, and all of this has been rather overwhelming. I truly am sorry to leave you to finish on your own. If it were up to me, I would say this is more than good enough and assure you that everyone would be happy with everything you've accomplished."

"But it's not you." Aria let out a defeated sigh, the rag in her hand slowly stopping in circling and coming to halt. "It's your father and his exacting requirements. You know… Mia sent word a few weeks ago. The baron hired her entire family on and has been lavishing them with praise for their work. They've earned bonuses paid out in *silver*, and she said they even get a day off each week."

A great amount of concern filled Bella at that moment. "You… what are you saying?"

Aria let out a deep sigh, shaking her head and motioning for Bella to leave. "I'm not saying anything. You've impressed me over these last few weeks. I never expected you would rise to the tasks dropped on you like this. Now, get going, or you *know* what the consequences will be!"

Bella waited a long moment, guilt filling her, before rushing away and leaving the woman alone. She hurried up the stairs, quickly sorting through her scant selection of dresses. Truly, the only option was the second gown she'd received from Signore Tobias, though the burnt orange coloration would wash her out. Even so, she rifled through her wardrobe as though a secret, unknown article of clothing would make itself known to her. No such thing happened, so

Bella gave a frustrated kick at the wall, softly singing her annoyance out into the world.

"*Rags and gowns, and nothing in between! The times, they're rich or they're super lean. Now I find myself just kind of stuck… if you could sew, well, then I'd be in luck!*" The last lines had been for the mice who'd immediately begun gathering all around her, and the image in her mind made her laugh. "Mice sewing a dress? You know what? Maybe someday."

After all, she'd been practicing with them as extensively as possible. Now they could dance, somersault, cartwheel, back-flip, and even help her clean. Perhaps, when she got her skill levels high enough, actually sewing might be something she could compel them to do. Before she went too far down that rabbit hole, Bella shook her head and firmly gripped the orange dress. "Today is absolutely *not* the day for experimentation."

She hurried down the stairs, planning on going out back through the servant entrance to get to the bath, but gasped in horror as the door opened. "No, father can't be here already!"

As someone stepped inside, she realized their build was completely wrong to be the Master Merchant. Squinting against the sun, Bella let out a deep sigh of relief as she realized it was Giada the younger, back from acting as a courier for her father.

"Well, you're certainly looking taller and dirtier than the last time I saw you." Giada chuckled as she glanced at Bella over the large box she was carrying in. She had never been one to stand on decorum, not that Bella minded in the slightest. While their age difference meant they weren't particularly close, Giada had known her mother, and she treated the young woman well.

"And you are looking… well-traveled?" Bella countered with an arched eyebrow, clearly scoping out the sunburns on Giada's neck and arms.

"Three months on the road will put some sun on anyone."

Giada swung the box down to the side, dropping it on the ground before stepping forward and pulling the young Beast Singer into a hug. "I met *Nobile* Alaric on the way back, and he sent me ahead with this dress for you. As a warning, he is very focused on his title and wealth right now—I'm certain the lovely lady he is bringing along with him has something to do with that. Make sure to greet them with every ounce of decorum you can manage. Now, we have some time—not much, but some—so I figured I might give you a hand getting this on. But perhaps... you need more help than with just putting it on?"

"Yeah, a bath can only help." Bella rolled her eyes, motioning for the servant to follow her. "I was on my way there already, and I would absolutely *adore* some assistance. How are you at plaiting hair?"

"Better than doing it on your own, most likely." As they quickly walked through the manor, Giada kept sweeping her gaze over the young woman. "Some time without your father looming over you has been good for your health, it seems. You seem stronger... more grown up. I had thought you'd be more lonely than you seem."

"Busy hands make it hard to feel lonely." Bella let out a scoffing laugh. "Father was at least correct about that."

She quickly bathed, washing the signs of hard work off of herself, trimming her fingernails, and using both coarse sand and a harsh bar of lye soap to get the grease off of her skin. After she got out, shivering from the cold, Giada wrapped her in a towel and began working on her hair while Bella dried off and began dressing.

After a few minutes, her hair was complete, and she was dry enough not to leave obvious spots on her new dress. Bella pulled the top off the box, finding a brand new dress, made of soft material. It was brown, quite plain, but suited her well. The darker material fit with the autumn season and would help mask how pale her skin had become from long days spent only indoors. "Huh. No fussy ties or laces? Has father finally taken my preference into account?"

The smile on her face drooped slightly as she glanced over at Giada, finding that the older woman was staring at the dress with a shocked expression. "What's the matter? Is something wrong?"

"It's... it's not for me to say, young mistress." Giada blinked rapidly, lips parted as she panted as if she were suddenly dizzy. "If I'm not wrong, you should need no help getting that on. If you would excuse me, I... I need to go speak with my mother."

Bella looked back at the dress, wondering what the issue was. With a sigh of frustration, she pulled it on and made sure everything fit as well as possible. "I hate having to puzzle out mysteries. Not her place to say? All that means is that I need to go into the situation blind. Wonderful."

Having finished sooner than expected, thanks to the assistance, Bella spent a few minutes wondering what sort of woman her stepmother would be. In the rare instances over the last few days when she'd seen Luca, she had inquired about Signora Matringa Treesbane, only to be waved off and reminded there was work to do. Then he would slam the door in her face. Bella couldn't wait to inform her father of the man's activities, so he could be dismissed from their service immediately. "Finally, someone who *deserves* to be thrown out on their rear."

The clattering sound of wagon wheels slowly began to fill the air, so Bella went back inside, exiting through the front door just in time for a carriage, followed by two wagons, to pull around the front. The wagons continued around the house, presumably to unload, while the carriage stopped just in front of her. Moments later, Luca came striding out of the house, dressed in an impeccable uniform, and he pulled the door open, while somehow managing to bow at the same time.

An elegant young woman, younger even than Bella, stepped out, followed by another, who was certainly the older of the two sisters. The eldest got her feet on the ground, sketching a shallow curtsy as she sized her up. "You must be our new stepsister, Bella."

The younger girl glanced at Bella up and down, raising her eyebrow and turning to the other, "Why would you think *she's* our stepsister? She's clearly-"

"*Lovely.*" A sharp word rang out from inside the carriage, followed by a tall, imposing woman in the most extravagant gown Bella had ever seen. First, her hand reached out of the carriage, gripping Luca's hastily outstretched palm, then she pulled herself up and out, settling onto the ground as if it were a great honor for the dirt. Bella felt her skin crawl as the woman's eyes roved over her body, searching her from head to toe. "Quite... *lovely* indeed."

Somehow, the praise didn't make Bella feel good; instead, she felt her skin crawl as she realized her father must have married whilst away, meaning this was *officially* her stepmother. The searching gaze bore into Bella, as if trying to make her feel inadequate. She grit her teeth, holding as still as possible as she waited in vain for her father to join this small entourage.

Yet, there was no sign of him, and after a few moments of awkwardness, she took it upon herself to make introductions. "Welcome to House Vigatori... Signora Matringa, and, um, stepsisters. I'm sorry, I didn't know you existed... that is, I didn't catch your names."

"Malvagio," the older one said in a bored tone, not bothering to curtsy in return.

"I'm Cattiva, but I still don't understand...?" The younger one was cut off yet again, this time by a jab from her sister.

"Signora Matringa is so *formal* for family. You may call me stepmother or Matringa... when there aren't others around." The new lady of the house stepped forward, motioning for her daughters to follow. "Bella, would you be a *dear* and start bringing in our luggage? The wagons are around back."

As the ladies bustled into the house, Bella had only one thought, which kept bouncing around inside her skull. "Oh, *no*. By the system, they're just like Luca?"

CHAPTER
SIX

BELLA STEPPED INTO THE HOUSE, straining to carry a suitcase in each hand. She set them down just inside the door, turning to go and retrieve the others when Matringa waved her over.

"Oh me, oh *my*. Those must be so heavy; what a *robust* child you are. Still, that can wait for the moment. You may give us a tour of the house, so we are not fumbling around like thieves." Signora Treesbane, or perhaps now Signora *Vigatori*, imperiously demanded as Bella stood in the doorway uncertainly.

"Of course, of course. But, if I may, where's my father?" The question had been burning inside of her from the first time she clapped eyes on the trio; she certainly had *many* things to say to him at this point.

Matringa rolled her eyes and let out a soft sigh of disappointment. "He was held up. Now, show us to our rooms, as well as the important sections of the house."

Bella nodded and stepped past the trio, striding into the house with the others trailing behind. She was pleased to hear Cattiva gasp at the sight of the wide marble staircase in the foyer. The arched ceilings led to the center focal point of the ceiling: an impressive silver chandelier, and each grand doorway had intricate designs carved into them. Her father had truly spared no expense making this place look as he imagined all noble houses would.

"*Do* stop your rustic gaping, Cattiva," Malvagio chided her younger sister, though she did so with an apathetic tone—like someone shooing away seagulls from someone else's half-eaten sandwich. For her part, Signora Matringa simply swept her gaze around the sight, expressionless as she beckoned for Bella to continue.

"I'm assuming this main floor is merely the kitchen and common areas? I would like to be directed to our chambers; the journey was longer than I wanted it to be." The words were curiously sharp, as though accusing Bella of being a bad hostess, despite not having expected to be the one showing them around.

Trying to make a better impression, Bella shook her head firmly and recounted, "In fact, Stepmother, this floor has a parlor, a sitting room, dining room, the great hall, and… and none of that matters right now, I see. Naturally, let us go upstairs."

Signora Matringa ran a finger along the handrail as they slowly and properly ascended the stairs, rubbing a coating of dust between her fingers which was so sparse as to be *almost*— but not quite—invisible. "The servants have been idle, I see. We'll take care of that as soon as Signore Alaric arrives home."

"I can personally assure you, nothing could be further from the truth." Bella's blood was boiling, though she forced a smile on her face as Matringa looked over at her sharply. Compounding the sudden concern was how her new stepsisters gasped and paused on the steps, glancing between Bella and their mother.

"Is that so?" Going by Matringa's twitching lips, she was *unused* to being contradicted. Her left hand came down on the railing and drummed along it. "*Humm…*"

The silence stretched for a long moment, continuing until the new Stepmother got her face under control, a slight smile on her lips. As she continued moving up the stairs, she lightly stated, "*Well*. Perhaps your standards are not the quality I strive for in my household."

Bella cast about for anything else to say, falling back on her duty as a hostess when nothing else came to mind. As they arrived at the first landing, she waved at the closed door. "Here is father's study, and on the next landing is the master bedroom. Allow me to show you where your things will be-"

"What could possibly make you *think* we would not want to peek into the study?" The words flowed from her mouth like honey, but were spoken as if to a very young child who had a hard time understanding simple concepts. "The lord of the house does his business here, providing for all of us, in this room. I'm certain it is going to be *quite* important for us to know all about it."

Bella inhaled through her nose, opening the door to the study without a word; though she did let out a soft mutter, "So anything I say is going to be wrong, huh?"

"Maybe you *do* catch on quickly. Still, such brazen impoliteness will not be tolerated going forward. Like your father, I expect you to be prepared for the rigors of court. That means knowing how to keep your thoughts on the *inside*." Matringa responded to the words under Bella's breath, causing the young lady to freeze. The older woman swept into the study, scanning the inside quickly, running her fingers along the leather-bound books and the walnut desk before turning, nodding, and stepping back out into the hallway.

Moving on to the master bedroom, Bella stepped back, relieved her tour was nearly over. Unfortunately, Matringa merely stepped inside, scanned the room nearly exactly as she had the study, and returned to the group. "Well? Lead on, I'm certain there is more to see."

"Oh. Um." Hoping the interaction would be as short as

possible, she moved down the hall and opened the door to her own room. "This is my room, though there isn't-"

"Goodness! It's *perfect!*" Malvagio exclaimed, stepping in and looking around, causing Bella to flush slightly with pride at how well she took care of the space. That is, before her new, elder stepsister continued speaking. "The lighting? How open of a concept it is? I simply *must* have this room as my painting space."

The girl turned to her mother with pleading eyes, but it was Cattiva who replied, "You can't *possibly* think that's acceptable. Look at the high ceilings! The acoustics in here are ideal! I must have it for my lute and singing practice."

Her temper flaring, patience with these intrusive people running out, Bella stepped up to Malvagio and poked her in the chest. "Is this some kind of sick joke? I've lived here my entire life, and I most certainly won't be giving up my bedroom. *Get. Out.*"

The two girls scrambled out of the room wide-eyed as Bella stormed out with them and slammed the door behind her.

"Oh me, oh *my...*" Matringa watched on with calm eyes, though her left hand drifted forward to allow her fingers to drum along the door frame. Speaking in a mild voice, she looked between each of the three. "Girls, girls. Living arrangements for everyone will be discussed *after* dinner. Let's continue our tour."

The woman glided away, leaving everyone to follow after her, including the bewildered and frustrated Bella, who called out, "Look, there are three other rooms meant as proper long-term living spaces, and each of them have almost exactly the same layout."

Though they visited each of the other prepared rooms, neither sister exclaimed excitedly over any of them. Even so, Matringa bid them to rest in one while she stepped away to have a private word with Bella.

"*Humm...* your father has told me much about you... for instance, before he left to come to me, you and he had a little argument." The tall woman looked down at Bella, looming over her with a simpering smile on her face. As Bella attempted to decide what to say, the Signora waved her words off. "No, no... I need no other details, child. I've heard all about it. There's only one thing I don't know for certain. Do you intend to give your father the oath he has informed you is necessary? *Today?*"

"I... um... this is a discussion on the system, and he..." Bella stammered in an attempt to buy a few moments to think, freezing as her stepmother's long fingers wrapped around the railing of the banister and squeezed hard enough that the wood creaked under her grip. Looking at the woman questioningly, the young Beast Singer frowned and decided to simply speak her peace. "I'd like to discuss this with *him*, as this is a matter between the two of us."

"Is that so?" With a flick of her wrist, Matringa dismissed Bella from her sight. "Very well, I suppose you should go about your day. I have no doubt you have chores to complete. Many, *many* chores. While you're down there, be certain to familiarize yourself with the serving staff I've brought along with me. Something tells me you're going to get to know them *very* well."

More confused than ever, Bella slowly descended the stairs. As warned, there were people she had never met before busily carrying in items, sweeping, mopping, and rushing to and fro. As the young woman took in the view of a manor with plentiful serving staff, she paused in horror before whirling around and looking up to face her stepmother, shocked and sick to her stomach.

The new lady of the house simply held her gaze, the simpering smile practically painted on her face as she gave Bella a slight nod. "It seems you noticed that each of the household's maids share a uniform appearance. Really, that dress fits you *perfectly*."

Attempting to even out her breath, Bella tried to count how long she was inhaling and exhaling, anything to give her mind a chance else to think other thoughts so she wouldn't start a shouting match with this new person in her life. Her breath came in for a count of four, was held for a count of four, then out the same. Even so, each inhale was ragged, shaky, just shy of a snarl.

Unable to risk opening her mouth for fear of her thoughts flying out, Bella turned and stomped down the stairs, going directly outside instead of to work. Her hands were clenching, teeth grinding, she furiously began muttering, "My status is lost? Fine, I never cared about it anyway. My father has turned me into less than a servant in my own house? *Fine.* They can't *force* me to keep acting like a servant. I have no doubt I'm about to lose my room to one of those spoiled brats, and... *why?*"

She let loose a stifled scream before returning her breathing to a rhythmic pattern—accidentally whistling slightly as she did so. Her Basic Skill, Animal Communication, activated instantly, though she didn't intend it. Even so, she didn't realize what she was doing until a rabbit hopped up to her, head-butting her leg until it had captured Bella's attention.

Too wrapped up in her thoughts to try and pretend she didn't know what was going on, she reached down and scratched the bunny behind the ear, and as it settled down, so did she. For several minutes, she simply stood there petting the creature, lost in her cooling anger.

"Isabella Vigatori, step away from that filthy, flea ridden *animal.*" Alaric's sharp voice cut her to the quick, instantly filling her with dread as she slowly looked up to see her father on a horse trotting toward her.

"Father!" Startled out of her reverie, Bella jolted upright, causing the nearly sleeping hare to suddenly leap away, its hind claws catching her on the leg. It was a shallow scratch, though deep enough to cause blood to bead just above her ankle.

"Bella!" Alaric swept off of his horse, marching over and crouching to inspect the tiny wound. Relief showed on his face for a bare moment when he saw it was nothing more than a scratch, and his demeanor immediately shifted. He smacked her leg gently on the wound, leaving a tiny spot of blood on his own hand.

"Is this what you want? What I have to come back to? A lifetime of scrapes and scars from filthy wild animals instead of listening to me? How is it that I can come home after three months of you practicing servitude, only for your first act to be flaunting your disobedience?"

This close to the man, even though her father's face was contorted with anger, for the very first time, Bella realized his eyes were watery. He was holding back tears? "Father, I don't *want* to disobey you. I don't want scrapes and scars; I didn't even realize what I was doing. I just needed something soft and cuddly to pet… something to take my mind off how rapidly things are changing."

"Bella," Alaric sternly stated, though Bella continued speaking as if she didn't hear him.

"I love animals, father. What happened to mother was horrible, but in all her time with you, doing what she loved, she was *happy*. Can you at least admit that?" Bella pleaded with her whole heart for him to understand, and for a moment, she thought she might have gotten through to him. He took a deep breath, his eyes traveling from her own to the scrape on her leg. "I just want the same for myself, *please*."

He opened his mouth to speak, only to be interrupted by the arrival of his new wife as she intruded on their moment. "Finally! There you both are. Bella, I know we just met, but is this really how you want to act toward me? Running off and leaving the work of the manor for people who don't know where things are supposed to go? I can certainly see why your father felt he needed a wife to help control you. I admit I'm quite disappointed to learn *exactly* how unladylike you actually are."

Signora Vigatori glanced between the father and the daughter with a shrewd look in her eye, "Unless, I'm entirely mistaken, and you came out here to give your father your oath in person? That would be the *proper* thing to do after months of him waiting for it."

The question hung in the air, and Bella turned back to her father, pleading with her eyes for him to say it wasn't necessary. Failing that, to say this was none of the woman's business. Instead, her father's eyes hardened, and he stepped back from his daughter, hands on her shoulders to keep her at arm's distance.

"No. No, she has *not*. Bella, being a Beast Tamer is a dangerous, unacceptable path. I stand by my decision. Until you make a system oath to renounce the class and all of its skills, you will be treated as one only on the fringes of this family. You will sup with us so I can ensure you haven't forgotten your proper manners, but I expect you to be up each morning lighting the hearth and staying too busy to pursue this failed desire of yours. Three months clearly wasn't long enough, and I suppose we'll just have to see how long it takes."

He stepped over to his horse stiffly, swinging a leg over and mounting it before extending a hand to his new wife. "Would you like to ride with me for a short while, Signora Matringa?"

"No, thank you, my dear. I'll walk back with Bella." The new stepmother turned to the girl she was speaking about, flashing a smile which didn't reach her eyes. "It seems we have much to discuss."

CHAPTER
SEVEN

THE WALK HOME, short though it may be, was extremely informative. "My staff was quite looking forward to meeting you. They've never worked beside a proper *lady* before."

Bella ignored her, staring straight ahead, refusing to give this cruel woman the satisfaction of seeing how upset she'd become. Matringa didn't seem to mind, merely humming softly at the attitude and proceeded to speak at her own leisure, "At least, I *think* they're looking forward to working beside you. As you would have noticed if you had introduced yourself as *instructed*, they don't speak very much. Not at all, in fact. Each of them was convicted of the crime of sedition and had been sentenced to death for speaking against the crown."

This injection of information earned a reaction from Bella. "You've brought *criminals* into my house? My father couldn't possibly know about this; there's no way he would allow such a perception of impropriety to fall on us. The house, his business, will be under *constant* scrutiny!"

At that moment, a pigeon swooped down and knocked off the tiny, impractical hat Matringa was wearing. Bella was too startled to stop it, though her hand came up to try and send the bird away. The pigeon came around once more, diving at the new stepmother, only for her hand to shoot out and catch the bird by the body. It blinked rapidly in surprise at the sudden grip, and Bella looked up at her new stepmother in shock.

"Oh me, oh my! What a nice little treat. I'll have the cook add this to the pot. Now, as I was saying before I was so *rudely* interrupted," Matringa drummed her fingers on her hip in annoyance, before allowing her left hand to drift upward and cover the bird's head. There was a muffled *crunch* before the woman continued speaking. "I have an acquaintance who collects voices. Though some think working with her may be a little fishy, *tee-hee*, I am able to *guarantee* their gossip will end. They were released into my service, and I am able to have indentured servants at a pittance, compared to the standard pay of hard-working staff. Quite a tidy little compromise, isn't it?"

She turned to stare directly at Bella, the little smile still on her lips. "It's wonderful to have options for those who don't know when to keep their mouths *shut*, isn't it? Now, as for your father, buying their contract means paying only a fraction of what he would otherwise pay his household. Not only does he know about it, he is *ecstatic* over the idea. *He* certainly sees the value in this method, which is why the other staff—other than the cook, apparently—will be dismissed right away. Not to mention, this 'Aria' was quite rude when I tried to have her woken up earlier."

"She's been working herself to the bone for *days* to get the manor ready," Bella managed to whisper around the terror making her jaw clench. She swallowed, slowly shaking her head. "Leave me alone. Leave *us* alone. Why are you so... so *wicked?*"

Something dark flashed in Matringa's eyes at that moment, but to Bella's surprise, her smile only widened. "Whatever do you mean? What have I done to offend you?"

Bella slapped her hand to the dress she was wearing. "For

starters, you sent me the dress of the rest of your 'indentured' servants. I'm neither a servant nor a *criminal*, and I don't appreciate the insinuation."

Her stepmother's eyes were wide and innocent, and her hand reached out to gently rub Bella's shoulder. "You must understand, I understand the minds of young ladies like your-self. I was young myself, once. I simply knew you wouldn't be giving your father an oath and renouncing your class, so I thought you may appreciate starting our relationship with at least a nice, clean garment meant for the toils ahead of you. I thought, well, I thought you would *appreciate* having something nice and easily replaceable."

"You're dismissing our servants-" Bella angrily continued, though the fury had dimmed as confusion crept in.

At this, Matringa pulled them to a stop, the limp pigeon swaying in her hand, and began speaking slightly more sternly than she had to this point. "Bella. My dear. Perhaps you just don't understand that your father has *no* money? He has lost more than half of his caravans and was up to his eyeballs in debt. I have many solutions to his problems. I have money from my previous husband that I am bringing into this house-hold, cost-saving management plans, and will be assisting him in selecting the most profitable routes for his trade goods—as I'm told your mother used to do."

"You... he... you were so harsh earlier," Bella lamely finished, breathing hard at the realizations being forced on her. "Father is-?"

"You realize I've been on the road for *weeks*, Isabella?" Matringa pulled her hand off Bella's shoulder, striding forward and forcing the young woman to begin following after her. "*Forgive* me if I come across harsh after not having a bath or proper meal in days, all while sitting in a bumpy, uncom-fortable carriage."

She continued with a dismissive wave, "Not to mention... none of these changes are against your father's wishes. This is his household, and I am now merely his wife. I bring improvements, that is all. This place has gone without a woman's touch for far too long. As far as his thoughts about you? I'm only biding by his decisions, even if I may have chosen differently. You know I saw the rabbit, yes? More free meat would be welcome, if it were up to me. But it is *not*."

Completely disoriented, somewhat ashamed, Bella followed her new stepmother into the house, and soon they sat for dinner as a family for the first time—she could barely manage to chew through the stew and roasted squab.

Things changed over the next few weeks, but surprisingly not even as much as when her father had left for nearly three months. Firstly, she retained her bedroom, and her stepsisters each had to choose a room down the hall, splitting the third on the main floor for their lessons. Though she felt slightly guilty over her outburst at the two, she still remained wary of losing her possessions and position to them.

First impressions mattered, and she was *not* the only one among them who had made a poor one.

Giada the younger was teaching Luca the minutiae of the outdoor chores—much to his disgruntlement. Apparently, being a First Footman was meant to be an *indoor* job. Aria was dismissed the morning after the family breakfast, though Cook quietly informed Bella that she'd been snapped up by the Baron, just as Mia's family had. As for Bella, with Aria gone, she was now considered the senior maid of the household. She was introduced to the three silent maids who had come along with her stepmother: Bebee, Cece, and Dedee.

While Bella was certain those weren't their real names, that it must be a cruel joke played on them by her stepmother, there was no way to know for certain. They couldn't speak and had sworn binding oaths not to write any information, unless directly ordered by Alaric or Matringa.

Lastly, she began to worry that perhaps she *was* having unkind thoughts for no reason—after their introduction, and her stepmother's explanation, there hadn't been a harsh word directed her way. Not only that, but she would step in on Bella's behalf and silence her daughters if they started to say became unpleasant.

But as the days continued passing, Bella slowly came to realize that it wasn't just harsh words which were withheld—practically *no* words were spoken to her. At dinner, there were new rules. They were there to eat, not to have discourse, all covered under the umbrella of 'your future husband will not want you mouthing off in front of his guests'. Since dinner was practically the only time they were all assembled, this meant the Beast Singer was surrounded by silence at all times. She was busy with chores, her father was in his study for the majority of the day, and her stepsisters were occupied with lessons taught by their mother.

Of course, every once in a while, she was tested on her own aptitudes, fully expected to maintain high marks in all of her 'courtly manners'.

Her stepsisters remained somewhat of a mystery to Bella, with the elder, Malvagio, being sixteen and only two years away from marriageable age—not to mention being able to unlock her Full Class at eighteen. Yet, she hadn't heard even a single mention of a suitor calling, or plans to make it happen. No one spoke of soirees or parties they should attend, and frankly, Bella thought the older girl needed those things. Even though Bella was easily able to see that the girl was a talented painter; so talented that it seemed unlikely she didn't have a class or skill dedicated to the pursuit, *everything* seemed to bore her.

Cattiva was fourteen, though she looked and acted younger, leading Bella to the misconception that they weren't the same age. She also idolized her older sister and tried to affect the same disinterest in the day-to-day routine, following Malvagio's lead. Even so, she was unable to mask her delight at the delicious meals they had or her happiness at the size and exquisite craftsmanship of the manor. It was strange to Bella, as she'd assumed her stepsisters were used to luxury, but apparently their late father had been far more frugal in his spending.

From what she could glean, their previous home had been decorated and dominated by the man, having few windows, trophies from animals he had hunted, as well as erring on the side of skimping on firewood and coal to warm the house. Overall, it had led to a dark and gloomy house, but now Cattiva seemed to be thriving.

The only downside to the same-aged sister was how she was used to getting her way in all things. She was dismissive of the staff, pretending not to see them in whatever room they happened to be in. Yet, she wasn't sure how to treat Bella, settling on hesitant nods should they meet eyes. Otherwise, they ended up avoiding each other.

Only one person really took the time to speak with Bella: Giada the Cook. Though she kept conversations light, really only speaking on the gossip and goings-on in town, it was the only conversation Bella had, and she treasured it. Beyond that, she'd been *throwing* herself into working with small animals wherever she knew she would be alone and had even managed to increase her skill level, after getting several mice to put on a play for her. Still, the conversations with animals were—by their very nature—one-sided.

Luckily, the volume of her singing didn't seem to matter as far as her skills went, meaning she could practically whisper her songs and still reach every animal in a certain range. When she was outside, she was often trailed by squirrels, groundhogs, rabbits, and even the occasional young raccoon. So long as they weighed less than five pounds, and their body was shorter than the length from her elbow to her fingertips, animals flocked to her.

Only *once* did she have an unfortunate encounter. While she was walking the grounds, a couple of months after settling into her new routine, her soft singing drew a small fox. It emerged from the underbrush next to the trimmed lawn, its movements jittery and erratic. Unlike most of its kind, this one had fur which was matted and unkempt, and its eyes were wild with a glassy sheen. As it faced Bella, the creature's black lips curled back, revealing its small, sharp teeth. Thick foam gathered at the corners of its mouth, dripping onto the cut grass as it took one step forward, then another.

Bella was wearing only her simple servants dress, not carrying anything she could use to fend off the diseased animal. A wind swept over the area, adding to the sudden chill crawling up her back. Knowing there were no other options, she sang out.

"Hello fox, I think you want to go away. You're sad and sick, not mad… so go and take a nap, poor lad?"

While it certainly wasn't the best song she'd ever come up with on the fly, it did its job. The creature stopped in its tracks, eyes rolling in its head. Bella repeated the song over and over again, slowly backing away. The fox was breathing heavily, continuing to let loose a whining snarl as her skills warred with the disease ravaging its body. As she paused to take a breath, the fox yipped, spun in place, and dashed into the underbrush around their estate.

She hurried away, casting glances over her shoulder and breathing a sigh of relief each time she saw that the coast was clear. Suddenly, she felt her arm warm up slightly, and information tickled her mind.

Skill increase! Minor Creature Control [Level 5 (Moderate) → Level 6 (Considerable)]!

Requirement to advance to level 7: Successfully instruct an animal you've not had contact with from a significant distance away—beyond immediate line of sight—to follow a set of tasks.

"What… what had been the requirement to go to level five

again?" She frantically tried to remember what it had said, though she'd expected to have plenty more time to study it. She had only just achieved level five a few days previously, after all. "What was it? It said something to the effect of commanding an animal to perform a task it is instinctually resistant to do? Something about a higher level of control over the rodent's natural instincts?"

Frustrated with her inability to remember the exact wording, she swiped along her arm to read over the skill in its entirety.

Advanced Skill: Minor Creature Control: Level 6/10.

When communing with non-magical minor creatures—size limit: the tips of your fingers to your elbow in body length, maximum of five pounds— you are able to exert [Considerable] control over their actions.

"The skill levels are coming faster... is it because I'm working on them more often? Or, wait, I remember something about this. Unless I'm mistaken, a long time ago, Mother told me it's easier to increase your skill level if you're in danger while practicing them. That's why people with combat skills flock to guard positions or the King's army."

She thought about the sick fox she'd just seen, unable to suppress a shiver. "If that's what it takes to progress faster... I think I'll just stick with slow and steady."

EIGHT

WINTER PASSED QUICKLY, with no changes, other than Bella's hands becoming harder, calloused, her body shifting slightly as she grew used to the harder lifestyle of being an indoor servant in a noble manor. The weather had been exceptionally harsh, setting her father's caravans back by months. He'd grown more and more tense as the weeks went by, often vanishing into his study for days at a time.

As spring came, and the snows melted, all of his planning turned into action. He left the estate behind after emptying out every last *scrap* of trade goods. Frankly, Bella barely noticed his disappearance, far too exhausted with the additional chores springtime brought, such as trimming hedges and weeding the garden in preparation for planting.

One morning, as she was coming in covered in a particularly noxious blend of soil and fertilizer, Bebee the maid suddenly appeared in her path, agitation showing on her face as she motioned for Bella to follow her. The young woman trudged along through the halls, pausing just outside the study and frantically pointing out a multicolored splatter on both the walls and floor.

"What am I looking at, Bebee?" The young Beast Singer

let out a grumpy sigh as she inspected the wide area which was now off-color, only to realize she wasn't about to get an answer. "Great, let's play a guessing game. I'm seeing reds, yellow, a tiny bit of purple... Malvagio? Let me guess, she spilled her paint and didn't bother to tell anyone."

Bebee bit her lip, throwing a worried look at the stepsisters' door in the distance, before quickly nodding. Bella forced a strained smile onto her face and reached out to give her fellow maid a reassuring pat on the shoulder, only for the woman to dodge; a bit of color appearing in her cheeks.

"Why...? Oh, I'm so sorry, I haven't washed up at all. Would you mind helping me out with grabbing a bucket? I have a solvent we can add to it, which might be enough to get this off." It took only a few minutes to return with a brush, mop, and hand rags. The mixture worked well, but slowly. They scrubbed and scrubbed, and only after they'd been at it for a while did Bella realize the other maid was looking rather frantic. "Did you have something else you needed to be doing? Go, I can handle this!"

Bebee shot her a greatly relieved expression, dropped her rag in the bucket, and hurried down the stairs, vanishing around the corner as Bella slopped some more water onto the ground.

"Malvagio, isn't it bad enough that you're cold and apathetic? Do you have to be destructive on top of it?" Only after she'd stated the words did Bella realize they'd been spoken aloud, and she pressed her lips together. "That's odd, I thought I was done complaining about them to everyone but the mice. Why do I feel so... *angry*, all of a sudden?"

She paused to reflect on her thoughts, the silence allowing her to notice that the angry muttering wasn't only in her own mind—there were malevolent, harsh whispers slithering through the door of the study. Trying to figure out what was going on, Bella stepped closer and pressed her ear to the wooden barrier.

"-useless, incompetent, nearly worthless!" a harsh voice she had never heard before rang out. Bella's forehead scrunched, and she tried to place the unknown person. However, there had been no indication of another person arriving at the manor—no riders had arrived, and there was nothing in her notebook about a planned visit.

Bella's eyes went wide as her stepmother's voice cut in, but whatever she said was spoken too softly to make out what she was saying. Either way, Matringa wasn't able to speak long before the cold, oily voice cut her off. "I only need to hear you say it will be here and be *ready* for when we move forward. You don't want to fail me *twice*."

Her stepmother replied, once again too softly for Bella to make out details. It seemed as if the proud woman was nearly begging for something, and it sent chills down her spine as Matringa struggled to get out each word. She intrinsically understood something nefarious was afoot, and she *needed* to know what it was. As the harsh voice began again, she grimaced in annoyance that they seemed to have gotten their temper under control and were now speaking softly. She strained to hear what was being said but only managed to catch snippets of the conversation.

"Limited number... truly cursed objects," the voice seethed. "You... *fullest* extent of its ability! Understand? *Well?* All the planning... the potential will be lost! The cost will be yours alone to bear, and I—what was that?"

Bella's head had gently bumped against the door as she tried to adjust her position, and she'd already started scrambling away as soon as she made the noise. By the time the entrance to the study was flung open, Bella was across the hall, up to her elbows in water as she vigorously scrubbed the wall.

Matringa glared at her for a long moment, biting her tongue as she held herself back from accusing the young woman of something. Finally, the stately lady decided on simply asking a question, "Whatever *are* you doing, Bella?"

Though her voice was harsh, Bella could still detect a hint
of deadly intent—as well as fear, going by how she clutched a
book in her hand like a weapon. Matringa's knuckles were
white and bloodless from the strength of her grip, but the
young woman pretended not to notice any of that as she
glanced over, keeping a mildly annoyed expression on her
face. "Hmm? Oh, Stepmother. Somehow, paint got all over
the wall and floor, as if by magic. Clearly it happened on its
own, as no one bothered to point it out early enough for me to
get it off before it set."

"Being passive aggressive is no substitute for *wit*, Bella,"
Matringa replied almost reflexively, relaxing as she saw her
stepdaughter acting no different than usual. "Well. Get back
to it, and stop lurking around. I'm trying to read; I don't need
to hear disturbing noises in the hallway."

As the door to the study began closing, Bella clearly heard
the woman mutter, "Perhaps I should put *bells* on them.
Servants popping up out of nowhere-"

As soon as there was a barrier between them, Bella
allowed herself to take a few deep, panicked breaths. "There
was no one else in there? Who was she talking to, then?"

Before she could relax fully, the door suddenly swung open
again, as if to catch anyone next to it off guard. Matringa
watched Bella carefully, and the young woman kept a carefully
confused expression on her face. "Good, good. I'm glad to see
you are behaving properly; for a moment there, I thought you
might be trying to find a new skill in skullduggery. I'm glad to
see that's not the case. Humm… why don't you join me for
tea? It's been… oh, months now since we've last *talked*."

Bella clearly remembered their last 'talk' and had no
desire to be threatened with strange magical effects or sold off
to some other household if Matringa could level a false accu-
sation against her and have her voice removed. Until this very
moment, she'd been trying to put her negative thoughts on
her stepmother out of her mind, but… someone in that room

had been talking about cursed objects. Only the most vile people imaginable had access to such magic, and already the young woman was beginning to go over all their prior interactions with a lice comb.

"Stepmother... if I don't get this off the wood soon, it won't be *coming* off." Bella half-heartedly waved her wet rag at the wall, sending droplets splattering across the floor.

"It will be taken care of. Put the rag down; join me in the study." Matringa half turned, then reached into the study and pulled out a bell. Holding it with her index finger and thumb, she gently shook it then waited with a patient expression on her face. Cece soon came rushing up the stairs, a pained expression on her face, which only faded as she got within a few feet of Matringa. "There you are, *finally*. Tea for Bella and me, sugar and cream. Send one of the others up to finish scouring the wall and floor."

Cece vigorously nodded, her eyes on the bell still held gently between Matringa's fingers. When it was set down, the maid seemed greatly relieved, sketching a curtsy, turning, and rapidly walking away.

Matringa watched her go, turning to Bella with cold eyes and a smug smile. "That one is an *excellent* maid. She's so very *motivated* to be prompt, professional, and discreet. How do you feel about the new help, Bella? Are they listening to you properly?"

"They're... very capable. They picked up on the needs of the household very quickly, and I don't think I've ever seen them idle." Bella felt as if her words were coming out slowly—she felt as if she had just missed something important, some threat or point her stepmother was trying to make.

"Humm... yes, of all the household staff I've gone through in my life—more than you could probably imagine —these three have been my favorite." Matringa motioned Bella into the study, sitting in Alaric's seat as the younger lady tried to get comfortable in the guest chair. They waited a moment as the sound of Cece's hurried steps in the hallway became louder, the maid popping in and setting down a tray a moment later. She poured the tea, looked to Matringa for approval, and quickly left the room. "That said…"

The stepmother trailed off, taking a long sip of tea and closing her eyes to savor it. "That said, with the way the world is going, they may need to be dismissed."

"What? Dismissed? I thought you'd purchased their contract, and they couldn't leave because they were criminals you were rehabilitating? Or something like that?" Bella looked at the tea in front of her, deciding against adding sugar to it, since she got the feeling she was there for some specific purpose. No need to be wasteful, when her mind told her it was unlikely she would be allowed to drink it in the first place.

"Yes, well, what with your father rushing to and fro with his work as a merchant, I've been appealing to him to invest in higher stakes. These *piddly* deals he's been brokering whilst wallowing away at the manor are beneath him. He's a *Master* Merchant, and he will never push through to level ten in his skills without taking risks." Matringa sipped her tea, staring at Bella over the rim of her cup.

When the young woman didn't say anything, Matringa let out a soft noise and placed the dish on its saucer. "However, taking risks means money will be extraordinarily tight until he is successful. Reduced in status as they are, these maids don't work for free. None of them, that is, save…"

Bella felt herself flush as her stepmother sent her a knowing look before leaning back in her chair. "It sounds like you're saying *I'm* a-"

"A loving daughter, yes." Matringa interrupted skillfully. "That's one of the reasons I was hoping to have this conversation with you. I was thinking perhaps *you* could speak with him, Bella."

Of all the ways this talk could have gone, this was not

what she'd expected. Bella let out an incredulous, bitter laugh, "Me? I haven't influenced my father in… well, a long time."

"I don't know about all that; you may be surprised what a heartfelt plea from a daughter can do." Matringa folded her hands in her lap, waiting for Bella's expected outburst.

She didn't disappoint. A deep snort shot out of Bella's nose. "I've been *pleading* to advance my class for over half a year now. You've seen how much good that's done. Alaric doesn't listen to me or care what I have to say. You think I can convince him to do anything? To that end, what are you even asking for?"

"*Alaric* now, is it? Oh me, oh my… as to what I'm asking, perhaps just that we could change his mind… together." Matringa dangled the offer in front of her like a sugar cube before a reluctant horse. "You have something you want from him, and I have something I want from him. If we work together, he won't know what hit him. He'll never stand a chance."

"You'd help me get an Advanced Class?" Bella shifted her gaze, staring into her untouched teacup. The strange noises she'd heard earlier were practically out of mind at this point, but she still didn't believe this conversation was happening. "You never told me exactly what it is you want."

"I want what you want, child. I want this family to succeed." The intensity in Matringa's voice caused Bella to look up, locking eyes with her stepmother. "When he comes back from his current sub-par sales trip, I want you to work with me to convince him to collect all of his funds and what I brought in, and do a *real* deal. I want him to run the sort of caravan he used to, the kind which brings in enough money to buy a noble title. Why, when he returns, he'll be so flush with success and excitement that we could go as a family to the Class Shrine. We could revamp the barn out back, restaff, and bring House Vigatori back to its rightful place."

As much as she wanted to agree, just to get an Advanced

Class and new skills to begin working on, Bella paused and considered the implications of the deal. "Matringa, a caravan like that, one that could bring in such a large sum of money… there's no way to do that locally. Even a single trip would take him months on end, possibly a year or more!"

"Yes, that would put quite the burden on you if you were the only maid. I understand," Matringa stated with a patronizing huff. "Are you truly going to be so selfish as to refuse some hard work when it will mean you get everything you want, and your father does the same?"

"No, I mean, wait… I'm not sure why I'd be the only one expected to help around here?" Bella waved that aside as her stepmother's face went hard, sitting up straighter as her thoughts gained clarity, "As much as Alaric and I argue, he's still my father, and I want him to be around. To be in my life. This winter was already difficult enough, and not seeing him for-"

"Just answer. Are you going to help me with this, or not?" Matringa interrupted coldly, staring at the young woman, who simply sat and tried to think. As the silence stretched, the stepmother merely scoffed and stood, waving both hands in a shooing motion. "You know what? Perhaps I was wrong to try and make peace with you, I suppose your father really did know what he was doing when he decided you should be a servant in this household. Get out of my study. Get out of my sight."

Bella's mouth dropped open, but the barrage continued, drowning out her attempts to accept the offer.

"I don't want to hear it. You were right in the first place; I'll handle this myself. You haven't influenced him in a long time, so why *would* he care what you had to say?"

CHAPTER
NINE

I<small>T WAS APPROACHING</small> summer by the time Alaric returned, but the intervening months had barely taken the edge off Bella's fear of Matringa. The young woman had thrown herself into her work, finding new and inventive ways to involve the creatures in and around the house.

Bella quietly took her seat at the foot of the table, as had become her routine, and served herself last. She braced for yet another meal swallowed in silence, only to join her father in confusion when Malvagio subtly cleared her throat to draw attention.

"Mother, I'm in dire need of new paints; my palette is almost exhausted," the oldest stepdaughter lamented. Her gaze briefly met her mother's before darting strategically towards Bella's father, Alaric, who seemed engrossed in his dinner, deliberately oblivious to the unfolding drama.

"She's not the only one! Another of my lute strings snapped today," Cattiva added, quickly following suit. Her complaint was almost casual, as she was struggling with a tough piece of meat. Only after a moment did her glance flit towards Alaric, signaling to Bella that this was an orchestrated event. Going off her last long-ago conversation with Matringa, she felt that she even knew what they were after.

"Now, girls, we shouldn't burden the dinner table with such concerns," their mother interjected with a practiced smile, slicing into her meal with a casual ease no one else was able to mimic, all while her eyes remained locked on Alaric to gauge his reaction.

"But it's of *utmost* importance," Cattiva insisted, dropping her fork with a clatter and earning a glare from Bella, who'd spent *hours* buffing nicks out of the silver. The younger stepsister's voice rose in a calculated whine. "If I can't practice, I'll never refine my talents. I'll end up performing in dingy taverns instead of palaces, and what suitor would have me then?"

Alaric chuckled at the overly theatrical display, but a sharp look from his wife quickly stifled him. He cleared his throat, attempting to interject, only to be cut off by Malvagio's escalating grievances.

"Mother, I'm just as stranded! Without the latest fashions, a decrepit carriage, and no social events of our own, how am I to be seen as a suitable match? One cannot simply attend balls without hosting in return. What would society say?" Malvagio, too, abandoned her napkin and mirrored her sister's indignant posture.

The stepmother allowed a tense silence to linger, her eyes sharply fixed on Alaric, who suddenly found great interest in his potato. Matringa cleared her throat, her voice silky smooth, yet laced with a hint of self-pity as she addressed the table.

"Ladies, we *knew* joining this household would bring changes. We're all making sacrifices. Your stepfather's manor demands a grander staff than it is able to maintain currently, so hosting a ball is out of the question. I *know* each of you has desires which are going unfulfilled. Even *I* dream of seaside vacations, but we must set such desires aside. Alaric is working on ventures that will prosper—his talents as a *Master* Merchant are beyond compare. Patience is key."

"It's been *weeks,* though," Cattiva interjected, tossing her hands in the air with a dramatic flair, her overacting cutting through the tension at the table and spoiling the drama the other two were attempting to push. "Mother, you promised I wouldn't have to sacrifice my music. You said I'd have access to the finest lute strings. Yet here we are, relegated to this remote place, far from the best suppliers. What's the use of marrying a merchant who can't procure simple musical essentials?"

Her complaint halted as Matringa's fist thudded on the table. "*Enough*, Cattiva! I will see to your needs *myself,* if I must!"

Matringa's eyes then shot towards Alaric accusingly, her frustration thinly veiled as she sipped her wine for composure. Malvagio chimed in with a dry comment, "Is that so? My paint, purple especially, is practically on another continent. What grand plans do we have for those, Mother? Shall we clatter across the lands in our worn carriage, becoming the mockery of high society?"

Her smirk was evident as she took a leisurely sip of her drink, reveling in the unfolding drama. Bella's father, having observed silently to this point, finally spoke with authority.

"Ladies. Let's not burden your mother with these… logistics. It seems I underestimated the needs of adding daughters to my household. This oversight is mine to correct, not hers." Alaric placed a comforting hand on Matringa's shoulder, and Bella saw the fleeting look of triumph that flickered across the woman's face, even if Alaric didn't. "I will ensure your needs are met. I have connections that will secure your items at a discount. As for social engagements, my neighbors know our situation. They understand why I don't reciprocate and would be *more* than happy to host you in your quest for a husband, Malvagio."

Here he paused, looking between Matringa and Malvagio quizzically. "You must forgive me for not realizing that a suitable marriage was a priority for you. This is the first time it's been mentioned in my presence, and I hadn't... anyway, as for the upkeep needed to ensure you don't look 'shabby', I'll have that taken care of."

He then confidently tore a piece of bread, his manner casual yet decisive. "I'll manage the upkeep myself. I can't imagine maintaining a carriage would be overly difficult."

"Well... there you have it, ladies. Problems... solved," Matringa smiled at her daughters, but Bella could sense the fury behind it. But, then, the young woman knew what her stepmother was trying to accomplish. The cold glare shot over to her, and Bella knew Matringa was laying the blame for this failed attempt at manipulation squarely at her feet.

But that wasn't anywhere *near* the end of it.

By the end of the next two weeks, Bella was prepared to fight her way out the door and make a merchant's journey *herself*, as the dinner complaints from her stepsisters had become a nightly ritual. So, it wasn't a big surprise when, after four full weeks of this treatment, her father finally announced he had agreed to put the entirety of his savings into outfitting a single caravan and heading south.

Though she had tried to speak her mind on the subject, Bella had always found herself interrupted by Matringa, one of the stepsisters, or called away for some suspiciously timed 'necessary' assistance. Yet, with his news, and the fact he hadn't yet made the investment, Bella finally ignored anything else and barged into his study when she knew he was alone. "*Father.*"

Alaric jumped in surprise at the sudden intrusion, accidentally knocking over a small quill and inkpot as he worked on his papers. "Bella! What are you doing, barging in here like that? Look at this mess I've made!"

Muttering furiously, the man quickly tossed aside his

papers, pushing his maps away, and began mopping up the liquid with his handkerchief, as he couldn't find anything else to do the job. Though she rushed forward to try and help, Bella was angrily waved off.

"I need to talk to you about this trip you have planned."

"I know you will be fifteen years old before this autumn, but the answer remains the same. Until Matringa and I agree you have sufficiently pushed away all distractions, or you swear an oath to me, you will not be upgrading your class!" Before Bella could get another word in, Alaric held up a hand. "Also, *no*, you will *not* be journeying with me. I'm going to be traveling for at least a year. The whole point of me marrying someone was so you could be raised with a mother's guidance."

"This has nothing to do with any of that!" Bella barked at her father, causing him to go very still and finally looked up to meet her eyes. "I need to talk to you about this trip."

"Well? You have my attention." Her father placed both hands on the desk and leaned forward, stooped over the mess. "I do hope whatever you want to talk about was worth the three sleepless nights I'll need to redo this paperwork."

"I need to inform you of something strange that happened in here several weeks ago." Bella pushed forward, ignoring the glare and any repercussions she may be earning herself. "Matringa was in here while you were on your last trip, speaking to some other... woman, or *thing*. They were discussing 'cursed artifacts', that they were in the house. Your wife was practically begging for more time, and I don't know what-"

"*Stop*." Her father's cold whisper was worse than any time before when he'd yelled at her. "I can't take this absurd tale, child. Do you even know what a cursed object *is*? Not only how powerful, and evil, and rare it is... but also how expensive it would be to casually own one? Not just in gold, but in danger? If there were even a *rumor* of a cursed object being in this house, the Kingsguard would raid our house, tossing every stone until they either found or did *not* find what they were looking for."

He slapped his hand on the desk when Bella tried to speak again. "Enough! You are threatening everything we have with this falsehood you don't understand, and for what? To keep me home? Prevent me from using my skills and business to enrich our lives? Are you bored or simply looking for revenge on the family for trying to steer you right?"

"None of that... I'm just scared," Bella told him, her voice barely rising above a whisper. "I'm not lying. I know what I heard, and you're in danger. As am I."

"I'm leaving by the end of the week, and that's the last I'll hear of this," Alaric told her sternly. "In fact, I want not a word spoken to me by anyone in this home until I leave. We're going back to silence at dinner, or your stepsisters can go hungry in their rooms. Every night it's, 'I want this, I want that'. Now I have to deal with *you* coming to me and trying to destroy us with rumormongering as I am pursuing our only hope? Just... enough."

Bella took a shuddering breath, determined to *make* him listen. She didn't expect him to walk around the desk, grip her arm with an ink-stained palm, and march her out of the study, practically throwing her into the hallway before slamming the door. She whirled around, raising her fist to pound on the wood, only to freeze in place as a sound reached her ears.

"Humm...?" Ever so slowly, the young woman turned, finding Matringa standing only a few feet down the hall. The woman swept past her, sending chills down Bella's spine, before gently opening the door and closing it *almost* all the way before turning and staring into Bella's eyes.

"What an *interesting* story you came up with. We'll have to do something about those lying words you spout. *Soon.*"

CHAPTER
TEN

KNOCK.

The single strike against her door woke Bella from a dead sleep, and she blearily sat up. "What? Why? What time is it?"

"Bella, I need you to come out here right now." Alaric's voice came through her door, and the young woman swept her covers to the side and launched out of bed. It had been several days since he'd thrown her out of his study, and in the entire time, he hadn't said a word to her. Peering out her window, Bella saw it was still full dark outside, several hours before dawn at the minimum.

"You're not leaving early, are you? You weren't supposed to leave until the overmorrow at least." Checking her nightgown to ensure she was decent, she threw open her door to find her father framed by light, far more than should be illuminating the hallway at this time of the day. "What's going on?"

"I'm sorry to say," Alaric stiffly informed her, his face seemingly carved from stone. "There's been an unfortunate accident."

A deep pit opened in Bella's gut, and her hands began shaking as she waited for more information. Instead of speaking, her father simply motioned for her to follow him, and led her down the stairs... then down again, into the servants area. As they got closer to the kitchen, Bella felt as though each step required twice as much effort as usual.

"-ate bad mushrooms. Thank *goodness* she had a habit of sampling the meals she prepared for us before serving them, or this could have been all of us." Matringa was solemnly finishing a conversation between the maids and her daughters as Bella was led in. "Ah, there's the last of our family. Why don't you sit down, child?"

The polite words were offset by the fact that all the chairs in the area were pushed in under the servants' table, and atop the table was the too-still body of Cook.

Bella's eyes were drawn to the corpse like iron to a lodestone, and anything else which was spoken was drowned out in the deep *buzz* filling her ears. Something touched her, and Bella jerked away, her eyes going wide as she realized she'd just flinched away from her father's hand on her shoulder. "I'm... I-"

"I understand, Bella. It's not the first time I've lost a servant, and I know Cook was especially important to you. She's been here since you were born, and I've always turned a blind eye toward her making you special meals. I understand this will be hard, but it is the duty of the family to take care of issues like this." Alaric's words practically bounced off of Bella as she turned her eyes back to Cook laid out on the table like one of her fancy meals.

"It's a true tragedy, Bella." Matringa's words cut through the haze around the young woman's mind, and she slowly turned to look at her stepmother, who, as always, was wearing a slight smile. "I know she was your most trusted confidant, and you would speak to her about practically *anything*. Hopes, plans, even gossip and wild tales. A young lady needs someone like that in her life. I know this might be too soon, but I hope eventually *I* will be able to fill that role for you."

The pit in Bella's gut suddenly felt very full, and she had to breathe deeply so she didn't lose what little there was remaining in her stomach. "This is… *this* is how I'm punished for speaking to my *father*?"

Even though the words came out as a whisper, she immediately had all eyes on her. Matringa shook her head sadly, sending a *significant* glance at Alaric before speaking gently, "Sweet child, I had just explained what happened before you got here. Cook had been preparing a stew, or perhaps a roast, I'm not certain. I have no culinary skills, after all. As far as we can tell, she was preparing everything and testing her food to ensure it was to our standard. There are mushrooms on her cutting board still, and she must have tasted them without realizing they were poisonous. I'm told they can look very similar."

Matringa stepped forward, opening her arms as if offering a hug, but Bella took a sharp step back, eyes never leaving the older woman. The stepmother dropped her arms and pulled a sad face. "I hope you realize, she *saved* all of us. Her final act, though fatal to her, saved the entire family from succumbing to deadly mushrooms as she did. Even though she'll never know it, she's a hero."

Bella took another step back, then another, and suddenly she was running out the door and pounding across the lawn.

A call came from far behind her, but she was already too far away for them to easily catch. "Not the barn, that's the first place they'll look. I don't want to be dragged home and made to act like everything is normal. She *killed* Giada! There's no way around it. She killed her because I told Father what I heard."

Finally reaching the edge of the maintained lawn, Bella pushed through the underbrush, tearing small holes in her nightgown as thorny brambles tried to slow her. Her heated breath formed clouds in the night air, each exhale sharper than the last as panic filled her to the brim. As soon as she'd stepped off the lawn, she was in unfamiliar territory—Bella had no idea where she was going, and she didn't care. "I need to hide… I can't let them take me back there!"

She repeated those lines over and over again… and the forest around her came alive.

The night descended into chaos as squirrels chittered furiously, screeching as they left their burrows and tree nests to dart from branch to branch, adding to the noise. Small birds were roused from their sleep, not daring to fly but still filling the air with piercing calls and flapping of flustered wings. Normally silent hunters, such as owls, hooted loudly to draw attention. Rabbits and other small creatures rustled through the underbrush—all in all, a massive distraction for anyone who might be following after her.

After running for several minutes, Bella tripped on an extended root and fell into a small clearing. She tried to catch her breath, but couldn't think straight to get it under control. "She had her Advanced Skill at Perfection. Herbs and fungi! Fungi means *mushrooms*! Cook Perfectly understood what mushrooms were dangerous, poisonous, this *can't* have been an accident!"

She felt something and sucked in a breath as her hand shot out. Her fingers met soft fur, and she let out a deep sigh of relief as she petted a rabbit, which had hopped into her lap. Moments later, there was another, then a squirrel. Ever so slowly, Bella felt her heart stop racing as she drew her fingers through the silky-soft fur of the creatures, which were now surrounding her on all sides. Without meaning to, she dozed off, only waking up as the sun began to rise.

Disoriented, sore, and what felt like an unnatural numbness filling her whole body, she looked around and found herself surrounded by forest animals: squirrels, rabbits, porcupines, raccoons, bluebirds, sparrows, and one owl perched above, which was looking at the feast below with hungry eyes. "Was I singing in my sleep? Or was it just the rhythmic breathing of sleep that drew everything in?"

Now that she was awake, the skittish wild animals began to scurry away, vanishing into the growth around her as quietly and suddenly as they had arrived. Bella looked up, meeting eyes with the owl. Ever so quietly, she began to speak, knowing the creature would understand her intent, if not her words. "I lost a friend today, Mr. Owl."

Whoo.

"Giada... our Cook." She hung her head, but her eyes remained dry. "I was careless, and I underestimated my step-mother. I don't know what she's doing, but I know she's doing something terrible. She's a terrible, *wicked* person, even if no one will believe me. Even if... even if I don't have any *proof*!"

Deflating slightly, Bella ever so slowly shook her head. "Going by Father's reaction, if I brought this to the constable, my family would be destroyed. Worse, they might not believe me,then they'd punish me for trying to bring down a noble house."

Whoo.

"The *kingdom* would punish me, Mr. Owl." Bella sadly stated. "I'm sure there are laws against this sort of thing. It would be all too easy to point at how I've been treated and say I was bringing the information forward only out of revenge. That is... unless I did manage to find proof about what she's doing."

Whoo.

"Matringa, my stepmother." The beginnings of a plan were forming in Bella's mind, and her breath started to steady. "If I hadn't been so blatant about working against Matringa, if I'd been able to hold back just a little and be subtle about what I was doing, maybe none of this would've happened. Maybe that's what I need to do? Pretend to give in, to give up? Be the perfect daughter, the perfect... *servant*. Ugh. Then, when I have proof, I'll figure out a way to get it in the hands of someone who can stop her. Like the king, or... maybe I could talk to her and have her advance my class as a reward for bringing down this fell plot."

Whoo.

"The Queen." Her head slowly began to nod, and Bella placed both hands on the ground, pushing herself up to a standing position. "That's something they do. They have the power to advance classes, just like a Class Shrine, but they only do it for people who have earned their favor. If stopping some cursed artifact from being used against the kingdom wouldn't earn that favor, I don't know what would. Thanks for listening."

Whoo.

"You." With a slightly wet chuckle, Bella firmed her heart and tried to figure out how to get back to the house she'd fled hours ago. After a few steps, she found herself scratching at her arm, finally looking down in annoyance… only for her eyes to go wide as she realized she had an update to her skill waiting for her perusal.

Skill increase! Minor Creature Control [Level 6 (Considerable) → Level 7 (Proficient)]!

Requirement to advance to level 8: Issue a long-term command or set of instructions that a small animal will carry out over an extended period.

"An 'extended period'?" Much as she appreciated the boost to her overall capabilities, Bella couldn't help but be annoyed by the vagueness of the skill increase requirement. "How long is that? Hours? Days? Years?"

Deciding there was nothing she could do but start practicing, the Beast Singer began an impromptu melody. "*Oh feathered friend, what do you say, could you bring me home to where I usually lay? I'm lost in the woods, now it's just you and me. Let's go, pretty please, without delay, so I don't end up in a bear's buffet!*"

A cardinal zipped down through the trees, bright red

feathers standing out among the greenery of the leaves. *Cheer, cheer, cheer!*

Bella followed along after the happy bird breaking through the underbrush only a few minutes later—finding herself slightly flustered at how little distance she'd actually put between herself and the house before passing out. "To be fair, I was still mostly asleep, and that was a pretty big shock to the system."

Arriving at the servant's entrance, she pushed in, accidentally knocking the door against the wall in her haste. A loud *bang* announced her arrival home, and she found herself frozen in place as four sets of bleary eyes turned to her. Out of sheer surprise, Bella found her mouth opening. "What in the *world* are you all doing at the servant's table?"

"See, there she is." Matringa tiredly said to Alaric, who had deep bags under his eyes. "I told you she hadn't gone far; I *know* you could feel it as well. Young ladies need privacy when they grieve, that's all. Bella, for your part, I know this morning was difficult, but we've all been worried *sick* about you."

The young woman simply closed her mouth, letting her eyes drift over until she was staring at her father, who simply watched on as Matringa launched into a full-blown lecture. Bella tuned out most of it, until one sentence caught her ears, and she jerked her head to stare at her stepmother. "-I know the cook's position must be filled, and as you can see, Dedee tried to fill in. While we are all very grateful, the food is... rather simple. I think Bella should take over the duties of the kitchen. She spent so much time with the cook, she must have learned *something* from her."

Without thinking, Bella scoffed and muttered, "Pretty sure you don't want me anywhere *near* your food. I'm a big fan of mushrooms."

"Excuse me?" The tone of the question was a bit *off* as it rolled out of Alaric's disbelieving mouth.

Bella froze in place, cursing herself for already forgetting what she had promised herself in the woods: she would act as though she'd been broken and gather enough evidence to destroy Matringa for good. Then, she realized everyone was waiting for her to speak, and they actually hadn't heard what she'd said. Trying to hold back her sigh of relief, the young woman cleared her throat and spoke louder. "I said, I'm not a very good cook. I don't know if you'd want me anywhere near the food. Plus, now I'm terrified of mushrooms."

"So don't *use* mushrooms, that's easy enough." Cattiva rolled her eyes and half lifted a hand while looking at Malvagio, as if to say 'can you believe her'?

"I have become quite used to good food in my household." Alaric, surprisingly, was the one to speak against the idea. "I really don't think-"

Matringa smoothly interrupted him, "Don't worry, darling, since you leave tomorrow morning, you won't have to think about this for a long, long time. By the time you return, perhaps you'll have even met a cook that you'd bring home with you. As for you, Bella, I'm sure you'll learn. You're a smart girl; you don't often make mistakes twice. Do you?"

"No, stepmother." Bella's gaze dropped to the ground, and she forced herself to swallow the words she had actually wanted to say.

"Good girl!" Matringa practically purred. "There, that's all settled. Let's all get some sleep... well, Bella, you look well-rested. Perhaps you could look through the recipes and figure out how to prepare some bread for a mid-morning breakfast?"

"I... of course," the young woman ground out as she felt the weight of her stepmother's stare. As she washed up and prepared to start the day with yet *another* burden on her shoulders, Bella whispered to herself, *properly* under her breath this time.

"This might just be harder than I thought."

ELEVEN

ALARIC'S DEPARTURE the following day was done without pomp and barely a word of farewell. With the death of her mother, Giada the younger had tendered her resignation, so the final non-indentured servant, Luca, went along with him. As the caravan was full of expensive trade goods, it was at another location, under a careful guard. The two men rode away, quickly becoming nothing less than figures in the distance, then they were gone.

As Bella watched them go, her eyes were hard. "I have a year to figure out what's going on here and gather proof to show Father when he gets back. On the plus side, I've figured out what the long-term instructions I'm going to give my animals are."

Reaching into one of the many pockets of her servant dress, she stroked the soft, fluffy fur of one of the house mice. "I think I'll call you Bert. You and Mert will be in charge of teaching the other mice what I teach you, though I may have you hold off on the waltz for now."

The crooked smile on her face fell all the way off as Malvagio strolled up to her, a bored expression showing as she delivered her message. "Mother wants to see you. She says 'now'."

"You know, Malvagio, it's so nice of you to seek me out to personally deliver a message. I think this is the first time you've ever come looking for me. Thanks!" The intense cheerfulness Bella wore like armor left her a stepsister blinking behind her, wondering if she was being teased.

Without waiting even another moment, Bella hurried into the house, going up to the study, where she assumed Matringa would be waiting for her. As she knocked on the door, the voice of the older lady drifted down from above. "I'm all the way upstairs, Bella."

The forced smile on her face faded away, though she worked hard to keep some semblance showing. Stepping up the stairs to the next landing, she found her stepmother waiting just outside her room, arms crossed and nodding to herself as if she'd just received a great revelation.

"Bella, with all of your tasks, I find that this room you've been in is a great waste of space." Matringa continued speaking, clearly thinking she was throwing Bella for a loop. But, in truth, the young woman had been expecting something like this since the day she'd *met* her father's wife. That it'd taken *this* long was already a boon. "There's so much more this room could be filled with! So much closet space is going to waste, and there's plenty of light you don't get to enjoy, as you're busy all day."

"Humm…" Matringa stepped into the room, walking over to the window and drumming her fingers along the sill. "Yes, I think this is the right decision for all of us. Given your new duties, it would be for the best if you had a room close to the kitchen. No one wants to have everyone shouting down the hallway like some hellion; I should be able to ring for breakfast and have it brought to me when I need it."

Casually waving at the closet, Bella's stepmother gave her an order, "Gather your things and bring them downstairs. We both know it shouldn't take too long. Humm... make sure to leave the bedspread; it matches the colors of the room so well. You understand this is for the best, yes?"

Bella let her eyes travel around the spacious room which had been hers ever since she could remember. The flowers on vines going up the left corner of the room had been drawn by her mother. On the right, her height had been marked since the moment she could stand still for her parents to measure her. Only her determination to play her part so she could effectively destroy this woman kept Bella from melting down as she quietly spoke, "I understand, stepmother."

"That's wonderful." Matringa started walking out of the room, turning back and pausing for a long moment as she looked at the downcast young woman. "I think we are not on as good of terms as I had hoped for when I first arrived. Perhaps, at that time, I was too hasty."

Bella looked up, though the hope in her eyes was dashed in the next moment as the lady of the house delivered a final blow just before exiting.

"Yes... allowing you to call me by my first name so familiarly... I think it has given you an inflated sense of disrespect for me. From now on, you may call me Signora Vigatori, Signora Matringa, or just Signora."

"As all servants would," Bella replied quietly to the empty room. She nodded to herself, longer than necessary or perhaps was healthy, as she digested the newest insults to her status and sense of self. "I'm going to figure out how to ruin you, *Signora*, and I'm going to *enjoy* doing it."

After gathering her clothing, she marched down the hallway and the stairs, heading to the kitchen and looking around with mild confusion until BeBee motioned to her with a kind expression on her face, opening a door directly adjacent to the preparation area. Bella nodded her thanks, glad at least the voiceless servants and she had a semi-decent relationship, after all the times she'd gone out of her way to make their lives easier.

There was a thin layer of dust over everything in the small space, as this would have been Cook's room, if she had used it. Instead, she'd spent most of her nights in the small house Alaric had gifted to her husband when he had been alive. Technically, her daughter, Giada, still owned the deed, but Bella was certain that wouldn't last long. She set her things down and tried to swallow down her anger.

The room next to the kitchen wasn't dreadful nor drafty. It just wasn't *hers*. Bella amended that thought a moment later, letting out a rueful chuckle. "It's mine now, I suppose. For as long as it takes for me to *win*."

With her meager belongings settled into the comparatively cramped quarters, Bella surveyed her new domain. It wasn't much, but for now, it would do. "This isn't going to just be where I come in at the end of the night and collapse into sleep. This is going to be my *war* room."

Bella plopped down onto the narrow bed, which took up more than half the room, pulling out the item which would be integral to her success: her task-list notebook. Ever since she had found out about her father snooping, she'd taken measures against it being read without her permission—more than just hiding it, she had figured out a way to write in a shorthand, which would be unrecognizable to anyone but her.

"First off, I need to get used to the layout of this new area." Mert, now an elderly mouse compared to when she'd first found him, crawled out of her pocket and peered up at her. "You've been with me the longest, so I need you to help me train the next generation of mouseketeers. They'll be my eyes and ears in the floors and walls, but it will be a dangerous task. Are you willing?"

She spoke to the mouse without attempting to use her Minor Creature Control, only communicating her thoughts and desires. That way, it was three times as gratifying when the mouse nodded solemnly, squeaking its desire to join her in this war of endurance. Over the next few days, she focused on training her squeaky allies, creating six different groups, which would each be in charge of searching through a different part of the house.

"Bert, Mert, Luke, Mary, Perla, and Suzy," Bella addressed the six mice she had chosen to lead the individual groups. They were standing on their hind paws, sniffing at the air as they tracked her movements back and forth in the small room. "I need comprehensive knowledge of what's going on in the house. The most dangerous area will be directly above my room, Father's study. Only the bravest and most noble among you should volunteer for this duty."

With a squeak, Mert stepped forward, his beady eyes bright with fervor. Bella nodded at him, acknowledging his intent. "Go and decide who will be in your charge, then. As for the rest of us... let's divide up the house."

Days passed quickly with all the things Bella needed to focus on, and her nights were long as she worked on using her abilities to communicate with the dozens of mice she needed for her plans. Over time, she implanted clear instructions, etching them permanently into their tiny minds.

However, they were still mice. There was only so much they could remember at any one time, so Bella worked to train them to follow certain key commands. When she needed them to search an area, she would softly sing, *"Avoid the light, search for the shadows, watch for the cats who prowl at night."*

To anyone who may have overheard her, the small song was gibberish. Yet, to the mice, every other person in the house was superimposed over the image of a deadly predator. As weeks turned to months, and the next generation of mice were taught not only by her, but by their progenitors, it got to the point where no one else in the house ever saw so much as a whisker.

As summer turned to autumn and into winter, the Beast

Singer created a half-dozen other small songs, though most of them were keyed toward helping her with her various tasks throughout the day. With the assistance of dozens of other creatures, even the most frustrating tasks Matringa threw onto her shoulders were completed with a smile on Bella's face. She could always be found humming, singing, to all outside appearances completely at peace with her new lot in life.

Eventually, even her sharp-eyed stepmother began letting her guard down, culminating in her joyful joke one night at 'family dinner'. "Bella, I've seen such improvement in you since your father went on his travels. Truly, I've greatly appreciated the change I've seen in you… especially your quiet focus on the tasks you're given. Perhaps the other maids' penchant for silence has been rubbing off on you!"

Between the lack of sleep, which made her mind feel groggy all day, and the work which hardened her body but caused her to constantly be filled with aches and pains, Bella simply didn't have the energy to even attempt a rebuttal as her stepsisters tittered and giggled. This turned out to be for the best, as Matringa broke into a smirk at the lack of response.

"Perhaps we've been asking too much of you, Bella. It must be difficult to get everything done and still have to sit here and dine with us each night, humm?" Signora Matringa traced her finger along the rim of her crystal wine glass, the small smile on her face widening fractionally. "Why don't you eat dinner as soon as it's ready? That way you don't need to sit and wait on us to finish? I'm sure it will be better that way, for you."

"Thank you for your consideration, Signora," Bella managed to murmur, staring down at the table…

…to hide the grin on her face.

TWELVE

As PER USUAL, winter passed ever so slowly, doing its very best to dig its claws in, only to eventually be dragged away by the heat of spring coming into full bloom. Just as winter refused to give in, so too did Bella find herself navigating the complexities of life with far more cunning, strategy, and more than a dash of mischief.

"The birds should be returning soon." She kneaded and pounded her fists into bread dough while offhandedly commenting to her loyal mice troops, who had yet to uncover anything of significance in the house.

On that note, Bella was becoming slightly frustrated at not achieving a new skill level with Minor Creature Control, though she was certain she had done exceptionally well at imparting long-term commands into the vermin of the house. Whatever benchmark of success the skill relied on remained hidden away, and she could only push herself to maintain long-standing commands, while training other animals in more complex variations in an attempt to push through to level nine.

Nevertheless, there were many small successes. For instance, though they hadn't yet found a cursed artifact, they had unearthed small treasures from Bella's past. Hidden in the walls where only mice could go to retrieve them, the Beast Singer had stored her mother's previously-thought-lost wedding ring, a silly drawing she'd made for her father back when she was six, a finger-long carving Mia's husband had once made for her, and many other small scraps of her former life.

She only let these trinkets come into the open area on days when she needed a boost, as she was certain Matringa would find some way to take them away or otherwise damage them.

Each day now began with the same monotonous routine, serving breakfast to her 'family'. As always, she delivered Matringa's breakfast at first light, never once failing to find her stepmother immersed in paperwork and barely acknowledging her presence. Bella would always set the tray down silently, never meeting the other woman's eyes, and being careful to never draw attention before swiftly moving on to serve Malvagio and lastly Cattiva.

The elder sister seemed to take offense to how Bella now seemed unstoppably cheerful, always demanding some item on the tray be redone, no matter if it were eggs, toast, or the rare sausage. Even so, after later collecting the trays, the redone item was almost always untouched on the plate.

For her part, Cattiva slept in as late as her mother would allow, and Bella had long since learned to be as stealthy as possible. The only time she had accidentally woken her slightly younger stepsister, Cattiva had screamed at Bella and hurled the plate of hot food at her.

After months of careful planning and interacting with the animals, Bella's understanding of her surroundings had given her an acute knowledge of what happened in the manor... which manifested as subtle acts of defiance. As she grew more comfortable with her command over her rodents, she began using the mice for more than scouting or chores. They quickly started to become accomplices in small pranks, which served to not only amuse her, but to subtly unsettle her stepfamily.

One of Mert's offspring, named Mert Junior in honor of his now-late patriarch, took to the pranks with extreme dedication. When Bella put together the breakfast trays, she always did so to the best of her ability, ensuring there was no cause for her to be reprimanded. After delivering the food, Mert Junior would patiently wait until after Matringa had sampled her food and drink, then he would sprinkle salt from his position on the bookshelf into her tea. It was never enough to cause a stir, just enough to pucker her lips and cause the woman some discomfort. In the best case, ruining her morning.

Malvagio was particularly fond of bread, and Suzy the mouse figured out—all on her own—how to gather juice from onions and sprinkle droplets on the morning toast. This went on so long, and caused so many issues, that Matringa and Malvagio eventually both appeared in the kitchen, watched Bella make the toast, both cut their own slices and took them back to their rooms.

On her way out, Malvagio drew a finger across her throat and pointed at Bella, "No more getting away with this. Mother's going to punish you for tampering with my breakfast the last few weeks, just you wait."

Not ten minutes later, the elder stepsister stormed back into the kitchen, shouting at Bella, only to be forced to leave the room by her mother—who found nothing wrong with the toast at all. Bella's stepsister had been nearly in tears and refused bread in the morning for the next few weeks.

These and dozens of other tiny, petty revenges were carried out under the guise of standard, routine service. Each day, Bella wrote the family's reactions in her notebook, which ranged from puzzled frowns and shrugs of indifference to abject fury when a tiny annoyance remained consistent. As she knew better than to witness their frustration on her own, Bella had to puzzle out the meaning of the mice's charades—which quickly turned into a happy game of its own.

When she eventually got it right, the tiny creatures were as excited as she was.

As the seasons changed, and Bella became more adept at understanding and manipulating her environment, her confidence soared. House Vigatori, which had felt like nothing more than a prison over the last few years, slowly shifted until it began to feel more like a chessboard. Each move was calculated, every player unknowingly put in their place by the ever-humming, smiling servant girl who was never once around to be blamed for their grievances.

Beyond breakfast, after Bella had gone to her father about the dark voice whispering to Matringa, she hadn't been allowed to work on the floor holding the bedrooms, nor the study. The three magically silenced maids took care of the duties in those areas, leaving Bella somewhat unsure of how her stepfamily spent the majority of their time—until one day, after Malvagio insisted on a particularly time-intensive breakfast being remade.

From past experience, Bella fully understood that the meal wasn't going to be eaten either way, though she couldn't *not* make and deliver it. Instead, she did several of her other chores, finally bringing the meal up barely an hour before lunch time. "She's definitely not going to eat this… hello, late breakfast for *me*."

Quietly entering Malvagio's room, she noticed her stepsister was already fully absorbed in the painting she was working on. Her brush was moving over the canvas smoothly, the easel placed perfectly to maximize the use of light pouring in through the window. Despite herself, Bella couldn't help but steal a glance at the painting itself.

She was stunned into stillness, and her eyes devoured the stunning rendition of the view from the bedroom window—an almost perfect recreation of the landscape from the edge of the house to where the old barn stood, though in a state of disrepair. As much as it irked her, Malvagio's artistic talent was undeniable: the colors were vivid, capturing the early morning light and shadows with a possibly literally magical quality.

Bella shook herself out of her stupor as she thought over the potential that this truly was a magical painting of some sort. She didn't know the class or skills her stepfamily had, but there was no way they were pursuing their interests with such intense dedication without an underlying reason.

As the young lady slipped out of her stepsister's room, her brow was furrowed in thought. "Do her skills help her create art, or do they allow her to insert some kind of emotion into the paintings she makes? From how it hit me... I want to say it's likely closer to the latter, but it could honestly just be that good. Talent like that couldn't have been given to a worse person, though."

Leaving her elder stepsister to her art, Bella passed by her former room, dark thoughts cut off by the sound of Matringa's harsh voice echoing out, the words aimed at someone other than herself for once. "Cattiva, what good is your talent if you don't make full use of it? You've learned to focus on one thing at a time, now bring it all together *correctly*. Subtlety is the name of the game with a talent like this, and if you can't pull it together, it's all useless in the end. You don't *want* to be useless to me, do you?"

There was a soft murmuring she couldn't make out, then in the next moment, the gorgeous strains of a lute filled to the air—strings vibrating in a mesmerizing melody Bella hadn't thought Cattiva could possibly be capable of. Leaning into the music, Bella found herself pressed against the wall, inching closer to the door. Just as she was about to reach for the doorknob, practically in a trance from how enraptured she was, an unexpected intrusion broke the Beast Singer out of the odd trance.

"Daa~nnce dAnce, *don't* yoU want to get up aannn~dd

daaance!" The discrepancy between Cattiva's ability to play her instrument and her horribly off-key singing was so atrocious that it was all Bella could do to keep from falling to her knees, clapping her hands to her ears, and begging for it to stop. Yet, it wouldn't have helped. For the first time, Bella understood what it felt like to be directly and clearly impacted by a skill an untrained person was using on them.

Cattiva's shrieking song echoed directly into Bella's head, and it was only then that she realized she was only hearing the melody of lute. Her younger stepsister *wasn't singing*. Even with how atrocious the singing was, Bella felt her feet shift, as Cattiva's song compelled her to dance. Happily, she was able to rebel against the mental demand easily, thanks to the assault on her senses; it certainly wouldn't do her any good to be caught snooping outside the room.

"Stop at *once*." Matringa's voice mercifully ended the compulsion, as well as the strumming of the lute. "You are doing the equivalent of screaming your words into my brain. How is it that you are so adept at the main portion of your talents, yet abyssally awful in the secondary? The thoughts and concepts you're meant to be pushing should be subliminal, not cymbals and *fireworks* going off in the mind of those who hear your music and alerting them to your influence."

"I work on this every *day*, Mother!" Cattiva seemed on the verge of tears, but Bella couldn't find it in herself to care. "It's so draining to push like this. I need to train by working with people who don't know what I'm doing and who don't have such powerful resistances, like you do. How am I supposed to get better, if I'm never truly allowed to test-"

"You *know* why that can't be allowed." Matringa's words seemed patient, but they held a sharp undertone. "If you were found to be capable of mind magic, and they could prove it, an oath to the kingdom or a cell would be the only option for you. Until you can *contain* yourself, you will practice in *secret*."

Bella's eyes went wide, and she immediately and very, *very* carefully began walking away. As soon as she was safely on the main floor, she reflected on what she'd just heard. Already, Cattiva was a terrible pest, but in a few years of continuous practice with her skills, especially against someone who could clearly notice and resist them easily, it was likely she would be an extremely formidable person.

"Mind magic, huh? I wonder if father knows about that very *unladylike*, illegal aspect of her talent." Bella felt a surge of excitement as the first piece of evidence against her stepfamily fell into place. Retreating to the servant's area, she began humming softly and quickly gathered mice from every nook and cranny. "This could backfire badly, but… I think I need to ask all of you to chew Cattiva's strings regularly."

Bella's hands clenched into fists as she looked at the ceiling above her, in the direction of the practicing musical mindweaver. "I can't let her get good enough to influence me or my father. Not until I've escaped, at the absolute minimum. Matringa can't be allowed to create stronger tools to use against us."

THIRTEEN

LATE IN THE SPRING, a thunderous clatter in the yard caused Bella to rush outside, coated to her elbows in flour. Her mouth dropped open as a dozen men drove draft horses forward to pull on the support beams of the old barn. Before she could do more than gape at them in surprise, a whip crack signaled the horses surging forward.

The enormous sound, which Bella now understood to be cracking beams, rang out once more, and the entire structure collapsed. "What in the ever-loving system are you *doing*?"

"Language, child." Bella flinched away as Matringa swept by her, casting a small smile over her shoulder. "The barn was gathering dust, and as you can see, it had become quite the hazard. Since we are planning on beginning to host gatherings after your father returns next season, I thought it would be best for us to start putting together some areas for entertainment. After this mess is cleared away, I'll have a walking labyrinth put together for couples to meander through as they converse."

"The chickens!" Bella sputtered, making a half-hearted gesture at the collapsed building.

"Oh, pish, you don't think I'd make it *harder* for myself to have a good breakfast, do you?" Matringa rolled her eyes and gestured to the other side of the yard, where a large crate was letting out soft clucking sounds. "They're going to use the wood and build a coop by the end of the day. Honestly, Bella, you think the worst of me for no reason at all."

As her stepmother marched away, calling greetings to the working men, Bella's lips went white from how hard she was pressing them together. She shook her head slightly, and spoke under her breath, "I've got reason, and I already have a little bit of proof. A couple more pieces... just a little more."

Time marched ever forward, and as the debris of the fallen barn was cleared away, the warmer season also brought about visitors. Townspeople came to call, oftentimes peddling simple wares, few of which were purchased. However, just before the official start of summer, a messenger arrived during lunch to announce that the Duca's niece was being married to a Conte who lived to the distant south of their manor.

"I do hope you'll pardon my intrusion, Signora Vigatori." The messenger, bedecked in the heraldry of the Duca, gave a proper courtly bow, "The Duca's niece was wondering if she and her group would be welcome to stop and have tea here tomorrow afternoon. It is late notice, and I've been instructed to inform you there will be no hard feelings if the answer is no. Still, I know they would welcome a small relief from their travels."

"Think nothing of it!" Matringa waved the man in then motioned for Bella to put together a plate for him, and motioned for the young lady to sit and eat with them, as it was a common occurrence. "Signore, it would be a great honor to host them. Please, rest a while before returning with our regards and invitation."

The man ate swiftly, thanking the family profusely before bowing and rushing away to mount his horse.

"Humm..." From the time he stepped out of the room, Matringa had gone silent, drumming the fingers of her left hand on the table as she contemplated the news. Finally, she turned to Malvagio. "Darling, I believe a *painting* is in order."

"Oh?" Malvagio responded in her usual bored tone, but Bella noticed her whole body had shifted, and she was practically vibrating with excitement.

"Indeed... wouldn't you agree that a guest of such *distinction* should leave with something to talk about? We wouldn't want her to have nothing to say after she leaves." Matringa had a strange glint in her eye, and her gaze kept coming to rest on Bella in a way the young woman didn't particularly like.

"Talk? You mean gossip." Malvagio shook her head, as if in disappointment, though a mirror of her mother's permanent smirk had appeared on her normally apathetic face. "What could we possibly have around here that would interest a newly married Nobildonna enough to tell her friends about us?"

"I'm certain there are a good many things you could consider. For instance, look at the four of us! Blended families such as ours aren't often found in the low nobility. Perhaps we could put together something which would help put to rest any rumors of disparities in the treatment between you girls?" Matringa abruptly stopped speaking as she caught Bella's intense stare. "Well, enough chatter about this, perhaps we should just get you started and see what you come up with."

Malvagio's lips were twitching in glee. "Can't wait."

"Don't be too abstract now; a caricature simply won't do. Something... realistic." Matringa seemed almost to be talking to herself as she followed her daughter out of the room, leaving the other two at the dining room table. As Bella attempted to puzzle out the meaning of the strange conversation, Cattiva continued horking down her food, showing no indication that the interaction had meant anything to her. There was nothing she could do at the moment, so Bella finished her food and spent the rest of the day wondering what terrible thing was coming.

The next morning, the family gathered in the courtyard as the procession began to arrive. Bella had been given the day off, instructed to dress in one of the gowns which matched her actual status, which meant Bebee had been given the task of serving the group their tea. The family as a whole sank into a deep curtsy as the Duca's niece, a lovely girl named Rosa, stepped out of the carriage while holding the hand of one of her footmen.

"Thank you for your hospitality, Signora Matringa," Rosa called in a sweet voice, "I cannot quite express to you how happy I am to get off the road for even a short while."

"Truly, Lady Rosa, it is our honor to be thought of," Matringa practically gushed as she stood from her curtsy. She half turned, gesturing to her daughters, who stepped forward. "Please, allow me to introduce you to my daughters, Malvagio and Cattiva."

Rosa greeted them warmly, gripping their hands and exchanging several hushed compliments. Then Matringa turned slightly further, gesturing Bella to step forward. "And this... is my *stepdaughter*."

Bella curtsied once more, blushing, although she wasn't really sure why. Something about how her stepmother had introduced her caused chills to crawl along her spine. As Rosa turned to greet her, the gracious smile on her face slipped away, and she physically recoiled. The gentile lady pulled herself together, politely curtsying at the young woman, but didn't approach or offer her hand. Instead, there was a carefully neutral expression on her face, which caused Bella to look down at her dress to see if she'd stepped in manure or something of that nature.

Matringa rushed the group inside, leaving Bella behind to follow at her leisure. As they made their way to the patio for the promised tea, she swung into the hall and decided to look at herself in the mirror. "Is this some court intrigue I don't know about? Am I wearing colors offensive to Rosa or her family? What could possibly-"

As she stepped in front of her reflection, Bella let out a shriek and stumbled backward, then lurched forward to check if she were seeing things. "What... what *is* this?"

The dress she was wearing matched up in the mirror, but nothing else did. Half of her normally golden, wavy hair was missing, as if she had mange like some wild dog. What remained was only scraggly wisps of hair limply hanging from diseased skin. Her eyes were mismatched, one too large, one clearly smaller, a brackish, muddy color instead of their normal bright blue. Opening her mouth, she nearly gagged as her previously straight, white teeth were replaced with snarled, foul versions of themselves.

Bella's eyes rolled up in her head, and only a swift intervention by DeDee, who'd been passing through to take care of some task, kept her from landing on the floor and hurting herself as she nearly blacked out. As her breathing slowly came under control, Bella gripped the other maid's shoulders tightly, shuddering in horror. "What have they done to me? How did they do this to me? When did... how didn't I *notice?*"

The maid had a grave expression on her face and nodded in understanding. She pulled Bella to her feet, a pained grimace showing for a moment before she gently slapped the young woman.

"I really, *really* didn't need that." Bella growled at her, her eyes snapping into focus as she stared at DeDee.

Instead of cowering away, the maid only firmly nodded at her once more and made a 'follow me' gesture. With the rest of the family safely on the patio, Bella was quickly led upstairs, into Malvagio's room. DeDee pointed at a cloth covered canvas, and when Bella threw it to the side, she found a portrait which perfectly portrayed what Bella appeared as right now—hideous to behold.

"She... she made me look like this? Is this what I look like now, forever?" While she wasn't exactly prone to vanity, such a monstrous alteration dropped on her was causing Bella to sink into panic.

DeDee shook her head sharply, going to the bedside and retrieving a hand mirror. As she flipped it around so Bella could see herself, she tried to look away, but DeDee grabbed her chin and forced her to look in the mirror. Then she reached up and grabbed Bella's hair, yanking on it gently.

"There's... there's no hair there, though?" Bella frowned in agitation as she realized her reflection and reality were not lining up. Ever so slowly calming down, she reached up and felt at her head and face. "I'm not bald... my hair is there, my eyes didn't get moved... this is an illusion?"

When DeDee nodded, Bella let out the deepest sigh of relief she'd ever managed in her life. "Do you know how long this will last? Hours? Days?"

Her fellow maid shrugged and held up one finger, then swung her hand side to side. Bella, having spent months practicing charades with much less human partners, immediately understood, "The first one, so hours, but you don't know how many?"

DeDee put her finger on her nose and nodded. Bella swallowed and took a few deep breaths, "So... Malvagio isn't just a fantastic painter, she can create illusions that match what she makes. Okay... okay. Thank you. I know you're putting yourself in danger for me right now, so I'll go join the tea. They've already seen me like this, but... actually, maybe I can turn this to my advantage."

Now calm and rational, Bella stood up straight and marched down the stairs, throwing open the door to the patio in time to hear Malvagio finishing her words to Rosa, "We try to help her stay up with the current fashions, but... you can only put so much lipstick on a pig."

One of Rosa's escorts noticed Bella marching toward

them, quickly clearing his throat and causing the engaged woman to change the subject. "I've heard Crown Prince Fella is doing well. Has he ever come through this area? Perhaps even visited the manor? It's quite charming here, like a fancy cottage in the woods."

Her voice was unnaturally high and pitched, and Rosa shifted slightly to keep her back to Bella. Cattiva leaned forward, fanning herself with one hand while miming a swoon with the other. "I've seen him when we've gone to town; he's never even slowed down while riding through town... but he makes such a dashing sight!"

"Donna Rosa, I need you to know-" Bella gasped in shock as Matringa stepped past her, sending a sharp elbow into her gut and knocking the wind out of her.

"Bella, are you quite alright, dear?" Matringa looked over and locked eyes with Rosa, deep pity etched on her face. "I know how quickly you tire these days, perhaps it would be best for you to go lie down."

"Not a *chance*," Bella growled, all thoughts of long-term strategy flying out of her head as she sent a burning glare at her stepmother. Though she was still struggling to take a deep breath, she moved forward again, only to be blocked by one of the footmen. He didn't say a word, merely swaying back and forth in front of her as if by accident, but obviously intentionally keeping her several feet away from the Nobildonna. "Signore, please-"

Rosa struck up conversation with the stepsisters once more, doing her best not to look at the scene playing out behind her. "Any word from the Lord of the manor? My father has expressed his deepest respects for Signor Vigatori, and since his regards, I'm surprised we haven't received a visit from him in... I don't even know how long."

"In fact, he's set to return in three days or so." Cattiva spoke out, startling Bella to silence.

She looked between her stepsisters, then Matringa.

"Really? Father will be back so soon? But... that'd be well ahead of schedule, is everything-"

Her stepmother glanced over at her, the pitying expression shifting into something... else. Shock, concern? "Indeed, a messenger arrived the other day. Now, for your *health*, it's time for you to go inside, right now. I don't want you to fall ill so close to his return."

Gripping Bella's arm with a hand like a vice, Matringa marched her inside and closed the door behind the youngster before returning to the tea party.

Bella didn't have to wonder for long why she'd been led away: passing by a mirror showed that the illusion was starting to fade. Her hair appeared fuller, her eyes returning to their normal, matched state, and—the largest relief by far—her teeth looked healthy once more.

"Thank the system, it's short-lived. Now I just need to find a way to get to Donna Rosa..." Bella grumbled as she waited for another opportunity to speak with the Duca's niece, only to be met with disappointment as the group was led around the house and into their carriages before clattering away a short while later.

When Matringa stepped inside once more, she raised an eyebrow at Bella and motioned to indicate the state of the house. "Well? Is now really the best time to laze about? Did you not hear me when I said your father would be returning in three days' time? There's work to be done."

FOURTEEN

"HEIGH-HO, THE MANOR!" Bella couldn't remember the last time her father's voice had sounded so jaunty, excited, practically *oozing* self-satisfaction. She dropped the mop in the hallway, rushing out the door before anyone else had a chance to get there first. As he stepped down from the wagon he was driving, she slammed into him, hugging him as though he were about to leave immediately.

"Well! It's good to see you, too, daughter. Let me take a look at you." Alaric gently pushed away from Bella and looked her up and down, his smile becoming even wider. "Look at the muscles on you! I haven't seen any other girl your age with such a proud physique. You are going to be the *bella* of the ball, Bella!"

Matringa appeared in the doorway, waiting just before crossing the threshold with her arms spread wide. "We've missed you, Signore Vigatori."

Alaric's happy smile turned back into a cocky one. "You wouldn't *believe* how successful my trip was, darling. Every item you suggested was purchased at a premium; I barely made it to my destination before having to turn around—I was completely sold out."

Her stepmother's face fell slightly, and she stared intently at her husband. "But you did go all of the way, yes?"

"Of course, of course! How else could I have stocked up on the local trade goods and come back to make an even *larger* profit?" Alaric threw his head back and laughed as he strode strongly toward his wife, sweeping in and giving her an intense kiss.

Cattiva poked her head out. "Welcome home, Father! Did you bring us presents?"

Bella flinched at hearing her stepsister call Alaric 'Father', glaring at the younger, disingenuous girl. He didn't seem to mind, however, and simply gave her a much more appropriate pat on the head, though she tried to duck away. "Presents, tales, *gold*… I have it all and more. *We* have it all."

Malvagio was nowhere to be seen, so Alaric simply shrugged and motioned for everyone to follow him. "Why don't we go to the dining room, and I'll tell you about my travels? I know! I'll hand out the gifts I brought when we get to the part of the tale of the town I bought them in."

The small group bustled into the dining room, with Alaric having to run back out and grab a large travel bag before starting his story. "The route I took, Matringa? I honestly couldn't *believe* how well you'd planned things. Barely two weeks into travel, I arrived in a large town, and from the moment I rolled in, I had people absolutely *clamoring* for my goods. I was barely able to keep enough to reach the port city and sell for an even higher premium. From there, I needed to buy a whole new stock of wares."

He pulled out a box roughly the size of his hand, scooting it across the table to his wife. "While I was there, I found something just for you. Go on, open it!"

Alaric beamed in anticipation as Matringa opened the gift, her eyes going wide as her eyes reflected the sapphire necklace and matching earrings. "Oh, my! It's beautiful."

"While I was in the port, I ran across a sea captain, who

informed me of a distant kingdom he was planning to sail to, which needed supplies. Unfortunately, he didn't have the funds to provide them... you know what I did?" Alaric smugly grinned, though everyone's eyes went wide at the thought of him giving a large sum of money to an unknown person. "That's right, I was able to broker a deal and join him on his journey at a *fraction* of what it would normally cost. I've been sailing for months now. Bet you didn't expect to hear that!"

"I... most certainly did not." Matringa's hands went limp on the table. "What about the route I had planned for you?"

"Worry not, Signora!" Alaric winked at her. "With the complete sale of the items you recommended, I had more than enough to fully fund the wagons to continue on the original path. I sent Luca with the wagons, with plans for us to meet at the port on the way back."

"You *split up*?" Matringa's eyes flashed with dark anger, and she reached for Alaric's arm, only to pull back at the last moment. Taking a deep breath, she pushed her cheeks up into a facsimile of a smile. "You are back here, and all seems well... so it must have worked out."

"Indeed, it did." Alaric's enthusiasm had dimmed slightly after seeing her reaction, but he continued on with his story. "I gave him strict instructions not to sell anything for a copper less than *my* prices. Of course, I was fully prepared to return to a fully-laden wagon as... well, Luca certainly does not have my expertise, does he? However, I came back to three-quarters having been sold, and the empty space filled with high-value southern goods. To say I'm impressed would be quite the understatement."

"I'm so glad everything worked out." Matringa took a deep breath. "Though I really wish you hadn't split up. I put so much... *effort* into planning that route for you."

"I hear your concerns, but what's done is done." Alaric dismissed her concerns with the wave of his hand, and Bella's eyes flicked over to see how Matringa reacted. Going by the glare, she could only assume that particular point in the conversation would be discussed further at another time.

"My sea voyage was the smoothest I've ever had. The captain said it would take five weeks to get there, but it only took four. When we arrived, I didn't have to take a step off the ship—the port authority arrived and bought everything we had brought without a single attempt at negotiation."

"That seems... unlikely." Malvagio stepped into the room, bringing her normal apathy with her. "They took everything? They didn't even ask how much it would cost?"

"I thought it was strange as well." Alaric nodded toward her to acknowledge her point. "But it seems a new sultan had just been crowned. Apparently, he was a prince from a neighboring desert kingdom, and he rode in on an elephant while tossing gold coins as if they were earned as easily as plucking them off a fruit tree. I gathered there was some unpleasantness with the Vizier, but now a full month of celebration was declared—hence the need for any goods they could get their hands on."

"Jaffery *fail-*?" Matringa's stricken response was bit off and hidden... from everyone but Bella.

Reaching into his oversized luggage, Alaric pulled out three boxes, handing one to each of the girls. All of Bella's attention was turned to the box, and as she pulled the top off, an intricate filigree silver necklace was revealed. It was certainly beautiful, and she smiled her thanks at her father but left the necklace in its container. Frankly, she knew it would break if she were to try and wear it whilst doing her chores.

Not to mention, it was practically guaranteed to vanish from her room when he next vanished from the house.

"-We drank a toast on our success as we were sailing home, the entire crew, and the following morning, the clear skies turned to dark clouds." Bella tuned back in as her father excitedly went over his adventures. "The more superstitious among the sailors were concerned that our celebration was premature, that we had angered Poseidon himself with our revelry. That night, clouds turned into drizzle, then into a raging storm!"

Bella's eyes went wide as she thought of her father being lost at sea, and none of them even knowing he had gotten on a boat in the first place. She clenched her hands together and listened as he spoke on. "As it turns out, the squall saved us! In the early morning, lightning was brightening the sky, and thunder was drowning out all sounds. We sailed right next to, and I am not exaggerating, *right* next to a sandbar where sirens and the like were set up, trying to lure the sailors off their boats. Thanks to the noise of the storm, we didn't lose a single man! Only a statue of a prince, sent as a gift from the sultan, but *I* didn't sign for it!"

From there, he mentioned returning to the port city and gathering Luca, then continuing on the planned route once more, now hauling exotic goods from across the sea. "Once I got there, I turned around and brokered deal after deal on the way home. Now I have shipments which will be coming into the area each week for the remainder of summer, able to turn around with three times the number of wagons full of goods —which have already been half paid up front by the buyers!"

"How exciting!" Matringa exclaimed as she lifted her glass. "A toast to the Master Merchant, and the good fortune of our family!"

"Hold…" Alaric's chest puffed out as everyone kept their glass hovering in the air, "When I say I've never had a more successful trip, I mean it, and the world agrees. You are looking at a *Perfect* Merchant, *not* a Master Merchant."

The room filled with gasping and excitement as he shared the news, though he refused to explain the details of the skill he'd unlocked upon reaching Perfection with his original mercantile skill.

After the excitement died down, conversation turned to the house and the state of House Vigatori.

"Tell me, how is everything here? The garden looks spectacular, the house seems in good order, how about the cook? I've been impatiently waiting for a proper meal."

Bella looked at her stepsisters sharply, but they seemed perfectly puzzled. Matringa faltered for a moment, shaking her head but refusing to meet his eyes. "I don't know what you mean, Signore. No cook arrived; we've had Bella in charge of the kitchen since you've left."

"Well! How about that? My deepest apologies; I sent him back on my very first stop." Alaric grumbled for a moment about 'directionally challenged chefs' before turning and looking over at Bella proudly. "Everyone looks well-fed; you've done well so far. Still! Tomorrow we'll go into town and hire some new staff. No daughter of a merchant as rich as myself should be the household cook. In fact-"

Matringa interjected in a huff before Bella could get too excited about his announcement. "Alaric… I don't wish to be the one to bring this up, but your daughter has still not given you her oath. Perhaps, after all this time working herself to the bone, she might be ready to do so now?"

The room was immediately filled with silence, matched only by the thick and cloying tension which sprang up between the stepmother and stepdaughter. For his part, Alaric simply took a deep breath, furrowing his brow and looking down at his teacup.

"Perhaps I have been too hasty in my previous decrees." His voice was low, yet firm. "Some time away, some success, may have given me a little… perspective. My daughter and I will meet later and discuss what is best for her. Either way, her time in the kitchen comes to an end. Now."

Working hard to contain her breathing and her disbelief, Bella simply remained seated, blinking rapidly. While she wasn't looking forward to declaring herself a Beast Singer now and forever, she hoped he wouldn't force her to refuse the system's gift any longer.

The following days were a whirlwind as her father went into town and hired five new maids, a trio of men to work the grounds, and a new, proper cook to feed the family. Money flowed like a river into and out of the house, and his new status as a merchant who had a Perfected skill caused a near stampede of guests and well-wishers who wanted to either hear more about it or get in on the ground floor of whatever his next venture would be. In fact, he was so busy that the promised conversation continued to be pushed further and further away.

Bella found herself with an incredible amount of free time, which she used to practice her skills in the wooded area around the estate. Her reasoning was very straightforward.

"Until Father and I figure these things out… it will be better to make myself scarce. If she can't see me, find me, or find fault in what I do, hopefully Matringa won't be able to do anything to keep me as a servant in my own home."

CHAPTER
FIFTEEN

As DAYS TURNED TO WEEKS, Bella's excitement over her father's decree began to wane. Each morning, he had a full schedule of anything from the new arrival of goods, potential partners vying for attention, to reveling and celebrating his success. The promised 'talk' never manifested, and though she didn't need to cook any longer, ever so slowly, Matringa stepped in to ensure she was given the hardest or most tedious tasks available.

Though Bella's hands were busy, her mind was free. Even if her hopes were fading, she finally settled on the method she would be using to convince her father to allow her to pursue her system-granted talents. "Numbers. Numbers and profit. My entire life, the only thing he's ever understood is calculations. If I could just get him to see how my skills will benefit the family business in the long run, maybe he would finally understand."

Once she had settled on this plan of action, the errors in how she had pursued this in the past became obvious. Bella scoffed at her past self, who was young and brash. "Of *course*, my arguments over the love of my skill and so forth didn't mean anything to him. All he would see is a dramatic child who likes soft and fluffy creatures, not a serious potential revenue source."

Over the next few days, while she was working, she made a mental list of all the things she could do with her gift which would make money, things which should appeal to her father as 'proper'. As soon as she was done for the day, she would write everything out in her notebook, creating an enormous list and flowchart which she could use as a visual model for him. "I can start by helping to train noble lady's pet dogs, or even hunting hounds, if I start while they are young enough. That might be tricky, since they grow fast... but the pets? I could earn myself invitations to all the noble houses in the kingdom if I show enough skill. If nothing else, that would gain Father additional business contacts."

Once she had put down everything she could think of for her current skill set, her mind turned toward the future. "If I get my Advanced Class soon enough, I might still have time to unlock my second skill before turning eighteen and gaining a Full Class. Perhaps that would allow me to train larger creatures, such as horses and the like. Father's caravans could be moving at speed once more, and if we expand our ownership of land, I could help to train the horses or oxen which would be tending it. Profit from all corners."

After several weeks of preparation, she had a full business proposition ready to go. It was time to stop waiting around to see if Alaric would remember his plan to speak with her. Grabbing her papers, she threw open her door and took a single step out, nearly running directly into Matringa—who was standing just outside her room with her hand lifted, poised to knock. "Oh. Step—that is, Signora Matringa. What can I do for you?"

"Let's talk, child." The woman swept into the small servants' room, pausing for a moment when she realized two paces had nearly brought her to the end of the available space. Bella took a deep breath—not *particularly* enjoying being called 'child' when she was approaching her sixteenth birthday at the end of this summer—but maintained a neutral, pleasant expression as she turned to face the woman invading her personal area. "I've spoken with your father, and he has agreed it's better for a woman to parent a girl than a man. After all, I understand what it is you need most, what you are thinking, and what you are going through."

It took significant effort for the young lady not to immediately shove her finger at the intruder and clarify that she was only 'going through things' because Matringa was actively seeking to wear her down. "That's very generous of you to offer, Signora."

"Isn't it, though?" Matringa's ever-present smile widened, "I'm certain you understand he is busy with his work and new partners. Frankly, it isn't a good investment of his time to waste it on teenage fantasies. So, to make clear what I mean, if you have anything you'd like to request of him, bring it to me, and I will give you your answer. If I can't, I will determine if it is a question worthy of his *very* valuable time."

Bella kept her mouth shut, simply looking at the smug stepmother showcasing a simpering smile. Matringa leaned forward, staring deeply into Bella's eyes. "Do I make myself clear?"

"I certainly understand what you are saying, Signora," Bella replied neutrally.

"Oh me, oh my!" The stepmother straightened up, looking at her stepdaughter with cold, calculating eyes. "I suppose I'll just have to *accept* that answer for now, won't I? It's what is for the best, my dear. On a completely unrelated note, with so many new faces in the household, we've decided that anyone who can't listen to simple instructions will face suitable consequences. The hired help will be outright fired, but in your case, we would simply have to find some other… punishment."

When the young lady simply remained silent, the smile

finally fell off Matringa's face. "Oh, child. Your father being home always causes you to act with such *defiance*. Truly, I don't know *why*, after all this time. Fine, keep your silence; I have another matter to discuss with you. With all this new staff, It wouldn't be proper for you to sleep in a room directly adjacent to all these unmarried men, especially unchaperoned as you are. As all the spare rooms have been emptied of furniture and filled with trade goods, I've made a new arrangement for you. A bed is being brought to the cellar, and a few of the new hires will be here shortly to move your personal items downstairs."

Bella's mouth dropped open in horror, causing the corners of Matringa's lips to curl as she finally got a reaction. Shaking her head and mock sadness, the cold woman spoke patronizingly. "All of that could have been called off, if I came here and found a dutiful young woman, as I've been trying to mold you into for the last… almost two years? Would you look at that? Time certainly does fly."

"Surely, it would make more sense to put the wares in the cellar?" Bella voiced the question in such a deadpan tone that even Malvagio might have been impressed. The thought of living in the damp, dark, and spider-filled cellar was rattling her, but she was determined not to show it.

"Don't be silly, child! Wares have intrinsic value, and they can spoil. Obviously, you've already been spoiled, so there's no more harm which can come to you." Matringa chuckled at her own wit, though Bella simply firmed her stance as though a fifty-pound backpack was being strapped onto her. "Don't give me that look. You moving to the cellar is not a debate. I'm simply informing you so you know where to go at the end of the day. I like to think of it as a courtesy, so you aren't looking around for your bed in a room filled with packages. You should thank me."

There was a lapse in the conversation where Matringa waited patiently, only to shake her head in disappointment.

"No thanks? I guess *next* time, I just won't let you know before changing things, then. Good to know."

Sweeping out of the room, the stepmother walked away without looking back. Bella waited a few heartbeats then followed after her. There was no hesitation in her step. She marched upstairs in search of her father, breathing deeply to try and clear the red tint from her vision.

Murmuring from the dining room caught her attention, and she burst into the space, already launching into a furious outburst. "Father, your *wicked* wife is moving me to the *cellar-*"

That was as far as she got before her father shot up from his place at the table, face draining of blood, only for it to come back in a rush, leaving his skin red and splotchy. "Bella, you could not have worse timing. If there is something that needs to be addressed, you will do so *privately*."

Only then did she notice the other two men in the room, both of which were sitting across the table from her father, a glass of fine wine in their hands. They seemed completely aghast at the intrusion and looked between Alaric and Bella several times before one leaned to the other, clearly meaning to speak quietly but failing to do so thanks to his slight inebriation. "In *my* household, children don't interrupt business meetings."

Hearing those words, Alaric's eyes went wide, and any semblance of kindness he was trying to portray vanished. "It's time for you to leave, this is not the time-"

"Then tell me a time that works for you. I'll put it on the schedule." Bella still had her notebook in her hand, and she flapped it slightly before opening it like a professional scribe. All three men now had shocked looks on their faces, and she froze as she realized how blatantly disrespectful she had just been.

"Alaric, I must ask." The deep voice caused Bella's father to slowly turn toward the speaker, looking for all the world as though he had been carved from wood. "Can a man who can't handle his business at home truly handle *our* business out in the real world?"

"It *will* be handled, Signor." Alaric flashed a glare at Bella. "I've been on the road, and have left her discipline to her step-mother. Perhaps for too long. Perhaps she's been too lenient and has been raising my daughter with values I do not welcome."

Matringa's voice rang out behind Bella, and the young woman immediately began shivering, "My deepest apologies, Maestros. This is entirely my fault. We will depart immediately and begin implementing *extra* etiquette lessons. Please don't hold a young woman's anger toward her father against her; it was the loss of her mother that led her down this path."

Bella felt a firm hand grip her arm, and as she was pulled out of the room with all the inevitability of a riptide planning to drown a swimmer, her father tossed out another decree.

"For the rest of the week, you are disinvited from dinner time with the family. You will also go without breakfast during this time. Perhaps a hungry stomach will teach you to focus your will and help you learn to keep your temper in check." Alaric turned back to the other merchants at the table, a sheepish expression the last thing Bella saw on his face before the door started to close. "My deepest apologies, please allow me to refill your glasses, and let's put this unpleasantness out of our-"

The door finished closing into its frame with the same **thud** of finality Bella would associate with her casket being dropped into an unmarked grave. Matringa didn't let go of her, not saying another word as she dragged her charge outside, around the house, to the doors of the cellar. She yanked one up and pushed Bella forward almost hard enough to cause her to fall down the stairs. "*Consequences*, child. There are always consequences for your actions."

Without further ado, Matringa shut the entrance to the cellar, leaving Bella in the darkness below.

CHAPTER
SIXTEEN

THE STEPS to the bottom of the cellar were uneven, forcing Bella to keep her hand on the wall as she descended, or she would trip and fall down the stairs. Only the thought of how much it would please Matringa if she broke her neck kept her moving slowly and cautiously.

As she stepped into the main portion of the cellar, she sneezed, only for the sudden burst of air to kick up dust. A moment later, she was coughing and had to cover her mouth and nose with her dress simply to keep from falling into a repeating cycle. Just as she thought everything was settling, someone walked overhead on the floor above, causing dust to rain down on her.

Her eyes were slowly adjusting, and Bella realized it *perhaps* wasn't as pitch dark down here as she had expected it to be. She found the source of the soft glowing: a set of thick, murky glass set on either side of the cellar, which were so dirty that even the filtered light coming through them was nearly extinguished. "How long have I been relegated to the position of a maid that my first thought upon seeing this area is how *badly* I need to dive into cleaning my room? Great."

Though she was angry with herself over *already* starting to consider this space as her own, Bella started singing her frustration to try and take note of it, so she could begin setting it aside. "*I've been sent to the dark, I've only arrived, but without help, I don't know if I'll survive. But I'll persist, I'll pay the price, so long as I have help from my darling mice.*"

Thanks to her mapping out the house with her small creatures, Bella knew they had access to this space as well. With only a few repetitions of her song, scores of mice poured through the ceiling and crawled down the wall. She watched them come, wondering how other people could be so disgusted by their presence. "Thank you all for joining me; I'm sure you're wondering why I've gathered you all here today."

Squeak, Mert Junior replied for the group, pantomiming confusion at the change in locations.

"We'll get to that, Mert." Bella put off the question for now, still too upset to want to discuss it. "First, I have to start with a question. Was I able to be clearly heard upstairs, or was it my skill reaching you?"

Mert Junior grabbed his oversized ears with his tiny paws, pulling them down so they were flat along the side of his head. Bella raised an eyebrow, nodding in understanding, "I see… so perhaps there is a small silver lining. We'll have more leeway with singing and planning down here. Well, to answer your first question, this is apparently my new room. It's nearly as large as my original bedroom, so we will have more space to train, practice, and continue the battle against the evil step-intruders."

Squeak! The large group of mice responded near-simultaneously, each of them standing at attention on their hind legs. Many of the smaller creatures looked around in confusion, only slowly mimicking the others around them.

Bella saw this and smiled happily. "Oh, some of you are new! Well, let's get acquainted. I'm Bella, and I'm going to teach you how to do *wonderful* things."

Squeak. Mert Junior reached over and patted one of the

young mice, nodding his head in agreement before standing straight once more. The Beast Singer watched on with amusement. She was almost positive she had seen the older mouse *wink* at the younger.

"The first order of business: I *can't* live like this." Bella swept her hands out to indicate the entire room. "I don't mean figuratively. I might actually die from exposure down here if this place doesn't get cleaned. I need large rags, soap, and perhaps a bottle of cleaner, if someone can figure out how to get it down here without putting themselves in danger."

"After that, I've been kicked out of dinner time and told I will no longer have breakfast." Bella nearly snarled at the thought but kept her voice even as she spoke to the mice—who could perfectly understand her, thanks to her Basic Skill being maxed out. "I certainly don't intend to go hungry, and since I'm not in the kitchen anymore, it's going to be up to all of you to figure out how to liberate enough food from the pantry for *all* of us. House Vigatori has *money* again, after all. They can afford to keep us *all* well-fed."

Only then did she notice she was speaking of the family as an estranged group and was slightly saddened by the realization. Bella shook it off, muttering to herself, "If it's the truth, it's the truth. What else will we need for the war effort? Shelter will be taken care of, food... water? I'm going to need to scavenge some canteens and dig a hole into the floor. Lastly... my final hope, Alaric, has failed me. I must plan my escape and start gathering money for travels."

Turning her attention back to the mice, she singled out Suzy. "You've been working with me for a year now; are you ready for a new task? Good. Coins, small pieces of jewelry, gems that fall out of jewelry and go otherwise unnoticed, I need you to start collecting *all* of it. Keep it in a place you can get it out, somewhere in the walls, but don't even tell *me* where it is. Perhaps a spot which connects to the outer portion of the house, so I'll be able to pull away a section of paneling and have it all fall into a sack?"

Suzy paused for a long moment, considering Bella's words, then nodded a single time. *Squeak.*

"Thank you. Money means freedom and the ability to go to a Class Shrine to advance my class. I'm certain Matringa made sure I have never gotten pocket money, as yet another failsafe to keep me dependent on them. I'll talk to the birds as well; I know they admire shiny things. If I can figure out how to get them to collect fallen things for me, we can start building a true hoard for our escape. I wouldn't leave you all behind, after all. Not forever."

This caused a slight commotion as the huge group of vermin started chittering amongst themselves, as if whispering excitedly. Bella understood their excitement. "I hope there was never any doubt that I'd bring you along. You've been helping me for so long, what sort of friend would I be if I didn't do the same for you?"

Having decided on her next steps, Bella took a deep breath—only for her nose to wrinkle as she was reminded of her unpleasant surroundings. The air was thick with dust, and a damp mildew scent she just *knew* would sink into her clothes if she let it. Looking around the space, the only good thing she could say was that it was a large, open area, and it *wasn't* the wine cellar. If it had been, she would have needed to deal with people coming and going in her room anytime there were guests or dinner time was approaching.

The area had been cleared for her imminent arrival, and crates, empty casks of wine, and other sundry had all been cleared out. While she considered the area, her mice had been hard at work, filtering up through the ceiling, rushing along their pathways. In the span of only a few minutes, the fastest among them was returning with a large rag clutched in its mouth. Within half an hour, a veritable army of rodents had returned, each dragging scraps of cloth or entire rags with them.

One particularly ambitious mouse carefully pulled along a rag, which was folded around another that had been soaked with a potent cleaner. She grabbed it right away, pulling it away from the sensitive noses of her companions. "That was *very* impressive! Don't put yourself at risk, but I can't thank you enough for this."

Before anything else, she set to work on the windows. Using the soaked rag, she scrubbed away at the thick glass, little by little wiping away the years of muck that had accumulated. "Only a few minutes into cleaning, and there's ten times the amount of light in here!"

She knew it was a bright day outside, but the warped glass shifted the light enough that it appeared to be a gray, cloudy day outside of her hole in the ground. With her surroundings now illuminated, Bella set the mice to scrubbing, with an additional instruction to notify her if they found any patches of mold.

Many hands, no matter how small, made the work go quickly. Each time a *squeak* rang out, Bella hurried over and applied the potent chemicals on the rag to the mold, knowing she would need to come back and do a more thorough job with a whole bucket of the stuff in the future. For now, she did her best to scrub it away, leaving a dense, medicinal scent behind which would allow her to easily find these patches when she was looking for them again.

The floor was packed dirt, so there was only so much her creatures could do to tidy it up, but soon a huge pile of dust and debris had been collected into the center of the room. Bella steadily worked on the parts of the ceiling she could reach, running a dry cloth along the seams of the wood and trying her best to remove all dust from between them. Bella chuckled to the mice around her. "While I desperately need a shower, a dust shower whenever someone walks overhead is certainly not what I have in mind."

There were few squeaks of approval for her wordplay, causing Bella to purse her lips and snort, "Tough crowd, huh? Not my best attempt, I admit. Don't worry, I'll have you laughing by the end of the day."

Though a part of her mind was on the task of keeping herself safe by having a clean environment to live in, she mostly allowed her body to carry out the familiar actions on its own as she considered other things. Every few minutes, she would pause to redirect the mice, who had organized themselves into teams of runners and cleaners—some going to bring the filthy rags to the laundry room then return with clean ones. Others focused on cleaning the walls and ceiling with dry cloths, and the last group collected the falling filth.

There wasn't much of a visual transformation, but the difference in comfort was extremely stark. Hundreds of spider webs had been taken down. Nothing sparkled, the area was still dark, but ever so slowly, it became a space someone could survive in, even if it wasn't yet somewhere someone could properly *live* in.

Hours passed, and the dark cellar, which had been all but forgotten by the family before, now was finally clean, the air smelling bland with an astringent tang. The floor was flat and clear, the walls mold free, and the windows were shining with a surprising amount of light as the evening sun directly beamed on the western wall.

Exhausted but pleased with the change, Bella carefully sat on the floor and reached out to gently pet the heads of the hard-working mice. She whispered to them, her voice warm with intense gratitude, "Thank you, my friends. This would have been a terrible trial without you."

After a few minutes of sitting in silence, surrounded by tiny bodies, the sound of many feet on the floor above her caused Bella's eyes to narrow. "What's going on? That's not stomping, but they're not just walking, either… it sounds as if someone is-"

Her eyes went wide, and she hissed at the mice to disperse up the walls and into the ceiling, "Someone's carrying a heavy object; it can only be the bed on its way down here! Run, there's nowhere for you to hide!"

CHAPTER

SEVENTEEN

THANKS TO HER FURRY FRIENDS, missing dinner with the family was nowhere near the punishment her father had intended to be. Then, after the first night of being stuck in the cellar, she was not just allowed but *expected* to be out of the underground space working again.

Thanks to the plethora of help in the house, she had to *volunteer* for a particularly tedious task—weeding the garden—and used the time away from prying eyes, especially around dinner time when she knew her family would be otherwise engaged, to sing to the outdoor animals. Crows, magpies, any creature under five pounds, yet strong enough to carry heavy coins were given the same request: find shiny things and put them in a hollow tree at the very edge of the property.

For the entire week, she repeated this request to any animal that would listen, imprinting into their minds her need. There were small issues, as the wild animals had never before done something of this nature. For instance, a large black bird dropped a gaudy ring onto her head as she was bent over, causing Bella to suck in a sharp breath through her teeth and grab at a now-throbbing part of her skull. "Put it in the *tree*, bird!"

Caw. The crow replied with a call that sounded a *little* too close to laughter for it to be an accident. When Bella bent down to pick up the ring, her eyes went wide, and she nearly refused to pocket the jewelry. It was lovely, and indeed very shiny as she had requested, but the fat teardrop diamond in the setting was absolutely enormous—there was no way she could sell this without someone considering it stolen.

Seeing as this was the very first shiny object which had been given to her, Bella had high hopes for what the animals would be able to find and collect on her behalf. Much to her amusement, or perhaps *bemusement*, on the sixth day of her banishment from the dinner table, she sneaked to the hollow tree and found a large assortment of everything from buttons to nails and hairpins. Letting out a soft grunt of disappointment, she was about to drop out of the tree when she saw a silver coin half buried under the other trinkets.

"Success! A dozen more of those, and I'll be able to pay for a class advancement. If the price hasn't gone up in the last five years… better make it fifteen." She placed the huge diamond ring in the hole as well, just to have some distance from it in case news of stolen jewelry began circulating. She spent the rest of the evening lounging in the sun, singing to small creatures, and generally relaxing.

It was strange to remember how, in the distant past, this had been a fairly normal way for her to spend her evenings. On the seventh day, she was honestly disappointed that the week of relief from dinner was almost up, as she had grown to prefer even working instead of the silent, tense dinners she was forced to endure with her step family. "Sure, the food is good, but I always leave feeling empty. What does it say about Matringa and her daughters that literal vermin are better company, by far?"

That night, barely an hour before dinner, there was a knock on the front door of the manor. To Bella's great surprise, instead of waiting for someone to let them in, the door flung open, and a lovely woman of indeterminate age practically danced into the building.

"Yoo-hoo! I've arrived, and all is right in the world once more! Bella? Boo-boo? Where are my two most favorite people in this whole wide world?" The beautiful voice seemed to fill all the empty spaces of the house, wrapping around Bella with the same warmth of a cat snuggling into her lap and falling asleep.

"*Bibbidy!*" Bella rushed through the house, nearly slamming into the woman as she wrapped her in a very tight, informal, unladylike hug… just as her father appeared at the top of the stairs.

"A-*hem*." The fact that Bella's eyes went wide, and the joy in her face drained away in an instant was not lost on their guest as Alaric cleared his throat in disapproval. Both of the women looked up at him, only to see the man standing with his hand holding onto the railing tightly, as though he were expecting to fall at any moment. "This is quite an unexpected visit, Maestra Bibbidy."

"Such formality, Alaric! Does one expect a sun shower in the middle of a cloudless day? Twins from a cow? How could anyone expect *me*? Still, such unexpected things always cause those who receive them to thank the system anyway!" A bolt of lovely silver fabric was pulled out of… *somewhere*… and dropped into Bella's arms. "You see, when one's godmother appears, the only thing expected is a good meal, companionship, and, naturally, gifts!"

At the same moment she said 'gifts', an intricate bottle of fine wine appeared in her hand, and she waved it back and forth to entice her long-time friend to come and have a drink with her. Alaric's stiff expression melted slightly, and he raised an eyebrow. "Indeed. I'd be more than happy to allow you to stay for a night. Bella, have BeBee fix up a room for her. Maestra-"

"Just *Bibbidy*, darling," the exotic woman chided her old

friend, a serious expression now on her face as she stared at the man. "How long have we known each other?"

"Sometimes I think *too* long... Bibbidy." Alaric gave her a sharp nod, turning on the stairs and speaking over his shoulder as he climbed back to his study. "Dinner will be in an hour; I'm sure you can get yourself settled. BeBee!"

The shout rang through the house, but he was gone by the time the maid arrived. Bella quickly gave her the instructions to make up a room, then turned back to her godmother and found Bibbidy staring at her, her eyes jumping from the maid to the young woman, clearly noting the fact that their dresses matched in form, function, and coloration.

"A room would be good, I suppose a light snooze would not go amiss. I'm getting on in my years, after all." Her smile was back in full force as she winked at Bella, a shimmer playing over her skin and leaving behind deep smile lines and white hair pulled into a tight bun. Then the vision vanished, and she was once more ageless, regal, exquisite. "It's good to see you looking so well, so healthy. I've heard... rumors."

At that moment, as the godmother's voice struggled to contain her emotion, the sound of distant thunder rumbling echoed into the room, though it had been a perfectly cloudless day only minutes before. Bella swallowed her discomfort, knowing all too well what the current gossip was—Rosa, the Duca's niece, had been telling anyone who would listen how wonderful Matringa was to care for such a misshapen, unfortunate creature as her stepdaughter. "It's good to see you again, Bibbidy. Things have been... hard, *wrong*, since Mother died."

The exotic merchant slowly bobbed her head. "I'll make sure to visit more often, sweet girl. I'm going on another trip soon, but I should be back before your eighteenth birthday. Years away, but not half a decade or more between visits. Now, I'd love to meet your new family, as well."

"Dinner would be an appropriate time for that; please

make yourself ready," Alaric called out as he reappeared, descending the stairs to come and speak with his oldest and most excitable friend. "Your room is ready. Allow me to show you the way."

"Has the house changed that much since my last visit, Alaric?" Bibbidy questioned him with a knowing look at his daughter. "Have even the places people *sleep* shifted?"

The master of the house cleared his throat uncomfortably, offering an arm, which Bibbidy took. They spoke together quietly as they ascended the stairs, and going by the sounds, Bella assumed their guest was being led to her old bedroom. As the door creaked open on the floor above her, the whole house seemed to darken for a moment as thunder rumbled once more.

"That sounded closer this time."

She peeked out the window, frowning slightly as she saw only clear skies. Alaric appeared at the top of the stairs a moment later. "Prepare yourself for dinner, Bella. Wash up and change; you will be joining us tonight. As for that cloth, put it in your room."

Even though she opened her mouth to protest that the bolt of cloth was far too fine to be put in the cellar, her father cut her off with a wave. "I want no backtalk tonight. I know what I've said before, but this is a special occasion, and you will be present. Go."

Walking slowly, feeling intensely uncomfortable, Bella started walking toward the servants' entrance, only for the main door to fly open and bounce off the wall. Matringa and her daughters, who had been out for an afternoon stroll, piled into the room, looking around frantically. Her stepmother's eyes landed on Bella, and she snapped her fingers at her to stop the young woman from walking out of the room. "What's happened? What's going on here? What did you *do*, you filthy little brat?"

The words came out in a rush, and Bella froze in place as

her sweating, out of breath stepmother advanced on her menacingly.

"My dear, what happened? Did you *sprint* home?" Alaric's voice impacted Matringa like a physical blow, and she whirled around and stared up, her face pale, sweat beading on her brow. "Are you quite all right?"

"D-don't worry, Alaric, I'm just suddenly not feeling well." Matringa certainly appeared as though she were on death's door. Bella stared at the panting woman, *willing* that hope into reality. Her stepmother spun to face her, catching her eye and frowning deeply. "Are you wishing *ill* on me right now?"

Luckily, her father butted into the conversation. "Matringa! That's quite enough. We have company for dinner this evening, and... do you *often* speak to my daughter this way?"

Matringa went even paler, if that were possible, taking a deep breath and running her hands over her rumpled dress. "Company? I'm in no state for company... who is here?"

"An old family friend. Bella's godmother and Elara's before her. I'm sure I've mentioned her before, Maestra Bibbidy B-" Alaric rushed down the stairs as Matringa's knees buckled, and she only stopped herself from falling by gripping Cattiva, nearly taking both of them to the ground. "Matringa!"

"We need to leave." His wife sternly turned to her daughters, who had remained silent up to this point. Looking at them, Bella realized they were far paler than usual as well.

"Leave? You're in no state to leave. At any rate, we have company. Do you have any idea how it would look to the public if my wife knew we were having dinner with a *fairy* and refused to meet her?" Alaric gaped at his wife, reaching out hand to steady her, only for it to be slapped away.

"It has nothing to do with her." Matringa was clearly lying, but it came out smoothly enough that even Bella nearly believed her. "The reason we had rushed home was because we had forgotten we are scheduled to be fitted for dresses this evening and needed a carriage immediately. We've been waiting weeks for this appointment; we cannot miss it. I'm sorry we'll miss dinner, but... her arrival wasn't *scheduled*, was it?"

"No..." Alaric admitted quietly, his usual demeanor returning, now that everything seemed logical once more. "She is unrepentant in her refusal to conform to the calendars of other people."

"Well, *proper* guests send word ahead of time. There's nothing for it, Alaric; please send my apologies." She turned and swept her hands at her daughters, all but shoving them out the door. "We will return tomorrow, hopefully by dinner time. After the fitting, we will stay in town and have the dresses altered for us upon the morrow."

In moments, Bella and Alaric found themselves alone in the entryway, blinking at each other in confusion at the sudden turn of events.

CHAPTER
EIGHTEEN

On her way to her new 'room' to get dressed for the evening, Bella was interrupted by Cece. The maid frantically motioned for the young lady to follow her, turning and presenting a midnight blue dress with a grand gesture. Looking between the gown and the beaming maid, Bella realized the clothes were for her.

"How did you get this? Modern lacings, elegant stitch work... I haven't seen this before. Did you take it from one of my step-sisters' rooms?" A frantic shaking of the head met Bella's question, followed by the maid pantomiming frantic flapping of wings, pointing into the distance, then at her own smile. "Did you... get this from Bibbidy?"

Cece pointed at her own nose, nodded, then winked at Bella. Then, she swept her hand around, indicating she would help Bella get dressed.

"Oh, no, you *don't* have to do that," she demurred while raising her hands, not wanting to ask so much of the maid. "There's so many things to be done, and I'm sure there is a better use of your time."

Cece raised an eyebrow and clicked her tongue, folding her arms and jerking her head to the side as if to say, 'get in here'. Letting out a laugh she couldn't contain, Bella stepped into the small room and allowed the maid, her *friend*, to help her with a task she had been doing on her own for years.

The dress went on, fitting beautifully, with the laces barely needing to be pulled to be set in the perfect position. After it was tied and settled, Bella was pushed down into a chair, and Cece's fingers dove into her hair, pulling, twisting, and braiding. There was a certain wonder, familiarity, perhaps even *trust*, in letting someone else do her hair. With her eyes half-closed, Bella allowed her mind to drift back to when this was a common occurrence... before she knew it, Cece was tapping on her shoulder to rouse her.

A hand mirror Bella recognized from Malvagio's room was lifted, and all thoughts of Cece risking herself fled as Bella looked at herself. Her hair had been brushed until it shone, twisted into a high updo to grant her height she did not actually have. Combined with the dress, she appeared taller, slender, older than her years. Perhaps even *regal*. Cece *tsked* and dabbed at the corner of Bella's eyes with a handkerchief, wagging a finger at her.

"Sorry... I didn't even notice you applying makeup. I must have been more tired than I thought I was." Instead of tears, Bella let out a laugh. "I didn't realize you'd be turning me into a princess for the night! Where have you been hiding these skills?"

Cece raised an eyebrow, dropping her chin and staring at the youngster.

"Ah, right. Far, far away from my stepsisters. Makes sense." Bella scoffed and shook her head, only realizing afterward that they had done so at the same time. "I can't thank you enough, is there anything-"

Di~ing a bell rang from the floor above, indicating dinner was about to be served. Bella looked at the maid with a sheepish smile, only for Cece to flap her hands to shoo her up and away.

Going up the stairs and over to the closed door of the dining room, Bella took a deep breath before firmly pushing them open and striding in. Her eyes landed first on Bibbidy, who was wearing a wide smile, then over to her father, who went pale as if he had seen a ghost.

Alaric stood from his seat at the table, slowly walking over to Bella, who stood stock still as if he were about to shout. Instead, he swallowed hard, studying her face intently. "Bella, when did you turn into a woman? I missed it, didn't I? You've grown up while I've been doing other things. You look... just like your mother."

He took her hand, kissing the top of it before pulling her gently over to her seat, getting her settled, and moving back to his own place. The entire time, Bella was blushing, not only from the compliment, but because her mind was spinning from the first sign of affection she had gotten from her father in as long as she could remember.

Letting out a long sigh as he sat down, Alaric softly chuckled, "My Bappy, reincarnated in her daughter's face."

"It was *Boppity*, Boo." Bibbidy reminded him gently. "You're an adult as well, but you never were able to get the inflection just right."

"She never minded," Alaric stated with a sigh, reaching for his cup.

"So, tell me." Their exotic guest smiled at Bella. "You have your mother's face, do you have her *talent* as well?"

The question was an innocent one, but in an instant, the soft environment thickened, punctuated by her father releasing a disgusted scoff. Bella sank in her chair, and Bibbidy looked between the two of them, her sharp eyes taking it all in. "Oh? Now here's a story I must hear."

"We do not speak about it. Move on." Alaric sharply waved his right hand, even as his left lifted his cup as though he could hide behind it. For the first time, Bella noticed a tinge of shame in his words and didn't know how to react to it.

"Excuse you! I will *not* move on." Bibbidy focused all of her attention on Bella, and let out a ringing, clear command. "Speak freely, child. This *instant*."

Ever so haltingly, Bella began to speak, not sure where she was finding the courage to do so in front of her father. "Yes, I take after my mother. I have the class 'Beast Singer' and-"

"How *wonderful!*" Bibbidy brought her hands together in an excited clap. "A class devoted to beautifying nature and the creatures in it. Did you know how rare that class is? Beast *Tamers* are one thing, but a *Singer?* Oh, the lovely things you'll... you'll... wait. By now, you must have had your fifteenth birthday. Beast Singer is a *Basic* Class, is it not?"

Even though her hands were still pressed together from her previous excited motion, Bibbidy's head turned with creaking slowness 'til she could stare at Alaric, who seemed to be doing his best to study the bottom of the inside of his cup. Unable to take the awkwardness, Bella cleared her throat softly. "You see... it isn't a ladylike class. Not proper for low nobles who are hoping to increase their lot in life. So advancing in it is out of the question-"

Bibbidy scampered from her position at the table, swooping in to wrap her arms around Bella. The comfort was a rare experience, as was being open, not to mention her father's silence at their actions. All of this combined to create a single tear she couldn't hold back, which was followed by another, and another... until she was weeping into her godmother's soft, fancy robes.

"There, there. All is well. For *you*." As their exotic guest gently pushed back the lock of hair which had fallen across Bella's face, she rounded on Alaric. "As for *you*..."

The light in the room flickered, and the candles seeming to dim, a chill filling the room, though a fire was roaring in the mantle. The shadows around Bibbidy swirled and danced, her features fading as her eyes shone with starlight bright enough to let off its own glow. "How *dare* you? How dare you tarnish and diminish Elara's memory by trying to make her child ashamed of the part given to her by her mother?"

"Now, Bibbidy, the way I raise my daughter-" Alaric started in a weak voice, as though examining his failings and finding that all his excuses were feeble.

"Silence." The word was resonant, echoing in Bella's mind and causing her to go still, her tears forgotten as she looked on in stunned surprise. Bibbidy reached out her hand, placing her palm on the wood of the table, leaning in slightly and refusing to allow Alaric's gaze to squirm away. "Did you think I wouldn't notice what has been going on here? What she was wearing when I arrived? You stripped her of her room, her status. You dare to reduce your daughter, *Elara's daughter*, to a mere servant in your household? You may speak, oh yes, you *will* speak. I demand answers."

"She is willful and well on her way to being unmarriage-able." The words were thin, almost questioning as they fell from Alaric's lips.

"*So?*" That one word was filled with so much power, so much fury, that Bella was surprised her father was able to push through.

"I'm keeping her *safe*." This was said with more convic-tion, and for the first time, Bella realized her father truly believed his words. "Her mother's death was a direct result of her talent, and I've seen the bloody consequences. It will *not* be the same for her."

"No, Alaric." Bibbidy let out a long sigh. "It won't. Oh, how foolish I have been, holding off on my visit to give you time to heal. Instead, I arrive to find deep scars and misalign-ment. Would that I would have been here to help stitch things into place."

Giving Bella a gentle pat on her shoulders, Bibbidy stood and slowly walked back to her seat, plunking down and staring at Alaric with kind eyes. "My darling Boo, who ever told you to fixate on Elara's death and ignore her *life*? She was vibrant and free. She lived loud and loved deeply. She was a force unto herself and made those around her better. Much better, in some cases."

She stared down her nose as she said this, and the snub caused Alaric to wither in his seat. "She was proud of her class, what she could do for herself, for you, for her family, who she loved more than anything. Now, you are trying to ruin the only bit of Elara you have left, trying to cut her out of your life entirely or reduce her to something you can mark down on one of your forms."

"She would have wanted our Bella to be safe," Alaric whispered, unwilling, perhaps *unable*, to acknowledge his failed parenting. "I can't let her become... not even for you..."

His words were disjointed, and as they trailed off, Bibbidy let out a deep grunt of annoyance. "I had hoped this would be a great gift, and instead it will become something *else*. Well, if you won't listen to me, maybe you'll listen to *her*."

With a careful motion, the visitor pulled a letter out of the air, setting it on the table and slowly unfolding it. Immediately, a voice floated up from the paper, filling the room with a voice no one had heard in more than five years.

"My dearest Bibbidy."

Alaric was suddenly sitting rigidly in his chair, looking for all the world as though he had been struck by lightning. "Elara? Wait, this is a letter to *you*? When did she send it?"

"Shh!" Bibbidy cut him off.

Unable to hear him, the enchanted recording of Bella's mother continued to speak into the now-silent room. "My little family is the greatest achievement of my entire life. Forget the foxes, the birds, the griffins, the kraken... the one thing we're never lackin' is love and laughter. You must come and get to know Isabella better; I know you'll love her as much as I do. She is an always-laughing, joyous girl who lights up a room when she enters it. I admit, she is always underfoot, always in my work, asking why, why, why... and I love it."

"She-"

"I said '*shh*'!"

"I know you had your concerns in my choice of husband, but Isabella is proof that I made the right choice. Don't get me wrong, he's still the quiet, calculating, collected man I married... but Bella brings out in Alaric a jubilation I did not think was within him. With her, he lets his guard down in a way that no other person, including me, has ever been able to match. As she grows, they will bring out the very best in each other, I just *know* it. Do you know she's already showing the early signs of being a Beast Tamer?"

Laughter filled the air, a wild sound which had no place in a 'proper' environment. "She's just like her mama! I'm so very proud... it won't be long before the three of us are traveling the world. Alaric will sell the most beautiful of wares, and of course, whatever he wants to bring along, and the two of us girls will amaze the masses with all manner of beasts. From those we train to those we sell, the world won't know what hit it!"

"Now, where do you fit into all of this? I was hoping you would join us, travel with us for a while, so you can be there to celebrate Bella's tenth birthday and the unlocking of her class when we are done with our next caravan run. I know it would mean the world to her; you've been there for all the momentous occasions in her life already, but... for some reason, I just feel that having you nearby is important. We love you, we *miss* you, and hope you can catch up; just get here soon! Ever yours, Elara."

The room remained silent for seconds that felt like an eternity, then, to Bella's dismay, her father let out a broken sob. "She invited you there to watch her *die*!"

"Alaric." Bibbidy spoke with such tenderness that the man managed to look past his current crisis and hear her. "She called me in to watch you *live*. All three of you. A life full of laughter and joy. Is that what you have? Is *this* what you want?"

He struggled, taking deep breaths through his mouth, slowly turning until he was staring at Bella. "But how... will you ever forgive me?"

They stayed in their seats, staring at each other, until Bella realized he was truly waiting for an answer. "I just want to be your daughter again. I want you to be proud of who I am now... not who I could be."

"I'll take it," Alaric fervently promised her, standing from his seat so quickly that it fell to the ground. He ignored it as he came around the table, mimicking Bibbidy's actions by throwing his arms around her and pulling her close. "I never could deny Elara, and I know this is what she would want. I must... I *will*... I *am* proud of who you are."

Cupping her cheek, Alaric pulled back and stared into his daughter's eyes, his eyes shining with unshed tears. "This I swear to you... things will be different from this day forth."

NINETEEN

AT BIBBIDY'S INSISTENCE, Bella returned to her old room, sleeping on a mattress dragged in from Cattiva's. Even though she slept among paints and broken instrument parts, it was the best night of sleep she had managed in what felt like years.

Waking up to the sun shining in her face, Bella forced herself to relax, though her ingrained instincts told her to get up and start cleaning, cooking, or some other menial task. Instead, she began to hum in happiness, soon finding a handful, then dozens of mice dancing around the room as birds swooped in through the open window to sing along with her sweetly.

A knock on the door announced her return to reality, and the voice of one of the new maids floated in. "Bella! Uh, that is, Signora Isabella, your guest is preparing to leave and wished to say goodbye."

Catching her breath, Bella grabbed a robe and wrapped around herself before running down the stairs. Just outside the front door, Bibbidy was inspecting a pair of majestic white steeds hitched to her elaborate carriage. The older lady looked up, eyes curled into crescents as she beamed at Bella.

"Lovely baby Boo, did you sleep well? Is all right with your world once more?" Then she let out a startled laugh as Bella crashed into her, wrapping each other in crushing hugs.

"When will you be back, Godmother?" Bella anxiously spoke from where her face was buried in the tall women's riding cloak. "Having you here has been so... so amazing. I'm afraid of losing... *you* again. Please stay at least a *few* more days. It'll all fade like a good dream the moment you're gone."

"Your father wouldn't *dare* break his promise." Both of them knew what the youngster truly meant, but Bibbidy merely rubbed a thumb across Bella's cheek and gave a cryptic reply with a tight smile. "I'll return when the rains shift, and the moon is hollow once more."

Bella lifted an eyebrow in annoyance, making Bibbidy smirk. With a kiss on the forehead, she pulled back and assured her goddaughter, "Sooner rather than later. Don't you worry. I expect to return to see great changes. More than that, *good* changes."

This last bit had been directed at Alaric, who had stepped outside and witnessed their final exchange. He replied to her with all solemnity, "I fully anticipate that you shall. Thank you for showing up, no matter how unexpected or unannounced."

"Mm." Bibbidy's smile tightened slightly. "I do so look forward to meeting the woman who captivated you so, on my next visit."

"Safe travels, Godmother." Trying to express all of the emotions she was feeling within her at the moment, Bella gave Bibbidy one, final, tight embrace, then stood near the door waving until the carriage was finally out of sight. Eventually, another arm dropped around her shoulder, and she looked up to see her father staring off into the distance.

"Come now, we must make preparations for our own trip." Alaric gently pulled his daughter into the house, waving uncertainly into the depths of the manor. "Why don't you go pack, and I'll make a list of supplies we'll need. It's a week-long journey to the Class Shrine and back—accounting for entrance time slots—so be sure you have plenty of clothes, linens, and toiletries."

She all but sprinted to her room in the cellar, quickly gathering her dresses and coat. Then, realizing she had no luggage, she ran up and grabbed a spare from a storage room, running back to her underground room and packing as quickly as she could. Bella was only halfway done when she heard the return of her stepfamily, or, more accurately, the frantic footfalls from the servant quarters just above her head indicating that the demanding group had returned.

Squeak.

"Mert Junior, as terrible as they are, there's no need for that kind of language." Bella chuckled to herself as she forced the final bit of the gown into the oversized bag. "I agree it's odd they completely missed her visit, but, and this might sound selfish of me, I can't help but be glad of it. Bibbidy is *my* godmother, and if they had been at dinner, things might have turned out very differently."

Squeak.

"Okay, fair, *perhaps* they would have been influenced by her to be better people as well." Bella rolled her eyes as she played out the one-sided conversation, not *actually* able to understand her mouse friend. "Yet, somehow, I doubt it. Matringa would have driven her out, then locked the door so she couldn't get back in."

Turning on her heel, Bella rushed up the stairs with her heavy pack, bursting into the house just in time to find herself in the middle of an ongoing argument.

"-is unacceptable! you can't just leave at the drop of a hat! You have responsibilities, business agreements, a *contract!*" Matringa was actually shouting at her father, causing Bella's mouth to drop open in shock. If this got out, it would cause a scandal of unparalleled magnitude. "All these wares are taking up every room in the house, and the entirety of our savings is on the line! This conversation must wait!"

Alaric shifted to the side, watching on in shock as a small vase flew through the air and smashed into the wall. "Control yourself! Signora, I've been derelict in my duties far too long already. I must make this right, and I must do so immediately. You—stop that at *once!*"

A ceramic serving platter spun through the air, impacting the wall just to the side of Alaric and peppering him with shards of broken crockery. "Your duties? Your *duties?* You are a *merchant!* Your duty is to complete your trades and become a successful man, not a useless person who takes weeks off at a time in favor of *one* person, when he has three others relying on him and dozens of deals on the line! It's unfair to Cattiva, to Malvagio, and to *me!* It's Signore *Treesbane* all over again."

Bella's stepmother collapsed into a chair, face in her hands as she began to sob—the very picture of a destitute, long-suffering widow. Realizing the coast was clear, Alaric studied his wife, brushed off his shirt, and pondered the situation. Finally, he took a deep breath, casting an apologetic glance over to his daughter as he began to speak.

"I am most certainly *not* your previous husband gambling away his fortune and finding himself at the mercy of unsavory debtors. However, you do make a valid argument. I'll start my journey earlier than planned and sell the goods we have in stock. *Then* I will return and take Bella to the Class Shrine. A small break between contracts is completely acceptable, valid, and will cause no issue." Alaric stepped closer to his wife, his attention entirely focused on Matringa, and his back to his daughter.

"I knew it." Bella turned away, feeling sick to her stomach as she saw her only opportunity for escape vanish right in front of her.

Then, her father spoke, slightly louder as if to ensure she heard him. "The inventory will go quickly; it's all highly sought after. No need for worries. Still, I've taken note of my failure, and Bella *must* be moved back to her room. During my absence, she must also be fitted for a new wardrobe. Servant clothing will no longer suffice. It is unacceptable, and I have no idea why I convinced myself to let it go on this long."

He glanced over his shoulder, meeting his daughter's eyes, and Bella found herself pinching her arm to make sure she wasn't asleep. In the moment his eyes were on her, the young woman saw her stepmother look up at her husband, disgust flashing across her face for a bare moment before a sickly sweet smile appeared on her face once more. "Of course, husband. After all, this is your household, to run as you see fit."

"Furthermore, she must be allowed to hone her skills as a…" Alaric swallowed hard, took a deep breath, and powered on, "as a Beast Singer. I've come around, and I see the value in what she can do. All the things I've taken from her in my ire must be returned, and more. Her lessons in preparation for her debut have suffered, and her hands have become calloused and rough. Cleansing baths, a soft wardrobe, and a return to her proper status should see her ready before achieving her Full Class in a few years."

"As you say, all will be done. I will see to it personally." Matringa nodded vigorously, and Alaric seemed content with the reply. She stood and took his hand, gently pulling him toward the stairs. "Well… I suppose we must make haste and prepare for your departure, if you truly intend to leave by the end of the day."

"Today? No, I didn't mean I would leave-"

"Signore, why would you remain here if you intend to start making sales immediately? We have the commodities on hand; we have the help we need. Get loaded and get on the way." Matringa paused, grabbed a bell positioned near the stairwell, and rang it vigorously to call for the maids. "The sooner you go, the sooner you'll get back, correct? Oh good, there's the help! All of you, begin preparing the goods for a long journey. Bria, go tell Marco he is needed, and ensure Luca is working to load up for a long journey. Girls!"

"Matringa, I'm not sure-"

"This is a full family effort, no idle hands, no time to waste!" Matringa ignored her husband's protests, turning to stare at Bella. "Perhaps you should raid the pantry? I'm sure your father would prefer to leave with a hot meal instead of relying on what can be cooked over a fire. Bebee! The heavy blankets; there's still a chill in the air in the early mornings. Cece, pillows, and why isn't Bria back yet?"

Father and daughter were both caught up in the whirlwind of activity, and the day flew by until Bella found herself standing in front of her bemused father. To his credit, he flushed slightly, needing to clear his throat and hold himself still as he met her eyes. "I'll return as soon as I'm able and make sure you have everything I promised. Forgive my delay, but… it *will* happen."

"Of course, Father," Bella replied in a defeated tone, trying her hardest not to wince as Matringa's hand landed on her shoulder and squeezed gently.

Alaric nodded at his wife, stepped forward, and exchanged an awkward embrace, then stepped back and nodded at the group as a whole. "Keep her safe. I look forward to seeing a girl well on her way to being a noblewoman on my return."

"Don't you worry; I won't let her out of my sight." As Matringa spoke, Bella felt a chill run down her spine. "I'll take care of her exactly as she needs until you return."

As the merchant and the start of his caravan rolled down the road, Matringa looked at the evening sky and turned to Bella. "I'm sure I don't have to explain to you how exhausting the day's work has been, but I, for one, have no interest in moving beds or preparing rooms this evening. Why don't you return to the cellar and get a good night's sleep? Tomorrow is going to be *quite* a long day."

CHAPTER
TWENTY

WHEN SHE WOKE UP, Bella threw the doors to the cellar open, only to find that it was a cold, dreary, overcast, and drizzling morning. After a moment of arguing with herself, she descended the stairs once more, pulling on her warm servant dress—hoping it would be the last time she needed to do so. "Suzy, what do you think my new wardrobe will look like?"

Sque~eak!

"Oh, I agree!" Isabella twirled in place, swooping into a formal curtsy. "I'll make sure it matches my skin tone properly, doesn't wash me out, and highlights my features correctly. It *will* look beautiful, thank you. The blue color of this dress my godmother left me is a good base to build on; maybe I'll pick out similar fabrics."

Now warm and prepared for the day, she hurried back up into the main house, only for the hopeful smile on her face to fade as she walked through the building. Her steps slowed as she found an oddly silent, dark house, without a soul to be found. Worried that something terrible had happened, she called out, "Hello? Is everything alright?"

There was no reply. After going to the kitchen and checking the servant rooms, she climbed the stairs and checked the dining room, peeked into the sitting room, and finally pulled open the front door to see if everyone had gone outside. There, she found herself stopping short in shock. "What in the world happened to our lawn?"

All the shrubbery lining the path to the house had undergone a sinister transformation overnight. Once waist-high, it now loomed over her with unnaturally thick, knotted, and gnarled branches, each bristling with vicious thorns. Almost in a trance, Bella walked forward, shifting her head back and forth to try and see through the thick foliage, but finding her gaze unable to penetrate the thicket. The once-familiar path now felt like the entrance to a dark maze, foreboding and impenetrable.

"Oh look, she's *finally* awake." Matringa's voice came from almost directly behind Isabella, startling her enough that she almost leapt into the plants, only the nearness of the long thorns convincing her to catch herself before falling into them.

"Step… Signora Matringa, I didn't see you there." Bella swallowed as she tried to appear properly contrite. "My apologies for oversleeping; the darkness in the cellar combined with the weather convinced me it was earlier than I thought. What happened to the lawn?"

Matringa rolled her eyes, pursing her lips before seeming to decide on a proper admonishment. "Bella, excuses are the tools of the weak-willed, and I will have no dealings with them. If you have something to say, say it. If it causes issues, accept your punishment and move on."

Bella fought to keep her face still, though her left eyebrow betrayed her slightly by ticking upward. "Well. I'm certain it won't happen again, once I'm properly moved back into my room. I'm sure the light there will be better than what I get in the *cellar*. In fact, I'm perfectly happy to go and get that started right now… where are the servants?"

"Where are the other servants?" The way Matringa

rephrased Bella's question made the Beast Singer tense up, but she held her peace for the moment. "All in good time, child. As for the hedges, as always, they are here to help keep out unexpected, *unwelcome* visitors."

"Bibbidy is *always* welcome. Father said so." Bella crossed her arms and spoke firmly, despite knowing she was likely skating on thin ice by using this tone with Matringa.

"*Humm?* Now he's 'Father' again, I see." Matringa cocked her head slightly to the side, the fingers of her left hand drumming on her hip. "But notice, child, you did not say she was 'expected'. I understand you are simply naive toward the standards of polite society, but welcome or not, someone showing up like that is exceedingly rude and *uncustomary*. The hedges, well, they're just a tiny little extra precaution to help hold people to the 'polite' portion of *polite society*. Whether we like it or not... there are rules to adhere to, otherwise we are no better than animals. Don't you agree?"

"I agree that rules are in place for a reason," Bella carefully replied, not breaking down and continuing to speak, though Matringa seemed to be waiting for something more.

"I see." Matringa gestured grandly at the hedges. "Well, the beauty of my flora is manifold, but has two particularly important purposes. Not only will it keep unwanted visitors out, it will also serve as a firm boundary to help keep members of my household inside... and safe. Exactly as your father ordered."

Three heartbeats passed before Bella understood what her stepmother had just said, and her mouth dropped as she did a double take at the hedges. "The shrubs won't let us out? We're stuck in here?"

She looked up and down the hedgerow, realizing there was no break in them whatsoever. Overnight, not only had they more than doubled in size, they'd grown along the packed dirt road used to come and go from the estate.

Matringa shook her head and let out an annoyed huff.

"How absurd. They'll part for whomever I *decide* they should. As I mentioned, your father charged me with your safety. I can't have you leaving the area alone, and this will also help keep out dangerous animals. When he's out of town, who knows what trouble you might find yourself in?"

"I've *always* been safe here."

Matringa reached out and patted Bella on the head as though she were an oversized puppy. "Of course you have. Yet, somehow, despite not obtaining your oath, your father's interest in you has changed. He relented on the position he held for years, after a single night with an uninvited guest. He's your father, and it is his decision. While it is not a stance *I* would take with such a willful child, if you are allowed to begin increasing your skills as he ordered, who knows what you might accidentally draw in? Though you can't control it, what would happen if your little tunes summoned a bear or, worse, an Ascended Beast like a *Dread Bear*? You wouldn't know, but it has happened to others more skilled than a child like you."

As frustrated as she was by this turn of events, Bella didn't know enough about her class or skills to truly argue and simply had to trail behind Matringa as she began walking back to the manor.

"Now, let's have tea and... talk."

"Yes, Signora," Bella's words came out tiredly, defeatedly, and she only realized what had happened when she saw the small, victorious smile on her stepmother's face. "When will I be starting my lessons with you?"

"As soon as I have time for them, we can begin." Matringa sat down on the patio, ringing one of the ubiquitous bells which seem to be sprinkled in every room of the house and now apparently outdoors. Moments later, a tray arrived, with milk, sugar, and a single cup of tea. The Signora took the cup and sipped at it, half-closing her eyes in pleasure. "Ahh... nothing better on a dreary day like today."

Bella waited a moment, finally asking, "So, what sort of lessons will I be having? Father had mentioned-"

"Isabella Vigatori, how would I have that information already?" Matringa firmly set her cup onto the tray, the annoyance in her voice taking Bella aback. "I already have separate lesson plans for Malvagio and Cattiva and have had a single night between learning that I need to put together additional lessons and now. Am I supposed to figure out overnight what it is you need to learn, then assemble the lessons? Do you not know that I already have expectations to meet, as well as firmly set priorities? No. *Patience* shall be your first lesson. I suggest you learn it well."

After a long stretch of silence, Bella found that she was tapping her foot, unsure what to do. She wasn't certain if she was about to be bored into submission, or what other strange punishments Matringa was going to dream up. A few moments later, she froze, eyes going wide as she saw several mice up here, drawn to the rhythm and unintentional activation of her skills as her breathing fell into sync with her footfalls. Mert Junior waved at her from the doorway, pointing his little paw at Matringa, then drawing one of his claws across his neck and nodding questioningly.

Ever so slightly she shook her head, relieved that the mouse immediately scurried away—as he was *Perfectly* able to understand her intentions, thanks to her max-level Animal Communication skill. A moment later, she went rigid once more as the other mice stealthily came closer, vanishing under the table. She wasn't certain what they were doing, but a moment later, Matringa frowned and began to move to look at her feet.

"Did you see the dress my godmother brought me?" Bella blurted out, desperate to keep her stepmother's attention away from the small animals. "I was thinking we could use it as a base for my wardrobe selection."

"Brought... *you*?" Matringa's scoffing reply hit Bella like a brick. "As I understood it, she brought that as a gift for the household, to say nothing about the bolt of fine fabrics you tried to hide before I returned home."

"No, it was a gift to *me*." Bella leaned forward, her brow furrowing as she glared at her tormentor. "The dress, the fabric, they were given to me, for *me* to use. Also, I 'hid' nothing. Father told me to put it in my room."

"Me, me, me." Matringa mocked her, appearing more bored than anything at Bella's outburst. "Do you even hear yourself? How selfish you sound? Malvagio is the one who will be looking for a husband first, and let's be realistic... the fabric would outshine you."

Bella felt her vision tunneling as she shoved herself to her feet, hands balling into fists as she held herself back from lunging across the table. "That fabric is the only gift I've been given by anyone besides my father in years, given to me from someone who loves me, with no strings attached. Give it back. It's *mine*."

"Ah, yes, there it is. The famous return of your temper as soon as your father gives you the slightest amount of attention." Matringa's lips curled in a sneer as she practically dared the young woman to come closer to her. "Let me tell you this, *child*. Your tone just cost you your room. Perhaps, once you learn to moderate your voice instead of acting like a rabid dog, we could revisit this topic. For now, go back to the cellar. Perhaps you can reflect upon what *else* could happen when you make demands you have no right to make?"

"That fabric," Bella hissed, "is *mine*."

Matringa showed a syrupy smile which only accented her icy-cold stare. She shook her head back and forth just a tiny bit, pouting as she sing-sang her next words, "And much like your room, it was taken away. Now... off you go."

For a few long moments, Bella didn't move, instead merely breathing deeply as she thought through her next action. Before she could do anything foolish, she felt several dozen tiny claws as the mice under the table scampered up her pants and hid under the hem of her dress. Breathing deeply, she turned and woodenly walked away, slowly returning to the cellar as ordered.

When she was alone, she looked down at her legs, finding a half-dozen beady eyes staring up at her. "Well, I don't know what I was expecting. I should know better than this by now, shouldn't I? Why do I always let myself think it'll change?"

Just as she opened the door to the cellar, she heard a crash and a clatter, followed by her stepmother loudly cursing as hot tea poured over her. Bella glanced at the mice, who quickly pantomimed what they'd done by tying a string to Suzy's leg.

"You tied her to the table so everything would fall on her when she stood up?" Bella chuckled softly, descending the stairs and carefully pulling the door shut above her.

"Be more careful in the future, but... *great* job."

TWENTY-ONE

THE NEXT FEW months would have been absolute tedium, were it not for Bella being able to practice her skills without interference. With no lessons, no chores, and almost no human interaction whatsoever, her days blended together— marked only by the solitary meals she ate each day. The new cook was adept in the kitchen but inordinately cranky. Bella was *certain* that was the reason Matringa had been excited to hire him in the first place.

As she was unwelcome in the main house, Bella filled her days by sitting in the cellar and working with her mice or wandering the estate grounds singing to the birds. The avian creatures were always sent away, instructed not to linger in the area or go anywhere near the hedges. If it weren't for the fact that Bella wanted to hide her association with the rodents in the house, she would never paint a target on her feathered friends like she was.

But, as she always had to remind herself, especially when she saw crumpled pigeons and thorn-pricked crows: Matringa could *never* be allowed to know about how she was *really* practicing.

One day, as she got out of bed, Bella's feet landed on the

dirt floor of the cellar and felt as though they were going to freeze off. "Whaa! No! Winter can't be coming early this year, there's no reason my floor should be this cold."

After getting ready for the day, she walked up the stairs and out of the cellar, only to find that a thick rime of frost had settled over the lawn. She hurried inside, only to find herself face-to-face with her stepsisters, who seemed just as surprised to see her as she was to see them. Cattiva stepped close to Bella, a strange, squinting expression on her face. Her younger stepsister raised a hand then smacked Bella on the shoulder.

A puff of dust escaped the fabric, and the stepsisters let out a scoffing laugh before turning and walking away from her without a word. Cece trailed after them, a laden tea tray in her hands. The maid winced in sympathy for Bella's dusty state, then jerked her head to the side. Correctly guessing her intention, the Beast Singer went into the kitchen, finding a thick, steaming pot of porridge that she quickly took a bowl of to try and regain some body heat.

"Bella? Bella!" Matringa called down the stairs, "This is ridiculous, why do I need to shout through the hallways like some common hooligan to get your attention? Cattiva told me you were down there; come up here immediately."

Luckily, she'd finished eating by the time her stepmother came searching for her, so Bella quickly brushed off her dress to try and make herself as presentable as possible, then hurried up the stairs. "I'm here, Signora."

"Finally. Today I'm going to… what… why are you covered in filth?" Whatever Matringa had been about to say fled her mind as she took in the dusty, cobweb-in-hair, mess that was her stepdaughter. "You're disgusting."

Barely holding back her shrug, Bella maintained her poise and calmly replied, "My apologies, Signora, it was too cold to go straight to the bath this morning. The dirt floor and constant rain of dust in the cellar doesn't exactly lend itself toward keeping me clean, but normally I'm able to wash up before-"

"Yes, the ground is cold. That's what *happens* this time of year." Matringa let out a sigh as she explained the situation as sweetly as possible. "I understand you aren't happy with that, and you want the floor to be covered. Yes?"

Narrowing her eyes in suspicion, Bella slowly responded, "Yes... though I would much prefer to just have my room back. I know this might be strange, but I never expected sleeping inside my own house to be a privilege."

"Of course it's a privilege to sleep in your *father's* house. You don't see the common rabble of the town trekking out here and hibernating through the winter like groundhogs, do you?" Matringa shook her head and looked to the heavens, as if to question why she'd been burdened with such a dense child.

Just then, the stepsisters entered the room, shooting Bella nasty looks when they saw she was a part of whatever they'd been called for. Matringa turned to them with a smile. "Good, you're all here. Now, we've received an invitation for a winter gathering. You may recall our *friend*, Rosa, who married the Earl?"

"Yes, of course!" Cattiva clapped her hands eagerly. "Does this mean we are going to be fitted for some new dresses? I love the winter style. Fur just *works* for me."

Matringa waited for her daughter to finish speaking, raising an eyebrow at the interruption. "Indeed, a better wardrobe is needed for all of us. However, in my mind, this would be a welcome opportunity to mingle with the nobility and perhaps spread the news of Malvagio's upcoming eligibility. Wouldn't it be wonderful to see her married up the social strata?"

"A new dress and new shoes, then." Malvagio rolled her eyes, as if accepting a dark fate. "Fine."

Cattiva butted in, "Mother! I want a new necklace-"

"Girls, girls, take it easy, we have *plenty* of time. Plus, we already *have* the fabric for your new dress, don't we?" Matringa let out a tinkling laugh, her eyes burning with excitement and ambition. "How about *you*, stepdaughter?"

The question threw Bella for a loop, as she had expected to be ignored and so had gotten busy plotting how she would retrieve her stolen fabric. "Me? I... need a new coat?"

She flushed as her stepsisters made scathing sounds of annoyance at her simple request, but held firm. Bella knew the ride to the Earl's manor would be multiple hours at the minimum, and it wasn't as though she were going to be allowed to curl up next to one of her stepfamily for warmth—she would choose to freeze before doing so.

"Done." Matringa took a sip of her tea, pointedly raising her pinky into the air as she sipped. Catching sight of Bella, she set her cup down and returned the stare in kind. "What? You can't imagine I would allow you to freeze when you are directly in my care? I can't imagine what kind of person you think I am, but I doubt you are fair to me in your thoughts."

"Fa-" Bella flinched and snapped her mouth shut before she could let her incredulousness overtake her sense of self-preservation. Again. "Thank you for your consideration."

Her stepmother ran a critical eye over the girls, then she turned to Bella once more and waved for her to go. "We'll find something for you to wear. Now, I've sent some of the servants to gather coverings for your floor, so your precious feet don't get *chilly*. Perhaps we'll find you some fancy *slippers* you can ruin by playing in the dirt as well."

"I've always *loved* slippers; thank you for your consideration." Bella replied monotonously, doing her best Malvagio impersonation. Matringa pursed her lips then gestured at the door once more, perhaps giving up on trying to goad Bella into 'earning' a punishment.

"Go get your room in order. In fact, it would be a good day for you to spend some time thinking over how you want your future to look. Make yourself a tray of food; no need to come back inside today." Matringa turned back to her daughters and began once more speaking excitedly of dresses, pearls, and pageantry, as though she hadn't just ordered her husband's child to suffer in solitude.

Doing just as ordered, Bella went down to the kitchen and searched for food, only to find that the bland porridge was the only ready and available food. For some reason, the pantry now had a thick padlock on it, barring her from making her own meals—at least without permission. "You want me to take enough for lunch and dinner? *Fine.*"

Bella grasped the large pot by its handles, hauling the entire thing with her and leaving a trail of steam in the frosty morning as she marched over to the entrance of her room. In her anger, she almost slipped on the top stairs, which had a thin sheen of ice on them, and forced herself to calm down enough to maintain her balance. Throwing open the door, she called out to her animals, "Today, we feast! Tomorrow, we…"

Looking around the room, Bella took in the sudden appearance of the huge piles of straw, which had been tossed into her room. "Oh. Look. The promised floor covering. Who needs rugs or blankets when you can nestle into dried grass, like a chicken?"

She walked across the ankle-deep straw, grimacing as she saw the long strands cling to her dress and socks. "This… this will not do. If I leave this as it is, I'm going to be infested by bugs on top of freezing to death. If only I could order crickets around as easily as a shrew!"

After sitting on the bed and staring at the intentionally frustrating situation her stepmother had created for her, the Beast Singer started looking at the positives of the situation. "Well… no one's expecting to see me for at least a day. I have plenty of food for myself and my friends, and, well, to be fair, it's already less damp in here. How can I turn this to our advantage?"

Beginning to hum as she thought through her options, Bella allowed her mice to gather in droves. "If you're all willing to help me, I think we can turn this into a huge positive. What do you think?"

Squeak! The reply was instantaneous and unanimous.

"Wonderful. Thank you all; you are kinder than you ever need to be." Taking a deep breath and clapping her hands, Bella let out a sudden, aggressive sneeze. She rubbed her nose, trying to get rid of the frown on her face. "We need to clean, organize, and create. Can I get half of you to move all of the straw from this half of the room to the other side, and the other half.... we need to figure out a way to turn all this loose straw into something dense. Could we weave it? Straw rope is a thing; it just isn't very strong, right?"

She joined the first group, using her hands and already straw-coated dress to scoop large swathes of straw off the floor and into the other side of the room. As she sang to pass the time, any scraps she missed were quickly gathered by her furry friends.

"In a cellar dim and cold, a girl and mice fight straw and mold! Together we toil the straw to shift, and you know what? With every bundle, my spirits lift!"

Bella found herself chuckling as she worked, not noticing that her happiness was infectious—the mice were working faster and harder at the same time.

"Scamper and hustle, little feet so spry! I'm tired and angry, but can't just sit here and sigh! Straw to the left, straw to the right, clear this cellar with all your might!"

Behind her, the second team of mice began to weave the straw together, their tiny mouse hands achieving a tightness of weave that larger human hands simply couldn't. As Bella continued to sing, the new straw rug continued to grow.

"Together we'll work, not one straw missed! In perfect harmony, we'll coexist. By noon today, our task will be done... just a girl and mice working as one!"

She kept practicing the song, adjusting it until she was happy with how it sounded, how it flowed. With her hands busy, and her mind working on a task, the hours flowed by. The Beast Singer made sure to give the small creatures rest as needed, doling out porridge when they were hungry but needing them to secure their own water when they were thirsty.

Before Bella knew it, the straw rug had grown to the size of nearly three-quarters of the floor's space, and she was out of loose straw. Taking a look at the weave, she was shocked by the perfection and density of the creation, "By the system! I bet I could use this to carry water, if I needed to. Great work, no… fantastic, unbelievable work!"

Squeak. The mice stood on their hind legs, kicking their feet as if embarrassed at the praise. They made a 'go on' motion, waving their front paws at her—all but one. One of the mice, an extra fluffy little guy she had named Gus, was doing something odd. Bella stepped closer, and found that the mouse was chewing on a small bug.

"Were you all eating the bugs in the straw as you cleaned and wove?" Many of the mice nodded vigorously, and Bella could only silently thank them, holding back happy tears as she thought of how terribly the day could've gone—how badly it was *intended* to go. "Thank you all… as far as I'm concerned, you've spun this straw into gold."

CHAPTER
TWENTY-TWO

SEVERAL DAYS LATER, Bella was called up to the sitting room, where her stepmother was waiting for her. Without a word, Matringa held out a long black coat. It was fluffy enough that it had to be stuffed with down, and while obviously not new, it looked *warm*.

Bella was delighted.

"It's wonderful! Thank you!" She took the coat, hugging it to herself while looking closely at the wooden buttons and running her fingers along the soft fabric. For a long moment, Matringa frowned, her brow furrowing as she tried to reconcile her expectations with this elated reaction for an old, heavily used coat.

Eventually, the Signora merely shrugged and allowed a smile to play about her lips. "Yes, well, Giada the Younger... the not-dead one, won't be needing it. Here, one of Malvagio's old dresses for you to wear as well."

"Giada?" Bella went stock-still, even as her stepmother perked up.

"Why, yes, she left it behind when she left town. Since both her mother and father have passed on, it was time for her to go as well. After all, the house was never theirs; it was merely a loan from our family to her parents, to use as long as they wished. Well, *they* aren't using it anymore." Matringa walked from the room, calling over her shoulder, "We're leaving for the Earl's estate within the hour. I suggest you put together your clothes and get the dress on."

Bella knew her stepmother wanted her to be upset about her childhood friend leaving the area, but she could only feel relieved that Giada had escaped Matringa's clutches. Taking only a moment to be thankful for this fact, Bella hurried down to her room and frantically began packing. After *significantly* less than an hour, her stepfamily impatiently began shouting for her to join them, and she rushed through the cold outside air with her sweaty gown clinging to her.

By the time the carriage began moving, she was decidedly shivering. To her surprise, Bella was seated next to Cattiva in the wagon, instead of on the driver's seat or some other ignoble position.

The ride passed ever so slowly, with each of the others simply staring at Bella, waiting for any small infraction they could use to nitpick her attitude, clothing, or whatever they could think of. The only silver lining for Bella—though confusing—was that Malvagio was *not* wearing a dress made from the fabric gifted to her by Bibbidy. Thinking about that, and trying to figure out why, gave her enough mental space to ignore the constant jibes.

Eventually, the stepsisters got bored and pulled out a book. Cattiva began reading, while Malvagio sketched away on blank pages, though she had to keep pausing, reaching under the sleeves of her dress to fiercely scratch at herself as though she'd fallen into a patch of poison ivy.

"Stop that, Malvagio." Matringa ordered her oldest daughter. "It's not going to help. You are only tearing up your skin; I told you already, we will fix this when we can."

After an interminable ride, they began exiting the carriage, but not before Matringa gave Malvagio a not-so-subtle nod. The older stepsister began whispering under her breath, touching the sketch she'd been working on. Before Bella could question their antics, a footman was reaching for her hand and pulling her out of the carriage.

"Welcome, welcome, *welcome* friends!" Rosa called over, her eyes landing on Bella and widening fractionally. "Oh! You look much improved from last time, I do hope you've gotten over whatever was ailing you."

Once more, Bella was excluded from the greeting hugs, but at least this time she wasn't literally barred from being near the Earl's new wife. The Beast Singer grumbled internally, swearing to herself she would soon find a mirror and figure out what illusion had been draped over her true appearance. Still, this time she knew better than to try and make a complaint or ask for help—at least until the illusion began to fade, then she'd actually have *proof* that she wasn't simply trying to cause damage to her stepmother's reputation.

They were escorted into the house, and Bella gasped at the sight of the packed room. It had been *years* since she'd been around more than a handful of people at a time, and she felt a rush of shyness. Remembering her etiquette lessons, she forced herself to begin taking even breaths. Her discomfort only grew as she passed a mirror, though this time around, her visage wasn't *nearly* so grotesque as Malvagio had forced upon her the last time they met with Rosa.

"I've got hair and teeth this time. I'm practically *beautiful* compared to last year." This time, the person looking back at her from the mirror was much more believable as a real person, instead of a caricature. Yet, there was no escaping the sheer unpleasantness she evoked in others. "Her artistry sure has progressed, hasn't it? Good for her... me, not so much."

She was seated at the table directly adjacent to Matringa, and immediately, servants began to filter past, putting snacks and treats on their plates. Bella looked around, noticing plenty of people diving in, and so she reached out and took a small bite of a sugar cookie, immediately beginning to hum in delight at the intense, sweet flavor. After a moment, she realized her error, scanning the room and noting a mouse staring directly at her. Changing her tune, Bella cautioned all small animals to stay away from the ballroom.

She had no doubt that traps and cats would be brought in immediately if a guest saw there was vermin scurrying about in the Earl's house. Murmuring to herself as she reached for another treat, Bella compared herself to those very mice and tried to figure out what sort of trap Matringa was setting up for her. "Gotta make sure I don't somehow use my class's powers and embarrass our host. I bet my tormentor would figure out a way to refuse to allow me to practice my skills."

Reaching for the fruit tart on her plate, she turned her head to the side and found Matringa staring directly at her. Bella froze in place, realizing a moment later that they were alone at the table. The Signora leaned in. "Why don't you go dance? The other girls were swept away barely moments after sitting down."

"Something tells me my current makeup just isn't to the tastes of the men dancing around in here," Bella replied firmly, leaving no openings for Matringa to jump on. "I didn't even notice them go; I've been enjoying the food too much."

"Well. No arguments *there*." The Signora gave a pointed look down toward Bella's stomach before turning to watch her girls dance. For a moment, Bella wavered between dropping the fruit tart or eating it, but she eventually shrugged and popped it into her mouth.

It was there to be eaten, and she rarely had such quality food these days.

A few minutes later, the dance ended, and the stepsisters returned to the table, winded but laughing. Their mother greeted them with a tight smile, causing both of the young ladies to cease their giggling and sit up straight. "I hope we all remember why we're here. Bella, at this point, why don't you just go over to the buffet directly? Perhaps you can even leave a few scraps for the rest of us."

"Absolutely, Matringa." Pretending not to understand how she was being insulted, Bella immediately took the opportunity to escape and leapt to her feet. She moved directly toward the area where food had been set out, ignoring the scoff behind her. Glancing over her shoulder, she noticed both of her stepsisters were on their feet, trailing along behind her. "Abyss, I'd been hoping they'd be focused on other things tonight."

"Would one of you pretty young ladies care to dance?" a man's voice called out just behind her, and Bella froze. She turned around, letting out a small sigh of relief when she realized the nobleman was speaking to Malvagio.

The older girl brushed her hair back over her ear, showing a bright smile before pointing the man at Bella, using the motion to hide how her other hand began vigorously scratching at her lower back. "I just came off the dance floor, perhaps I can convince you to twirl about with my stepsister for a song or two?"

Though he appeared disappointed, the man turned toward Bella, only for his polite smile to become strained. "Ah, unfortunately, I see my good friend has just arrived, and I must run to greet him!"

Even though she knew exactly what was going on, Bella felt a flush of humiliation tinge her cheeks red. She ended up standing next to the buffet for so long that Matringa herself finally marched over, hissing at her angrily, "How long are you going to stand here? Are you just eating directly out of the chafing dishes like this is a pig trough? Get back to-"

Before she could spew any more of her vile words, no matter how muted they might be, a small dog jumped out of a nearby lady's arms and rushed toward Matringa, growling and snapping. Bella hummed softly, thinking calm thoughts, trying to get the small creature to go away, but the dog refused to stop, even when his owner tried to call him back over and over. Finally, a man stepped forward, heavily relying on a cane and scooping up the pup.

"Come now, what are you yapping about? Forgive us, Signora, he's but a puppy, and we've been having the most difficult time finding a qualified trainer." The gentleman bowed as gracefully as his apparent injury would allow. As for the dog, it had stopped snarling, but it was still staring Matringa down, showing its teeth and letting its tongue snake out to lick at its lips every few seconds.

Oddly enough, Matringa had gone pale over the encounter, though she attempted to gracefully excuse herself from the situation. "Think nothing of it."

She swept away, and the elderly man turned to Bella with a far different expression on his face. "Signora Vigatori, you don't seem to be having much fun. A sweet girl like you should be right in your element here."

"I don't get out... much." Bella finished her statement somewhat lamely, unsure what to say at the moment. She didn't fail to notice she'd been called a 'sweet girl' and not a 'pretty young lady' as she had been hearing her stepsisters being called all night. Still, she found herself relaxing in his presence, especially with the dog staring at her with its ears up and a clear smile on its face. "What's his name?"

"Pacatezza." The man vigorously pet the dog, and it leaned into the open hand happily. "I call him Paca for short. I had been hoping naming him 'calmness' would help, but it doesn't seem to be working, as you have no doubt noticed. But... you know what?"

The old man leaned in conspiratorially. "You may think me an old fool, but I think dogs have a way of knowing who are good people and who aren't. Nobody in the dark wants to be found out, but dogs? Dogs know. They're too pure for the darkness of this world, and they'll warn you about it, if you listen. But… to be fair, he barks at everyone. Everyone but you, I guess!"

Letting out a deep laugh, he nodded at her and walked back to his wife, speaking softly to his puppy. Moments later, a young man—just a little older than Bella—stood from the table and walked over to her, a smile on his face. As he got closer, she realized he stood at least a head taller than she did. The smile on his face exuded confidence, though he had an air of a scholar about him. Stopping an arm's length away from her, he sketched a bow, his curly brown hair bouncing gently as he completed the motion.

He looked up, deep brown eyes swirling with a strangely intense reflection of firelight meeting her own baby blues; intelligence, curiosity, and a hint of mischief within them. As he opened his mouth, his clear, articulate words reinforced her supposition of his intense tutelage. "I beg your pardon, had I managed to lay eyes on you sooner, I would have earnestly requested the honor of a dance. Is there some *small* chance you might forgive my oversight and find room to grant me that privilege?"

"Um. Me?" Though she was trying her hardest not to look around and see if he was speaking to someone behind her, Bella still found it hard to believe he was looking directly at her.

"Only if you are free, of course…?" He let the question linger until she finally remembered her manners and nodded frantically. With a grin, he took her hand and led her to the dance floor.

They swept around the room once, Bella concentrating on not stepping his feet, while he concentrated on studying her. As they twirled past candles, the flames flared higher, causing their shadows to dance along the walls and light to continually shift the contours of their faces. For some reason, the music continued on and on, far longer than any of the songs before.

Finally it ended, and her only dance partner of the

evening stepped back and bowed. Bella curtsied in return, feeling breathless and light-headed, but unable to keep the smile off her face.

Paca barked, drawing their attention to the older couple who were on their feet. "My apologies, it seems my parents are eager to return home. I won't forget this dance. Perhaps we will meet up at another such locale in the future?"

Before she could answer, he swept away, only to be replaced by Matringa in the next moment. As the Signora opened her mouth to speak, Rosa stepped closer, staring at Bella incredulously. "By the *system*, dancing agrees with you! You must come back again. Why, you nearly look like a different person."

Matringa flinched at Rosa's words, as though she'd been physically struck, her eyes flicking back to Bella and turning calculating.

"Mother, I need-" Malvagio stepped forward and whispered to her mother, but Bella didn't hear what else she said. Her eyes were drawn to Malvagio's neck, where an aggressive rash was spreading from under her dress.

Matringa noticed as well. Very quickly, she thanked their host for the lovely evening, politely refused an overnight stay, and hustled her charges out to the carriage.

CHAPTER
TWENTY-THREE

SPRING HAD NEVER SPRUNG SO BEAUTIFULLY, at least in Bella's mind. By the time all the snow had melted, and she was free to sit outside and watch the birds, the Beast Singer had—out of sheer boredom—worked with her mice to weave not only a continuation of the floor mat, but also wall coverings and an entire reupholstering of her mattress. The room might've smelled like a hayloft, but it was as intricately decorated as anywhere else in the house, if not as expensively.

Even more wonderfully, spring meant the return of her father. At least, by the end of the season. She couldn't wait to get to the Class Shrine, upgrade her class, and find any, any, *any* reason to never return to this house.

A frown touched her lips, and Bella muttered to herself, "Then again, I'll only be almost seventeen... everyone automatically unlocks their Basic Class, their 'child' class, at ten years old. Anytime after turning fourteen, they can unlock their Advanced Class, but no one's considered an adult until they unlock their Full Class, their 'Adult' Class, at eighteen. Even if I get to the Class Shrine, I won't be considered an adult until the unlock *after* this one."

A noise on the patio behind her startled Bella, and she

looked over to find Cattiva staring at her with an annoyed expression on her face. Her younger stepsister flopped into the chair opposite Bella. "Don't you have better things to do than sit outside and stare into the distance all day?"

"Literally no, Cattiva," Bella replied with the exact same amount of acid in her tone. "Your *mother* made sure of that. Also, just because she talks down to me doesn't mean I'll let you do the same. Believe me when I say I can make your life just as uncomfortable as you make mine."

Cattiva leaned back, surprised at the strength in Bella's tone, then her face went flat and unreadable. "I think you should be careful how you speak to your betters."

Even though the words came out of the face of a petulant sixteen year old, the way they were said with such confidence and surety managed to send a chill up Bella's spine. Cattiva not only believed the words, she very much so *meant* them.

Keeping her own face neutral, to hide how unsettled she felt, Bella crossed her arms and raised an eyebrow. "Sisters are usually in the same class of people. Not to mention, I'm older than you. You live in *my* father's house."

"This argument is beneath me." Cattiva shrugged prettily then sat primly in her chair, mimicking Bella's earlier position as she stared at the sky. A moment later, she let out a shriek of disgust as a bird flew overhead and dropped a present into her hair. Flinging her chair to the ground as she rocketed to her feet, Cattiva ran off to clean herself. "I *know* you did that!"

To add insult to injury, Bella called after her, "I don't know why you're so upset; some people think that's good luck!"

Even though she actually hadn't had anything to do with the insulting 'gift' from the passing bird, Bella knew she'd be blamed for it. As she ruminated over this thought, she started hearing the sound of someone breathing heavily. Her eyes drifted to the side, only to land on a man standing at the edge of the patio, breathing heavily and staring at her with bloodshot eyes as small rivulets of actual blood poured off him from dozens of locations. "Wah! *Abyss!*"

"Pardon my intrusion!" The man quickly held up his hands and waved them to show he wasn't armed. "I am but a messenger, delivering a letter."

"To the *patio*? At the back of the house?" Even as the words fell from her mouth, Bella felt bad for speaking them. "No, I'm sorry, I'm just still startled from your sudden appearance. Why are you here instead of at the front door? Why are you *bleeding*?"

The young man blinked and looked down at his arms, where thin trails of blood were running down his skin. "Oh, yeah, that. Something's wrong with your hedges; I ran around the entire property looking for a way in. The thorns got me, is all. That's also why I'm here instead of at the front door. I wasn't sure which way I was supposed to go. Anyway, the letter is from Signore Vigatori, meant for Signora-"

"I'll take it." Bella firmly held out her hand, and the man reluctantly dropped the letter into her waiting palm. "Can I help clean you up? I have a wash basin just on the other side of that wall, and-"

He shook his head, wiping his arms mostly clear of the dripping blood. "Can you just point me toward the gap in the hedges? Maybe throw a couple copper my way for prompt service?"

They stared at each other for a few moments as the young woman tried to figure out how to get him out of here without alerting the entire household to his presence. A thought struck her, and she whistled a few bars. "Why don't you take a seat, and I'll figure something out?"

The young man sat down, frowning and letting out a sigh of annoyance as she joined him at the table, unfolding the letter and immediately beginning to read. "Hey, I thought you said you'd-"

"Just a moment. *Please.*" Bella turned her full attention to the document, ignoring his annoyed muttering.

To the residents of my household,

I'll cut to the chase. The odds of me returning home this season are... slim. It pains me to write this, as I long to see familiar faces, dine at my own table, and sleep in my own bed. Yet, it seems that no matter what I do, our wares are simply not selling. I have taken the same path as my last route, as the towns had seemed in such dire need of the goods I provide. We had all hoped they would remember us fondly and greet me with open arms and coin aplenty.

Unfortunately, the farther we go from home, the worse the news becomes. A strange sickness has befallen these towns, and no one is willing to leave their homes for fear of growing ill. No markets are open, and I've been needing to go door to door to sell even the most meager of goods. Even then, I've been chased off more doorsteps than I care to count.

I must adjust my travel plans, taking a route not yet traveled. As I'm sure I don't need to tell you, if I fail to sell at least two wagons worth of these goods, we will be ruined. Matringa, I must ask you to halt the plans on the extensions of the manor. The luxury goods such as paints and high-end instrument accessories are not forgotten, they will just be brought home later than anticipated. Bella, I will be sending another letter to a friend to come and escort you to the Class Shrine; I have not forgotten my promise.

I know you will all be fine until I can make it home, but be safe and make me proud.

Cordially, Alaric Vigatori.

"That's father, alright." Bella shook her head sadly, "He signed it 'cordially' to his wife and daughter."

Moments later, a shadow flicked across their table, and

three copper coins tied together with string bounced on the table with a sharp note of metal on wood. The messenger scooped up the coins, nodding at Bella as she folded up the paper. As he turned to go, she took a deep breath, "Would you like more coin?"

Turning back, the young man raised an eyebrow, a wry grin on his face. "Does a wolf poop in the woods?"

"I... believe so?" They looked at each other for a moment longer, then Bella held out the folded message. "If you deliver that to the front door and don't say a word about letting me read it first, I'll make sure it's worth your time."

"A little family drama, huh? Sure, why not?" The young man took the envelope, winked at her, and took off running. Bella waited a handful of minutes then stood from the table and walked inside, moving slowly through the house so she could arrive just as Bria closed the door in the messenger's face.

"Who was that?"

The maid looked at her with sadness in her eyes. "Never you mind, young miss. A letter arrived for Signora Matringa."

Bella cocked her head, trying to show her interest, "Oh? Who is it-"

"*Surely* you are not badgering the hired help in a blatant attempt to gain access to my private messages?" Matringa called imperiously from her perch on the stairs above them.

"It's *Isabella*, Signora," The Beast Singer replied with confusion in her voice. "My name isn't Shirley."

"Daft child," Matringa grumbled as she stomped down the stairs. "Get out of my way. Bria, the mail."

Snatching the letter, the stepmother went back up the stairs, closing the door firmly behind her as she entered the study—as it wouldn't be proper to slam it behind her, and she was nothing if not the paragon of etiquette.

Slowly, carefully, Bella allowed a drawn-out sigh of relief to escape her lips. It had worked, and now there was no reason for her stepmother to suspect she knew exactly what had been written in the letter. Her eyes narrowed as she stared up at the hallway, "Let's see how much of a lie you're going to tell me. If nothing else, it'll be a good baseline for future conversations."

Moments later, Matringa reappeared at the top of the stairs and called out, "Bella! Come back here; I have received word from your father."

The young lady had stepped out of the room and waited a few moments to return, as though she hadn't been skulking about. "The letter was from my father? What did it say? Is he almost home?"

Her acting seemed satisfactory, or at least Matringa was too focused on her own thoughts to notice anything strange. "Your father won't be returning this season; it appears he's run into some trouble on the road."

"Oh no! Is he okay? When will he be back, did something happen-"

Matringa held up a hand, palm toward the young woman, and Bella bit back her words. By the flash of delight that crossed her stepmother's face, perhaps her acting fearful and scared had been a bit *too* good. "Hush, child. Apparently, he's been running into some sickness along his usual route. It's nothing to worry about; this is what *happens* as winter ends. People get sick. Still, it's delaying him. I'm sure he'll send word when there is news to be had."

She turned to leave, but Bella called up after her, "Is that all? May I read the letter? Surely, something awful must have happened if he's not going to make his normal timeline; he's a *Perfect* Merchant. A few people getting the sniffles shouldn't be enough to stop him."

"I've given you the information, and now I must make preparations." Matringa turned back, all fake smiles gone from her face—which could've been cut from stone with how still she was keeping it.

"As I'm sure you saw, this letter didn't arrive with a sack of gold so I could pay the servants, and it makes not a single mention of *forthcoming* funds. Since this is the case, I must dismiss the excess staff, cancel the expansion projects, and generally make other people's lives harder by having them lose their jobs with us. I hope you can find it in your heart to allow the needs of others to take precedence over *you* reading a letter from Daddy."

As her stepmother stormed off, Bella turned and walked away as well, keeping her face neutral. If she hadn't already read the letter, she would be retreating to the cellar and furiously pacing until she did something foolish about the missive.

Instead, she decided to do something completely unrelated to the letter, but possibly even *more* foolish. Upon returning to her room, she calmly looked around at the mice who were waiting for her, drawn by her having been walking and breathing in a rhythmic manner, understanding her intentions to have them gather.

"Tonight's the night, everyone. It's time to get my fabric back."

CHAPTER

TWENTY-FOUR

"*CAN'T STEAL what's already yours! My mice, I'll need your help with this quest. It's not about being the best dressed; it's about being able to rest.*" Bella softly sang her song, repeating it over and over as she clearly visualized what needed to happen.

She knew the mice had a deeply ingrained knowledge of the intricate pathways through the house and had been trained for a full generation at this point on remaining hidden while carrying out tasks of both reconnaissance and sabotage. But tonight, they were going to fulfill one of her original goals: getting into the study and taking something Matringa was hiding from her.

In her mind, Bella laid out the plan, singing her intentions into the minds of the creatures around her. Over and over she repeated her song, only drifting into silence as the last of the small animals vanished into tiny holes in the ceiling. "*Can't steal what's already yours…*"

Then she let out a deep sigh, carefully sitting on the bed and settling in to wait. At this point, there was nothing to be done, nothing except hoping everything would turn out as she'd envisioned. Right now, she was trapped in the dark, both figuratively and mostly literally. Between the extreme flammability of all of her decorations and her stepmother refusing to allow Bella to take an 'expensive' covered lamp to her room, as night settled in, the only illumination in the cellar was a soft glow sneaking between the slats of wood above her.

Minutes stretched to an hour, and she had long since began pacing around her room from sheer nervousness. Every sound felt amplified: footsteps on distant floors felt like drums being pounded. The soft rustle of woven straw under her feet was comparable to crunching through leaves in autumn. What she *didn't* hear was tiny claws scraping on wood or the soft sigh of fabric snaking through tunnels in the walls.

Finally, there was a muted **squeak** from one of her mice, the signal she had taught them when they needed to make sure the coast was clear. "Yes! Come in, come in!"

One by one, the mice appeared out of the shadows for only a moment at a time as they darted through the lines of light drawn on the floor. Her heart leapt at the sight of them, relief washing over her as she counted each tiny little head. "Are you all safe? That took far longer than I expected... I'm so sorry, I shouldn't have sent you on such a selfish mission."

Mert Junior came to the front of the group, but as he got on his hind legs, he stared at the floor instead of meeting her eyes proudly as per usual. Bella's lips pressed into a line as she saw his dejected posture and crouched down to offer a hand to him. "You didn't find it? Or you couldn't bring it back? That's okay, don't worry about it."

Sq... squeak. The leader of the mice shook his head, followed by what Bella could have sworn was a sigh, before he looked back and motioned with his paws.

A carpet of mice surged forward, and Bella's eyes widened in delight as she saw the fabric she'd been gifted appear. They went even *wider* when she saw that each mouse was carrying cloth, but none of it was connected. The sparkling blue fabric was in tatters, shredded into strips and patches without the help of scissors or a sharp knife. Bella's hands trembled as she picked up a piece, holding it in the light to see the damage that had been done.

Tears stung her eyes as she looked at the gift that had been stolen from her, and her heart ached as she realized that Matringa hadn't destroyed the fabric for any purpose but spite. Her stepmother knew exactly how much the fabric had meant to Bella, and instead of making something beautiful with it, even if it was for someone else, she had done her best to outright destroy it. "Why would she do something like this? Why would she *save* it? Was she going to show it to me in a moment where she needed to cause me grief?"

To her surprise, as she collected more and more of the scraps, Bella realized the majority of them were covered in a thin layer of soot. She wasn't sure what to make of this, until finally something clicked in her head, and she turned to look at Mert Junior. "Did you pull this out of the *fireplace*? She tried to *burn* it?"

Squeak. Mert nodded solemnly.

"It wouldn't burn...?" Bella turned the fabric over and over in her hand, trying to figure out what that meant. "Maybe... when I saw it for the first time, it glowed for me. Maybe that wasn't just my excitement; maybe it's *actually* magical cloth. Bibbidy has never been one to take half measures with things, and if she has access to magical goods, some of her business practices would make more sense."

Turning her attention to the mice, who'd all been waiting silently, sadly, she put a smile on her face and looked around at all of them. "Thank you all so much for working on this, and... who knows? If this was magical cloth, maybe there's something else special about it. Maybe we can salvage something from this mess? At the very least, we'll keep it around to patch up my dresses when they get damaged. Would you all do me another favor and hide this in the walls for me?"

Squeak. Without another word, the mice rushed forward, swirling around her and lavishing her with hundreds of tiny hugs. Then, one by one, they accepted a scrap and ran it up into the ceiling and from there into their hidden places in the walls.

Bella dropped heavily onto her bed, utterly spent from the bitter emotions she was feeling. Throwing an arm over her eyes, she took a long inhale, slowly letting it out and trying to bleed off her anger at the same time. "Well, at least *they* couldn't use it, and if Matringa was trying to burn it, there shouldn't be any reason for her to notice it's gone."

As she lay there, the almost-adult woman slowly drifted off to sleep, and the night slipped by.

Wham.

The sound of her door being thrown open hard enough to bounce off the stone foundation startled Bella out of her sleep, and the intense light of the lantern caused her eyes to water. Not knowing what was happening, she scrambled away from the intrusion, freezing in place as Matringa's voice rang out with frigid malice.

"Where is it?"

Still half asleep, though her adrenaline was surging, Bella looked around the room frantically. "W-what? Where is *what?*"

"You *know* what is missing!" Matringa hissed at her. "That *cursed* cloth vanished overnight, and the only person who would want to have anything to do with it is *you*."

"Cursed?" Luckily, Bella fixated on that word instead of showing any guilt to indicate she knew what Matringa was talking about. "Something *cursed* was in the house?"

Matringa went silent for a long moment, the lantern highlighting her face in an unflattering way as she stared at her stepdaughter. Enough time passed that Bella was able to gather her wits about her, and she stood up straight and met the eyes of her father's wife. Both of them knew there was something dark and cursed indeed going on, but Bella couldn't accuse her, and Matringa would never admit it.

Instead, she stepped forward and slowly swung the lantern

to the side, looking for any hint of blue in the room. "Yes, *cursed*. I don't know why she did it, perhaps out of jealousy of your father reaching Perfection in his Merchant Class skills, but the woman you had thought of as a friend, *Bibbidy*, put a nasty curse on the cloth she brought for the household."

"For *me*," Bella growled before she could stop herself.

Matringa paused for a moment, her eyes darting back to lock on her stepdaughter. "Yes, for *you*. How lucky *for you*, after it was made into a dress and worn by Malvagio, its dark magic was activated and affected her instead of *you*. The first time she tried it on, the threads of the cloth dug into her skin, causing a painful, itching welt to appear. Over the course of the night, it spread as a rash until almost every inch of her skin was affected."

Bella blinked at that information, her mind flashing back to the night of Rosa's party, when Malvagio had been scratching at herself. Matringa continued her tirade, slowly advancing on Bella as her voice became more and more heated.

"We had to *tear* the dress off of her, cutting it off in some places where it had dug into her skin. Even then, it continued to try and come after her, and we needed to absolutely shred it before it stopped. Then, we tried to burn the material, only to find that it wouldn't hold any heat. So, yes, it was meant for *you*. The cloth, the curse, and the suffering it caused. *You* are *welcome*. I'm sure you'll be pleased that my daughter suffered instead of *you*, the intended target."

"She would never try to hurt me," Bella managed to squeak out as she looked up at her stepmother looming just in front of her. "Something else had to be going on."

Matringa scoffed and stepped back, though her line of vision was still darting all over Bella's dress, hovering on her pockets. After a moment of hesitation, she turned and started walking around the room, continuing to look for any patch of blue. After a few minutes where Bella's dread mounted, she finally gave up and instead looked at the surroundings and decorations.

"Oh me, oh my." She bent down and ran a finger over the woven straw mat that covered the floor. "You *have* been bored, haven't you? What an *industrious* little thing you are, child. All made out of *straw*? Rumple would have a fit of glee if he saw this…"

The last line had been spoken so softly that Bella almost missed it, but she made sure to burn the name Matringa had spoken into her brain. The stepmother hesitated as she looked around the room a few more times before finally scoffing and walking toward the stairs out of the cellar. "If I find you had anything to do with that fiasco, or are hiding the material for some reason…"

Her voice trailed off as she climbed the steps, leaving the rest of her threat unspoken. Bella stayed where she was until the oversized, horizontal cellar doors slammed closed, only then did she allow herself a quiet moment of relief. "Thank the *system* I've always had the foresight to have my creatures hide everything for me. If she asked me where it was, I could've honestly said I have no idea."

It was morning already, but only by the technical definition. Still, there was no way Bella was going to be going back to sleep, so she changed and got ready for the day. Leaving her room, she went up into the main house, finding it dark and nearly as cold as her underground room. Though she walked around the servants' area, the only people she found were the three silent maids.

"Looks like the cook and newer staff were already fired. Did she throw them out just before bedtime?" Bella shook her head at the absolutely *shocking* behavior Father's wife would exhibit whenever he wasn't home. Since the rest of the house was so quiet, she also moved around stealthily, trying not to wake anyone.

Gathering an armful of wood, she went to the main floor

and began stacking it in the hearth. Just before she reached for the tinder, she froze in place as she heard Matringa's voice floating down the chimney from where it connected to the study.

"No… it's just *gone.*" Matringa gnashed her teeth loudly enough for the *click* to be heard. "There was no sign of it in her room, and she gave away no hint that she knew what had happened to it."

A few moments of silence passed, then the stepmother spoke again as if responding to someone who'd been speaking quietly. "I suppose that *is* possible… but if the magic had faded enough for it to finally catch on fire, why wouldn't it have done that the first few days? Yes, I *understand* what 'fading' means. I agree, it couldn't have been her, but… no, you don't need to-"

At that point, Matringa must have moved away from the fireplace in the study, since the conversation became too distant for Bella to hear.

In the next moment, the Beast Singer's arm flared with a gentle golden light.

TWENTY-FIVE

BELLA RAN her fingers down her arm, looking at what the system had updated for her. Exactly as she'd hoped, her Minor Creature Control skill had finally increased after years of dedicated, focused, intentional effort... and she couldn't even pinpoint *why*.

Skill increase! Minor Creature Control [Level 7 (Proficient) → Level 8 (Extensive)]!

Advanced Skill: Minor Creature Control: Level 8/10.
When communing with non-magical minor creatures—size limit: the tips of your fingers to your elbow in body length. Maximum of five pounds—you are able to exert [Extensive] control over their actions.

Requirement to advance to level 9: remain focused on and complete a task in only 1 hour which would require a team of three Proficient humans a minimum of 24 hours.

"That's... *absurd*!" Bella read over the requirement three times, four, completely shocked at how difficult it was. "It took me what, two years? Two *years* to move from Proficient to

Extensive, now it wants me to complete the work of *three* of myself yesterday in an hour? That's…"

She quietly raged for a short while, trying to think of any loopholes or ways around this ridiculous requirement. "Okay, there's nothing in the message that says it has to be only my animals who are working on it, so at least I can work *with* them to speed it along. Still… I can see why people get stuck in the upper levels of their skill and never reach their Breakthrough Skills. By the *system*, if this is what the advancement in the Basic Class looks like, what will my Full Class look like?"

Musing on that thought, Bella lost track of time as she envisioned the potency and impressiveness of her future classes and abilities.

Still, all good things come to an end, and as soon as the sun had peeked over the horizon, Matringa called all the girls to the dining room to discuss the changes in the manor. The expectation that there would be food to buffer her from her stepfamily failed, being the very first change Matringa pointed out.

"As you can all see by this *empty* table," the woman grumped at her charges, "as soon as I informed the cook we would no longer be paying him, he left without even preparing the next day's food. Needless to say, he did *not* get a recommendation on the way out. We are down to only three maids, and so we're all going to have to make some sacrifices on our expected comfort."

Bella's mouth was completely dry as she waited for the inevitable reassignment of her servant duties. Even so, the young lady thought back over the letter that had arrived from her father and realized Matringa was going far beyond what he had stipulated.

Alaric had called for *extra* projects to be halted, such as expansions and unnecessary ornamentation. He most certainly hadn't even hinted at firing the entirety of the staff. Knowing the answer, but wondering how her stepmother would spin things, Bella cautiously questioned, "Is this what father asked for in his letter?"

"Oh me, oh *my.*" Matringa raised an eyebrow at her. "Perhaps your lessons on logistics from your father are even more distant in your memories than I had expected. Let me explain, child. We must pay the price of preparation, or it will cost us a princely portion when it's time to pay the piper, if his product isn't purchased."

"Ugh." Bella let out the softest of noises at the condescending comment, though luckily, her stepmother moved on quickly.

"Now, as I said before, *everyone* will be making sacrifices." Matringa spoke sadly, shaking her head as she looked at her daughters as though they were going to need to sell their home, dresses, and wear the clothing of paupers. "Malvagio, Cattiva, both of you will now be responsible for cleaning your own rooms and making your beds. You will also be in charge of cleaning up after yourself in the lessons room. Bella, as you are the only one with experience, I'll need you to return to your tasks in the kitchen to ensure we all have the *strength* to get through this difficult time."

Bella stared at her stepmother sullenly as she was saddled with the task of cooking, a constant effort with so many people in the house. Surprisingly, that was the only task she was given —at least for now. "So... I'm waiting to hear the part where *everyone* is making sacrifices? Are they going to help out with anything actually *useful* to the family?"

"Is the firing of our maids not *enough* for you?" Malvagio shook her head with a small roll of her eyes, looking at her mother for vindication. "She said we need to make sacrifices, not *suffer.*"

"Not now, girls. Bella, I've no intention of going over matters of the estate with you. I'll take care of all of us, you just do what is asked of you, like a good little girl." Matringa waved them off and stood wearily. "Since we are all sacrificing breakfast today, I expect lunch at the proper time. Unless you think you have enough time to dawdle, you ought to get started. Off you go… *go* on. Weren't you just complaining the other day about having nothing to do? I think this works out well for everyone involved."

Remembering she was supposed to be playing a part was the only reason Bella kept her mouth closed and started walking out of the room. Before she could make it, Matringa called out as if she'd just remembered something, "The menu today calls for seven bean soup, but your dear sister Cattiva has troubles eating the split peas, so be a dear and pick all of those out."

Bella continued onward as though she hadn't heard anything, but knew if she didn't accommodate her stepsister, there would be some severe, ridiculous punishment headed her way. "Pick out the peas? Why? That's the most bizarre ask I've ever had for meal prep."

After making her way to the kitchen, she quickly realized *exactly* why she'd been given such a seemingly simple task. The contents of the soup were dry currently but had already been mixed in a large container. Dried peas were absolutely *tiny*, and the task would take her hours if she tried to do it by hand. But if the beans weren't put on to soak, and soon, they would be too tough to eat, even if she boiled them the entire time they were cooking.

That meant lunch would be late, which would throw her into a spiral of punishments and continuously failed tasks— clearly the point of the task she had been given.

"Nope, I'm *not* letting this happen," Bella snarled as she lifted the pot of dried foodstuff. She walked to the back of the kitchen, raised an eyebrow at the fact that the padlock on the pantry was gone, and stepped into the small room, closing the door behind her. "I refuse to give in when she sets me up for failure."

Humming a few bars to try and even out her voice, Bella prepared her throat and softly sang out:

"Mice on a mission, come sort with ease! Tiny paws quickly separate these peas. Beans to the left, in neat little rows. I'll help out; it's how our teamwork grows!"

She laid out a tablecloth, carefully pouring the contents of the pot onto it. Immediately, a dozen mice swarmed through the mix, tossing peas out ever so quickly. A quarter of them were set to the side to cook and give back to the mice as thanks for their help, while the other portion would be served with dinner so there would be no wastage. Even with as quickly as she could scoop the beans and peas into separate areas, the mice were able to move faster, and soon she was looking at a pile of mixed dried beans and a separate, much smaller, pile of peas.

"That took... *minutes*." The gears in her head began spinning, even as she thanked the mice and promised them cooked peas later in the day. "Maybe it *is* actually possible to complete the next level increase quest?"

The next task was soaking and boiling the beans, so she got the kettle on the stove and bustled around the pantry, putting together a simple salad along with toasting some bread with minced garlic and butter. "It's a simple but filling lunch. Any reasonable person who eats at our table should be satisfied. Which means... I guess I should be prepared to be punished for *something*, since there are no reasonable people in the house besides the servants."

Once everything was ready, she checked the time and found that she had another two hours before she needed to serve everything. Knowing no rodents would get into the food, she covered everything and put it away. Then she went upstairs and set the table.

Matringa walked in as she was putting down the last of the cutlery and was wondering what to do next. "Bella? What are you doing in here? Should you be *idle* at this moment? Perhaps my instructions for the day were *unclear?*"

"Not at all, Signora Matringa." Bella responded in the same deferential tone she'd always spoken in while playing her part as a servant. One half demure, one half respectful: the perfect recipe to remain invisible to her stepmother. At least, unless she was specifically *looking* for trouble. "The beans are soaking, and everything should be ready just in time for lunch."

"I suppose we shall see, shan't we?" Matringa looked around the room suspiciously, then she slowly walked out and up the stairs to the study, going by the sound of her footfalls.

Deciding against remaining in an area where she was an easy target, Bella returned to the kitchen and began cleaning up in preparation for starting on supper. After she got a large pot of water boiling, she poured it into the wash basin and swirled some soap around in it. Thankfully, the water cooled quickly, with only the pots and pans with the most caked-on burns having been left in to soak. When it was cool enough to work with, she plunged her hands in and began scrubbing, only to flinch away as she heard a **plop** and felt a spray of sudsy water on her face.

She glanced to the side, finding a trio of mice standing on the counter and working together to push a cast iron pan into the wash basin. Letting out a stunted laugh, she helped them out by picking up the pan and setting it to the side. "I appreciate your eagerness, but I can't imagine the uproar that would ensue if I washed a cast iron pan in soapy water. Can you bring me the spatulas instead? Feel free to enjoy the batter on them."

Several squeaks of excitement came moments later, and from that moment forward, each dish sent over had only the faintest sheen of scraps on them. Even pans with charred remains were cleaned as the mice happily ate what humans couldn't or wouldn't. When the last pan had been pushed into the water, the mice stood and waited for the next task, so Bella shrugged and tore a rag into small pieces for them.

Squeak?

The muted sound called her attention to the floor, where dozens of other rodents were waiting to be a part of the efforts. She happily handed them soapy rags, and they began scrubbing the floor.

Soon, she was nearly done with the dishes, far sooner than she'd expected to be. By the time she needed to start pulling lunch out, the floors were swept and mopped, the countertops cleared and cleaned, and all in all, Bella had a pristine workspace. "Thank you all; I'll prepare a special meal for you later. Why don't you all run along now; I'll finish up here?"

The kitchen cleared out, and Bella began putting serving dishes on her tray to haul upstairs, when she saw Gus waiting next to the soup pot, staring at it hungrily. "Poor little guy, I saw how hard you worked on those peas! Sure, why don't I-"

"Who are you talking to?" Malvagio's voice rang out from the doorway, causing Bella to jump and nearly send the soup flying. She barely managed to catch the pot in time, causing her stepsister to screech and flinch away in fear of having boiling soup dumped on her. "Honestly! What's *wrong* with you? Are you trying to disfigure me with boiling soup because I asked you a question?"

"Sorry, sorry! I was lost in my own little world there. I was talking to myself and wasn't expecting someone to answer." Bella dipped her hands in the now-cool water of the basin to try and remove some of the pain from grabbing the hot pot, then grabbed a hand towel, dried herself, and dropped it on the tray to cover Gus.

Malvagio watched on suspiciously, looking around the room to see if perhaps one of the silenced maids had been present, before finally huffing and returning her gaze to Bella. "Speaking to yourself isn't a healthy habit. Now, the only reason I'd come down to this *pit* is because Mother told me to come and remind you about the peas. Lunch is coming up, and now that the soup is hot and everything is soft, it's going to be a lot harder for you to finish on time."

"Thank you for the reminder," Bella replied calmly, turning to stare at her stepsister blankly. "You should go back upstairs; it's almost time to eat."

Malvagio didn't move, instead stepping forward and leaning against the counter as she studied the younger woman. "So… you just cook, clean, and talk to yourself in here?"

"Are you volunteering to come keep me company?" Bella challenged her, pushing the tray closer to Malvagio. "The work is pretty much done this time around, but I suppose you could do the absolute bare minimum and help carry it upstairs."

"I'm certainly not about to lower myself to doing *kitchen work*." The typically apathetic artist spat to the side, leaving a wet splotch on the recently cleaned floor. All mirth and joking mannerisms drained out of Bella as her stare turned into a glare.

Pointing at the floor, Bella calmly stated, "You're going to clean that up, right now. Do you know how people get sick? Disgusting behavior like that. I don't know what makes you think kitchen work is so beneath you. Life skills aren't something to look down on. Being *useful* isn't something to be mocked."

"Pshh." Malvagio scoffed even as Bella stepped closer to her. She watched her younger stepsister with a hint of nervousness but tried to hide it behind her standoffish thoughts. "Our usefulness is so much more than you could ever dream of. *We're* going to change this world. You? You're just learning that you're in your rightful place—serving us. Someday, you'll go too far, and Mother will take you to her friend along the ocean, and then we'll not have to put up with your incessant complaints. Believe me, the rest of us can barely *wait* for that day to come."

The threat touched a deeply held fear of Bella's, a concern which had been in the back of her mind since the three silenced maids had been introduced to the household. Even so, all the reminder did was make her even more angry. "I told you to clean up that spittle."

"Make me." Malvagio barely got the words out before her smug smile turned to rigid fear as Bella lunged forward, grabbing the front of Malvagio's dress and yanking on her. Muscles built by years of hard work in the house barely strained against her stepsister's comparatively willowy form. In an instant, the stepsister was on the ground, being pushed back and forth like an oversized rag to clean up the spittle. "You! You *wretch*! You scullery maid! Get *off* me!"

Bella let her go and stepped back, a smile firmly in place on her face. "I'd like to remind you not to make a mess in the kitchen. It's not good for your health."

"I'm going straight to Mother!" Malvagio swore as she scrambled to her feet and out the door.

"Perfect. Let her know lunch is ready."

TWENTY-SIX

LUNCH WAS A STRAINED AFFAIR, though to Bella's surprise, Matringa didn't immediately call her out or punish her for the fight. Her older stepsister sat across the table, glaring at her... unless Bella met her eyes. Then she would flinch away and pretend to be studying something in the room with undivided attention.

Everyone seemed to be waiting with bated breath as Bebee ladled out the soup, serving the meal for the fractious family. Each person had a chunk of toast and salad, but only Bella began eating as soon as her portion was poured into her bowl. Each of the others dug in with their spoons but spent the first half minute pushing aside beans, searching for a single pea without avail. None of them found one, and she didn't miss how they glanced back and forth between each other as they came to realize she had succeeded in the task.

"Humm..." Matringa drummed the fingers of her left hand on the table, smiling over at Bella happily. "I'm so glad you were able to make the soup to my standards. Cattiva is most displeased when she has to suffer through eating that particular vegetable. Yet, *I* look forward to having cooked peas with dinner. That won't be a problem, will it?"

"Of course not, Stepmother. I was more than happy to make sure there was no pea in the pot." Bella returned calmly, "Still, I made sure to separate them out and save them in a saucepan. Waste not, want not, as my father used to tell me."

"Yes…" The drumming of her fingers continued, and Matringa took a deep breath. "On that note… your father."

Now she had everyone's attention, and Signora Vigatori let out a long-suffering sigh as she stared up at the ceiling dramatically. "I've been waiting to make this announcement until we were able to come together as a family, and I think now is the time. Let's all support each other in this, but… the fact of the matter is, the head of our household continued on farther and farther to try and make his sales. He will be sailing with the *Triste Mietitore*. We anticipate his current journey could take another year, potentially a year and a half between the travel, sales, and building long-standing relationships in those communities."

"That's a-" Bella managed to catch herself before she called her stepmother out for lying, but as Matringa had been expecting an outburst, her stare was already piercing the younger woman.

"What is your issue, child?" Matringa hissed at her in great agitation. "Can I not get through *one* announcement without being interrupted? Go on! Tell me what is so important that I can't speak first in my own house."

"I'm sorry, it's just… that's a… long time for him to be away. I just miss him, is all." Bella finished lamely, not able to meet her stepmother's eyes for fear of saying what was truly on her mind.

"This is our life savings we're talking about. The entire fortune of House Vigatori is on the line." Matringa's voice rose into not *quite* a shout by the end, but close. "Your father is doing what needs to be done so we are not left destitute! Already, I am preparing to make even more sacrifices to our comfort than I ever thought I would need to do."

"More? What more must we give up, mother?" Cattiva was the one who interrupted this time, throwing her fork—and the speared piece of lettuce—onto the table.

"Cease your pouting, Cattiva." Matringa's shoulders slumped as she voiced what was going through her mind. "If we do not hear from Alaric after another nine months, I will have to sell the contracts for Bebee, Cece, and Dedee. Even with as little as it requires of us to take care of them, we could at least have a small influx of coins to put behind your dowry, Malvagio."

"What then, Mother?" The oldest stepsister slowly lowered her spoon. "What if we don't find a suitable suitor swiftly? Am I to start mopping the floors like a spinster in her mid-twenties who couldn't secure a husband?"

"We'll burn that bridge when we come to it, darling." Malvagio let out another sigh then put on a slight smile and turned to look at Bella. "Luckily, we have someone here who already knows the intricacies of the household and what all needs to be done. A toast to Bella, who will help us push through this tough time, no matter what!"

As the stepsisters raised their glasses in a mocking salute, Bella stared at her stepmother with dark eyes. "Really? This is all so very sudden and seems rather unlike my father. I'd like to read that letter. Just to try and better understand his reasoning, that is."

"Humm…" Matringa shook her head sadly, though her twitching lips betrayed her internal laughter. "As much as I wish I could let you do that, dearest Bella, in a fit of pique, I'm ashamed to say I threw his letter into the fire. You may not know this, but you're not the only person who sometimes struggles to keep their temper under control."

"Let me get this straight, *your* daughters are going to take care of their bedroom. Meanwhile, *I'm* supposed to take care of all the rest, tend to the garden and animals, collect eggs from the chickens, *and* cook for the family? This certainly doesn't seem right, or anywhere near fair."

"Comparison is the thief of joy, child," Matringa calmly took a sip from her glass, "And *fair* is where you go for pony rides and spun sugar. I don't think you should partake of either of those concepts. It's not good for your skin. Wrinkles."

"Comparison? *Comparison?* There is no comparison! You intend to work me like a beast from dawn to dusk, while you and your spoiled *brats* lounge about-"

"Silence!" Matringa sounded angry, but her eyes were glimmering with victory. "You sit at our table, dining with us, anything to complain about what is necessary? We haven't even gotten to the point where this is a reality, being mere speculation of what could happen three-quarters of a *year* from now, and you're already throwing a tantrum! Of all the ungrateful people in my life... and to think your father spoke so highly of you in his letter. He would be *so* disappointed. Between this, and what you did to Malvagio earlier—she's going to have a *bruise*, Bella—I think you need some time away from family meals. You can start by leaving now."

Having somewhat expected an outcome like this, Bella had long since finished her soup and bread, which meant she only had to leave approximately half her salad untouched. She didn't wait to be told twice, getting up and storming out of the room.

Contrary to what she was certain her stepfamily was thinking, Bella wasn't angry at her father for being gone, nor was she truly unhappy about having tasks looming over her in the future.

"If Matringa is saying he'll be gone for a year, it'll be at least one and a half, or two." Her hands were shaking from adrenaline as she balled them into fists. "He'll be too late. I'll miss my opportunity to get to a Class Shrine and gain an Advanced Class. Even if I eventually manage to go and get my Full Class, I'll lose out on skills that would make me valuable to the world. I won't have even *half* of what a different candidate would have to offer, which means no apprenticeships, no skilled labor jobs. I'll be trapped here, likely even without an opportunity for *marriage* as an escape."

Her eyes burning with determination, Bella walked out of the house, into the cellar, and quickly scooped a few sets of clothes into a woven-straw satchel. "I'm not going to stay here and be experimented on by these terrible people. Even if I can't afford the offering to get into a Class Shrine, I'll find someone from the Sect of... what did he call it, so long ago? Sect of *Scoprire*! I don't care how unlikely it is, I'll get out there and find an awakening artifact and advance my class. I can always unlock my Full Class later, after I earn enough money. It doesn't have to be on my eighteenth birthday—I'll wait until I'm *twenty*, for all I care!"

Plan set, she began singing softly, not saying any words but still calling her trained mice to her side through sheer intentionality. This time, she didn't hold back at all, and every mouse in the house poured into her room. Looking around at the scores of rodents, she nodded and turned to the door without a word. She marched up the stairs, a living carpet swarming along behind her.

Bella rushed across the lawn, running in a straight line to the hedges closest to the hollow tree at the edge of the estate. As she got closer, the bushes twisted, straightening slightly to show the dripping thorns along their branches. Even so, she went up to them, carefully reaching out to grab an area without thorns and pushing it to the side. It squirmed in her grasp, popping back into position and leaving a deep scratch from wrist to elbow.

As blood flowed down her arm, Bella looked down at the wound in shock. She began to shake, lips curling back from her teeth as she tried to contain her anger. Dropping her satchel, she pulled out the clothes, wrapping them around her arms, then even putting her hands in the bag for extra protection before *shoving* forward once more.

The hedges pushed back against her, moving as she moved, unnaturally refusing to allow her to pass. "Some kind of skill... this must be Matringa! Well, two can play that game!"

"*Nibble, gnaw, chew, and bite! We won't give up without a fight!*" She sang to her mice, who swarmed forward and joined in the battle against the hedges. "*Crunch, munch, and devour! I must be gone within the hour!*"

For a moment, the surge of tiny teeth chewing through branches and roots seemed like it would be enough. The plants shuttered, shrinking back as an opening slowly formed. Then, one of the mice bit into a bulbous growth on the lowest part of the hedge.

As it popped, a thick green smoke belched forth.

TWENTY-SEVEN

ANYWHERE THE HAZE REACHED, the mice started coughing, then dropped to the ground convulsing. Seconds after they were first touched, they stopped moving.

"Back! Get back, everyone!" Bella frantically called, and the mice rushed to obey. Even so, less than forty of them were able to get away from the writhing hedges, thorns, and deadly smoke. Before she could somehow convince herself this was a natural phenomenon, Bella watched as the roots of the hedges lifted out of the ground, wrapped around the fallen rodents, and pulled them below the surface.

For far too long, she simply stood there, staring at the now-innocuous hedgerow in horror.

"Oh me, oh *my*." The simpering faux concern drifted into her ears, and Bella slowly turned to watch as her stepmother stalked across the lawn. "You're so angry about possibilities that you would endanger the entire family by trying to destroy my beautiful plants? *Humm…*"

Matringa came to a stop, taking a moment to admire the despair on Bella's face. "It seems we're going to have to make some changes around here sooner, *far* sooner than I thought."

Bella felt completely numb, unable to respond in the

slightest even as her stepmother had the cellar doors at the top of the stairs fitted with an oversized padlock. She simply sat on her bed, replaying the memory of her valiant vermin being viciously victimized by the vindictive vines. The few dozen who'd survived had scattered only after Matringa had arrived on the scene, and her stepmother barely commented on them —but she *had* seen them.

The young woman barely mustered the energy to glance up as Signora Vigatori suddenly loomed in her doorway, staring her down with cruel delight. "I certainly hope you can understand the need for this extra layer of security. How am I supposed to keep this estate in check if I don't even know if you are in your room when you're supposed to be? From now on, you will have a curfew. I will *personally* ensure you are in your room before going to bed myself."

Even as the words echoed in the small space, Bella felt as though she were watching herself from a distance. All she could see in her mind was herself in the cellar for two more years, eight, who knew when it would end? In fact, why *would* it end, when her servitude directly benefited her stepmother? Until she was at least eighteen, even if she managed to call for help and someone bothered to listen, Matringa could simply point out the fact that she was taking care of her stepdaughter as legally required.

"Are you even listening to me?" Matringa's sharp words cut through the haze around Bella's mind, and she nodded ever so slightly. "Good. Now, come with me, we're going to have our *second* family meeting of the day. Look what you're doing to us, Bella. You're making us act like executives who can't make a decision. Your father would be ashamed."

After deciding her stepdaughter was moving too slow, Matringa gripped her arm and practically dragged the young woman up the stairs, and into the dining room, where Malvagio and Cattiva were already waiting. As she was sat down, Bella's attention was drawn to the three silent maids, who were staring at the ground, refusing to meet anyone's eyes.

"It appears the changes we discussed are going to come sooner than I'd expected, and all of you can thank Bella for the shortened timeline." Matringa began without preamble, not even bothering to sit. "As I can't keep track of my plants and an errant *child's* whims, the contracts of the staff shall be sold off *immediately*."

"Mother! No!" Cattiva's gasp almost gave Bella a spark of hope, but it was immediately followed by, "You said it would be almost a year before we had to manage our rooms; why do we get punished for something we didn't even cause?"

"It *does* seem somewhat unfair." Malvagio agreed with a rare show of solidarity with her sister.

"Enough. The maids are leaving. Their bags are already packed; we're only waiting on the carriage to arrive. I'm retaining a part-time servant for chores outside the estate, such as fetching us our weekly supplies. However, there will be no more outside influences living in the estate with us." Matringa turned to her daughters, who seemed ready to explode with indignation. "I understand the frustrations you two must feel, but I've no desire for Bella to intrude into our space. Remember how we talked about sacrifices that needed to be made?"

Malvagio and Cattiva's eyes darted over to their stepsister before they nodded in reluctant understanding. Matringa inhaled, straightened her posture, and waved at the maids to exit the room. "The lock on your door will remain as long as I deem it necessary. Actions have consequences; it's time you learned that lesson. Perhaps a firm hand is what's been needed this whole time… well. We'll find out, won't we? Your father wants you safe. You are the most safe right here, but apparently you need chores to keep you away from idle, dangerous behaviors."

A loud knock on the door interrupted the rant, and the

women were ushered out of the dining room and into the entryway. One of the silent maids opened the door, stepping aside as a man with a long, ragged beard and mustache stepped in.

"Signora, I'm here to pick up your baggage and drop off your order."

"Thank you kindly, Scagnozzo," Matringa responded with great familiarity, causing Bella's gaze to sharpen as she looked between the two of them. "The speed with which you can accomplish tasks never fails to astound me."

The man smiled broadly, revealing rotten teeth, "That's the reason the coins sing for me, Signora. Here's your crate; I've already been paid, now come on, baggage."

He motioned for the maids to follow him, nodding at Matringa before tossing the small amount of luggage onto his wagon and hoisting the silent maids up. Ignoring the reins, Scagnozzo lifted a whip and flicked it at the single horse, causing it to surge forward in a panic and yank its burden away from the manor with a rapid clatter.

"Were you all aware we had a *rodent* infestation?" Matringa's inquiry drew Bella's attention over to her step-mother, who was pulling apart the crate with an astounding amount of brute force. "Well, Bella the *basic* Beast Singer certainly did. Instead of dealing with the issue, she fed them *our* food, trained them in *our* house, and tried to turn them against *our* first line of defense. Imagine what could have happened, who could have been allowed into our home, if she tore down the only protection we have against the world outside this safe space?"

The wood finally gave way with a cracking groan, and six obese black cats stalked their way out of the container, hissing with clear wrath as they looked around the room. Slowly, all of their eyes came to rest on Bella, and she felt a shiver run up her spine and took an involuntary step backward. Instinctively she called out with song, "*Run*! Run! As fast as you can, don't let them catch you, you're the-"

"Too late for that!" Matringa shouted with fury as the cats scattered into the house, yowling with hunger. "My sisters saw fit to lend me some of their pets, and they are *fantastic* hunters."

The oversized cats were as dark and malicious as they appeared at first glance, and within minutes, they began to bring back one tiny body after another.

Matringa grabbed Bella's chin and forced her to look into her eyes, "This could have easily been your task, something *you* handled for the family. These creatures are filthy and could easily be spreading pestilence in our house! What are they doing when you aren't around? Eating the walls, destroying our home? How would you know? As soon as I saw them around you, the cause of so *many* little annoyances came to light."

Bella was released, and she staggered back, clutching at her chin where she could already feel a pair of bruises forming. Matringa wasn't finished with her, instead jabbing a bony index finger at her face. "I know what your father said, but I can't in good conscience allow you to keep practicing these disgusting skills. I'll take that oath you owe him, or you'll be working in this house each day until you *drop*."

Silence filled the air for a few long moments, with the stepmother waiting impatiently and the stepdaughter keeping her mouth closed with all her might. The staring contest continued long enough that Cattiva and Malvagio became uncomfortable, fidgeting in the background, before their mother began shaking her head and chuckling from sheer anger. "Defiant 'til the end, aren't you, Bella?"

Still, the young woman refused to say a word.

"Good... very good." Matringa stepped forward and clenched her hand around her stepdaughter's arm once more, dragging her through the house as she marched along. "This is exactly how I prefer you. *Silent.* Let's make this a regular thing, shall we? Unless one of us speaks to you directly and asks you a question, you are not to speak at all. Anytime I hear you doing so out of turn, I will find a way to punish you, do you understand?"

Once again there was no answer, so Matringa suddenly paused and rounded on Bella, her grip tightening to the point of being painful. "Let me make myself understood, when we ask you a question, you *will* answer. Do you understand?"

"Perfectly," Bella growled out her answer, not bothering to hide the intensity of her own emotions as she glared at her stepmother in return.

"Then what comes next should be no surprise." Matringa's voice was almost a whisper as she trembled with anger at the disrespect in her stepdaughter's tone. Bella was shoved into the entrance of the cellar, missing her step and falling down the stairs.

As she lay at the bottom, trying to catch her breath, the young woman stared up at the silhouetted form of Signora Vigatori. Her father's wife shook her head once, then reached over and slammed the door to the cellar closed. *Click* went the padlock, followed by Matringa stomping away.

Now alone in the dark, Bella finally allowed tears to run from her closed eyes.

CHAPTER
TWENTY-EIGHT

BELLA LISTLESSLY CLEANED THE WINDOW, even as she wistfully stared through it, watching the birds fly south before the snow became too thick to find food.

She had passed most of the year in silence—even when she was alone. Far too many nights, she'd noticed that the lines of light coming into her room from above were... wrong. It had taken her several days of trying to figure out what was going on before she realized that one of her stepsisters had been positioned above her in order to see if she was singing or speaking after being locked in her room for the night.

It wasn't every day, but sometimes, it was just too difficult to know if she was imagining their presence or if they were actually there. The terror had led Bella into silence, and as far as anyone knew, there she had stayed.

She glanced at her left arm, taking a deep, shuddering breath as she ignored the impulse to look at her class and skills, knowing nothing had changed. Nothing except her age. Now that she was seventeen, the clock was ticking down. If she turned eighteen without getting an Advanced Class, all she could ever get was her Full Class—wonderful on its own, but drastically weakened without the supporting skills she would've gained during her progression of an Advanced Class.

Sweeping her gaze around the room, Bella noticed Malvagio sitting on a couch with a sketch pad, turning away before her stepsister noticed her staring. If there was one thing that built a small scrap of dark satisfaction in her heart, it was that she wasn't alone in this joyless environment. With no entertainment and almost no one to order around, true smiles had become more rare than mice in the manor—unless they were smug smirks or facsimiles generated by watching Bella suffer more than they did.

Bella got back to cleaning, as she didn't want to be forced to find a way to steal enough food to eat today if she were caught being lost in her thoughts. Her stepfamily no longer put on a show of treating her with any sort of fairness or false kindness. No, that had been swept away the same day a letter had arrived at the end of summer, just before her birthday.

This one, Matringa had not just *allowed* her to read, but had stood and waited as she did so.

Dear Vigatori family,

My name is Hugo Amatore, and I was the owner of the ship Triste Mietitore until a few weeks ago. Sadly, upon the return trip from Swarvit- tica, the whole ship fell victim to the plague as they were coming into harbor. As such, it was not allowed to dock while the sickness ran its course.

Unfortunately, on a ship, there is no reprieve from such an illness, it makes its rounds, and makes them again. As such, there were no survivors aboard the Triste Mietitore, and we were instructed by the harbormaster to burn the ship until it sank, along with whatever goods were aboard, to prevent the spread of disease.

As the owner of the ship, it fell to me to take down the words of the living

*at the time it was anchored a mile from the harbor, as the local doctor
warned this outcome may indeed be the case. Alaric Vigatori was among
the living at this time, and I will recount to you what he had to say. Please
forgive any flaws in my rendering of said last words, as they were being
shouted at me from ship to shore:*

*'To my wife, I'm sorry I've failed you.
To her girls, I wish I had more time to get to know you.
To my daughter, you are a credit to <u>both</u> your parents.'*

*There is no doubt Signore Vigatori intended to say more, but he was
wracked with coughing at this time and could yell no longer. I am told he
succumbed to his illness only hours later.*

*I understand the position this puts you in both personally and financially,
and all I can offer are my condolences. If it is any consolation, myself
and my business partners are out thousands of gold but will not be coming
to collect from your family. Signore Vigatori convinced several of us to
invest in this venture of his, but his contract was airtight in the event of
his death or a failed...*

Nothing else in the letter had mattered to Bella, which was
good, as it had fallen from her nerveless fingers. Matringa had
caught it then walked away without a word of either condem-
nation or condolence. It had been a breaking point for the
young adult, and combined with watching her tiny trained
friends be slaughtered for her escape attempts had completely
smothered all shows of open defiance.

"Maybe I should have learned my lesson with what
happened to Cook. Then again, even if she killed me and got
away with it, who would clean up after them?" Bella froze in
place, thinking over the last few seconds and wondering if she
had spoken her thoughts aloud, and if so... had anyone heard
them? She didn't look around, not wanting to appear nervous,
as that would certainly be enough for the others to realize

she'd broken their arbitrary rules. When no gleeful comments came, Bella relaxed fractionally and got back to work.

Though her hands were busy, the rote nature of the work allowed her to sink into her thoughts and daydreams. A small trill of fear wriggled through her as her thoughts turned once more to the rumors of plague creeping closer and closer to home. Though it had killed her father, Matringa seemed completely indifferent to the rising fear of what few acquaintances had bothered to continue writing after the passing of Alaric.

In fact, she openly mocked those fearful nobles by reading their letters aloud at dinner to amuse her children—the only reason Bella knew something was going on at all. Apparently, the symptoms involved fever and chills and dark spots creeping along the body. The mortality rate was *astounding* and brought low seven of every ten people it touched.

"Why are *you* in here?" Matringa's voice made Bella flinch, and she whirled around as if she'd been caught *smashing* glass instead of cleaning it. "Malvagio, why is she in your room?"

"Oh, I don't know, Mother." Malvagio let out a huff of annoyance at being interrupted in her sketching. "Maybe it's because, no matter how many times I clean my windows, the birds keep fouling it? Or perhaps it's because I'm not a chimney sweep?"

"I told you both she was to stay off this floor." Matringa continued speaking to her daughter, completely ignoring the fact that Bella was still in the room with them. "Figure it out. Isabella, leave. No, go back to your room. I told you not to come to this floor; you *will* listen to me over other people. Even my daughters."

Bella didn't bother to fight, instead she simply bowed her head, trudging out of the room, down the hall, the stairs, outside, finally closing the cellar door behind her and stepping on to her woven, straw flooring. With a soft sigh, she sat down on her bed and shook her head, "I can't believe…"

"…how *easy* they're making it for me."

She began tapping on the straw next to her, and three dozen mice rushed into the area. These were no longer the fluffy, cheerful, pristine creatures Bella had trained over the last few years. Instead, they bore the marks of survival: scars across their bodies where fur no longer grew, some limping along, while many of the rest were missing entire limbs. Those weren't even the worst of them; that unfortunate title went to those who didn't answer the call, the mice who were even now filling the bellies of Matringa's vile cats.

Still, their eyes were sharp, even sharper than their predecessors, as her current vermin had a glint of battle-hardened resolve showing as they waited for Bella's commands. "Mert the Third, Gus Junior, Suzy… I know it's been hard, and we've all lost someone important to us. But we're running out of time. I know it's not fair of me to ask this, but… I used to tell your parents or grandparents not to take risks. Not to be seen. Well, that time has passed. Now all I can ask of you is… don't get caught. I need you to delve deeper and find me the proof I need, before I need it. The first chance I get, I need to run. The *only* way I'm coming back is if I can be at the front of an entire platoon of soldiers."

Mert nodded his tiny head solemnly, being much less vocal than his predecessors, thanks to Bella's example of silence at all hours. As the mice scampered off, Bella reached out and picked up Suzy before she could go too far. "Wait for a few moments, would you?"

Suzy let out a soft sigh, ears drooping as she nodded. Bella sucked in a breath, "So you know what this is about, then. I'm sorry, but you're getting old. The average lifespan of your kind is only two years, and these cats are lowering that even further. I need you to select one of your litter who will be in charge after you are gone. A clear line of succession would help me greatly if the worst came to pass."

Once more, the mouse gave a small nod, before hopping

to the ground and scampering off. With that unpleasant task taken care of, Bella turned to look at a group of small animals which had gathered behind her bed, and she began tapping her foot with a regular beat as she began working on their regular training schedule.

"Raccoons, we're going to start with you tonight; you're almost too big for me to directly control." Bella spoke in the softest of whispers. "But we don't really need that, do we? So long as I train you right... you'll be ready when the command comes."

The furry bandits bobbed their heads, showing their sharp teeth in response to her internal, constant anger, though her expression remained placid. "After that, I'll need the moles to get ready; we're going to need another storage area for non-perishables. Has anyone seen the shrews? I need them to be able to distinguish between female guests and the people who *live* in the house. We almost had an unfortunate incident the other day when our supplies were dropped off."

Even if there weren't dozens and dozens of these creatures, as they didn't reproduce and grow as quickly as the mice, Bella knew that all she needed was time. Each of these critters had been trapped on the estate when Matringa expanded her foul hedges and likely would've already died out if it hadn't been for the Beast Singer's training, as well as impressing upon all the birds of prey in the area to leave the land-locked creatures alone.

"Wait a second... where's Stella?" Of all the animals she smuggled into and out of the house, Stella was the most worrying. Depending on what she had managed to eat that day, the skunk either would or would *not* be influenced by Bella's Minor Creature Control.

Just moments before Bella began to panic, the black and white creature she could just barely influence poked her head up through a small pile of straw that had been collecting at the corner of the room. "Oh, *there* you are! Don't scare me like that, Stella, you're far too important to the plan for you to get caught this early."

Hiss. Stella's mouth went wide, and she whipped around, lifting her tail threateningly.

"That's right, Stella." Bella's eyes twinkled with dark delight. "*Exactly* like that. Your training is almost complete."

CHAPTER
TWENTY-NINE

She had expected the winter to be one of seclusion for her family, between the rise of the plague and the family in public mourning for the loss of her father. But as midwinter approached, Bella found herself being called to the main floor to help her stepsisters get dressed for a party they'd been invited to attend.

Surprisingly, the stepsisters seemed not at all excited as they put on lacy gowns and pearl necklaces with matching earrings. Cattiva in particular was outspoken, taking out her ire by throwing clothes and other small items onto the floor and making Bella retrieve them for her as she stood in front of a full-length mirror to check her appearance.

"We were a last-minute invite, *Mother*. You know what that means? It means someone else canceled, and they needed to invite *anyone*. Who else but us, who they know have no other commitments or invitations? That's what this says, so why would we go?"

"An invitation is an invitation." Matringa swept into the sitting room, fully dressed and ready for the evening. Bella's eyes were drawn to the shining emerald necklace she wore, matching earrings, a ring on each finger with the same stone.

Specifically, they were drawn there because she had never seen this jewelry before. "If you'd like to stay behind with Bella, just say the word. Speaking of, child, *why* are you staring at me?"

"Signora Matringa," Bella responded slowly, knowing better than to keep her mouth shut after being asked a direct question, "I was under the impression the family was destitute. When the ship was burned, our life savings burned along with it. How is it that all three of you are wearing new dresses? New jewels? What's going on?"

"Somehow, I'm still surprised you haven't learned your place even with all you've been through. What makes you think I owe you even the *least* explanation?" Matringa shook her head in mock sadness, stepping in front of the mirror to adjust her accessories. "I suppose it doesn't hurt for you to know. You do realize I'm quite a wealthy woman in my own right? Oh, go on, speak those words you're so desperate to shout as a little treat for learning to hold them in."

"Signora… if you are wealthy, why did you insist my father pour all we owned into going out on the road to make sales?" Bella tried to swallow her anger, in hopes of getting more information.

"Oh me, oh my…" Matringa turned to look Bella directly in the eyes. "What are you insinuating? You are correct, he poured all *he* owned into his venture, as well as what small portion of my wealth I allowed. The sales were for *him*, to help him achieve higher levels in his Merchant skills. Did you not realize how, when he followed my directives, he reached *Perfection* on his first trip? He had an opportunity to achieve his Breakthrough Skill and couldn't help himself. What else?"

"Then… if you have so much money, why get rid of all the staff? Why live like *this*, forcing me to try and do the work an entire household should be doing? You must know it's not enough, that the estate is suffering from neglect no matter how hard I try-" Bella's words halted as she realized Matringa was staring at her, the malicious smirk on her lips showing that the woman was just trying to give her enough rope to hang herself.

"I wasn't going to gamble my fortune on his success. As for the estate? If it can't stand on its own, it shouldn't. I married into House Vigatori for my own reasons, specifically the noble title I gained by doing so. Your father married me for my money. It was a simple business transaction, and both of us knew what we were getting into. Why should I reach into my coffers for upkeep, when I will be moving onward and upward as soon as I get the chance? I should think *not*."

Bella remained in place as the room emptied out, her stepfamily exiting the house and entering a carriage, which rolled up directly adjacent to the door to ensure they wouldn't have to endure the cold for a moment longer than necessary. Her thoughts were swirling but kept coming back to one bright moment in that conversation that played in her mind over and over. "She's going to move on as soon as she gets the chance? I'll be rid of her, and I won't even have to do anything? Perhaps that's why she's so eager to find Malvagio a 'proper' suitor."

With the house to herself, she went about her business, first chasing around and trapping the cats in Malvagio's room. Only when she was certain all six of the little monsters were stuck, Bella began singing out.

She threw open the windows and doors, allowing a flood of birds and bats to zip in and swirl around the open area. Her battle-scarred mice made a cautious reappearance, and Bella tried to decide what her next action should be—but her exhaustion almost overcame her.

"At least with this much help, I might actually be able to finish all the chores soon enough to take a rest." She finally gave in to her needs, instead of seeking out her desires, and used the bonus help to go through the manor room by room on the main floor and servants area, using the birds to dust, beat the curtains, adjust the furniture, rearrange pillows, gather all the discarded clothing her stepsisters had tried on and tossed to the side.

In only a few hours, Bella had caught up on everything she needed to do for the day. Her thanks was the only thing she could give her creatures, but she did so profusely. They never seemed to mind not getting treats or trinkets, which could've been an effect of her skills, but she wasn't the sort of person to demand work without reward. At least, not usually.

The thought of attempting to escape crossed her mind, but Bella was certain she knew why her stepmother didn't have that concern. It was a bitterly cold night, and wet snow was falling heavily outside, though the wind was not blowing too hard. She was certain that if she tried to go through the hedges, they would simply wrap around her and hold her still, allowing her to freeze before Matringa returned home. Even if they didn't, it was unlikely that she'd be able to make it to town without taking serious injuries or terrible frostbite.

Even then, she would simply be returned here by a well-meaning stranger when they found out she wasn't yet eighteen and unmarried. Bella shuddered to think what would happen if that scenario were to play out.

Instead, she went to bed early and caught up on sleep, waking the next morning feeling well-rested and ready to function at a high level once more. This turned out to be a great boon, as her stepfamily arrived home very suddenly and practically shouted their conversation back and forth from sheer excitement.

"Can you believe there were three entire *barrels* of cider?" Cattiva's eyes were bright as she paused to look at her sister's reflection in the mirror, since Malvagio was practically preening at her own appearance. "There's no way we got through even one of them, right? That means they spent a handful of silver on just that, all for it to be *decoration*!"

Malvagio waved her sister away with a knowing smile. "It wasn't simply for them to show how opulent they were. From what I heard, they were using it as a way to build goodwill with the villagers. Some kind of charity event so they could help out the fearful peasants. No one wants to go out and about as the plague gets worse."

"They're so afraid of getting a little sick. That was the younger brother of the king, nothing's going to happen to *them.*" Cattiva scoffed and shook her head. "Silly if you ask me, both for the host to buy into it, as well as to purchase so much for no purpose. They're going to be drinking that for weeks, unless it goes bad, and they have to dump it."

The older stepsister rolled her eyes. "Sure, but *they* don't know nothing's going to happen to them. At least, not until…"

Just then, both of them noticed Bella had entered the room, and the conversation died instantly, only to rekindle with a clear shift in their tone. Cattiva let out a high-pitched giggle then used her shoulder to bump her sister, "No wonder you danced with Enzo *three* times. Nephew of the king, so he'll be a Duca someday? I'd say that's a fair suitor, wouldn't you?"

"Yeah, if he wasn't so dreadfully boring." Malvagio paused for dramatic effect. "All he spoke about the whole night was how bitter their serfs are becoming. Morale is low! Sales are down, which means fewer taxes! Blah, blah. All the boring parts of politics, without being able to have a taste of the pie for myself."

Matringa's reflection appeared in the mirror, causing both her daughters to go quiet. "Well… if you want *excitement…* perhaps I should tell you what *I* learned last night?"

All three of the girls listened attentively, though Bella made sure not to show even a *hint* of interest in the conversation. The stepmother came closer to her daughters, looming large in the reflective surface. "They plan to resolve those exact issues. As a matter of fact, they have a plan in place already. You see, at the spring equinox, there's going to be a royal ball."

"No!" Cattiva gasped, practically trembling in excitement.

"Who all knows this? We have to get fitted for dresses before this becomes public knowledge; what will the fashion be? By the *system-*"

"*Cattiva*!" Matringa flinched away from her daughter. "Watch your mouth!"

"Sorry, Mother! I... forgot." the younger of the stepsisters practically whispered her apology, shrinking in on herself under her mother's glare—a look Bella had only seen directed at herself to this point.

Matringa waited a few moments longer, showing her dissatisfaction through silence before finishing her thought. "You got excited for the *party*, and that's not even the *interesting* part. The Crown Prince comes of age on the equinox, and with the surrounding kingdoms struggling so much with plague, the Queen doesn't want to invite sickness into our lands. According to our host last night, as a way to bring the population together, the Prince will be engaged to someone... from here."

"From our house?" Cattiva's hands went up over her mouth. "Is it going to be Malvagio or me?"

"From within our own country, you dolt." Malvagio's words were harsh, but they saved her younger sister from a more in-depth berating via their mother. "Who all is in the competition?"

"It's not for certain yet." Matringa admitted her lack of knowledge graciously. "It is certain the equinox ball will be happening, but the court is still in deliberations as to who should be allowed to vie for the prince's hand. Half of them want the Royal House to marry from the nobility, while the others think he should quell tensions by raising a commoner. As for me? I think it will be somewhere in the middle... perhaps a low nobility house which was raised from commoner status through sheer grit and determination, perhaps?"

"That's *us*!" Cattiva scream-whispered excitedly. "I knew that's what you meant from the start, Mother!"

"Hmm. Good, you positioned us well." Malvagio nodded at her mother thoughtfully. "I admit, I'd had some doubts over the last couple years. Anyway, if that's how it's going to be, I guess I have a few months to prepare the finest, most detailed painting of my life. I'll try to accept his proposal graciously."

"Hey, it could be me!" Cattiva exclaimed with a troubled expression. "You can't just assume you're going to get the best of everything because you're the oldest."

Malvagio looked at her younger sister then rolled her eyes over to stare at her mother. "Thoughts?"

"If she could bring her talents to an acceptable level, she might have a real chance." Matringa stated lightly, though her words caused Cattiva's face to crumple. "Now, don't act like that. You still have a few months; who knows what could happen?"

"There you go, nothing else to be said, is there? Now, I'm going to go take a nap. I need to get plenty of rest so I can be ready to hear you all calling me 'Your Highness' in a few months." At Malvagio's words, the trio walked away, leaving Bella to pick up their discarded garments and properly hang them. Cattiva's voice floated down from above, her petulant tone carrying words that made Bella's blood run cold.

"Couldn't we just bring a few villagers in for me to practice on? No one's going to miss them once the plague gets here, and it's not like the hedges are going to mind taking care of what's *left* of them."

CHAPTER
THIRTY

"HONESTLY?" Bella muttered to herself as she slammed her fists into the dough the next morning, pounding all of her frustrations away on the innocent concoction. "I'd be *perfectly* fine with her being the princess if they walked out of my life for the rest of it. What has the kingdom done for *me*? They can suffer her temper more readily than I."

She didn't slack on her chores or noticeably change her routine. Even so, Bella's thoughts were completely focused on the equinox ball—which was coming toward her at what felt like breakneck speed. This morning was particularly grump-inducing, as an official invitation had arrived from the palace. Specifically, a separate invitation had arrived for Malvagio, Cattiva, *and* Bella... as well as a single chaperone.

Bella had no desire to go, especially not after she'd seen the utter glee Malvagio had exhibited upon handing her the invitation. Her stepsister had been practically vibrating as she gushed, "You're going to look *so* amazing, Bella. I can't wait for you to try on what I've... what Mother decided you should wear. But, well, *I'll* be doing your makeup. You're going to have all eyes on you, I guarantee it."

"*Grrr...*" the Beast Singer-turned-maid growled as she punched the dough harder. "*Must* they humiliate me on top of everything else?"

In the next moment, a bucket full of icy cold water with chunks of snow floating at the top washed over her, and Bella let out a shrill scream. Eyes blazing, she turned—and clenched her jaw to remain silent when she found her stepmother staring at her.

"Oh me, oh my... *now* you want to follow the rules about only speaking when spoken to? Interesting. I hear a cold shower each morning would be healthy for your skin. Perhaps it would do you some good? Imagine how clean a bath each morning would make you feel."

Bella's eyes flicked to the side; the servant's bathing area was outside. Were she to plunge into it in the current weather conditions, there was a good chance she would freeze to death. She held her tongue, knowing arguing would only turn the threat into a certainty.

"Now, if you cannot be relied upon to be *gracious* when we take you to the ball, I'll need to make alternative plans. Is that what you want?" Matringa's voice was as cold as the water still dripping from Bella's servant gown.

"No, Signora." Bella mumbled the words around her chattering teeth, her body desperately shivering to try and bring back some heat. "I don't know what came over me just now."

"Mmm." The woman watched her with hard, beady eyes. "By royal decree, all eligible ladies are to attend the festivities at the equinox. You *will* be going, as many people already know about you. Even so, no one will be surprised when you leave early, due to your fragile health. Let me be clear... you will make an appearance so the royal decree is followed to the letter, then you will return home and go into the cellar. You will not come up those stairs until I return home. Now, Bella, I *will* have your oath on this, or I will need to take *drastic* measures to ensure your safety this upcoming evening."

Matringa seemed to be waiting for an answer, but Bella knew better. She hadn't been asked a question, and her stepmother was attempting to bait her into a punishment. As the seconds flowed by, and the expression on Matringa's face became more unpleasant, Bella thought she had perhaps misread the situation. Just before she could panic, Matringa's face smoothed out.

"Ah! I see... good girl." There was a crooked smile on her face, but in her stepmother's eyes was only pure satisfaction. "So, will you give me your oath, or will we think of something else?"

"Do you want a pinky promise, or...?" Bella hesitantly inquired, already nervous about such an act. While it was not crossing one's heart, a pinky promise—when broken—literally caused a person's finger to wither and fall off.

"No, there's plenty of trouble you could get into with only four fingers on one hand." Matringa allowed her eyes to sink slightly lower, and she stared with unrepentant excitement at the racing pulse showing in Bella's neck. "You'll cross your heart. That way, I know you'll take me seriously."

"But... if I cross my heart," the young woman slowly spoke, not certain if she were speaking out of turn or still answering the question, "I could *die*."

Matringa raised an eyebrow at her. "You could *die*? Are you actively planning on disobeying me? If not, there should be no issue at all. You'll go downstairs, and the next morning, you'll be able to come up without any fear of reprisal whatsoever. You'll even get a system mark of trustworthiness for a fulfilled oath, won't you? Those are all the rage these days. Helps people find the *good girls*."

Now that it had been pointed out, it was quite obvious Matringa had no such mark. Bella decided against commenting on that fact, taking a few moments to think over her options. Ever so slowly, she spoke her thoughts aloud. "Signora, is it wise to invoke the system for such a minor thing? If I recall, oaths like that are powerful things, and can have... unexpected effects."

"Nonsense!" Matringa waved off her concerns, even as her expression hardened, "You want unexpected effects? Try *refusing* the oath."

Her words had been spoken with heat, but Bella wasn't about to be pushed or bullied into making a binding promise, not for any reason.

She continued to hold her silence until finally Matringa grit her teeth and allowed a concession, "If you're really *that* worried, child, I'll even change the wording a little. Repeat after me. I, Bella, swear to return home from the equinox ball at the Spring Palace when told to do so by Signora Vigatori. Upon returning home, I will go to my current room, not ascending the stairs unless given permission by Signora Vigatori, *or* until ten in the morning the following day, whichever comes first."

"I... okay." After thinking over the offer a few times, Bella gave a hesitant nod and repeated after her stepmother.

"Now, make an 'X' over your heart and say that you cross your heart and hope to die." Matringa practically whispered the final command, her eyes boring into her stepdaughter as she waited to ensure the young woman couldn't slip in any other statements.

"Cross my heart and hope to die." As Bella made the motion and spoke the words, there was a bright flare of golden light in the air over her chest. A moment later, it sank into her skin, and she let out a gasp as she felt a sensation like a warm hug directly on her heart. As the feeling passed, she looked over at Matringa, expecting to see smug smiles or hear haughty words.

Instead, her stepmother was facing away from her, one arm up as if to shield her eyes, and was breathing heavily. Without turning back to look at her, Matringa spoke in a soft voice. "That will suffice. I'll have your gown ready for you shortly. I'm glad we are getting back into a mindset of mutual trust."

The older woman hurried out of the room, leaving Bella wondering what, exactly, had just happened. Before she could decide what to do next, whether that would be changing into something dry or finishing her work with the bread, Matringa's voice floated back to her. "There is one stipulation… you will not be allowed to lollygag about. Before we set off for the ball, all of your chores must be done, as well as anything else I deem necessary. Don't worry, if I think back on how easily you were able to handle the tasks I've given you in the past, *why*, you should have no problems whatsoever!"

Bella winced at that; there was no way she'd be able to use her animal friends to help clean the house or sort things while her stepfamily was in attendance and attentive to her. She fully understood her stepmother's true intent: by the time she went to the ball, Bella would be utterly exhausted.

It was unlikely she would be able to make trouble, even if she wanted to. Abyss, it would be hard enough for her to stay on her feet. Most likely, this would be the excuse given to their hosts to send her home early.

She tried to get back to pounding the dough, but simply couldn't function through the body-aching cold of her wet clothing. Deciding she needed to put off her current task for the moment, Bella bit her lip and rushed out of the kitchen, around to the back, and hurried into the cellar. She entered her room, closed the door behind her, and rushed over to her makeshift wardrobe to switch out her dress.

"Kind of surprised how warm it is in here, if I'm being honest with myself." Bella grumbled as she stripped and changed into a dirty gown. She'd been putting off doing the laundry, hoping for a warm, sunny day to do the painfully lengthy task. "Between the straw accouterments and being underground, it at least stays a nice, consistent temperature..."

Her fumbling fingers slowed, and Bella thought over the agreement she had just made with her stepmother. "Something I just said... what... being underground, it stays a consistent temperature?"

Bella looked up, her eyes going wide as a plan suddenly began forming in her mind. "The Spring Palace is only an hour down the road via carriage. It's too far to walk, but everyone *and* their daughter will be going to the ball. Could I get there on my own?"

She fought with herself for a moment, trying to determine why her mind was prodding her into action, but she finally remembered a conversation from long ago. "The Royals can advance people's classes directly; it's one of their abilities as leaders of the nation! Usually, they do this to show favor, but on a night like the prince's birthday, perhaps they may be more willing to throw around a bit of power as a show of solidarity with the people. But... how can I work around the oath I just made?"

As she thought, Bella was snapping her fingers, caught between the need to figure this out and get back to what she was doing before she was missed. Her intent rippled out, and a rustling in the straw behind her caused Bella to spin around in fear of finding Matringa sneaking up on her with another bucket of ice water. Instead, she found the coterie of eclectic animals staring at her.

Just like that, she had her answer. Bella froze in place as everything came together. "Matringa will be out of the house the entire night. She believes I will be here, because I'd otherwise die, thanks to my oath. But if I could get to the palace and get my class advanced, I could vanish. If I'm not here, and I have skills, I'll be welcomed elsewhere. That means I'll need to figure out a way to get past the hedges. Not only that, but since I swore I wouldn't go up the stairs after coming down here…"

She stepped forward and held out a hand, petting the enthusiastic mole that lurched forward to meet her. "Well… maybe we could think of a way to work around all of that, together? After all, we have nothing but time."

CHAPTER
THIRTY-ONE

THAT NIGHT, Bella was pacing in the cellar, her fingers tracing along the intricate straw weavings hung on the stone wall as she tried to formulate the last portions of her plans. "The most direct route out of here and to get under the hedges, would be to dig south, along the wall of the house and under the front lawn. I'd prefer to go under and across the road, but I'll take what I can get."

Kneeling down, Bella gently lifted the edge of the dense straw mat that served to keep her floor covered, revealing the cold dirt she had despised when she was first banished to the subterranean living space. Now, all she could feel was gratefulness and gratitude: escape would've been all but impossible from any other room of the house. "This can work. Alright, my friends, here's the plan…"

As she whispered, the cellar filled with the scurrying of tiny feet and squeaking of mice herding the other, less well-trained animals closer. Soon, she was surrounded by dozens of tiny staring eyes and whiskers twitching with anticipation, even as her own adrenaline began to spike.

"We're going to dig a tunnel right through here, under the cellar and out past the estate. This is… if this doesn't work, or if we're caught, I don't know what the punishment will be. That means, above all else, we need to be careful and stay hidden."

Quickly, as quietly as possible, she began laying out her plan for each of the different types of animal. "Bert, you're going to be in charge of sounding the alarm. That means a mouse in every possible location, passing information on the whereabouts of my stepfamily at all times. If they step outside for any reason, all work on the tunnel has to stop *immediately*. Matringa has some connection to plants, but she's never clued me in on what exactly she can do. That means we have to assume she can get information from them. That means no exposed roots; we need to dig deep."

Bert squeaked in approval, looking over at Mert the Third in slight confusion. Bella shook her head, turning to the mouse in question. "You have a special task, Mert. You and your most highly trained group are going to be making sure the cats stay busy. You're going to need to find sharp things, like nails, and start injuring those foul creatures when they reach into your mouse holes. Above all else, your group will be tasked with keeping those *things* as far away from the servant quarters as possible. Lure all six of them to the attic as often as possible; get them used to staying far away, so they can't hear what we're doing down here."

Squeak. Mert agreed to the deadly task with a firm nod of his tiny head. He raised a paw, and a dozen mice shuffled toward him, pulling out needles and other small implements they had already been carrying around.

Bella swallowed hard, knowing some of them would likely be taken by the creatures Matringa had brought into the house. "I can't imagine being as brave as you. Thank you."

Mert paused for a moment to make sure there were no other orders, then he led his group away. Bella watched them go, then turned back to hand out additional tasks. "Suzy, you're going to be in charge of the digging team. I don't want you in there digging, but I need you to keep everyone on task, make sure they keep the tunnel stable, and make it large enough for me to get through. I really, *really* don't want to go inside, only for it to become my grave."

"Moles, chipmunks, you are my main digging group, but bring in any creature willing to help and listen. I'll come into the tunnel when possible and sing to any creature outside your range. Hopefully, the farther we go, the faster the work will become."

With the sentries in place, Bella carefully rearranged the straw to give the creatures access to the tunnel. "Suzy, I can't risk having a person-sized hole here. Until the day we're going to use it, the first foot or so of the tunnel needs to be only large enough to let your team in and out. The day we use it, we'll quickly dig out the rest of it, but if it gets discovered, I can hopefully play it off as something I didn't notice before. Keep it small."

"*Squeak!** Suzy promised as the mole came over and started tossing dirt into the air.

"I don't know if this is going to work, but we have two months until we find out." Ever so quietly, she sang a soft rhyme, putting all of her intent and visualization of the needed tunnel into the words: "*Dig, my friends, dig deep and far. Keep it hidden, or I'll bear the scar.*"

Bella stepped away, knowing there was nothing else she could do at the moment. She went to bed, but even as she started to doze, she could hear the burrowing team tirelessly working, their small paws and claws churning through the earth with remarkable speed. As Bella drifted away, she heard Suzy intermittently directing her crew with soft, chirping squeaks.

When she awoke, Bella checked on the progress her creatures had made overnight and set up additional precautions. She carefully smoothed the straw matting, put together a small team of mice to clear away the collected dirt, and even had a few sections of the flooring torn out to be replaced because it had gotten noticeably filthy.

"Suzy, I'm going to add this to your duties as well," Bella informed the sleepy mouse. "You don't have to do it yourself, but make sure some of your people are sweeping out anything that can give this away. Keep it clean; make sure it matches the rest of the room. There can't be anything, not a single thing, to grab Matringa's attention."

As she prepared for the day and stepped out of the cellar, Bella's heart was lighter than it had been in a long time. "Escape route in progress, plan in motion. I just need to continue my charade of obedience and never give a hint to my stepmother or stepsisters of my true intentions. All I need now is enough evidence to expose Matringa and get the kingdom to stop her. But, failing that, the night of the ball… I'll vanish forever."

Her day began normally, filling up her time with cooking breakfast and preparing the rest of the day's meals. If they wanted to have bread in the evening, it needed to be prepared early, so it had enough time to rise and be cooked by lunch or dinner. Peas needed to be sorted out of mixtures, vegetables had to be cleaned and laid out for easy access, and any meat needed to be carefully portioned. A roast was a twelve-hour process, including the slow cooking of it, and each part needed to be done in order, long in advance of actually sampling the dish.

After nearly two hours of work, Bella had finished her preparation for that day's meals, and the sun was just beginning to come over the horizon. Almost at the same moment she laid the cheesecloth over the dough to let it rise without getting any bugs or dust in it, she heard a bell ringing from the floor above.

Following the sound, Bella walked up the stairs, hesitating at the base of the second staircase until Matringa stepped into view. "What are you waiting for? Did you not hear the bell? Get up here."

"Signora, I was concerned, as…" Before she could explain how she wasn't allowed upstairs, Bella had to dodge to the side as the bell on a handle whipped through the air where her head had been a moment before.

"Who gave you permission to speak?" Matringa practically growled as Bella looked at her in shock. "No one else will ring these bells. When you hear one of them, you're to come *immediately*. Now, in preparation for the upcoming nuptials of one of my daughters to the prince, there's going to be a few changes around here. First, they need to become reacquainted to being waited on. That means, every morning, you will be serving breakfast in bed to both of them, and I will take mine in the study."

Bella took a breath, remembering only at the last second not to speak out.

Matringa had paused almost hopefully, only to grunt and continue moments later, "Their hair needs to be done, their makeup applied properly. Then you'll help them get dressed and take dishes away while they prepare themselves for their lessons. In the evening, before you clean the mess left by dinner, I expect their hair to be brushed, linens turned down, and nightgowns laid out. You'll also remove their laundry and make sure it is folded and returned within three days."

Almost sick with the sheer amount of extra work which had just been piled on her, Bella still only nodded and let out a deep internal sigh. She knew exactly what this was really about: Matringa wanted her too exhausted to be thinking about the upcoming ball and certainly too busy to try and make trouble.

Luckily, she'd gotten that all out of the way the night before.

Matringa's piercing stare bore into her for a moment longer, before the wicked stepmother finally turned away, her lips curled into a smug smile. She lifted the bell in her hand, placing it on a floating shelf, which must have been installed the night before. Its prominent position was certainly intended to draw the eye, a clear reminder to Bella what her new and very real station in this house was meant to be. "You are dismissed. Better get moving."

Knowing exactly how much had been dropped on her shoulders, Bella turned and practically ran down the stairs, into the kitchen to try and get ahead of the intensified laundry list of chores.

First, she needed to divide up the breakfast she had just prepared, setting each meal on a tray, then each tray on a larger carrying tray so she could manage all of them at once. Bella had been preparing breakfast long enough that she fully understood they needed to be meticulously arranged to meet her stepmother's exacting standards, or the plate would be thrown to the ground, and she'd be forced to start over.

Each plate had an exact amount of fresh fruit, a small pastry, hot tea, a folded napkin, as well as a single sugar cube for each person. She added cutlery and hard boiled eggs, making sure to take off the shell just before hurrying up the stairs. Bella delivered the trays one by one, starting with Matringa in the study, who looked over her work and begrudgingly nodded, accepting her tray and waving the young woman off.

From there, Bella went to Malvagio's room, waking up the eldest stepsister, who glanced at the spread and barely acknowledged Bella before attempting to go back to sleep. "I'll be back shortly to do your hair and help you get dressed."

"What?" Malvagio looked up at her blearily. "Wait, you're not even supposed to be in here."

"New rules, apparently. Get ready, because I'm going to be here until your hair is done, and you're fully clothed. I'm sure you're *exactly* as excited about that as I am." Bella stepped out of the room as her oldest stepsister groaned in annoyance, though by the sounds of cloth being thrown around, she had actually gotten out of bed.

Next was Cattiva, and Bella made sure to treat the situation as delicately as was required. First, she set the food down on a nightstand on the opposite side of the room, then walked over to the bed and tucked in the sheets her younger stepsister was sleeping under. Taking a deep breath, she got close to Cattiva and shouted, "*Wake up!*"

"Ahhh!" Cattiva let out a primal scream that started as shock but morphed into absolute fury over being woken up so roughly. She struggled back and forth, only to find that she wasn't *quite* tied to her bed, but it was a near thing. "I'm going to rip your hair out! No, I'm going to find a pair of scissors and cut it *unevenly*! I'll tell everyone you did it yourself, and they'll believe me because they already think you're falling apart-"

"Yes, yes, you're *very* scary." Bella patted the top of the comforter gently, treating her younger stepsister like a caged, soaked cat. "Your mother has ordered me to bring you breakfast in bed, do your hair, and help you get dressed and ready for lessons. Every. Single. Day."

"You'd better *not* be serious, you-"

Cattiva's threat was ignored as Bella swept out of the room, only pausing for a moment at the door. "Don't worry, over the next few months, we'll get to know each other really well. You might want to be careful how you act in the morning, since, you know, now I've been *ordered* to be in your room. While you're asleep."

As her younger stepsister's half-awake mind realized what was being said, she lapsed into silence.

The real work had only just begun. She brushed Malvagio's hair until it shined like polished mahogany, styling it meticulously, thanks to her stepsister's ridiculous demands, then tried to apply makeup on someone else for the very first time ever. It was a disaster, and she ended up needing to scrub

Malvagio's face and try again and again, until finally her hand was slapped away, and the older girl did it herself.

The situation repeated itself with Cattiva, until she was finally kicked out of the room with the breakfast dishes in hand. The younger girl shouted after Bella as she hurried to get the last tray from the study, "Can't you do anything *right?*"

"Well. It certainly sounds like they are up and ready for lessons." Matringa eyed her stepdaughter, who was already sweating profusely from the strain of doing tasks she'd no experience or affinity with. "Look at you. Ten hours of hard work in the kitchen, and you barely glimmer with humidity, but a fraction of that time spent acting like a girl your age, and it looks like you ran inside to escape a deluge. You'll just need to get plenty of practice, it seems."

The rest of the day went fairly normally, though she was delayed from her normal routine by nearly two hours already. Adding on collecting the laundry from her stepsister's rooms, washing and wringing it out, only to hang it up in a spare room to dry cost her additional hours after dinner.

Evening crept in then rushed past as she scrubbed the dishes, the pots and pans, and the counters before finally putting away the final dish and glancing out the window. Bella was dismayed to see the stars already bright in the night sky, but she had at least finished for the day. She trudged toward the door, her limbs heavy and her eyelids drooping.

"All done?"

Matringa met her at the door, and Bella was too tired to react with anything more than a simple, "Yes, Signora."

"Oh me, oh my. This is working out even better than I expected, Bella. What a *fantastic* day it's been." Matringa followed her to the cellar while wearing a broad smirk—causing the young woman no end of anxiety—only to wait at the door as the young woman stumbled over to her bed and collapsed into it. "Sleep well. Tomorrow will come all too early."

By the time her stepmother had climbed the stairs, closed the cellar door, and *clicked* the padlock into place... Bella was breathing softly and evenly, her eyes firmly closed for what remained of the night.

The next day dragged on, and the week was absolutely brutal. By the end of the second week, Bella was only able to stay on her feet through sheer force of will and a constant reminder to herself that the end was in sight. After the second week, she finally acclimated to the schedule somewhat and was able to regain some of her mental clarity.

After that point, she made sure to get up extra early, place her mouth next to the entrance of the tunnel the animals had been digging out, and sing to the voles, moles, and burrowers to join in and help. By the end of the first month, Bella was terrified that they wouldn't make it in time. According to Suzy's charades, they'd only reached the edge of the manor itself and were only just beginning to expand past the foundation of the house.

However, each morning and each night, she would place her face into the opening and sing into the tunnel, her words echoing from farther and farther away each day. From what she could glean from the mouse's frantic attempts to communicate back to her, additional animals often burrowed in and began to dig in shifts.

Finally, with only a week to go before the ball, Bella found herself numb to the situation. As Suzy attempted to explain how far they had gotten over the last couple of days, Bella simply shook her head uncomprehendingly and allowed a tired smile to tug at the corners of her lips.

"It doesn't matter, sweet mouse. This is a good plan. Even if the tunnel isn't done by the time the ball comes around, we'll be able to escape. What's another few weeks, when I've had to function like this for years? At least she'll probably relent when there's no obvious way for me to make trouble."

"*Squeak!*" Suzy angrily stomped, pointing at the tunnel and nodding firmly.

"I believe you, you'll get it done in time." Bella used a single finger to pet the mouse's head. "But right now, I need to get back to it. I need a dress for the ball, and apparently one is arriving for me today."

She set the elderly mouse down gently then stumbled toward the stairs up, her exhausted mind clouding her thoughts. "*Gotta get a dress to wear to the ball, figure out a way not to fall, somehow I'll show them all.*"

Singing her song gently as she climbed the stairs, Bella failed to notice how Suzy went still, staring after the human that had trained her since she was a kit.

THIRTY-TWO

PRINCE CINDER

PRINCE CINDER DROPPED into a plush chair, pouring himself a cup of coffee to help regain some clarity after the intense physical training of the morning. He pulled a face as the room-temperature liquid swirled into the cup; clearly the pot had been sitting on the counter for quite a while. He stared into the mug, lost in his thoughts until his mother's voice entered his ears, and he broke from his musing.

"Julia turned up missing." The Queen swept into the room, her voice as even as usual, though the slight uptick in tone at the end of her sentence highlighted the fact that she was practically frantic, on top of being quite displeased.

"Turned up missing." Cinder tried out the words, tilting his head slightly as he watched his mother go to the desk and frantically begin flipping through papers. He raised an eyebrow, then glanced back at the coffee he was swirling his finger in, which was now steaming. "That's better. Mother, that's the oddest turn of phrase I've heard from you in a while. Remind me why this is such an issue? Who is this... Julia?"

That earned him a swat on the arm from a rolled-up scroll as the Queen gave him a stern glance. "Julia. Cinder, we've been in communication with her for the last year. The *Match-*

maker? The person who can ensure that your partner has an auric imprint that matches your own, the one individual we can point at and blame if your bride turns out to be unfit for the station she will earn upon wedding you?"

"Seems odd to need someone to blame, is all," Cinder commented, noncommittal, as he watched her continue to push papers to the side, "Plus, I think this may be the first time you mentioned her by name. It's been 'Matchmaker this, Matchmaker that', all for me to still have doubts that this hard work will end in an engagement. We both know we have three allies with eligible daughters who have been less-than-subtly requesting to present them for half a decade. I'm still of the opinion that we're going to need people who are friendly to us, if we want good trade relationships instead of war when this plague runs its course."

"*Now* you want to comment on your future commitments?" The queen paused to rub the bridge of her nose. "You know what they say about you? Day after day, all the prince ever does is practice, practice, *practice*. There's so many questions I have no way to answer, Cinder. Does he have a type? Is there a particular area he would like to pursue for his Conjoined Skill? Does he at least *enjoy* the hunts leading up to his birthday and the ball? I have no idea!"

Cinder only smiled and shrugged from his seated position. "You were the one who was so intent on ensuring I had the very best education and was devoted to developing my class to the point no one could contest my right to rule when the time comes. Is it my fault I fell in love with what the system granted me? Do I have a type? Yes, most certainly I do. Is there a particular area I would like to pursue for my Conjoined Skill? But of course. The answers to those questions are simple."

He lifted his right hand, staring into his palm as flames sprang into existence, reflecting in his eyes as he twirled the glowing plasma around. "Someone *fiery*. Full of passion, able to compete with me, so both of us can ascend through the levels. Someone with a powerful skill which will allow me to manifest my own in a new, unique, potent way, and she, hers."

Only after a few moments of silence did he look away from the blaze in his palm, meeting his mother's concerned glance.

"This, Cinder. *This* is why I worry about you. Wanting to grow and learn what the system has in store for you is perfectly natural, but this... *fascination* you have with the fire you create? I worry that, when the world sees the smile on your face when you are burning targets in a field, they might think you are deranged. No one wants a tyrant king."

Cinder's wide smile faded somewhat, becoming strained. "Isn't this the entire reason we decided on this... let's call it a *plan*? Get the common people to love us while avoiding the scrutiny of the high nobility? They will turn their anger and avarice toward the interloper in their midst, practically forgetting about me as I handle what needs to be done as King. I'll be free to pursue my... studies, and a commoner gets to live a life they never dreamed of. The population hopes they could be next, and the nobles are satisfied because one of their rivals did not become stronger. As for the rest, I just worry about what comes after."

"Well, if the plague continues spreading at the same pace, we might not need to worry about *that* for too long," the queen grumbled as she got to the bottom of her stack of papers, shoving them to the side when she didn't find what she'd been looking for.

"If it helps, I have been enjoying the hunts." Cinder's words earned him no love from his mother, though she did scoff as a slightly annoyed smile appeared on her face.

"You have a quick wit, I'll give you that." His mother took a deep breath, finally sitting in her chair and looking at her son. "You push buttons and push buttons, but then you say something *charming*, and it all seems to work out. I hope, for her sake, your future wife can handle being around you without her head spinning right off."

"However, as for the dancing and socializing in the evenings…" Cinder trailed off, as his mother let out a low groan.

"Yes, I fully understand how little you enjoy that. I *perfectly* recall how I needed to intercede before you lit that one poor girl's hair on fire." The queen shook her head and chuckled, "I can't imagine what would have happened. I know what you say, but it's still hard to understand."

"Ha! First of all, you know it wouldn't have hurt her." Cinder snapped his fingers and pointed at her as he recalled the same evening. "It would have simply been a flash flame to distract her while I slipped away. Why do I even need to explain this? She thought she could lie to *me* right to my face. For future reference, when someone deeply unpleasant backs me into a corner then talks *at* me for an hour without being able to make up for it with good conversation or a cheerful attitude, why is a sudden fire *not* the perfectly reasonable response?"

"She was perfectly lovely, Cinder. Besides, people aren't *supposed* to know about the lie-detection artifacts nor the protective talismans you wear. That would remove most of their usefulness. So, of *course*, they think they can lie to you." The queen paused to think for a moment. "Who actually was it… the stepdaughter of some minor Merchant if I recall. Vago? Lago? I forget her name. Yet, the choices which made you happy that night utterly astounded me. The one you actually decided to dance with? I thought perhaps she had been touched by the plague. Frankly, I nearly had the guards separate you."

"I have no idea what you mean. She was perfectly lovely and was clearly someone who worked to remain fit and healthy. She had a glow to her unlike any of the other nobildonna in attendance."

"Yes, yes… as you say…" They met eyes across the desk, hers blue, his a deep brown—so long as he actively contained his abilities. Otherwise, they swirled red and white, a maelstrom of energy that shifted the way he perceived the world.

"It's called a heat map, Mother. You know it's real. Otherwise, that assassin would have succeeded against Father a few years ago, instead of simply giving him a permanent limp."

Haaa. The queen let out a deep sigh, shaking her head at him as she pursed her lips. "Must you throw that in my face every time the conversation edges toward what you can and cannot do? I understand you're powerful, that's the entire *point* of our family line. Also, the reason I need *Julia* to be found!"

She turned her attention away, focused once more on the paperwork on her desk. Cinder knew she had settled into a bad mood, so held his tongue as he studied her. Queen Liora carried herself with dignity, her posture perfect, even though she was grumbling while throwing things around at the moment.

The golden 'X' on her right cheek was a symbol meaning she was recognized by the system itself as a valid and system-approved ruler of the kingdom. The same symbol on her left cheek showed her as someone who was married, which would be the only mark Cinder himself would be gaining until his parents stepped down as rulers to make way for him and his future queen.

For now, he was simply happy to be given the space he needed to pursue his own desires. "Just because we are selecting someone next week doesn't mean we will be *forced* to wed, correct?"

"You know the answer. I need to send the guards out to begin searching for Julia," Liora snapped at him. "How many times must we go over this, Cinder?"

"At least once more, Mother." Cinder sent a crooked smile her way, "Just for my peace of mind."

She slapped her hand onto the table. "No! Even if you

find someone who would be a good match, there are all manner of things to check before you will be *allowed* to get married. Forced? By the system, if you *get* to get married before you are thirty, consider yourself lucky. Background checks, personality matching, skill defining… all of it is absolutely necessary before we allow someone any kind of control over the kingdom. The vows of marriage can be twisted by the wrong person, and we will not allow that to happen under any circumstances."

"Good. I *do* wish you would explain the stipulations in the invitations, as the staring has gotten quite intense. I can barely ignore it these days. Quite often, I wonder if this is how my sandwich feels at lunch time, the last thing it sees being my smiling face." Cinder gave a dramatic shiver before sending a piteous look at his mother. "They don't see me; they see what they can get out of me."

"Ah, yes. My son, the veal," Liora drolly commented. "Were you not so fascinated with lighting everything around you on fire, you would be much more open and excited about the possibility of making a match."

"The world is a match, Mother. Of course I want to light it up," Cinder quipped back at her.

"You need a hobby."

"I have one; it's not my fault you don't like it." Cinder and Liora watched each other for a few long seconds, both smiling at the other. "Truly… I do worry sometimes about this bold new plan of yours. The second I am among the public, all eyes are on me in a way I've never felt before. There's nothing respectful about the stares; it seems almost… desperate."

"There's a plague." Liora shrugged at him, the least proper motion she'd made since entering the room. "Desperate times, desperate people. This shouldn't be shocking, Cinder."

The prince continued his tirade as though she wasn't trying to deescalate the situation. "Conversations have been falling apart like never before. 'Do you like horses? Oh, yes, I *love* horses, I'm just absolutely terrified of riding or being near them!' It makes all my formal appearances quite disingenuous. Conversely, *I* can't be casual, or they begin to make plans to move into the palace."

"Yes, that was an... interesting month." Liora chuckled at her son's 'misfortune'. "Luckily, we were able to convince their neighbor to return the deed to their estate, so long as they returned the money they paid for it. I don't think they were able to rehire all of their staff. Still, not our problem, and thankfully, they never will be."

"There's just so much about this situation I am deeply uncomfortable with, and I'm greatly unimpressed with the people who are throwing themselves into my arms in an attempt to pull the crown with them as they step back."

Cinder's words were very bleak, making the Queen's eyes snap over to him and frown, all levity vanishing as she considered him. "The ball is tomorrow night, Cinder. I'll tell you what... if you promise to be pleasant and spend a little time with a woman who interests you, and be *open* to the experience, knowing that we will *ensure* you are not trapped into marrying someone you despise.... I will open the firing range for you for the morning. I'll even clear out all the staff, and you can have free rein until tea time."

His eyes lit up, and the queen smiled at him warmly. "I fully understand how much you love your hobbies. As a word of advice, perhaps you *don't* let your wife know exactly how much you enjoy burning things until you've been married for... let's call it a year?"

"You make me sound like some kind of monster, Mother." Cinder chuckled as he stood and bowed. "I'm a perfectly normal person. I'm not cruel, I don't hurt others, I just love the way the power feels and how I get to see the world in a unique way. I know it's not a big deal to you, but... just know, you have a deal."

THIRTY-THREE

"ARE YOU *QUITE* CERTAIN, YOUR HIGHNESS?" The high level Captain of the Royal Guard looked around the massive open meadow as though assassins were hiding behind the daffodils. "I know Her Majesty the Queen permitted this outing, but I'd been hoping you would be open to an escort. Only for your safety. I would even swear to tell no one of your deeds this day, even if... perhaps you have a young lady from one of the noble families meeting you out here?"

"Nothing so risqué, Captain." Cinder could only chortle at the insinuation of impropriety. "I am merely going to be working out some frustrations and practicing my skills. Since my powers are meant for defense of the Kingdom, I simply want to keep them as private as possible."

The Captain raised an eyebrow, bluntly scoffing and shaking his head. "With all due respect, you've had tutors cycling in and out nearly a decade. Everyone knows you are gifted in the extreme with fire magics. Is one more person, your *sworn guard*, who has only your best intentions at heart, going to impact that so much?"

"You caught me." Cinder rolled his shoulders and smiled

at the man who had been guarding him since he was five years old. "I just want some alone time to blow off some smoke."

"So…?"

"So stand back, don't make a sound, and tell no one what you see here," Cinder finally relented, knowing he would keep hearing complaints until he gave in.

"On my honor and position. I will only speak to *you* about what I see here and only when no others may overhear. May I lose the ability to speak at all if I betray your trust in this matter, Your Highness." The man swore in return, a slight sparkle of system energy fluctuating in the air around his mouth. It was a common oath among people who had the trust of high-level nobles and statesmen.

Also…

"That's completely unnecessary, and you know it." Cinder shook his head as the guard settled into position, hand on the hilt of his sword and already scanning the horizon for threats. "But, have it your way."

Prince Cinder stood alone—at least, as alone as possible—in the meadow, the morning sun shining happily across the cheerful scene. Bees were buzzing from flower to flower, huge columns of gnats were swarming above warm spots, and all in all, it was an idyllic area. After one, final, concerned glance over at the Captain, Cinder lifted his right hand, generating a small ember which rolled back and forth between his fingers.

The flickering flame glowed brightly against his skin, licking and reflecting off of his pale fingers, even while refusing to burn him. It rolled into the palm of his hand, and he clenched his fist, furrowing his brow for a moment as he concentrated. Then, his hand sprang open… and the small spark erupted into a maelstrom of fire.

"Abyss!" Cinder heard the guard curse and flinch some-where behind him, but then the man was gone from his mind.

All that remained was the freedom of the flames.

Twisting his wrist, the wild burst of plasma condensed

down, then shot from his hand as a howling spike of energy. Hundreds of meters distant, a wooden target exploded into burning splinters, most of those being reduced to soot, ash, and cinders before they reached the ground. "Haa! *Yes!* Mother, I hope you added in a few durable versions, but I always love the surprise of an erupting target!"

Bright red flames licked the air in the distance, thick smoke curling up into the sky. Cinder clapped his hands together, pulling them apart and generating a cloud of pure heat between them. It roared like a living beast, and he watched it burn with a smile so wide it felt as though it were trying to shred his cheek muscles. His eyes flicked up, his gaze coming to rest on another distant target. Stepping forward, he shoved both hands at the dot in the distance, and the burst of heat erupted outward, spiraling forward and flaring into bright flame as it traveled.

As it soared along, close to the ground, all life below it was snuffed out, a trail of black following along seconds after the beam had already passed over. So hot was the energy that nothing caught on fire, simply being reduced to ash and embers. He had accurately struck the target, but unlike the first, it didn't erupt. Instead, it began to glow a cherry red, slumping in on itself and melting into a pool of glowing liquid, which smoked and warped the air above it.

Cinder stood still for a moment, panting heavily as he considered the target, his breath mingling with the sparse smoke rising into the air. "Let's see... had to be some kind of metal, I'm betting it was cast iron. I should *hope* Mother knows better than to waste precious metals on target practice."

"By the system!" The awed voice floated to Cinder's ears, and the prince grimaced in annoyance.

"Captain, if you're going to comment on every little thing I do, perhaps it would be best if you *left?*"

"Won't hear another peep from me, Prince Fella. Pardon my intrusion."

"Very well." Cinder grunted, keeping his voice low and controlled. He took a few moments to roll up the sleeves of his tunic then spread his arms wide. Closing his eyes, he breathed deeply for a few moments. When they opened once more, the iris and pupil had shifted, a pure white at the center swirling out into a perfect representation of flames swirling *inside* his sensory organs.

He looked around the meadow, staring at the flows of heat in the air and on the ground, choosing a thermal updraft and snapping his fingers. Fire appeared midair, following the warm air down and striking the ground before exploding into a sphere nine feet wide. Cinder raised an eyebrow, murmuring critically, "Not as fast as lightning, but we're getting there. Perhaps by the time I reach Perfection? Still, that *should* be very difficult to dodge…"

After a few moments of pondering, he once more spread his arms wide, as though preparing to give the world a hug. Sparks began popping into existence around him, floating through the air almost gently. "There we go… tight control… keep them small, keep them-"

The Prince chose a dozen nearby targets, perhaps fifty meters distant. Controlling his power carefully, he aimed and—

Whoom!

The sparks around him exploded into massive, blazing comets that streaked through the air all around him, each arcing through the sky before accurately slamming into their target. A dozen explosions within half a second returned a deafening roar, the instant smoke and flame blocking his view of the targets, which had *certainly* been obliterated.

Cinder dropped his arms to the side, letting out a grunt of annoyance. "Abyss… another failure."

"Fail-?"

"*Captain!*"

"What a *lovely* horizon." The Royal Guard began

humming softly, pretending he wasn't sweating profusely at what he was seeing.

Choosing another of the myriad targets set in the field, Cinder narrowed his eyes and extended his arm. A single spark appeared at the tip of his finger, and a moment later, the man-shaped mannequin was immolated...

...as well as nearly twenty feet around it.

"Why!"

A huge fireball detonated in the center of the meadow.

"Can't!"

The air shimmered around him as twin orbs of fire were conjured in his hands before being hurled simultaneously, crisscrossing in midair before separating in the distance into two distinct targets with a spectacular display of fire and fury.

"I!"

Flames collected around his arms, only to wash out of him as a river of destruction. All grass in front of him, for nearly a hundred meters, was reduced to ash.

"*Control* this?" Sweat was trickling down his face, his breathing was heavy, and even as he railed against his lack of fine control, he relished every moment of being able to use his power as he wished. Letting out a roar, he raised his arms high, summoning a wall of fire that swept across the meadow like a tidal wave, consuming everything in its path. His ears filled with the crackle of burning grasses, water hissing as it was vaporized, and a low thunder as the air itself violently shook.

He took a deep breath, dry air racing into his lungs and almost causing him to cough. Cinder turned to the captain, his swirling eyes capturing the attention of his guard and causing him to gulp. "Well, what do *you* think? I've talked to tutors, mages, every scholar who might be able to weigh in."

"I think that was downright *terrifying*, Your Highness," the man replied honestly, working to keep his voice even as he did so. "Frankly, you don't even seem winded. I don't know what resource you expend when you generate your flames, but you certainly seem to be ready to keep going."

"I have almost no limits on what I can do with fire, Captain. But that's not what I was asking." Cinder casually waved a hand at the scorched meadow, which was mostly hidden behind a thick layer of smoke, no greenery or life to be seen within it. "Like I said, I've studied the theory of all this since I turned ten and gained the ability to commune with flame. But, no matter where I look, what book I read, what sage offers advice, I can't keep the flames in check. I want to be able to earmark a single object and send a spike of heat through it."

The Captain glanced at the meadow, "Looks to me like you can take down pretty much whatever you want to at this point. Mastery? Perfection?"

"Merely *Extensive*." The Prince let out a long-suffering sigh as his guard gulped. "That's right, only level eight with this skill. Imagine what Perfection will look like. But how am I supposed to get there if I can't keep my flames condensed to a manageable size as soon as they are more than a foot from my body?"

"Ohhh." The Captain blinked a few times, suddenly realizing the real problem being presented to him. "So you weren't *just* working off anger there; that's the *minimum* size of your use of power when you use it?"

"I want to be able to contain a burst of flame within a spark." Cinder held up a hand, showcasing a spark which danced above his palm, "sending it through a distant enemy without destroying everything around them. What if they are an attacker hiding in a crowd? I can't simply *blast* my citizens just to get the one offender."

"Eh..." The guard shifted his palm side-to-side. "Depending on the circumstances... and you *are* a prince..."

"Captain!"

"I'm joking, I'm joking! No, unfortunately I think you are

already doing the right thing. Theory will only take you so far." The royal guard looked past the prince, considering the destruction in the distance in a different light. "You gotta practice. If you don't work hard now, figuring out what *doesn't* work, you'll never be able to do it. But perhaps, with enough practice and the right incentive, when the moment comes where you need to keep it in check... you will."

"Ah. You think I should join in a border war. While I love the feeling of progressing my skills and the way my power leaps to fulfill my will, using it on *people* isn't something I'm in a hurry to do." Cinder nodded with agitation. "Beyond that, their Highnesses will never approve of me going to the front lines of war."

"Skills level up the fastest under duress, and wartime or at least *combat* is certain to get you there." Seeing the prince's face, the guard could only shrug. "I'm not calling for conflict, just stating a fact. Don't worry, I'm sure you'll find plenty of deeply uncomfortable situations over the next few weeks. Doesn't your birthday celebration last an entire week? Seven entire days of partying, and every young woman in the kingdom fighting for your hand."

Cinder looked as though he'd bitten into a lemon, and the captain let out a roar of laughter. After a few moments, the prince joined in, chuckling ruefully. "Well, I guess I'd better get back to it, then?"

"Yeah, probably for the best. We're running out of time until you need to dance the night away."

Fire swirled around the prince, twisting and weaving together as it raced toward the sky, only to loop downward and spray along the ground in a line, as though a dragon had just passed over a battle line and immolated it. Flames, both reflected and generated, showed in his eyes as he watched the world warp under his assault.

"Yup. It's a hard life, but someone's gotta live it."

THIRTY-FOUR

BELLA STOOD in front of the full-length mirror, the reflection showing a pale, weary ghost of a girl framed in an elegant, completely out-of-style dress. It was slate gray with intricate embroidery subtly hinting at an allegiance to a foreign kingdom. Overall, her appearance was that of an exhausted person who was perhaps attending the royal ball to create some anti-kingdom sentiment. "No one's going to be sad seeing me leave tonight, that's for sure."

Though she kept the thought to herself, simply smoothing the bulky gown over her hips—which were completely hidden by the severe cut of the fabric—it seemed her stepmother had some idea of what she was thinking. Matringa's fingers dug into Bella's shoulder as she twisted a strand of hair into place *just* shy of painfully. "You will hold still, child. I don't care if you are fine looking like a slovenly mess when there are no guests around, but you certainly will not do so in front of the entire kingdom."

Bella didn't even bother to acknowledge the words, her mind almost completely numb from the exhaustion weighing on her. After the dress and hair was in place to her stepmother's satisfaction, Bella stepped into a pair of large, clunky shoes which would be better worn by a servant who needed to slosh through mud. With a hint of amusement, she realized they actually fit the dress quite well. A moment later, she was whisked out of the way as Matringa and her daughters checked their appearance one last time before leaving the way to the waiting carriage.

Malvagio and Cattiva fussed over their gowns and hair, debating on the best way to sit so as to not wrinkle their gowns, their banter and excited laughter filling the warm afternoon air as they clambered inside. For her part, Bella woodenly stepped in and plopped down, simply glad for the opportunity to *sit* for a short while. She'd been up since just after midnight, working on all manner of tasks Matringa had listed out for her, which needed to be done before luncheon.

Only after she had sat almost perfectly still, nearly asleep, did Bella realize there were hours and hours until the gates of the Spring Palace would open, not to mention the start of the equinox ball itself. Their destination was only a single hour away, even if they took their time. Though she knew better than to question Matringa's choices, she still wondered why they would risk their appearance and comfort like this.

Half an hour later, the pieces started to fall into place: they weren't going directly to the Spring Palace.

Instead, the carriage driver, a greedy, greasy man hired by Matringa for his ability to handle the horses, drove them to a house just inside the gates of the city. Bella watched carefully, not saying a word as Matringa pulled a small package from beneath the wagon and handed it to the lady, who cracked the door open after it had been knocked on.

No words were exchanged, only meaningful glances, then the carriage was away once more. Four more such stops occurred, each following the exact same pattern: Matringa grabbed a parcel, handed it to whatever woman opened the door, then they got moving once more.

As the last of them was delivered, a strange tension in the

carriage vanished, and the occupants relaxed considerably. Malvagio and Cattiva sank into their seats, speaking in a tone filled with obvious relief about their chances of enticing the Prince. Failing that, they discussed which Duca or Conte they would be willing to settle on.

Matringa herself was wearing a smile like a cat who had gotten the cream, her usual stern countenance softening as she allowed herself to look forward to the evening.

Only Bella became *more* tense, but she did her best to feign sleep instead of showing her suspicions. Something about those packages was gnawing at her, so she made sure to remember the route they'd taken to each of these abodes, burning the locations into her mind strongly enough that she would never forget where she needed to one day lead a troop of soldiers.

Their delivery route had taken them almost all the way back to the original entrance of the city, having circled the entire population center over the course of several hours. Just before five o'clock in the evening, they joined the main thoroughfare, forcing their way into the traffic of hundreds of carriages going toward the same destination. Then, another hour passed with them moving forward ever so slowly, only then arriving at the visitors' entrance to the Spring Palace.

The carriage rolled through the grand gates, then up a winding cobblestone road, finally stopping at the base of an intricately carved marble staircase. Half a dozen footmen in bright livery stood forward, ready to rapidly assist them out of the carriage and get it out of the way so the next arrivals could escape their enclosed space. Mind wandering slightly, Bella stared at the stairs, wondering if the carving was purely ornamental, or if it had some other purpose, such as providing stable footing during rainfall.

"Stay close to me, Bella." Matringa's hand firmly grasped Bella's arm, pulling the young woman out of the carriage and causing her to stumble as her feet met the ground. "Come now, we have requirements to meet and appearances to maintain."

"By the *system!*" one of the footmen muttered, looking away in a hurry as Bella and Matringa both turned to stare at him. The Beast Singer let out a sigh of annoyance, knowing by his gaze studiously avoiding her that Malvagio's 'talents' had come into play once more. As they began walking up the stairs, she could hear the man speaking in a low voice to one of his colleagues, "I know the Queen ordered all eligible women to attend, but, there's gotta be a *reasonable* limit, right?"

As they reached the top of the stairs, crossing into the interior of the building, a wash of cool air flowed over them, and Bella let out a small gasp of surprise. Matringa rolled her eyes and shook her head, "Of course, they have ways of keeping their guests cool, Bella. Keep your mouth closed; you're attracting flies."

Hundreds of people had already gathered in the grand antechamber, which by itself had more square footage than the entirety of Bella's home put together. Enormous doors which must lead to the grand hall were closed and wouldn't open until the official start of the ball that evening.

Even so, there was more than enough to capture all of Bella's attention. The room was created to impress visitors, and it most certainly worked on her. The vaulted ceilings shimmered with crystal chandeliers, the light of hundreds of candles sparkling across marble walls inlaid with gold. Servants swept around the room, holding platters of finger foods and chilled drinks.

Courtiers and nobles mingled in clusters, laughter and conversation filling the air to the point of turning into a constant droning roar. Matringa kept a tight grip on Bella's arm, steering her around the room with clear purpose. They paused often to exchange pleasantries with other nobles, Matringa's smile as insincere as their polite comments about how 'good of a person' she must be to constantly make sure her late husband's daughter got out of the house to experience the world.

Not one of them spoke directly to Bella, avoiding her, as she had become accustomed. She played her part, remaining silent, appearing wistful and sickly as she was not-so-gently paraded around. Still, she made sure to keep her eyes moving, noting important people and especially exits. She counted the guards, checking their position as they either roamed through the crowd or remained stationed next to the doors where people could easily access them if an issue arose.

Malvagio and Cattiva had been given leave to walk around on their own, and they flitted from group to group, exchanging pleasantries and gossip as anticipation built: it was almost time for the ball to begin. Finally, the noise in the room died in a wave, the silence causing the tension to rise to a peak.

"Welcome, my loyal subjects, to the Spring Palace." Queen Liora raised her hand, her voice clear and melodic as she addressed the hushed crowd. "Tonight, on the day of Prince Cinder's birth, we come together to celebrate as a kingdom, a people, and a family! I look around this room, and I find nothing but beauty and elegance, and so… I have a special request."

Bella felt a few mocking glances land on her as the Queen spoke, but she casually ignored them, knowing she wouldn't be here long enough to truly get upset over anything that happened. Instead, she memorized the Queen's face, making sure she would be able to recognize her, no matter what situation she was in later this evening—this person was one of the few with the power to directly advance her class, and she wasn't going to fail over something so simple as not being able to pick the Queen out of the crowd.

Dozens of servants stepped into the room, each holding large boxes filled with the exact same object. The Queen reached in, pulling one out and holding it in the air, "In the spirit of allowing my son to choose his future queen based on more than a glance, tonight will be a masquerade ball! You *don't* need to wear one… so long as you don't enter any farther into the palace, that is."

She paused to allow some polite laughter. "Anyone found not wearing their mask within will be asked to leave, unless you are only here as a chaperone. If that is the case, you may instead ask for a mark on your hand, but you will be automatically barred from so much as *approaching* the prince for the remainder of the evening on pain of removal from the event. That is… if you could even find him. Young ladies are not the only ones who were invited to the ball tonight, and all the young gentlemen shall be wearing a matching mask and outfit! Enjoy your night, and let the fun begin!"

As she finished speaking, the crowd erupted into applause, and the doors were thrown wide open, revealing a huge area set up for dancing, dining, with dozens of private alcoves for discussion. Each of the private areas had a guard standing watch, both to ensure the people within were given privacy, as well as to act as an official chaperone so the overprotective mothers and fathers among the crowd wouldn't need to worry over impropriety.

The crowd began filtering in, receiving either a simple mask to secure over their face, or a mark on their hand which let off a surprising amount of soft light. The reason for the glow became obvious as they stepped into the room, only to find it insufficiently lit by candles. The chaperones stood out because of this, the magical stamp acting as both a notice for the guards as well as providing an appealing silver light, which added a veneer of excitement and magic to the proceedings.

"You have one hour, Bella," Matringa hissed into her ear, though she maintained her polite smile. "If you do anything to draw undue attention to yourself, you'll find yourself locked in that hole in the ground you call a room so fast your head will spin. Maybe it'll spin right *off*! Understood?"

Bella nodded mutely, answering after a momentary delay when she saw that Matringa wanted to hear a verbal reply. "Yes, Signora. Frankly, all I really want to do is try some of the food before I need to leave."

Matringa stared at her a moment longer before slowly shaking her head. "All of this finery, enough wealth and drama to tell a thousand stories, and you are drawn to the buffet like a moth to the flame. I don't think I'll ever understand you, child. Away with you. Know I will be keeping watch. One. Hour."

The orchestra struck up a lively tune as Bella plodded toward the food, her mouth watering as she got close enough that the delectable aroma overpowered the cloying scent of perfume filling the rest of the room.

For a brief, blissful hour, Bella allowed herself to forget the weight of her stepmother's demands, the unpleasantness she was certain would start up again the next day, and the looming deadline of advancing her class. Instead, she stood next to the sumptuous buffet, reaching out for a dainty fruit tart and savoring the burst of sweet fruit and sugar mingling with a hint of lemon.

After half an hour, she could hear people whispering and laughing at her, but she simply continued moving along the table. Scooping up a bacon-wrapped fig here, a handful of toasted almonds there, spending nearly five minutes chewing through a chunk of glazed ham. More than anything else, what drew people's eyes to her wasn't how she was enjoying each texture and taste—it was that she was eating at all.

Everyone else was either attempting to maintain an appearance or was simply too nervous to eat. Near the end of the hour, the simple treats were replaced with a dinner spread, and what she'd been sampling was put on platters and began circulating on the shoulders of servants. Only then did other people begin enjoying the food as well; but by then, Bella had already filled a plate with tender slices of roast duck, mashed potatoes, and several other hearty options she had been missing out on.

"Well, *you've* certainly solidified the opinion other people have been forming of you." Matringa's quiet voice signaled the end of the night for Bella as the stepmother began leading her toward the door. "I certainly hope you enjoyed *gorging* yourself and staining not only your dress but the memory of your father's good name."

In a louder voice, Matringa spoke to Bella almost gently, "You did have fun tonight, didn't you, Bella? What nice people our hosts are. Yes, the cookies *are* very sweet. It's time to get home now. Let's go, dear!"

As the carriage came around, and Bella was pushed into it, she settled in for a relaxing ride home. The driver got them moving then poked his head in after the palace was well behind them. "Pretty fancy in there? Would it be worth doing again?"

"Yeah." Bella let out a soft belch. "It's a hard life, but *someone's* gotta live it."

The man let out a laugh, shook his head, and urged the horses on.

THIRTY-FIVE

BELLA WAS SHAKEN AWAKE a short while later and blinked in surprise as she looked around. She expected to be back at House Vigatori, with the greasy driver tossing her out so he could get back to his own bed, so she couldn't quite believe her eyes when she saw the familiar face of her godmother, Bibbidy.

"You don't have much time, sweet girl." Her Godmother smiled sadly. "I feel the power of a system oath in your heart. Already it is calling you, reminding you to fulfill its purpose."

"Bibbidy?" Bella felt as though she were dreaming, but when she reached out, she took her Godmother's hand. "You're really here? What's happening right now?"

"I'm giving you a gift to help you do whatever you are *going* to do." The ageless woman informed Bella. "I can't imagine you haven't figured out how to escape this binding in your heart. All I can do right now is give you a bit of hope and a present that's just for you, not to be shared or taken by anyone else."

Swiping at her eyes, Bella did her best to wake up and focus on the present moment. "I need to get back to the palace. Unless... why didn't I think of this before?

Godmother, do you have an Awakening Artifact? If so, I won't even need to risk myself-"

Already Bibbidy was shaking her head, so Bella went silent to hear the explanation. "No, even I have only seen such things a few times in my life, and always just before they're used by another. Items like that call to the worthy among those who are seeking them. They can't just be casually found. Listen, time is almost up. I've paused the thoughts of the man driving you home, and the horse is moving as slow as I can convince it to go. Still, that will wear off far too soon."

"She's *evil*, Godmother. I don't know any other way to explain it." Bella burst out, unable to contain herself in front of the one person in her life she trusted. "It used to be that everything she did seemed almost normal, a natural progression. But now that Father is dead, she's given up almost all pretense. I'm escaping tonight, one way or another."

"No, dear. You *must* go back." Bibbidy held up a hand to forestall the explosion of words Bella was about to unleash on her. "Until you are old enough to unlock your Full Class, her being your guardian is not in word only. It's a binding power, ancient even when I was young. Unless she fails in her guardianship, she'll always be able to find you and has the legal and magical right to bring you back and punish you. So long as the punishment is commensurate with the rules you broke, no one will even know."

"Then I have to get the palace to hear me out-"

"I'm *certain* she's told you many times not to damage the reputation of House Vigatori." The enigmatic merchant stopped Bella in her tracks. "A rule so long-standing, so potent, would allow her to take you down with her. No, you must be more subtle until *she* oversteps. You'll notice, you went to the ball tonight, though I'm certain she wanted nothing to do with that? That's because it was ordered by the King and Queen; they would know if someone disobeyed them and come to find out *why*."

"There's so much I don't know, and all of it seems designed to trap me." Bella took a deep, steadying breath, knowing there was no point in being furious about things she couldn't control. "You said you were going to offer me some hope? I could use a little bit of that right now."

"Hah! I bet." Before anything else, her Godmother swept Bella into a hug, holding her tight for a few long seconds. "I'll be waiting out here, carriage ready to rush you to the Spring Palace as soon as you get out. You won't need to count on the charity of strangers, hoping against hope you'll find someone going to the ball hours late. Second…"

She swung her hands through the air, gentle light like that of the stars twinkling for a moment. By the time her fingers had descended to nearly Bella's midriff, they were holding a box. "…a present for you!"

Feeling a bit nonplussed, Bella lifted the lid, revealing a pair of slippers which each appeared to be made from a single piece of sparkling crystal. Her eyes went wide as she lifted the seemingly delicate shoes, then she looked at her godmother in confusion. "Crystal slippers? I can't imagine how much these cost to make, but, Bibbidy… these must be incredibly delicate. Not to mention how they'll probably chafe, or even perhaps tear up my feet."

"That's where you're wrong, my sweet." Bibbidy cupped Bella's cheek in one hand, "You know I'm a Fairy, yes? Do you have any idea what that truly means? I see you don't, so I'll explain. It means I've achieved maximum rank with my Full Class skills from the system and gained access to the secondary system. Instead of gaining skills and abilities, I gain reputation with the system. Now I can complete tasks *for* the system in return for rewards of significant value. For instance, these *glass* slippers. Not crystal."

Bella looked down at the shoes once more, feeling a strange pull on her senses as she tried to turn away. "It feels like they *want* to be looked at."

"They do!" Bibbidy replied chipperly. "Practically no one will notice them, except for anyone who holds malice toward you. *They* will only be able to stare at your feet when you wear these, and they won't even realize they are doing it. They'll simply be judging your shoes. Whether it's a person or an object, if something is meant to harm you, they will only be able to come after these slippers."

Bibbidy smiled kindly at her favorite young lady. "I'm certain you have no idea the difference between Magical items and Enchanted items, but I'll explain someday in the future. Just know that these are the latter, granted directly from the system to me, for you, for nearly a decade of my devoted service."

"It's too much!" Bella immediately tried to return the slippers to her godmother. "You worked more than half my life for these? You musn't-"

Bibbidy pressed the box more firmly into Bella's hands. "Wear them, Bella. They are meant for you and *only* you. A system guarantee. If you somehow manage to lose them, they'll always find a way back to you. Someone else attempting to wear them will experience intense discomfort, in the most egregious cases of theft, possibly even losing their toes. They will protect you... like I should have been able to do."

"Bibbidy, no, you *can't* take the blame for the way my life went." Bella's words were soft, and she feebly attempted to hand the shoes back once more.

"We're approaching your destination." Bibbidy pushed the door of the carriage open. "I'll be waiting for you at the end of the road; don't keep me there for too long! We'll talk more on the trip back to the Spring Palace."

Moments after her godmother had vanished, Bella almost fell back in her seat as the vehicle sped up. The voice of the driver echoed out, "Hyaa! You falling asleep on me, Trotter? Twenty minutes to the stable; don't give up on me now."

A moment later, Bella nearly panicked as she realized her hands were empty. She looked around the small space, unable to find the box with the slippers no matter where she looked. "No! It can't have been a dream!"

The carriage came to a halt moments later, and her door swung open. The driver, clearly exhausted and annoyed, held out a hand for her to grab. "Let's go, missy! I get paid double tonight, so long as I drive you all there, bring you back, then bring them back later. Get a big fat tip for making sure you go into the cellar, for some reason?"

Distraught and confused, Bella took his hand and stepped out onto the road.

Clink.

She froze in place for a moment, glancing down and lifting the hem of her dress to reveal the glass slippers, already in place on her feet. The driver didn't notice, grumbling about late nights, but as Bella led the way, she felt like she was walking with a pair of incredibly comfortable, well-tuned wind chimes on her feet.

"Alright, there you go." The driver held open the door of the cellar for her, confusion writ large on his face. "I've done some odd, some might even say questionable, things for a bit extra pay, but this is one of the stranger ones. Everything okay? You, uh… need help?"

Though she fully understood what he was actually trying to say, with Bibbidy's warning in her mind, and the man being on the payroll of her stepmother, Bella decided to play dumb. "No, I can manage the stairs myself. Thank you for your kindness this evening. I'll see you… another time."

"Uh. Yeah." The man lowered the door gently behind her as she stepped down the stairs.

Bella descended into darkness, stepping into her room and feeling a bizarre *click* in her chest as the next portion of her oath came into effect. At the same moment, her left arm began to tingle, and the system whispered about her skills into her mind—though she barely noticed it over the surge of adrenaline flowing through her.

"Well, it's official. If I go up those stairs before being summoned by Matringa or tea time, I'll fall dead on the spot. I can only hope the system won't punish me for the loophole I'm about to use."

Squeak!￼ Suzy sounded off as soon as Bella closed the door behind her, and the mouse was sure the human was alone. *Squeaky squeak squeak, squeakers squeak squeak squeak-*

"Whoa! Slow down, Suzy." Bella shook her head sadly, wishing not for the first time that her Animal Communication Basic Skill allowed for two-way communication instead of only one. "I didn't suddenly figure out how to speak mouse; you're going to have to show me just like usual."

It was strange to hear a mouse sigh in annoyance, she had to really *listen* for it in order to catch the slight sound. The mumbled *squeak* was just *extra* in Bella's opinion, but she followed the frantically motioning mouse. To her surprise, they didn't hurry toward the escape tunnel—instead, Suzy led her to the opposite side of the room, to an overturned straw satchel. The mouse pointed at it, doing her best to smile up at the human towering over her.

Bemused but happy to play along, Bella pulled the bag open, going stock-still as she saw the glimmering blue and silver fabric within. "Suzy, this is supposed to be hidden in the walls, why did you bring all the scraps of this cloth here?"

The tiny mouse let out a growl of frustration, pointing at the bag several times and squeaking in annoyance. Bella reached in and gripped the shredded fabric, marveling at how soft it still was, and pulled. Her eyes nearly popped out of their sockets as she *continued* to pull, revealing *not* an armful of rags, but a unified, shaped outfit.

The dim light worked against her as she held up the garment, but Bella gasped anyway. "It's a dress! You made me a dress? How'd you manage to… look at the stitch work! It's as though the fabric was never sewn together. No, it *wasn't*! It was woven? That's not… *possible!*"

Suddenly, her left arm blazed with pearlescent light, shining intensely in the room and turning night into day. For a few, long, glorious moments, she beheld the most wondrous dress she'd ever laid eyes on. It was a simple garment, functional, but would hug against her tightly. The silvery portions of the fabric seemed to drink in the light pouring off of her, and even when the moment passed, the gown glowed softly in the darkness.

"What… what just happened?" With shaking hands, she reached to her left arm and pulled two fingers along the exposed skin, nearly fainting as she saw what the system had in store for her.

Skill increase! Minor Creature Control [Level 9 (Master) → Level 10 (Perfect)]!

Basic Class: Beast Singer
Basic Skill: Animal Communication: Level 10/10.
When vocalizing in a melodic manner, animals can [Perfectly] understand your intentions. Unless you do something to enrage them, non-magical creatures will go out of their way to protect you.

Advanced Skill: Minor Creature Control: Level 10/10.
When communing with non-magical minor creatures—size limit: the tips of your fingers to your elbow in body length. Maximum of five pounds— you are able to exert [Perfect] control over their actions.

You have earned access to your Basic Class Breakthrough Skill. Touch a Class Shrine to activate it!

"I reached *Perfection?*" Bella shook her head in mute confusion, "How? I was only at level eight the last time I checked, and it's not like the system is *subtle* in letting me know when I've fulfilled the requirements of upgrading. Two levels at the same time, that can't be right!"

She swiped her arm again, reading over the information, nearly in tears as she tried to understand why, *how*, she'd progressed so suddenly. "It's been so long, then…? Wait, *was* it at the same time?"

Bella thought back over the events of the night, and realized there'd been another moment where the system had poked at her. Slowly, she tried to piece together when things had changed. "When I got down here, I felt the oath settle in my heart, but I also heard the system whispering. Did something else happen at the same time?"

Squeak! Suzy nodded frantically, with great frustration. She began pointing at the other side of the house, where a mole had just popped out of the ground.

"The tunnel is ready? You made it in time? You *did* it!" The wheels began to spin in Bella's mind, and a nearly manic chuckle burst from her lips. "You worked with your friends to put my dress together, because I sang a sad little song about needing a dress the other day? At the same time you show it to me, the tunnel is completed? Which came first? Which one of those was the requirement for increasing which level?"

Ska-wea~ak! Suzy hopped up and down in agitation.

"You're right! It *doesn't* matter!" Bella finally shook off the shock she'd been trapped in and stuffed the dress back in the small satchel. Then she rushed over to the tunnel, pulling back the woven, straw mat to expose a hole just large enough for her to squeeze through.

"Tonight, I'm *taking* my life back!"

THIRTY-SIX

AFTER QUICKLY SWITCHING out her fancy, Matringa-provided dress for a simple, already-dirty servant's version, Bella stuffed the straw satchel down the front and carefully pulled herself into the tunnel head-first.

As it was still spring, the dirt around her was damp and cool to the touch, barely firm enough to remain in place as she began crawling forward, jamming one elbow forward at a time and pushing through. Small scrapes began to accumulate as she shoved past small rocks, her hair was gaining filth, and she was certain the makeup that had been applied on her face was thoroughly mixed with mud.

None of it bothered Bella, not in the slightest.

Instead, the scent of fresh soil filling her nostrils smelled like *freedom*. It might be just for a night, but she'd take it. The tunnel sloped gently downward as Bella pushed on, a necessary countermeasure against the hedges she knew she would need to go under. When it finally evened out, she picked up a little bit of speed, thanks to being able to use her arms and legs in tandem to shimmy along.

The excess speed may have been a mistake, as she brushed against the walls more than she should, and small sections of dirt began crumbling around her, falling onto her back and legs in soft clumps. She froze, cursing softly under her breath as dirt continued to drip onto her, even though she wasn't moving. "Don't collapse and bury me here, come *on!*"

Instead of a full collapse, there was just a small *slump*. With her left knee pulled forward to push against the ground, only her right leg was caught in the sudden shift of soil. Then the tunnel stabilized, and she began breathing once more, not even sure when she'd begun to hold her breath. She tried to push forward and nearly panicked as she found that her right leg was firmly held.

Bella swallowed down her fear, breathing steadily. "I still have air; that means the way forward is still viable. I just need help."

Putting her needs into song helped center her, as it was a near-constant action she had taken over the last half decade. "*Voles and moles, please come to my aid? Dig through this soil, as swiftly as you can toil! Those with quick little feet, please clear my path and help me retreat!*"

Though her voice wavered, she continued singing the song, having it echo back to her along the remainder of the tunnel. It resonated, causing small bits of dirt to rain from the roof of the tunnel, but she held herself as still and steady as possible. She waited to hear a reaction, only needing to do so for a few moments before the faint rustling of tiny paws scurried toward her.

Relief filled her so fully that it turned into water and leaked from the corners of her eyes. "Th-thank you for coming so quickly."

Even though she couldn't see who she was speaking to, as she was literally underground at the moment, moments later, she felt soft fur brushing along her as animals crawled over her body. They began furiously churning the dirt around her leg, managing to release her from the weight of the earth in under a minute. As Bella wriggled free, she began moving forward once more, barely able to stop herself from rushing again.

She wanted *out*.

Her wish came true only a few minutes later, as she pushed through the end of the tunnel. She squeezed into the open air with a grunt of effort, needing to force her lower half through the narrow opening—only to shoot out like a cork being released from a bottle of champagne. Bella tumbled forward, but even as she got scratched up by the wild growth along the side of the road, she could only feel gratefulness for having gotten out alive.

Breathing deeply, she took a moment to look up at the sky, taking in the vast field of stars. "Okay, it worked, but that sucked *so* much."

She stood and turned to run down the road, only to freeze in place and slowly turn back to look at the open mouth of the narrow passage. "Bibbidy... she told me I need to come back. That means I need to get through that collapsed section. You've all done so much for me already. I'm so sorry, but I need you to keep going."

Holding her thought clearly in her mind, Bella sang out at the top of her voice, knowing no one was around to hear her. *"Dig, my friends, shore it true. Make safe the path I'll need to pursue. But wait, there's more... we'll need it closed by morning light, one side must collapse and be hidden right."*

She only got through one repetition of the song before shrieking and flinching to the side. The underbrush along the side of the road, and well into the forested area, practically *exploded* with noise and motion as dozens and *dozens* of creatures swarmed past her—responding to her call without hesitation. Bella watched in dazed amazement as the numbers continued to increase. Against their nature, the animals worked in unison to repair the tunnel, visible only by how much dirt began flowing out of this end only moments after the first group had reached the blockage.

"Was it because of how loudly I sang?" Bella whispered to herself as she watched the incredible efforts of the small animals. Slowly, her eyes widened as she saw the creatures swarming in and out. "No, this is more than just being *loud*. Most of these have never been touched by my song, but now they are instantly tamed and trained? Is *this* what it means to reach Perfection with my skill?"

Remembering why she was out in the first place, Bella crouched down and looked at the small creatures without interrupting what they were doing. "Thank you all, and I'm so sorry I need to leave now. I want to help, but I need to go."

There was no response, but she hadn't been expecting one. Without another word, Bella turned and fled down the road, running as fast as she could in her shining glass slippers. Her breath misted in the cool night air, her heart racing as her eyes sought out any source of light. She knew her godmother would be waiting for her, she just didn't know exactly *where*.

Just as she started to feel her heart catch in her throat, a flicker of light on the connecting road drew her gaze, and a moment later, she saw Bibbidy standing beside the ornately carved carriage she lived in and did business out of.

"There you are!" Bibbidy was clearly trying to hide the concern in her voice and only partially succeeding. She ushered Bella into the bright-orange carriage, not at all worried about getting mud on herself. "Horses, to the Spring Palace, if you will. Bella, let's get you cleaned up. I'm sure the prince would choose you even if you were covered in muck, but getting close to him necessitates hygiene."

"Choose *me*?" Bella barked out a laugh of surprise. "Bibbidy, I don't care about that at all. I don't want to be the *princess*, I want one of them to unlock my class for me. The nearest Class Shrine is hours away, and I'd never make it there in time. Since I have access, and it's the prince's birthday, I thought perhaps they might want to make a spectacle of their generosity."

"Not the worst plan I've ever heard. Actually, it's *quite* well thought-out," Bibbidy stated after a moment of contemplation. The inside of the carriage was larger than its exterior suggested, filled with polished wood, soft cushions, and a small compartment with a door Bella couldn't guess the purpose of. It was this door that her godmother pushed her toward, "I'm going to show you something *truly* magical tonight, Bella. This is called a shower."

The young woman pulled off her mud-caked dress at Bibbidy's urging, wrapping herself in a towel as Bibbidy stepped into the small space, murmuring a few words under her breath and tapping a flat pane of metal. To Bella's surprise, the top of the chamber lit up, and water began pouring to the ground. "There we go! I adjusted it to be comfortable for you; I tend to like it hotter than you would enjoy. In you pop!"

Bibbidy placed small jars inside the door, then stood to the side to allow Bella to preserve her modesty. She stepped in, marveling at the steaming water and the way it seemed to actively seek out the mud both in her hair and caked onto her body. When she held up her hands, the dirt under her fingernails washed out with only the gentlest of urging. After only a few moments, she felt cleaner than she had in nearly her whole life.

Then she turned her attention to the jars, finding them filled with luxurious soaps, hair oils, exuding an assortment of fragrant scents. Bella lifted one to her nose, blinking as she tried and failed to understand what she was smelling. "Bibbidy, what are these supposed to smell like?"

"It's amber, sandalwood, and bergamot!" the muffled voice explained. "The soap uses a base of charcoal, burned down from cedarwood, with just a *hint* of cinnamon tossed in for fun."

"Smells like... I'd expect a man to smell?" Bella called

back uncertainly. "Is this the right container? Not to be ungrateful, it's just-"

"The room will be absolutely stuffed with the rancid scent of overpriced flowers, to the point even those without sensitivities will have their eyes watering." Bibbidy's voice was calm, but firm. "If you go in there smelling *clean*, associating yourself with things the prince is known to enjoy, I'd give you better than even odds of getting close to him. In fact, he might directly introduce you to his mother, and you can make your request with him supporting you."

"Oh, well *yeah*, in that case..." She began scrubbing herself down with the soap, trying not to miss an inch of her skin. Then she switched to a liquid soap meant for her hair, scrubbing it out thoroughly while leaving a warm, woody aroma reminiscent of campfires behind.

As soon as she decided she had finished cleansing herself, the water in the chamber simply vanished, leaving her completely dry. The door opened a crack, and a small bag was handed in. "Fresh under clothes! I'll look through my stock and see if I can find a dress in your size-"

"In my bag, under the servant's dress!" Bella called back as she quickly clothed herself. Moments later, there was a gasp from the main portion of the carriage, and she kicked herself for not opening the door to see her godmother's reaction. Rectifying that, she poked her head out, and Bibbidy looked over at her with tears in her eyes.

"You used my gift to you for such an important night? I'm honored." Bibbidy took a deep breath and handed over the dress. "Get it on, then I'll do your hair and makeup. You *already* have the best shoes for the night."

Bella lifted the dress above her head, poking her head through the shimmering material and simply allowing the fabric to unfurl. It dropped down over her, catching in all the right places to show off her curves and sparkling like starlight on water with the captured afterglow of her skill reaching Perfection.

"It's perfect on you, even better than I'd intended." Bibbidy looked over the gown with a critical eye, shaking her head slightly as she saw exactly *how* perfectly it had been created. "I don't know how you did this, but I recognize that glow. I always knew you were talented, but... did you reach Perfection with your *Basic Class* Advanced Skill? I've never heard of anyone doing that before."

"I got it just tonight, between you sending me in the house and me coming out." Bella twirled to test out the range of movement afforded by the dress, sending sparkling light shimmering around the interior of the carriage. "I didn't expect this, though. Was it supposed to happen?"

"Yes, indeed." Bibbidy wiped at her eyes, the smile on her face showing that the few escaping tears were ones of happiness. "The material was meant for you; it will always stay perfectly clean. When it senses filth, it tries to scour it, so it will also help you out. That function can be a little... *aggressive* at times."

Bella thought back to when Malvagio had worn a garment made of this cloth and nodded slowly. "That actually makes a few things make sense."

"Oh? I'll have to hear about that. Another time." Bibbidy trailed a finger along the sleeve of the dress, just above where Bella would read her class information. "As to catching the light, magical cloth meant to help others see you will always hold onto light from the system and shine with it until *it* decides to fade. I never expected it to happen this quickly, of course. Most people don't have the light of the system shine on them until the day of their wedding, when they gain a system mark."

The young woman was sat down in a chair, and Bibbidy quickly began twisting and pinning Bella's hair into an elegant style with a series of deft movements. Tiny flowers were woven in as well, yellow torch lilies which complimented the shimmering silver blue of her dress. "Just another little representation of fire to draw the eye. It might help, it might not."

When she stepped forward to begin applying makeup, Bella stopped her godmother. "Anyone wanting to approach the prince tonight will be wearing a mask; the queen surprised everyone by turning it into a masquerade ball."

Seemingly unsurprised, Bibbidy simply quizzed her, "What color is the mask, and how much of your face does it cover?"

"It's silver and covers from here to here." Bella touched her face on her forehead, just below her cheekbone, then held her fingers up to frame her face.

Bibbidy set down the makeup kit she was about to use, rummaging through a small box and pulling out a completely different one. "Good thing we know about that before you get there—just another tiny advantage you'll have over the others. Believe me when I say the small successes will add up quickly. We'll do just a hint of gloss on the lips, a blend of soft silver and blue on your eyelids, and silver sparkles on both cheeks just under where your mask will cover."

As she finished with all the preparation, the carriage came to a sudden halt. Bibbidy pulled Bella to her feet, her eyes darting around as she looked for any flaws. "You're perfect, darling. Go in there and win their hearts, and graciously accept the favor they'll offer you."

"Thank you, Godmother." Bella took a deep breath and reached for the handle, only to feel a gentle tug. She looked back, seeing that Bibbidy had more to say.

"My dear, I have only one more thing for you. You must leave here and be back in the carriage by midnight at the *latest*." There was clear frustration in the ageless woman's expression. "It'll take at least an hour to get back to the estate, and unlike our journey here, we will likely need to deal with traffic. You must be back in your room before the guardianship magic alerts your stepmother to your absence. This happens at the second hour of the day, *every* day. If you aren't where you are supposed to be, she will know *immediately*, and so will you."

"I understand; I'll be here." Bella nodded firmly and opened the door. The footman, who was reaching for the handle, leaned back, his eyes going wide as he let out a low whistle—*quite* a different reaction from when he'd barely attempted to hide his disgust at her appearance earlier in the day.

"By the system." A goofy smile started to spread on his lips. "I don't suppose you might be a lowborn looking to have a dance with a servant of the kingdom?"

"Don't worry about that." Bella brushed past him without accepting the outstretched hand. "As *someone* once told me, there's gotta be a *reasonable* limit to who you approach."

The other footman chuckled at his misfortune, though none of them seemed to associate her with the poor, bedraggled young lady who'd arrived earlier that day. As Bella walked up the stairs, her shoes chiming gently as glass met stone, Bibbidy's voice floated to her one last time.

"Remember, Bella! Nothing good happens after midnight!"

THIRTY-SEVEN

PRINCE CINDER

PRINCE CINDER STAGGERED to the refreshment table, reaching over and snagging a cup of ice-cold punch. Tossing it back in one quick pull, he grabbed another before swaying slightly in exhaustion as he turned to survey the grand ballroom. As he slowly sipped the second drink, he watched as lines of masked dancers swirled around, dancing to the lively tune the musicians were playing. Between the formal wear, the masks, the lowered lighting, and the bright glow coming from the attending chaperones, it was a chaotic kaleidoscope of color and motion.

"Whew… lots going on here," he muttered to himself, not expecting an answer but receiving one anyway.

Another guest, a young man, clapped him on the shoulder, Cinder's mask doing its job by not allowing the person touching him to know who he was. "Isn't this *great?* By the system, that prince of ours is a celestial-touched *hero*. I've never had so many beautiful women fighting for the chance to talk to me, let alone *dance* with me! This may be the best night of my life. So far, if you catch my drift."

"Yeah, that's one way of looking at it." Cinder chuckled in reply, taking another sip of his drink before continuing, "On the other hand, if I have to look into another set of wild eyes clearly trying to see through my mask to figure out if I'm the prince or not, I might just have to bow out for the rest of the evening."

"Good thing there's just a touch of skill applied to these, isn't it? Only way for them to come off is if we take them off ourselves." The unknown young man shook Cinder slightly, the grip on his shoulder not letting up even a little. "The last dozen in a *row* tried to pull it off of me, anyway. I extracted a promise of a kiss before showing I wasn't our valiant leader. Again… it's been a fun night."

Cinder rolled his eyes at the antics of his fellow, sighing inwardly while tugging at the collar of his suit. Though it was his birthday, it was starting to feel as though he were the prize on the inside of a pinata, and his dance partners were simply trying to buffet their way through his colorful wrapper to see what they'd won.

Even worse than the people who *didn't* know him were the ladies of high nobility that could pick him out by his posture alone. Out of sheer angst over knowing they weren't in the running for his hand, they'd been sending clearly unacceptable partners over whenever they could manage to do so. He had always been gracious, dancing with them, holding a short conversation, perhaps sharing the hors d'oeuvres making their way around the room.

But there was a reason they were unacceptable.

Almost all of them completely froze up, barely managing to speak a word out of sheer fear of the difference in their stations. "Dozens of young maidens fair, yet not even one had time to prepare? A barmaid, a milkmaid, a seamstress, a nurse… there's been that, and so *much* worse."

"Hey, that rhymed!" Cinder's new friend excitedly pointed out. "Do you attend the university? Sounds like you just came up with that, so you've got to be one of the scholars, yes? I heard the royals hired the entire class of male students who were approximately the prince's age to come and make it harder to find him. Do you like it there?"

"The university is... *exemplary*. The care, devotion, and coinage the king and queen have poured into it are enough to make my jaw drop to the floor. Truly, they have given the kingdom a wonderful gift." At that moment, the enormous door from the entry of the palace swung open, drawing Cinder's attention. "Oh? Is someone new arriving? I can't imagine anyone leaving before we kick them—er... before they are asked to leave."

As expected, a young woman stepped into the room. She was shimmering softly in the warm glow of the chandeliers, or so he thought, until the door closed and cut off the light from outside the room. In fact, her silver-blue gown was sparkling like the torches of an army on the move, which showed she was one of the wealthier attendees. Over a dozen of the high nobility were wearing dresses with magical threads woven into them, but no matter how many times he saw something similar, it was still an eye-catching design.

Surprisingly, the makeup she was wearing and the bright yellow gems in her hair complimented her mask perfectly. Cinder frowned at that realization, as no one should have been given advance warning of the masquerade portion of this ball. He was fairly certain no one who had arrived had yet departed, as again, they *wanted* to be here. "Let's see who you really are..."

The Prince knew all the highborn ladies quite well, having grown up with them, studied with them, been annoyingly *courted* by them. Activating his Fire Communion skill caused his eyes to light up with a smoldering glow and essentially allowed him to ignore the barrier of the masks, which had been specifically designed to allow him to peer through them. To his astonishment, while he *did* recognize her, she wasn't one of his peers. "Where have I seen you before...? Ah, that's it! At the Earl's estate. We danced, if I remember correctly."

To his astonishment, his skill picked up a faint coating of what seemed to be *soot* of all things covering her skin and coating her hair. To his eyes, it was no different than if she had just crawled out of a chimney. His skill loved it, and his curiosity was thoroughly piqued. Cinder began walking toward her of his own volition, yet another first of the night.

As he got close to her, the surprises kept coming. The incredibly expensive, elegant magical material of her dress had been used to create a gown with a simple cut, which fit her exceedingly well, but was certainly not the current fashion of the court. What he had taken at a distance to be yellow gems in her hair turned out to be fire lilies, his favorite flower, for obvious reasons. He came to a stop in front of her, just as the young woman stopped looking around the room and admiring its design.

"Well, *you've* certainly done your homework on the prince." Cinder chuckled softly at her blatant attempts to appeal to his personal desires. He waited for her to answer, but she merely looked at him in confusion.

"I'm sorry, I don't know what you mean… Signore?" Her tone was polite, but it *was* clear she didn't want to be having this conversation. "I'm so sorry, I don't mean to be rude; could you direct me to the queen?"

She'd stepped closer so she could be heard without shouting over the cacophony of the area, and the prince found himself surprisingly drawn to her. Something… something about her was very, very different from everyone else he had spoken to over the course of the evening. When he realized what it was, Cinder's mouth moved before his mind managed to add a filter between his thoughts and his tongue wagging. "Ah, that's what it is! You do not carry the overpowering scent of Eau de Toilette like the rest of them!"

They stood there, staring at each other, for a few seconds before the young woman took a step back and to the side.

"Thank you? I... don't worry, I'll ask someone else. I hope you have a pleasant evening."

Cinder found himself stunned as the girl in the sparkling gown gracefully glided away. After a few moments of cursing himself, he started chasing after her to better explain himself. "Wait! I've been churlish. Please, allow me to-"

Then he realized he was practically running after someone who was clearly trying to get away from him, and Cinder paused in place, realizing what this must look like to anyone watching. He stepped to the side, moving at a sedate pace back to the refreshments area, internally groaning and wondering what hole he could burn into the ground to hide himself. "Well, that's the end of *that*."

Break over, the musicians of the orchestra got back to work, filling the room with even more sound as those who had stepped away from each other got back out on the floor. Rolling his shoulders, he prepared himself for several more hours of being asked to dance; only to go still—like a hunter spotting a deer in the woods—as the mysterious young lady stepped up to the refreshment table and scooped up a fruit tart, popping it in her mouth before chewing with gusto and clear enjoyment.

Realizing he might have a second chance to make a first impression, he stepped up and offered his hand. "Pardon me, would you care to dance?"

There were dozens of other young men who looked exactly like him at the ball, so when she looked up and hesitated, wincing before answering, Cinder had to wonder if she had recognized him or simply had no desire to partake of the night's festivities. Even so, she reluctantly took his hand, and they stepped out onto the floor.

"Careful, this close, I may actually smell terrible. Who knows?" she deadpanned at him, leaving Cinder feeling like he was about to sink through the floor from sheer embarrassment.

"Please, that was very unlike me, it's been a long... *long* night." She didn't say anything, but her lips softened slightly at his pleading apology, even curling into a small smile.

"I can understand *that*, at least. This has been going on for hours at this point, yes? I'd be surprised if you weren't getting tired. I suppose I can forget our first conversation, if you wouldn't mind helping me find the queen? The king, maybe?"

At the repeated request, Cinder frowned slightly, his mind going back to the horrible night in the not-distant-enough past when an assassin came after his father. "Might I ask... *why* are you seeking them out so boldly? I'm sure you understand, there are guards preventing anyone from getting too close without a valid reason."

"Abyss, no, I didn't think of that." She bit her lower lip quite adorably, and it was only after a moment that Cinder was shocked to realize he had *considered* it adorable.

He stepped away immediately.

"I'm sorry, did I step on your feet? I got distracted." The sheer nervousness with which she asked that question calmed the prince down slightly—no one who was here to strike a blow against the ruler of the kingdom would be overly concerned about his toes. He glanced at her feet, planning to brush off her concerns and find an excuse to leave, only to realize they were clad in perfectly clear crystal.

"No... um. No. You didn't." Internally wrestling with himself, Cinder couldn't find a reason not to step in and begin to dance once more. "So... could you tell me why you need to meet the queen? Unfortunately, the king isn't feeling well this evening and is not in attendance."

"Okay... but only if you promise to keep it to yourself." Her words made Cinder's mask-concealed eyebrow lift, but he nodded anyway. "You see, I've been unable to make the journey to a Class Shrine, and I was hoping she was feeling generous tonight. I want to advance my class, but even before that-"

"You're already eighteen? Yet you haven't made it to a Class Shrine?" His question interrupted her thought, and she stuttered to a stop. "Wait, that can't be right. You have to be under twenty years old in order to be considered anything other than a chaperone for the evening, but I just turned eighteen today, and you seem younger than I am."

As soon as he realized he had all but *announced* who he was, Cinder's internal cursing ramped up even higher. He expected her to turn into a quivering puddle of nerves in the next instant, but instead all he received was a brilliant smile.

"Oh! Congratulations, and happy birthday! Did you get to unlock your Full Class today? What was it like? Is the skill you gained in line with the ones from your other classes? Wait, did you even *like* the skills from your previous classes? I heard that, if you get your skills to a high enough level, the system will grant you power in such a way that everything works together. Was that your experience, or-"

Seemingly realizing that he'd been given no chance to respond, she blushed prettily and winced, her nose twitching to the side as she sketched a smile. "Ah… sorry about that, I really like my skills, and I'm hoping to unlock something which will bring them even higher. That's why I wanted to meet the queen; sorry if my excitement killed your fun just now."

"*No!* Ahem… that is, no, in fact skill progression is one of my favorite topics," Cinder admitted, just as he realized they were standing still in the middle of a dance floor. "Come with me, let's talk. I might be able to help you."

They walked over to one of the small private alcoves, surrounded by silence as soon as they sat down thanks to the muffling magic woven into the drapes around them. Seeing his dance partner look at the cloth excitedly made him change his opinion of her yet again. This was no High Noble masquerading as someone else; this was someone who had truly not experienced the life of those in high society.

"Might I get your name?" he graciously questioned her, in his mind quite conspicuously not offering his own first. "You can call me... Ash."

"My name is, um, Bella," she replied uneasily, leaving him to wonder if she had also given him a false name.

They made polite conversation for a short while, discussing the thrill of advancing their skills and classes. Both of them agreed that there was no better feeling than seeing their personal power increase—something that was inherently theirs, which hadn't been given *to* them and couldn't be taken *from* them. The more they spoke, the more Cinder found himself enjoying the conversation. Finally, he offered a piece of information as a small boast, hoping to impress her.

"I actually *didn't* unlock my Full Class today." He leaned in and whispered to her, delighting in the way her eyes went wide, and her mouth made a small 'o' of surprise. "You see, I have a very powerful Advanced Class, with skills that give me strength beyond even most people who have unlocked their Full Class. My mother says it is due to my lineage being carefully selected and pruned, but in reality, it's just because I love what I can do so very much."

"Why *wouldn't* you unlock your Full Class right away? Wouldn't that just give you more to work with?" When Cinder realized that Bella didn't instantly grasp why he wouldn't immediately step into the next realm of power, he was left wondering where she'd been educated.

Leaning back slightly, he folded his hands over his lap, a smile with just a *hint* of smugness added to the mix on his lips. "I'm on the verge of reaching Mastery level nine with my Advanced Skill. There's a good chance I'll earn my Breakthrough Skill in the next couple of years. I'm willing to hold off on advancing my class so that I'll have an incredibly potent skill at my fingertips. It will give me a level of power and an edge no one will be expecting."

To his surprise, she didn't seem nearly as impressed as he

felt she should be. Instead, she seemed to be chewing on something, though he was certain she had finished the fruit tart a while ago.

Finally, she looked up at him and sheepishly let fly her words. "Is a Breakthrough Skill that powerful? Is it useful enough that someone might want to take someone with it on as an apprentice, even if their other skills are Common?"

"Oh, yes." Cinder nodded knowingly. "Though, I doubt anyone who has a Breakthrough Skill would be someone else's apprentice. No one gets there without years and *years* of dedicated effort. If I manage to achieve it before I'm twenty-two, the system might even give me bonuses toward the power of my next class. *That's* what I'm really after."

"Okay, *that* sounds awesome." Once more, Bella hesitated, and when she spoke next Cinder couldn't believe what he was hearing. "Is that something the queen could unlock as well? The system tells me that even though I earned one, I need to touch a Class Shrine to unlock it."

THIRTY-EIGHT

THE TWO OF them sat in their small alcove, both staring at each other without saying a word. Ash raised an eyebrow, his skepticism barely concealed by the mask he was wearing. When he finally broke the silence, his tone was laden with doubt. "I've made several conversational faux pas with you today, and I don't want to make another... but... you're claiming to have earned a Breakthrough Skill, *and* it's unawakened? I suppose I don't need to tell you how unlikely that sounds?"

Bella nodded earnestly, feeling a mix of nervousness and hope churning within her gut as her companion eased back in his seat. "I have it, just waiting to be unlocked, I simply have no way to make it happen. If I could meet the queen, do you think she would do both for me? Skill and class? Is that something she even *can* do?"

"Now we're back to you wanting to meet the queen." Ash's voice sounded very disappointed, causing Bella to be taken aback slightly. "Look. This is going to sound perhaps a bit, well, arrogant of me-"

"No! What? *You?*" Bella's laugh turned nervous after a moment when his face remained impassive. "Sorry, I was just... you know, the perfume thing, the entitlement when speaking, the lack of proper... *ahem*. What I *mean* to say is, please, enlighten me with whatever you need!"

"Huh." Surprisingly, some of the suspicion she could see in Ash's eyes had faded after her abrasive comments. "Then I won't hold back. Frankly, the fact that you are so insistent on meeting with one of the royals puts a bad taste in my mouth. I don't suppose you know that it's been less than a year since my... *king* survived an assassination attempt?"

Bella's gasp and the way her hand went to cover her mouth put her conversation partner further at ease. He watched her carefully, but continued speaking after only a momentary pause.

"Secondly, there's always the chance that you are some High Noble's attempt at getting around the restrictions the queen put in place for the evening. You are covered in items which have aspects of fire, and the main point of our conversation this evening has been on advancement and skill gain. Either you are very well-trained and very well informed about the prince and his habits... or you are being genuine, which I hope you understand seems less than likely, since you are at this ball."

He stopped speaking, staring at her intently, and Bella felt her cheeks flush. "I'm so sorry, I'm not sure why talking about my skills would be interesting to him, but I'll readily admit my godmother chose my accessories for the evening. I'm not sure what they have to do with the prince, but she told me there was a good chance he would appreciate them and potentially introduce me to the queen. You know... so I could advance my class?"

"So you say." He took in a deep breath, letting it out through his nose, even as his lips twisted to the side in contemplation. "Okay. I want to believe you, and I have a couple reasons to do so. First, I actually quite enjoyed our conversation. Second, you don't seem to have any grudge that you are here to settle. Third... well, Paca liked you a lot, and my father always told me to pay attention to animals when they judge people's character."

"Paca?" Bella blinked in confusion several times, wondering who this mysterious stranger could possibly be. "Who's Paca?"

"My father's dog, Pacatezza," Ash told her with a smile, lifting a hand and motioning at the guard of the alcove to come close. "You may not remember this, but we've danced once before. You even met my father at that time, and he seemed to like you. He's a fantastic judge of character, so I'm going to give you the benefit of the doubt. Even so... trust, but verify."

The guard stepped close, and Ash spoke quietly into his ear. Turning away from Bella, he lifted his mask, replacing it in the next moment as the chaperone nodded his head solemnly. He stepped back, and Ash turned to look at Bella once more.

"As my friend here is going to be running off to acquire something for me, we can't remain here any longer. No chaperone, no hidden private alcove to chat in." Ash stood and offered his hand to help Bella up. "Would you be so kind as to accompany me to the balcony? It'll give us the most privacy I can afford us, and I don't know about you, but I could use some fresh air."

"Sure?" Bella stood and walked next to Ash, wondering at his identity as they moved through the dense crowd of people. Casting a few confused glances his way, she murmured to herself, "Can just anyone order the guards around? He has to be at least a high noble, right? Maybe he's the earl's brother or something? Maybe a nephew? Why else would he have been at that party? No... there wasn't anyone wildly powerful there; Matringa would have *never* let me attend otherwise."

Feeling more confident in herself after making that realization, Bella stood a little straighter and looked around the room a bit more blatantly. Then, she nearly froze in terror as she realized nearly every eye in the area was on her. Specifically, Bella's eye had landed directly at her stepfamily, who were glaring at her in absolute disgust. They were only a double arm's-length away and didn't even try to keep their voices down as they discussed her.

"Sure wish *I* could have thrown a fortune at a dress I'll only wear for one night." Malvagio sneeringly told her mother and sister. "At least she's going to be going home in pain tonight."

"No joke. *Crystal shoes?*" Cattiva shook her head in mock sadness. "Have you ever heard of something else so likely to tear the skin right off your feet as you dance?"

"Girls, *girls*," Matringa called out calmly, though her tone made Bella begin breathing heavily with fear. "Don't forget yourselves. We are low nobility and lucky to even be here. The reality of the situation is, even though her father must have spent more coin than our entire estate is worth for that outfit, the very fact she is wearing it means she's precluded from joining in the competition. *She* will never be *our* queen."

"But we could easily be hers by the end of the night," Cattiva stated slowly, the covetous stare in her eyes sharpening as she examined Bella's shoes further. "I don't suppose a queen could order her subject to hand over certain... shoes?"

Ash cautiously placed a hand on Bella's elbow, pulling her along through the crowd. Though he spoke at a normal volume, due to the cacophony of the ballroom, his words came to her ears almost as a murmur, "Everything okay? You're as pale as cold ash."

Not trusting that her voice wouldn't be recognized, Bella only nodded and began walking quickly. When they got through the final fringes of the crowd, the hot and humid air was replaced by a cool night's breeze, a welcome relief after the intensity of the last few minutes. They walked slowly to the railing of the balcony, standing in companionable silence and watching the stars twinkling far above.

"Are..." Ash paused, closing his mouth and looking away without finishing his thought.

Bella stepped closer to him, shivering slightly as the wind picked up. "What's on your mind, Ash?"

"No, it's rude, and that's pretty much all I've been to you all night." He turned to look at her, a rueful smile on his face. "All I can do is beg forgiveness for how I've acted this evening. I don't have excuses, at least not good ones. I'm tired, and I've been worried for my parents' health for a while. It's made me a bit... distrustful."

"In that case, now you *must* tell me what you were going to say," Bella firmly stated, her eyes locked with his through their masks. "I think we could be friends, were the circumstances right. We'll probably never see each other again after tonight, so you might as well speak your mind."

The man let out a deep sigh, lifting a hand and rubbing the back of his head. "I was thinking the same. About us being friends, that is. That's why... well, you don't need to try and impress me with talk of a Breakthrough Skill. Instead of trying to activate it tonight, we could simply part ways, and you could tell me you are more inclined to go to a Class Shrine. Then, I at least wouldn't be able to know for *certain* if you were only-"

"Ash, why would I lie about that? It's an easily proven statement, isn't it?" Bella lifted her right hand, pulling back the sleeve of her left arm. "Look, I'll-"

"*Bella!*" Ash hissed in surprise, grasping the cuff of her sleeve and tugging it down. "I can't ask you to show me your class or skills, that's... that would be the height of impropriety! That would almost be the same as having a matchmaker determine the synergy between our classes for the creation of a *Conjoined Skill*."

She blinked at him several times, unable to determine

which question she wanted to ask first. Finally, she decided on the one that interested her the most. "A *what* skill?"

"Oh, for the love of the system. A *Conjoined Skill.*" Ash lifted an eyebrow and shook his head slightly. Seeing no reaction from her, he tried again. "The skill which is gained by the union of the two highest skills of a couple who undergoes a system-witnessed marriage? If someone saw you showing me your skills, they would think I asked for it, which would be no different than my asking for your hand in marriage!"

Bella felt like the wind had been knocked out of her, and she directly took a step back, away from both him and the balcony. "*What*! That's not... I'm sorry! I didn't mean to try and... actually, no. I've no idea what I'm apologizing for."

Taking a deep breath, she tried again. "Whatever you are doing to try and unlock this skill for me, I want to do it. You don't need to worry that I'm lying to you; I can prove it to you one way or another."

She wiggled her left arm at him, letting out a giggle as he shifted away like she was trying to tether his arm to hers with a manacle. As soon as he realized what he was doing, Ash paused and allowed a slow smile to spread across his face. "Ah. Well, I'm glad. I appreciate that you are so forthright. It's... refreshing. Now, I didn't get an answer, might I have your acceptance of my apology for my behavior this evening?"

"Sure, Ash." Bella continued to grin at him, rolling her eyes as she finished with, "Just don't let it happen again after tonight."

Before he could join in on the banter, three guards stepped out onto the balcony. Two of them were flanking the third, who was carrying a small chest on a pillow. With careful strides, they made their way directly over to the duo, and the chest was opened with a flourish.

Radiant, silvery light of the same coloration and quality of the energy captured by Bella's dress seeped out of the small box. It seemed to move almost slowly, as though it was a mix of luminescence and fog, washing over the small group of five and instilling a sense of peace in them.

On a small cushion in the box was an intensely glowing 'X', which seemed to be made of pure power.

She stared at the strange item that had been revealed, wondering what it could possibly be, only to feel her jaw drop as Ash casually reached out and picked it up. He gently tossed it in the air a couple times, catching it and grinning at Bella as her eyes tracked the motion. "Have you ever seen one of these before?"

"I have absolutely no idea what that is," Bella admitted instantly, unable to tear her eyes away from the two intersecting lines settled on his palm. "It looks like... like a... system mark of marriage? But glowing, and silver instead of gold?"

"You're pretty close, actually," Ash informed her gently, his voice lowering as he turned very serious. "As you can see, I can hold this and absolutely nothing happens. This is an Awakening *Shard*. It's not a full Awakening *Artifact*, which can advance classes and the like, but it is enough to awaken a Breakthrough Skill if you truly have one ready. If you touch it, your skill will awaken without fail, and the Shard will instantly be consumed."

Bella swallowed, resisting the urge to snatch the Shard out of his hand long enough to ask a question, "You're certain it's okay that I use it?"

Ash let out an unflattering raspberry, shaking her out of her intense stare at the glowing object. "Yeah. This has been sitting around gathering dust for a *long* time. It's a whole lot easier to go to a Class Shrine than to send a request for an Awakening Shard from the palace. With how difficult it is to achieve Breakthrough, and the royals being able to directly awaken skills and advance classes, this is literally the first time this has even been brought out. *Please* use it so the storage space can be used for something else... if you can."

The note of challenge in his voice caused Bella to look up and meet his eyes, which were staring at her unflinchingly. She felt just a *hint* of anger run through her, reaching out without another word. Before her hand could fully close around the glowing 'X', it brushed against her palm and was *sucked* through her skin.

"Celestials, she was telling the truth!" Ash barked in awe and surprise, blinking in the sudden darkness.

Bella couldn't hear him.

Her ears were filled with the sound of dozens of wind chimes gently swinging through the air, and her vision was completely blocked by a wall of light with text forming on it as the system directly assessed and spoke to her for the very first time.

Codex Arcane Ledger fractional access requested.

C.A.L. is assessing…
requirements for Breakthrough have been fulfilled!

Checking all system merits.

Basic Class:
-Basic Skill: **10/10.**
-Advanced Skill: **10/10.**
Total: 20/20.

<u>Bonus points</u>
-System merit (Unique): Child Prodigy (Achieve Breakthrough in Basic Class before 18th birthday) +20.
-System merit (Epic): Gift of Patience. Achieve Breakthrough in Basic Class by not advancing your class at 14 years of age. +15.
-System merit (Epic): Incorruptible Youth. Achieve Breakthrough in Basic Class while under the direct influence of a Witch, without succumbing to villany. +15.

-System merit (Unique): Apex of the Generation. Be the first person in your generation to achieve Breakthrough with a Basic Class skill. +20.
Total class points to be applied: 90/20.

Generating Basic Class Breakthrough Skill...
Skill generated!

Breakthrough Skill: Serenade of the Swarm. 0/10.

The user of the skill can channel their voice into a melodic call, summoning a vast number of creatures to a specified area. Upon singing, the user will immediately direct a swarm of, at minimum, 100 creatures, each weighing up to 10+[0] pounds, to a specific area. The size and duration of the swarm increases with the duration and intensity of the singing. With concentration and continued singing, the user can [Not] choose which species answers the call with greater accuracy.

Caution! The summoned creatures retain their natural instincts. If the creatures are outside the size range of the user's ability to control with other skills, they may attack whatever is within the target area.

Requirement to advance to level 1: begin to sing, intending to activate the skill for the first time.

Epic and Unique merits unable to be applied to Basic Class skill. Granting rewards or boons based on assessed needs. Assessing...

Gift of Patience (Epic). Boon granted. You may now choose which class you want to unlock at a Class Shrine, or through other means of activation, when unlocking a class, so long as the minimum requirements are met. For example, you can choose to unlock your Advanced Class instead of your Full Class, even when you are eighteen years of age.

Incorruptible Youth (Epic). Boon granted. You are able to visualize cursed energy when it is in your presence, and will automatically begin to disperse it, so long as the source is destroyed or you are in direct contact with the energy.

Apex of the Generation (Unique). Your next acquired skill will be upgraded to contain at minimum five modifiers.

The vision from the system ended abruptly, causing Bella to sway in place.

Ash stepped forward and caught her before she could fall, steadying her even as he looked into her eyes with something approaching awe. "I can't believe it... I'm *so* sorry I ever doubted you!"

Before Bella could find her voice to reassure him, the sound of a bell boomed out from atop the palace. She blanched, clutching at Ash's hand as she found her balance. "Ash. What time is it?"

"The process took a surprisingly long while, but we didn't want to interrupt you." At Ash's words, she looked around and saw a crowd had gathered to see what was going on.

"The *time*, Ash!" Bella looked back at him frantically, her glare boring into him as she waited for an answer.

Finally he did so, waving his hand as if to push her concerns to the side.

"It's a quarter after midnight. Bella! *Wait!* That's not important right now. You're a perfect ten!"

SHE WAS STRUGGLING to escape his arms, as Ash had reflexively clamped down when she turned to run. "Bella! What's the matter with you? You need to come with me and meet the queen, you don't understand-"

"*You* don't understand!" She frantically yanked her arm away, turning and diving into the crowd. He moved along with her, keeping pace despite her desperate speed.

"With a Breakthrough Skill, you are a strategic resource of the kingdom," Ash informed her with all seriousness. "You *have* to meet the queen. It's not a request, it's the law."

Barking out a laugh, Bella kept going, her eyes on the doors in the distance. "Pretty sure it *is* a request, Ash. First off, *you* can't tell me to do anything. Secondly, I'm seventeen years old, and I'm pretty sure there's no law about people under eighteen needing to go serve the country if they have a Breakthrough Skill. Third, there *is* a law on the books which is going to potentially cost me my life."

"A law? Are you a criminal?" Ash finally slowed down, falling behind her slightly.

Bella shook her head in annoyance, looking back over her

shoulder to call out, "No, but I'm bound by what my guardian decides for me until my birthday. I'm not supposed to be out tonight."

Ash drew himself up. "You are most certainly supposed to be here, by the decree of the king."

"She figured out a way around that. There was nothing that said I had to *stay* here. She brought me, then sent me home. You have to understand, she's not just cruel, she's a total..." Bella came to a halt, freezing in place as the merit the system had granted her suddenly made sense. She whirled around, "Ash. She's an *actual* Witch. The system gave me an achievement just now for not giving in to her dark powers, and I didn't understand it until just now. You need to help me. Bring an entire unit of soldiers to find me. Please. Figure out how to help me, and I'll find a way to repay you."

"How am I supposed to-"

Before Ash could finish his thought, Bella pulled off one of her shoes and stuffed it into his hands. "It's Enchanted; it'll always find its way back to me. Oh! My name is Isabella Vigatori, of House Vigatori. She keeps me in the cellar."

Then she turned and ran, leaving the startled man behind her holding a shining shoe.

Bella's heart was pounding like a drum as she rushed through the huge entrance hall of the castle, her uneven footsteps echoing off the hard surfaces each time her right foot came down, and the single slipper clattered against stone. Thankfully, the servants saw her coming, opening the door enough to allow her to burst through without slowing down. At the bottom of the stairs awaited her Fairy godmother, impatiently tapping her foot as she waited for Bella to make a reappearance.

"Start going!" Bella shouted out as she raced down the marble stairs. "I'm late! I'm so sorry!"

"*Hyah*, Descartes!" Bibbidy snapped her fingers, and the

horse started trotting away. Bella rushed in just before it picked up too much speed, the door slamming behind her as she threw herself into the moving vehicle. "Quickly, my dear, tell me what happened. I know you wouldn't be late if you had your own way."

Bella tearfully filled her godmother in as the carriage raced through the city, the bell of the clock tolling to signal that it was already half past midnight. Panic filled the young woman as they thundered along, swerving around corners with the wheels rattling violently against the cobblestone. "-he handed me a glowing 'X' and... time just zipped by. My Breakthrough Skill awakened-"

"You already have your-" Bibbidy closed her mouth with a tiny *click*. "Sorry, finish your tale!"

She did just that, even explaining the system merits she'd earned and what they must have meant. When Bibbidy heard about the Incorruptible Youth merit, she went pale and seemed just shy of nauseous. The Godmother lurched forward and threw her arms around Bella. "My poor, poor sweet girl. I had no idea it was *that* bad."

"I always knew she was a terrible person." Bella's muffled voice came from where her mouth was buried in Bibbidy's shoulder.

Shaking her head, Bibbidy leaned back and met Bella's eyes with her own. "It's far worse than that, my sweet. I've told you that I'm a Fairy, which means I have maximized my positive reputation with the system. A Witch is diametrically opposed to me. They've taken their class, their gifts from the system, and twisted them toward dark purposes. The system is neutral, granting power for achievements no matter how wonderful or terrible they might be. However, where my rewards are things that will better myself, my community, my kingdom, the world... hers will always work against that."

Bella's eyes went wide. "Godmother, before the ball, she

started dropping off packages in unsavory locations. I think she has something terrible planned."

Bibbidy nodded sharply, though she patted Bella gently and stepped away. "Of course she does. By the way, now that the system has confirmed her status for you, telling people she's a Witch will not be reputation destruction—it'll just be the truth. You cannot be magically punished for telling the *truth*. Just so you know. Now, let's get you out of those nice clothes and into something much filthier."

As the streets blurred past them, finally giving way to open countryside, Bella exchanged her beautiful, shining dress and glass slipper for the mud-stained servant's dress she'd arrived in. At Bibbidy's insistence, she sat on the nicely cushioned seat and fretted about dirtying it. As the minutes sped by, and the horse galloped as fiercely as it could for the sustained jaunt, the tension in the carriage continued to increase.

Bibbidy made some light conversation, asking questions about the ball, as well as assuring Bella that she would be returning to the palace immediately upon dropping Bella off. "There's no way I'm leaving you in there, and I'm a Fairy. They'll have no choice but to believe me. It's just... it might take a while for them to mobilize. Taking down a true Witch is no mean feat, and they'll want to bring out the powerhouses."

"Please, as long as I know I'm not going to be left there, I can hold out as long as I need to," Bella bravely swore to her godmother, though internally, she wasn't so sure. "I've always thought she was evil, and now that I know I'm right, what actually changes? I just need to keep my head down."

"Just don't do anything to give her cause to hurt you." Bibbidy fretted suddenly, tears in her eyes as she took Bella's hand. "I couldn't bear to live with myself if I had to leave you, and you weren't there when I came to pick you up. You're safe until your birthday... or, at least she can't do anything outside the scope of her authority to you without the kingdom collapsing in on her with their weapons drawn."

They began approaching the estate, which Bella only knew because her godmother let her know. The carriage didn't slow, and the surroundings were utterly alien, foreign to the young woman who had spent the vast majority of her life in one small area.

Then, all at once, the carriage lurched as they skid to a halt, and Bibbidy threw the door open. "Go, Bella! There's no time!"

Bare feet hit the grass, and Bella rushed down into the ditch next to the road. For a few frantic moments, she couldn't find the tunnel opening in the darkness, but luckily a high-pitched *squeak* drew her to the hidden entrance. "Suzy! What're you doing all the way out here? An owl is going to scoop you up for breakfast!"

Squeak!

"You're right, no time to talk." Bella dove into the tunnel, pushing through as quickly as she dared. Approaching the halfway point, she tensed, waiting to run into a barrier that would spell her doom. Instead, she found that section in particular had been reinforced with a lattice of sticks, as though dozens of birds had built a sideways, sturdy nest. She squeezed through without even brushing against the walls, showing how much work the creatures had been doing in her absence.

The end of the tunnel was in sight, and she squeezed her way up and into the room with a sigh of relief. "I made it in time, didn't I?"

Just before she could pull her foot out of the tunnel, a strange tingling settled into her toes—as though they had fallen asleep. It was unnatural, instant, *magical*. Bella's head swam, and she nearly vomited as she realized the clock must have just ticked over, and Matringa would be alerted to the fact that she was ever so slightly outside of her room.

"No…" Her eyes darted to and fro, trying to think of a solution. After a handful of minutes spent panicking, she woozily shook her head and focused on the one thing she could do. "I need... I need to save them. She'll hunt every last one of them down."

Swallowing hard to moisten her throat, Bella tried to sing, only to need to force herself to clear her throat when the words wouldn't come. Finally, she managed a croaking song, which was slightly distorted by her tears. *"Fluffy friends, heed my call! Through this tunnel escape, one and all! Run and flee to safety's arms, far from danger, far from harm!"*

A trickle of animals quickly became a flood as every mouse in the house left, some more reluctantly than others. Hedgehogs, voles, Stella the skunk, every creature that had to walk on the ground to escape the estate came in, went down, and vanished.

*"*Squeak*."* Bella's attention was drawn to Mert the Third, who was standing on his hind legs next to Suzy. The little mouse was glaring at her defiantly, shaking his little head.

"I know you're brave, little one." Bella forced a smile onto her face and crouched down. "But right now, I need you to listen. I have certain protections... but you have nothing but me, and I can't do anything for you right now. I know you want to protect me, but please... don't make me watch you die."

Ever so slowly, the mouse bobbed his little head and started helping Suze the mouse back into the tunnel, even as she resisted slightly. When the last of the creatures had finally vanished, and nothing in the house was stirring, certainly not even a mouse, Bella pressed on the edge of the tunnel as hard as she could.

The ground where the tunnel was buried began to sink, the soil shifting and mounding inward slightly before fully collapsing, as it was intended to do. Dust blew out of the opening in a huge gust, causing Bella to turn her head and close her eyes. When she opened them and turned back, there was only a shallow depression where the tunnel entrance had been only moments before. A spark of inspiration struck, and she grabbed one of her hidden water skins, pouring it into the space to make a shallow puddle.

"Now all I need to do is get Matringa's dress as clean as possible and make it look like I was working... not working to escape."

FORTY

PRINCE CINDER

Cinder turned and walked away from the doors of the palace, knowing there was nothing he *should* do to catch up to the fleeing Bella. He held the glass slipper in his hand, staring at it with confusion. "She gave me her shoe. *Why* would she give me her shoe? She already told me who she was and where to find her. What am I supposed to do with this?"

Returning to the masquerade, he put an easy smile on his face and started making his way through the people lost in their revelry. Even as people brushed past him, tried to speak with him, or otherwise impeded his progress, the prince never stopped his steady pace across the space. He had a goal, and he was going to achieve it.

That was what he did. That was who Cinder *was*. He made progress happen.

Finally, he arrived at the area reserved for the royals, needing to remove and set his mask to the side to get past the guards. He stepped forward firmly, feeling the weight of displeasure in his mother's stare as she watched him approach. "Your majesty, I-"

"The whole point of wearing the mask, Cinder, is so no one can be certain where you are at any given time during this party. I did that for *you*." The queen interrupted him immediately. "Why would you then go and throw that all away when there are hours remaining until our guests go home? As soon as you step away, you're going to be swarmed. You *know* this."

Cinder bowed sharply, knowing better than to cause a commotion in public if he wanted his imperious mother to listen to him. "It's a matter of some urgency, your majesty."

"It better be." Queen Liora grumbled for a moment, only to go still and look at him with suddenly-sharp eyes. "It couldn't be... that you found the woman who will be publicly betrothed to you?"

"No!" he yelped in reply, letting out a nervous chuckle at her now-arched brow. "I had three guards with me who can attest to what I'm about to tell you. A young woman was here, wanting nothing more than to speak with you and advance her class. For some reason, she's been unable to get to a Class Shrine and so was hoping you would do it for her as a gesture of goodwill."

"Not a terrible idea, frankly," the queen mused. "It's been quite a long time since your father or I directly advanced someone not of the high nobility. Actually, yes, bring her here."

"Well, *abyss*, I would have loved to know you'd be so open to doing that." Cinder sucked in a breath through his teeth, "So..."

"What did you do, Cinder? Just spit it out. Did you have her thrown out?" Liora leaned slightly to the right, putting the pads of her fingertips against the temple of her forehead. "By the system, sometimes the hints of paranoia I've seen in you since your father was attacked-"

"Mother!"

Cinder broke protocol, causing her to look up at him with a freshly-sharpened glare.

"I was just worried... that she may not be who she said she was." The glare softened at this, and Liora sighed softly at being proven correct. Cinder pressed on. "She claimed to have earned her Breakthrough Skill, but had not yet awakened it. Wanting to keep some distance between you and her, but also wanting to give her the benefit of the doubt, I had one of the guards fetch the awakening shard that's been rotting in the vault since grandfather was king."

"I hope you put it back after you finished indulging her braggadocious fantasies." The Queen shook her head slightly. "Wait, why would you want to give her the benefit of the doubt? How long were you speaking with her? Cinder... what color are her eyes?"

"That's not important... they're blue, with a small, brown section in her left one." Cinder sputtered slightly as his mother clapped once, a wide smile blooming on her face. "Stop that! She's in trouble. She ran out of here, saying something about magic laws that would get her in trouble if she were discovered out of her house?"

"Impossible." The queen shook her head. "I decreed that every qualified young lady be allowed to attend. That would supersede any other guardianship magic."

"I said the same thing, but she said you hadn't put anything in the decree about *staying* here." At Cinder's words, whatever Liora had been about to say didn't come out of her mouth. "Apparently, she was brought here, then sent home early."

Liora waved over a guard, speaking to him quietly for a moment before shaking her head and returning her attention to Cinder. "No, the only person who went home early was Isabella Vigatori. She's a sickly, misshapen young thing who isn't all there. Apparently she arrived, rushed to the food and gulped down as much as she could before being sent home for the sake of her health. You remember her, she was at the party we went to quietly for your second cousin and his new wife Rosa. You danced, for some reason that still eludes me."

"Yes, that's exactly who I'm talking about." Cinder's face

twisted slightly as he thought about what his mother had just said. "Isabella Vigatori. Why do you keep calling her sickly and misshapen? She's as lovely as anyone I've ever met."

"You... are joking?" Liora studied her son then shook her head. "Isabella is certainly a common name, perhaps in her haste to leave, her words became garbled?"

They stood in silence, both of them uncertain why they were unable to properly communicate with each other. Cinder tried again. "You saw her with me, or at least your guards did. She was in the luminous dress, and she... here! She gave me her shoe."

"What in the-?" Liora leaned away as Cinder offered her the glass slipper. "Why would she give you her *shoe*? Wait... my crown is... it *can't* be. Put that on the ground, right now."

Hearing the seriousness with which she was speaking, Cinder set the shoe down and stepped back hurriedly. "Are you worried that it might be coated in some kind of contact poison? I don't think she-"

He and his mother both gasped as the shoe shifted in place, the toe sweeping around to point south and a little east.

"It's *Enchanted*." Leora breathed lightly then looked up and met her son's eyes directly. "The Awakening Shard. It activated, didn't it?"

"It did." Cinder bobbed his head. "She told me it was from her Basic Class, that she hadn't even unlocked her Advanced Class yet. But, that's why she was here in the first place. She didn't even know you could do both. Frankly, she didn't seem to know anything about skills, nor your role, at least not what someone of her age and status should. There's more. She said her guardian is a literal Witch and that we needed to bring soldiers with us to rescue her. Mother... she was *terrified*."

"That settles it then; it can't be the same person." Liora sat back and tossed her hands to the side in a light shrug. "The guardian of the house is Signora Vigatori, a widow now that her husband has been taken by plague in a distant land. They've been at functions and events many times over the last years, and never once has there been a complaint against them. They are perfectly lovely, by all accounts."

"Moth-"

"We are in *public*, Cinder," Queen Liora quietly spoke over him. "Please remember that. Guards, I need my advisors. Cinder, pull up a seat."

A trio of nobles ranging from elderly to quite spry hurried over a few minutes later, their eyes shining with curiosity as they looked between the two seated royals. The queen looked stately and calm, while the prince was slumped in his seat and clearly frustrated.

"How wonderful!" The eldest of them smiled as he walked past the guards. "It appears you must have chosen our future princess, Your Majesty. Might I be the first to offer my congratulations, as well as the first to ask who it is? I know my daughter was attending; she was wearing the most lovely yellow-"

"No, it's not that." The man appeared slightly crestfallen, so Liora reassured him by saying, "The princess has not been chosen. However, we are seeking out a mysterious attendee who fled rather suddenly. Prince Cinder was with her as she awakened a Breakthrough Skill, and she fled without registering it with the crown."

There were gasps from the advisors, who turned to each other and murmured for a long moment before turning back with solemn expressions on their faces. "That's quite the crime. Do we know what her power set was, how dangerous she will be to bring in?"

"She's not dangerous," Cinder grumpily stated, sitting forward in his chair. "She broke through in her Basic Class. As far as I know, she's not even breaking a law. There's nothing that says someone too young to have their Full Class must register their skills."

"Her Basic Class?" Liora tilted her head at him. "Then it's even *more* important we find her."

"What do you mean?" Cinder balked at the sheer edge in her tone. "Why is that so important? I've never heard of anyone achieving Breakthrough in a Basic Class skill."

"*Exactly*, Cinder." The queen motioned for the advisors to stand closer and kept her voice down as she explained, "If she truly did so, that would make her the first to unlock the third skill of a Basic Class in... as far as the written history of our kingdom goes. She must have gained a truly impressive system merit for doing so, which means whatever she does next will be incredibly impactful. You say she hasn't unlocked her class? I want to do so personally, so we can bring her under our wing."

"How shall we proceed with finding her, your majesty?" The middle-aged advisor questioned as he stroked his long beard in contemplation. "Do we have a name, a lead on how to find her?"

"Only one lead, but no name." Liora's answer caused Cinder to jerk his head to stare at her in shock. She rolled her eyes at him, continuing by saying, "She gave a false name to the prince then ran away as soon as her skill was awakened fully. We *must* assume she has an extremely dangerous new skill."

"She didn't give me a false name, she..." Cinder swallowed as four sets of eyes turned to stare at him pityingly. "She wasn't like that."

"An Enchantress, perhaps?" The youngest of the advisors finally spoke, nudging his senior and winking at him. "Let me guess, love at first sight?"

"She gave the name Isabella Vigatori, but everyone knows the Vigatori girl is frail and sickly and has gotten worse after the loss of her late father." The queen shook her head at Cinder crossing his arms. "Prince Cinder, that's hardly the type of girl to galavant around at balls and leave behind her footwear. Well, actually, the second part might make more sense if that were the case. But she left behind *Enchanted* footwear. Not just magical, not simply skill-touched. Enchanted."

A guard stepped forward and adjusted the slipper, only for it to twist and point in the direction the mysterious young woman had fled not long ago. Cinder shook his head and reiterated, "She told me who she was. She's in danger. We need to send guards to bring her safely back here."

The advisors chuckled slightly, even as the queen raised her hand to silence them. "My son, what we need right now is a creative solution. Not to simply smash our way into some unfortunate low noble's home and destroy it over a young woman falsifying information about herself. We also need to do this within the bounds of the laws of our kingdom."

"Yes!" The youngest advisor snapped his fingers, pointing at the shoe. "Making a law targeting only a single person will not mesh into our ward structure. If we want to do this right, we should do it just as we did the masquerade: a royal decree that whoever the slipper belongs to must return to the castle and marry the prince!"

"Whoa, what, *no!*" Cinder nearly fell off his chair as he thrashed backward, away from the grinning advisors. "That's not what this is about! There's a powerful young woman out there who didn't register with the crown, that's *all!*"

"I second the motion." the middle aged advisor stated, while trying to hide his grin. "Clearly, the young prince has deep, convoluted feelings about this young woman. It's more than anyone else can say about another of the fine ladies of our realm."

"A grand search throughout the kingdom!" The eldest advisor tapped his cane on the ground in excitement. "Every maiden shall try on the slipper, and thus we shall find your mysterious damsel and return her to your side!"

"I'm telling you, I *know* who she is." Cinder pointed at the shoe in frustration. "The slipper is even telling us where she is. All we need to do is go and find her, and if it points another direction, we just keep following it!"

"Think of the celebrations, your majesty! Each village we get to we could hold a festival, bringing life back to the populace!" The youngest advisor was speaking again, absolutely ignoring Cinder and leaving the young man to seethe. "We shall leave no foot untested!"

"*Why not?*" Cinder barked at them in frustration.

"Well..." The youngest advisor hesitated, but the middle-aged one smoothly stepped in and filled the silence.

"You *are* the Crown Prince, Your Highness. This entire event has been put together strategically, with a clear intent of improving the lives of your people. Now, as we search for the young maiden who mysteriously vanished after the prince so desperately wanted to speak to her? The people will be expecting a show, and we shall give them one! Plus... what young woman here *won't* think it is herself? If you think your desired lady is truly in danger, then putting the royal procession together quickly and publicly closing in on her location may be able to forestall any untoward activity."

"Good enough for me." Queen Liora clapped her hands and smiled at her advisors. "Send everyone home, and let the slipper saga commence!"

FORTY-ONE

BELLA

THE NIGHT PASSED FITFULLY for Bella as she tried to get any sleep she possibly could, but only managed to snatch small sections of shuteye. Early, very early, she heard her stepfamily arrive home. They burst into the house, practically *shouting* in excitement, with Cattiva running around and sending plumes of dust falling from the floorboards above Bella's head. The one voice the Beast Singer was dreading the most, Matringa, was silent.

She waited and waited, but soon the noises faded away, to be replaced by total silence as the exhausted group went to sleep. Bella let out a soft sigh of relief, allowing her eyes to drift closed and sleep to take her. Just before she fully dozed off, she allowed herself to subvocalize her hope, just to get it out into the world around her. "Maybe she didn't notice?"

An unknown amount of time later, Bella suddenly sat bolt upright in her bed, her breathing suddenly sharp and echoing in the stillness of her room. She gasped for breath, clutching at her heart as it hammered against her ribs. She shivered as she sat in her bed, the air around her thick with the weight of stillness and the unseen. Bella cast her senses around the inky darkness, searching for anything that could have ripped her from her uneasy slumber... but there was only oppressive darkness in all directions.

Ever so slowly, her heartbeat began to slow, and Bella realized it was even quieter than usual in there. Without even a single mouse remaining in the manor, there was no one cuddling up to her to provide a modicum of warmth, sense of community, or connection. She started to lie back down, grumblingly resigning herself to stress-induced nightmares. Pulling on her blanket, she turned over and stretched out her arm, only to freeze in terror as her fingers met something unexpected.

It wasn't fabric, the wall, or the woven straw decorating her space. It was colder, harder. Without even realizing it, she allowed her fingers to trace the contours of the item, and her breath caught in her throat when she realized it was the arm of a chair.

Turning her head slowly, straining to peer through the darkness, Bella finally made out a faint silhouette. There was a figure sitting on the chair, calmly waiting for her to wake up.

"*Humm...*" Matringa shifted slightly, the sound of her fingers drumming on the arm of the chair as loud as thunder in Bella's ears. "Don't *you* sleep deeply. That must be nice. The sleep of someone with nothing to hide."

Bella was rooted to the spot, every instinct within her screaming that the danger she'd felt in her nightmare wasn't a figment of her imagination. It was simply the presence of the woman who governed her fate with a quiet, terrifying malice. She fought against her desire to scream in surprise and fear, falling back on her habits over the last several years of learning to stay quiet no matter what.

"I'm surprised, child." Matringa shifted to the side and struck a match, the light blinding Bella enough that she had to turn away. The lady of the house put the match into a covered lantern, and soon a bright glow illuminated the entire room. "It seems like you understand your place, it seems like you finally know better than to fight against reality. Yet, tonight I *know* you were not where you were supposed to be."

As Bella blinked away the blurry vision left behind by a bad night's sleep, combined with the sudden brightness, her eyes refocused on Matringa... and once more, she had to stifle the urge to let out a shriek.

Sitting upon the chair was her stepmother, of that there was no doubt. But now? Now Bella saw another layer to Matringa, as though a translucent veil had been draped over the overbearing woman. There was a malevolent force clinging to the woman like a second skin, oozing an aura of decay and corruption that Bella could nearly *taste*. The dark energy seethed around her, dark tendrils rising and twisting in the air as if seeking out a new host at all times.

Luckily, Matringa took her widened eyes and fearful expression as confirmation of Bella's misdeeds, instead of as recognition of the darkness she held within her. The older lady leaned forward, and Bella's brain nearly shut down as she tried to maintain her composure—the cursed energy reached out and brushed against her own skin, cold and clammy as it caressed her cheek. Yet, instead of completing the motion and touching her skin directly, it diverted around her like a gentle breeze flowing around a boulder.

"Where does it *tingle*, Bella?" Matringa's sickly sweet tone sent Bella into yet another tailspin. For a moment, the young woman thought the Witch in front of her had realized she was being protected by the system boon given from her merit of Incorruptible Youth.

Luckily, at the very last moment, Bella realized what she was talking about, bowing her head both to appear shame-faced *and* get the stomach-churning visage out of her sight. Realizing she'd been asked a direct question, Bella responded thickly, "the toes of my left foot, Signora Vigatori. I don't understand why... I was simply washing my feet in the basin over there, and suddenly I went numb."

Matringa's finger drumming slowed, coming to a stop after a long moment, though she remained staring at Bella, scanning her face for any sign of guilt. Then, in a flash of abrupt motion, she practically *flew* across the floor and ripped the carpet of woven straw away from the wall where Bella had pointed. The small depression, still half filled with water, greeted the intense, focused eyes of the Witch.

Though Bella could barely see in the darkness of the room, for some reason the darker, cloying energy surrounding Matringa remained visible at a distance. Her stepmother remained still for a long moment, staring down at the depression in the ground, before turning around to look at Bella.

Then she turned fully around to face Bella.

The incongruous motion made Bella's head spin, as she realized Matringa's foul power had shifted to look at her before her actual body did. That at least explained how she had noticed some of Bella's trespasses in the past, when she'd mouthed off at the Witch's back, thinking she wouldn't be seen doing so.

"Only your toes, you say...?" At a much more human pace, Matringa sauntered over and grabbed Bella's blanket, tossing the entire comforter halfway across the room with a casual motion to the side. Then she gripped Bella's ankle, staring intently at her toes. "So it is... so it is. Well, a breach of trust is a breach of trust, child. I'm going to have to take those toes."

"*What?*" Bella reflexively tried to pull away, but she couldn't break her stepmother's iron grip on her ankle. She thrashed around, but Matringa simply stood there, bored, as though holding the leg of a toddler throwing a tantrum. "Why would washing my feet make me lose my toes?"

"Because, Bella... that is what I'm *allowed* to take," Matringa stated in a calm tone, as though she were ordering a sausage for breakfast. "I see that this room is not nearly as secure for you as it should be. I didn't realize it was practically falling apart... how easy would it be for you to burrow your way out like a little *rat*, if you had the mental capacity to have thought of it before now? Let's take this inside, to the attic."

"S-Signora! Please! What's happening right now?" Bella's voice warbled as the Witch turned and simply started walking, not releasing her grip on the leg. The young woman dropped from her bed, hitting the ground with an **oof** before skidding along the woven straw. Then she was bouncing off each stair as they ascended to ground level, and finally, they stepped out into early morning sunlight. For a moment, Bella was shocked by the amount of outdoor light—it was far later than she was expecting.

In the next moment, Matringa let out a howl of pain, even as Bella felt a constriction on her heart vanish.

A golden 'X' appeared over her chest, fading after a long moment into a clear, hollow version of itself, which floated up and sank into her skin, permanently tattooing itself on her left cheek with a feeling like a feather gently tickling her. She'd forgotten this secondary function of the oath she had sworn to Matringa—to not ascend the basement stairs until told to do so—the golden 'X' on her heart had been transformed into a mark of someone who had fulfilled the most sacred of system oaths.

Bella watched as the presence of the system energy flowed through her, directly impacting the cursed energy surrounding Matringa's hand where it was wrapped around her ankle and *blasting* the darkness away. As soon as she was released, Bella backpedaled, scrambling across the ground as she tried to escape the maniac who was trying to take her toes off.

A moment later, she let out a scream of frustration as her stepmother appeared next to her, once more gripping her leg and inspecting her foot. It was only as Matringa let out a growl of absolute fury, like a wounded, rabid dog, that Bella's panic subsided enough for her to observe what was happening. Firstly, her stepmother's hand was bleeding freely, the skin blistered and torn where the system's energy and her own over-flowing evil had competed for space... only for her to lose. *Badly*.

Secondly... her toes were no longer numb.

Even as she had that realization, Bella was abruptly tossed to the side as Matringa let out a deep scoff. "I can't believe this... *that* was enough to reset the skein of the local ward structure? Well, Bella, looks like you get to keep your toes today. Now, we've all had a long night, and I'm certain everyone would appreciate a hearty brunch. Better get to it."

Ready to do anything to get away from her malicious step-mother, Bella scrambled away from her position on the ground and fled to the servant's area immediately. With shaking hands, she gathered the ingredients from the pantry. Once she had everything arrayed before her, she glared and tried to command her hands to steady themselves.

They refused.

"Fine! If I can't control it, I'll *use* it." Bella worked with frantic energy to control her breathing as she grabbed a whisk and tried to hold it still, ending up instead blending the eggs by using the involuntary motion alone. "Hah. See? Even when I'm out of control, I can be in control."

Making sure to always keep her back to a wall and one eye on the door, she fried up thick slices of bacon, toasting the bread and laying it in a pattern pleasing to the eye, setting whipped butter in a small carafe next to it. Just as she finished with the main foodstuffs, the spicy aroma of black tea filled the kitchen, the herbal scent fighting against the overpowering stench of bacon grease.

By the time everything was loaded up on a tray, Bella felt extremely drained, certainly too tired to be as scared as she'd been. She hauled everything up to the main level, mutely setting out plates and silverware around the cupboard dishes. Her stepfamily had begun to gather, still buzzing with the excitement of the previous night.

"-and what do you make of those absurd crystal shoes?" Cattiva was saying to her older sister as they burst into the dining room. "Abyss, I can't get them out of my head! It's just so... so *tacky!*"

"How could those ever be appropriate footwear? Let alone when you're at a party where dancing and moving around is *mandatory?*" Malvagio agreed with a dramatic roll of her eyes. "I suppose I could see it if someone was on a throne and didn't need to move at all, but how did they *not* break?"

"Maybe they did! Maybe that's why she ran out suddenly, to find someone to heal the shards jammed into the bottom of her feet," Cattiva excitedly postulated, a wide grin spreading on her face. "That would make sense, as they sent everyone home right afterward. They needed to clean all the blood off the ground!"

Matringa stepped into the room, and all conversation died instantly. The powerful Witch stalked over to her seat at the table, gracefully seating herself before allowing her daughters to follow suit.

"That's enough, girls. Bella here had a lonely night and a good life lesson this morning. Why don't we all take turns listening to her as we break our fast? Bella, why don't you tell us, in *exacting* detail, what you did after you returned home last night? After all, you were washing your feet near the second hour of the morning! Surely you were doing something interesting, something you wouldn't mind sharing?"

Bella choked on nothing, her face going red as her mind went blank. Internally, she quailed as she silently begged the universe for any kind of reprieve.

"Well? Don't keep us waiting, I'm sure it will be *riveting.* Nothing like a little look into your life to keep us on our *toes.*" Matringa's voice took on a sharp quality, clearly demanding an answer instead of asking for one. As Bella's jaw worked silently, Matringa stared at her then slowly began standing from her seat as no words were forthcoming.

Just before she could punish Bella for not answering, a firm knock on the front door resonated through the house.

Matringa and Bella stood silently staring at each other for a long moment, before the older woman put a sickly sweet smile on her face and turned away. "Now, whoever could *that* be at this hour?"

FORTY-TWO

GIVING Bella a glare of warning as she stalked out of the room, Matringa marched to the main door and yanked it open.

Bella was standing near the door of the dining room and peered through the crack between the door and its frame to try and see what was happening. All she could see was a sudden tension in her stepmother's posture before she was roughly shoved out of the way by Malvagio.

"Move!" the older girl hissed at Bella, who flinched away in horror as she saw the dark energy surging through her step-sister. Unlike with Matringa, there was no blatant aura of darkness and corruption; instead, it seemed to be slowly gaining in power. She was well on her way to being a Witch but had not *quite* crossed that threshold.

With that thought in mind, she turned to look at Cattiva, staring intently until the wisps of dark energy made them-selves known, crawling on the younger of the stepsisters like spiders scuttling into and out of hiding spaces. "Can you still be saved?"

In her surprise, Bella had accidentally spoken the words out loud, though very softly. It was enough to make her disgruntled stepsister glare at her, but not enough to make her comment.

"Signora Matringa, my apologies for the interruption of your morning," a powerful voice practically shouted into the entryway, the voice clearly well-trained and used to speaking to large crowds at a time. "It's-a me, *Dario*, the King's Herald, here to deliver the decree of the crown in person!"

From her new position as the last in line of the snooping trio, Bella could just barely make out her stepmother's motions as she swept into a stilted curtsy. "How very gracious of you, Signore. What can House Vigatori do for our kingdom?"

There was a sound of vellum flapping; no doubt the man was opening a scroll with a dramatic flourish. "As of this morning, a royal decree has been signed by the Queen's hand! Crown Prince Cinder will be leading a royal procession from town to town, seeking the young woman who filled his heart with fire during the masquerade! There is to be a festival in each town nearest the largest concentration of attendees, and all eligible young women who attended the ball are hereby ordered to present themselves to the prince when he arrives in their towns."

The authoritative voice cut off, and a long silence stretched before Matringa realized he had finished. "Do you speak for the Kingdom at this moment?"

"Indeed I do!" the man bellowed jovially.

Matringa allowed herself a polite chuckle. "In that case, perhaps I can make a complaint known through you. This is highly unusual and puts us in an awkward position. We are exhausted from the masquerade this last evening, as wonderful as it was and are ill-prepared to travel today."

"Not to worry!" The man leaned forward, finally coming into Bella's field of view, and she recoiled as she saw him wink salaciously at the Witch. "You will not have to travel at all! In fact, the prince himself has decided they will arrive here at luncheon instead of pressing on to the next town over. His

Highness felt it necessary to extend his personal presence, sending me ahead to deliver this decree in person to permit your household ample time to prepare for a private visit."

"He... the prince is coming *here*?" Matringa inquired incredulously, only her hand trailing along her dress to smooth it out betraying a hint of nervousness. "I have... there's no... we will be unable to host, as we have nothing prepared! Our servants were given the day off for the holiday of the prince's birth. I'm honored, but-"

"Not to worry, the procession will be bringing its own food, and your family is personally invited to dine with the prince!" Dario the herald paused, and when he spoke again, it was in a much more reasonable tone, conversational even. "Look, this is off the record. I've heard that the prince was quite taken with a conversation with one of your daughters last night. He sent me ahead, personally, to make sure you knew he was coming. You have perhaps... two hours? Less, most likely, but he *will* be arriving."

Through Matringa's sputtering combination of denial and thanks, the herald was clearly quite accustomed to dealing with all manner of nobility, from the highborn to the newly raised. No matter what she called after him, he refused to give any further details, simply bowing slightly before spinning on his heel and fading away like fog in the wind.

"A movement skill? I guess that explains how we got past the thorns." Bella muttered softly.

Thankfully, her words were hidden by Malvagio and Cattiva immediately scrambling into the hallway, squabbling with each other in raised voices. The younger of the two was the loudest. "He must be coming to see *me*! I danced with him twice, I'm sure of it, and I talked the *whole* time!"

"Stop deluding yourself; clearly, our conversation was what he's remembering. I know how to give *and* take, to bestow an arrogant meatsack like the prince to feel self-important." Malvagio seemed to be trying to maintain her apathetic air, but the trembling and smile forcing itself onto her lips belied her attempt at being casual.

"Girls, it could be either of you." Matringa set aside her hesitation after a moment, clapping her hands once and pulling all attention to her. "We only-"

"Couldn't be Bella, though, could it?" Cattiva cattily called, casting a condescending glance at her stepsister. "Not unless he's here to charge us for all the desserts she gobbled down in the handful of minutes she managed to make a pest of herself at the masquerade."

"I heard about that from at least three different people." Malvagio huffed and shook her head in annoyance. "Mother, please tell me she's going to stay out of sight. We don't need to be embarrassed."

Matringa nodded serenely, the burgeoning twitch of her lips blooming into a full-blown smile as she listened to her daughter's speak. "Never fear, Bella will be in her new room, preparing it for herself. I guarantee it will take days of hard work to make it livable… especially since my kitties seem so hungry today. There's not a mouse to be found, no matter where they look!"

Suddenly caught in the middle of a conversation she didn't want to be in, Bella simply hung her head to stare at the floor, folding her palms in front of herself in an attempt to become invisible. The sudden silence stretched thin, and Matringa finally snapped.

"Go now! Time is flying by, we must all prepare ourselves immediately. Bella. You are to see to it that they are both beyond presentable… they must be *exquisite*! Once the prince arrives, you are to go directly to the attic and begin cleaning. Do *not* test me, not today. Girls! This could be the chance encounter we've been waiting for!"

- PRINCE CINDER -

"Julia was found this morning," the captain of the royal guard quietly murmured into the prince's ear as they rode along at the head of a caravan stretching nearly half a mile. The wagons were full of foodstuffs, the covered carriages being mobile kitchens meant to feed whatever town they rolled into. "First confirmed case of the plague within the city."

"I'm sure Mother is devastated." Cinder shook his head as he replied, "I assume we are keeping that particular piece of news... rather quiet?"

The captain simply nodded his head solemnly, allowing the conversation to die. Cinder looked around, taking in the endless distractions such a well-stocked caravan could offer. Each portion of the caravan was bedecked in the colors of the crown: blue and gold. To his mind, they appeared as a winding sea serpent swarming with activity and noise. Hundreds of people were necessary for the planned event, and he'd brought *all* of them along.

"This time, when I find her, I'll have plenty of witnesses ready to verify my words." Cinder's leather glove creaked as he squeezed his hand into a fist, still intensely annoyed with how the masquerade had ended the night before. "All of this to find someone who we will, no doubt, throw to the guard if her ability has any combat application at all. Otherwise, we are just blowing wagon-fulls of gold coins to find someone Mother wants to hire."

Leaning in, the captain raised an eyebrow and reignited the conversation. "Is that so, my Prince? I was under the impression that you were rather taken with our runaway princess-to-be. You know... based on the stories *you* told me? *I* heard that you even knew what color her eyes were. Now, if we were just looking for someone who was evading us, or the crown wanted to hire, I would agree that this is wasteful. Conversely, if we are looking for one of the future leaders of the kingdom... well that puts a different spin on things, doesn't it?"

The clattering of wheels and the steady clopping of hooves filled the air between them as Cinder's face became more flushed, his jaw tight so he didn't open it and give the captain further ammunition to use against him.

Desperate to turn the conversation, he allowed the news of the plague arriving in the capital to come to the forefront of his mind, and a frown overtook the hard clenching of his lips. "How could the plague enter the capital? I was assured we had checkpoints in place to ensure no one who was sick could enter. Not just people, animals, plants. So... how? A disease cannot simply *ignore* the system's magic, can it?"

"That's a good question, your highness." The teasing tone the captain had been using moments before was nowhere to be found. "I'm sure you understand we have been frantically organizing to see if our ward structure has been tampered with. The best enchanters and artificers are already going over the designs, resetting them in some places to test their effectiveness. If it isn't a failed design... there's always the possibility that it was done by design."

"You think someone is *intentionally* spreading plague into our kingdom?" Cinder's voice was as low as he could keep it and still be heard. "I can't imagine any of the surrounding kingdoms doing something so egregious, especially when we have no quarrel with them currently."

"People will do strange things when there is sickness about, my Prince." The captain turned and shot him a wince. "Perhaps even fly into a rage that they've been sick, or lost someone, and see a kingdom, such as ours, which is as of yet untouched, only to blame us for their misfortune. Then... well, they figure out how the disease is spreading and make that happen here. But, we only got started this morning; we can't assume such terrible intentions until we rule out simple negligence or ineffectiveness."

"Hmm. I hope adjusting the kingdom's wards didn't have any unintended consequences." Cinder tossed that around for a few moments, before leaning toward the guard. "You will make sure to remain vigilant, yes? I know you have your doubts, but I want a *thorough* sweep of House Vigatori while they are distracted by the festival in their front yard. Bella told me there was great danger there, and I am inclined to believe her, for some reason."

"Understood, my Prince." After confirming with all seriousness, the captain cracked a grin. "I bet *I* know the reason. Mwah, *mwah!*"

Cinder shook his head and looked away, unable to meet the eyes of his trusted protector when he was making kissy faces at him. "Perhaps a year of patrolling the border on horseback with a *very* thin saddle will get you to calm down? Imagine that, the glorious war hero, Justin Williams, returned to the same place he made a name for himself originally?"

"No need for threats, Your Highness." The captain's grin shifted slightly, almost becoming a leer. "All they do is prove me right. Can't just banish all of your problems."

The caravan continued to roll along, past fields and forests. When they had been moving through the city, people had cheered and waved, collecting into a huge audience that followed behind them until they were outside the walls. Everyone seemed so sure that when the prince came back, they would be meeting their future queen. As he thought back over the events of late last night, into early this morning, the intensity and passion with which Bella had spoken of her skills, even *he* began to see the appeal.

"Perhaps... they can't be right, can they? There *are* worse choices than someone like her. At least she's someone who understands the draw of pursuing Perfection."

FORTY-THREE

BELLA

"THOSE ARE SOME INTENSE HEDGES." Bella deepened her voice as she made up the conversation that must be happening among the people in the procession driving onto the lawn at this very moment. "Yes, indeed, obviously, those are *completely* natural. Let's walk past them and expect to be able to leave whenever we want. Because, why *wouldn't* we be able to?"

She shook her head angrily, looking away from the window and dashing away the tears threatening to fall from her eyes. "I asked him to show up with an army, and he brought a *parade*. This is everything that's wrong with this kingdom."

Looking around the intensely cluttered attic, Bella felt her heart sink as she took in the thick dust swirling in the air in the light coming through the only window. "Not looking forward to breathing that in, but what am I supposed to do about it? When's the last time anyone was up here? Is this a storehouse? Feels like one."

There was a jumble of furniture covered in thick sheets and even thicker dust. Chairs were stacked atop each other, and trunks and boxes lay filled with yellowed papers, old books, and half-melted candles she recognized from the few times they entertained important guests. Worse, cobwebs stretched across the entire room, except the areas she'd passed through—those webs had collected on her clothes. Or in her hair.

"It's not often I wish I had different powers, but being able to sing to insects and have them listen to me would be really nice right about now. Ugh... why couldn't she have *started* me up here? This is basically a playground for mice." She turned back to the window, grabbing the lever and shifting it back and forth again, hoping that, this time, it would open farther than a crack. No such luck. "What corner of this place do I want to turn into my room? There's no way I'm going to be able to make headway on this without cleaning supplies."

Resigned to simply breathing in mold and thick dust for a while, Bella remained at the window, trying to get as much fresh air into the mix as possible. Her eyes widened as voices floated up to her, and she pressed her ear to the small gap to listen in.

"Those are some intense hedges!"

Bella nearly dropped to her knees as an intense groan of annoyance escaped her.

"If you have time to act like a gardener, you have time to peel those potatoes. Get to it!" Bella had heard enough professional chefs in her life to recognize one who was particularly harried. "We need to make a feast here, then do it again three hours down the road! What was he thinking, that lovesick-"

A pounding on the door two levels below her caused the entire house to vibrate, followed by an overpowering shout from the herald that had visited earlier. "Open up in the name of the King! Ladies of House Vigatori, you are hereby *ordered* to attend a feast in honor of Crown Prince Cinder!"

Bella's eyes went wide, and her smile was even wider as she turned and threw herself across the room toward the door. "It's a direct order on behalf of the King; I can't *not* listen!"

Just as she reached for the handle, something shot out of

the keyhole, grasping for her outstretched fingers. She pulled back just in time, as the thin, brown object shivered and grew spikes. Then it swung back, slapping into the door and digging into its thick wood. "Is that... that's a hedge!"

The stick quickly grew across the door, and soon there was a barrier of leaves and thorns between herself and the exit. "This... she can't do this! It's illegal! Not to mention..."

Bella's protests faded as she realized her wicked step-mother likely had no compunctions about sacrificing a door to keep her away from such a heavily armed and armored group of people who *might* take her seriously, if she were to complain about her situation. Seeing no other option, she slowly returned to the door, keeping one eye on the hedge to make sure it didn't grow into the room or come any closer to her.

"An *order*? I'm delighted you're so excited to meet myself and my daughters." Matringa's sickly sweet voice drifted up, and a flash of color down below was enough for Bella to realize her entire stepfamily had walked outside wearing bright dresses and shining jewels. "For, Your Majesty, your *desire* is our command."

"Yes, well, my command is *also* my command." As the person who must have been the prince answered in an annoyed tone, Bella's eyes went wide.

"Ash?"

"I seem to recall the order being for all the ladies of House Vigatori," the prince's voice continued with a sophisticated drawl, "I was under the impression, from my second cousin by marriage, Rosa, that there was another under your care, Signora."

"You must mean Bella." Matringa's voice was packed full of sorrow. "Yes... she was with us until very recently. You see, she did attend the festivities yesterday, but on her way home... well, she was on a very careful diet, as certain items caused her throat to close up. Unfortunately, while she was at the ball last night, she must have eaten something that didn't agree with her sensitivities. I didn't notice, and the driver didn't understand what to do. I'm sorry to… *ahem*… she's no longer with us."

"Wh-!"

Rustle.

As soon as Bella started to shout in anger, the twigs and leaves of the hedge which had grown around the door shifted violently, many twists of the roots dropping to the floor and snaking toward her. The rest of the word caught in her throat, and the hedge stopped moving as soon as she went quiet. "It's going to be like that, is it?"

"I… see," the prince stated in a tone that indicated he didn't quite believe her but was trying to show sympathy for her loss. "If you wouldn't mind, I'm certain some of my stewards would be quite willing to go in and fetch her body so she could be laid to rest-"

"It's been taken care of, Your Majesty." Matringa swept into a curtsy, "Might I… if you'd be so kind, could my daughter Cattiva play a short song of remembrance for the poor waif who lost her life late last night? It would mean a great deal to us to have you all participate."

There was no answer, but Bella could only assume the prince had nodded his acceptance, as only a moment later, the first sounds of a lute being strummed drifted on the breeze. Cattiva's voice softly came along with the music, heard more clearly than even the herald had been.

"Let's raise our glasses, let's delight! Poor Bella went quietly into the night. She'd want us to think of her with dance and song, so with merry hearts try to join along!"

Bella shook her head as Cattiva's cloying song bounced off of her. For a long moment, she'd been tempted to forget she, *herself*, existed. But no matter how potent her stepsister's skills had become over the years of practice, they couldn't do *that*. With a sobering realization, Bella amended her thinking.

"They can't make me forget I exist... yet. By the system, that's *dangerous*."

Almost everyone was standing perfectly still, watching and listening as Cattiva continued to strum and sing. But as she started her second verse, Prince Cinder suddenly flinched and looked down at a small satchel at his side in confusion.

"Leave her in the shadows we cast, tonight let's make our happiness last! Forget her story, just focus on now. Today's about joy, let me explain how-"

"Stop *singing*! At! Once! Guards!" Cinder roared in anger as he pulled the glass slipper out of his satchel. "She's affecting our minds!"

Bella clasped her hands together over her mouth to stop from shouting in excitement—the shoes were meant to redirect malicious attacks aimed at Bella to the *shoe*. Perhaps, because the song was meant to make them forget her, the shoe's power expanded and protected Ash... no, Prince Cinder.

"That's a baseless claim, Your Majesty!" Matringa gasped out as she stepped in front of her daughter. "She was simply playing a song; is it her fault you all got caught up in her talent? What's making you act this way? A shoe? Why are you holding a woman's shoe, especially such a gaudy one?

"Captain Williams, you are to enter this estate and look for anyone hidden away or proof that Isabella Vigatori is indeed dead." Cinder half-turned away from Bella's stepfamily, though he made sure to keep some of his focus on them. "Guards, detain them until we can ascertain their talents. Herald Dario, return to the Spring Palace immediately and bring an introspector here. Something's not right."

"Prince Cinder!" Matringa's voice remained calm in spite of the tension of the situation quickly ramping up. "This is completely unnecessary. I don't appreciate these accusations, nor will I have you going through my house like some kind of common bandit. There are laws in place you are breaking simply by *making* such demands!"

For a long moment, there was silence as Cinder contemplated the glaring Signora. As seconds ticked by, Bella's heart sank. She just *knew* he was going to turn away and leave.

"I suppose I'll just have to explain myself to the people who make those laws," Cinder finally spat out, taking a step toward the entrance of the building. "You know, the King and Queen? I like to call them *Father and Mother*."

"You... *little*..." Matringa took a deep breath, then another, finally letting out a slow, dark chuckle. "So this is how it's going to end? After years of effort, after marrying that *worm* of a merchant and having to fight day in and day out with his daughter, only for her to defy me at every opportunity? After all of that... I'm exposed because a spoiled prince who's using a *shoe* of all things to prevent bewitchment ignores me? You want me to be a criminal? *Fine!*"

The hedges, which had been wide open across the driveway into the estate, twisted and shifted, closing off all exits from the area. Then tendrils of sticks, vines, and thorns shot out of the dense shrubbery, grasping anyone and anything nearby.

"She's a *Hedge Witch!*" Captain Williams bellowed out as he reacted instantly, drawing his sword and charging at the three members of house Vigatori on the lawn; who simply scoffed at him with sneering expressions, vanishing from view as Malvagio pulled out a paper and flicked it.

"No! They can't get away!" Bella breathed in panic, as quietly as she could. "Someone out there, please, *stop* them!"

Brawwah!

The frantic activity on the lawn slowed as all eyes turned to the six enormous black tigers that had just burst through the windows of the manor and let out an earth-shaking roar.

"Bewitched Ascended Beasts! To me! Form up and prepare for battle!" Cinder lifted his sword, glowing with an intense light, then swung it down, pointing the tip of his blade at the charging creatures.

A thick column of fire burst out, catching one of the surprised creatures in an immolation and utterly consuming it. Bella stumbled back from the window as a blast of hot air swirled upward, narrowly avoiding the shattering glass of the window as it rained into the room.

"He can make tigers *explode*, and I can *ask* mice to do things for me? No fair!"

FORTY-FOUR

THE DEATH of the first tiger sent the others into a rage, all five of the enormous Beasts focusing their fury on the source of the flame: Prince Cinder. Bella had rushed back to the blasted-out window, the cacophony of battle drawing her to return, even though the shards of glass cut into her feet. Angry roars were countered with grunts of exertion and sharp orders from the royal guards protecting the prince, and huge paws were caught on the standard-issue kite shields they were required to carry at all times.

Intense flashes of fire lit the front yard of the estate brighter than the noontime sun, leaving spots of slowly fading light in Bella's eyes as she tried to see what all was happening. Cinder's voice, intense yet calm, floated over the sounds of the melee for a moment, "They are too close! I can't crisp them without risking-"

"*Lances*!" An authoritative voice cut off the prince just before a series of strikes landed on the raised shields, blocking the deadly claws and majority of the force but sending those impacted stumbling back. "If we can't destroy them at a distance, we'll cut them down piece by piece. Fear not, Your

Highness, though they're formidable, we have them outnumbered and outmatched!"

From where Bella was standing, she could see that the guardsman was not merely offering platitudes. Though the front line had been pushed back, more warriors were arriving by the moment, each clearly trained for such dangerous encounters. The tide began to turn against the rampaging beasts, as the coordinated defenders adjusted their tactics and methodically pressed each advantage they earned for themselves.

Another of the beasts was felled, a huge splash of sickly black blood pouring out of its corpse as it was beheaded to ensure it wasn't just playing dead. Seeing one of the tormentors of her small fuzzy friends being put down like the rabid beast it truly was, Bella leaned forward against the remnants of the shattered window, a deep feeling of satisfaction filling her. With a third of the creatures put down, the others turned desperate, fighting to destroy as well as break through the line of guardsmen.

Another of them was culled, and the defenders of the kingdom pushed forward to finish off the final trio.

"They're going to win!" Bella's eyes were sparkling in exuberance, but a sinister rustling from behind her drew her attention back to a more imminent concern. The hedge—which had sealed her into the attic—was shifting, twisting, becoming more gnarled and lively. Moments after she looked over at it in concern, thick vines began dropping out of the main body of the hedge, immediately growing thorns dripping with dark liquid along their entire length. They started stretching toward her, moving slowly, as they were catching on the floor and cutting through it with just a hint of resistance—like a knife going through very cold butter.

Cold dread settled in her chest as Bella realized Matringa must have decided to eliminate her. As the deadly vines inched toward her, the fear turned to fury. "After all this, after you've been caught out, you're trying to destroy me out of... what? Spite? No matter what Cattiva's song might have made you think, I'm *not* going to go quietly. If I'm going down... you're coming with me!"

Drawing in a deep breath, and knowing full well that making noise would cause the hedge to grow toward her faster, Bella began to hum, quickly raising her voice into a powerful crescendo and tapping into her Breakthrough Skill for the first time.

"Rise small creatures, from field and glen; heed the call from my voice again! Swarms assemble at my command; with Serenade of the Swarm, I make my stand!"

Skill increase! Serenade of the Swarm [Level 0 (None) → Level 1 (Minimal)]!

Requirement to advance to level 2: Create a swarm of no less than 500 creatures.

Perhaps it was because she was so deeply in tune with her skill at that moment, Bella didn't even need to double check the information that had been inserted into her mind. She just... *knew* what the system was telling her. It almost distracted her enough to falter, but just before the magic could be broken, Bella belted out her next verse.

"Fleet of foot or swift of wing, find that Witch and make her sting! Nip and gnaw, claw and bite. Surround Matringa and, for once, fill her *with fright! It's a lot to ask; it's not just for a thrill... force her to contend with my Breakthrough Skill!"*

As Bella's magically potent song lifted into the air, two things happened simultaneously. First, the hedge in the room with her vibrated violently, thrashing around and absolutely *shredding* the floor and furniture between the two of them. Second, the sounds of battle, shouting, roaring, clashing of metal... all of it was completely overwhelmed by the cacophony of nature itself screeching into action to answer her call to arms.

From hollows and nests, from every crevice a creature called home, animals erupted into motion. The first to arrive were birds, those able to simply fly over the line of protective hedges. Sparrows, robins, cardinals, then crows and larger birds such as chickens that exploded out of their coop in the distance. Screeching and intense flapping of wings made it hard to hear anything else, and the day itself seemed to turn into dusk with the presence of so many creatures flying to and fro.

"-happening? Is this the Witch?" a fearful voice called out, barely able to be heard. Bella winced as she realized some of the creatures she was calling might be attacked by those trying to rescue her. She kept her mind carefully focused on Matringa, hoping the animals wouldn't so much as swerve too close to the royal procession.

Next came the hustle and bustle of small mammals, the vast majority of them trapped outside the estate. A quick glance out the window showed Bella that they were throwing themselves in droves against the hedges, causing her to nearly choke up and stop singing when she realized she didn't have enough control over the Breakthrough Skill to get them to stay away from the deadly flora.

Wham! Rii~i~ip!

Bella dodged away from the window as a thorn-coated branch burst through an armchair and shot toward her, slamming into the wood of the wall hard enough to shake the last bits of glass out of the window frame. It twisted back and forth, tearing a huge gouge out of the wall before swinging around, as if trying to find where she had gone. Continuing to sing as loudly as she could, Bella carefully made her way around the obstacles filling the attic, knowing that the magic of her song would reach farther than the sound of it.

A high-pitched feminine scream shattered the air, followed

by the sounds of delighted birds as they found a target and began swarming it. Screeches of pain followed a moment later, and Bella winced as she recognized Cattiva's voice through the crying. She amended her song slightly, adjusting the intent of her targets slightly, *"Not that one, she's too small; go for the hidden one who's very tall!"*

Then she returned to singing her first portion of the song once more, hoping it would be enough. Snippets of conversation from down below started floating up, only able to be heard thanks to whatever skill amplified them so powerfully.

"-the last of them, find the Witch!"

"Birds got one-"

"Step aside! Cinder, I need that *ashed*!" Following this shouted order, there was a flare of light that turned the gentle sunbeams in the room into an almost palpable force. "This section of hedges is out of the way; get the non-combatants out of here!"

"The hard part is going to be-"

"Someone find the *hostage*!" Cinder's bellow made the fearful expression on Bella's face relax slightly. They were coming to find her. She hadn't been forgotten. Moments later, there was a familiar **slam** as the front doors were hurled open, along with the muted sound of glass breaking as what must've been the full-length mirror in the entryway was destroyed.

She sang at the top of her lungs, doing her very best to be a beacon for the guardsmen searching her out. The very air around Bella resonated with melody and power as she directed countless small creatures outside of her field of vision.

"I can hear her! Up the stairs, go, *go*!"

The floor shook as heavily-armored men charged up the stairs, their weight and strength causing the poorly-maintained manor to creak and groan in protest. As they approached, the hedge moved faster, frantically swinging around and obliterating whatever it touched. When it felt itself touch something at least as large as a chair, the thorny branch would wrap around it and squeeze until it exploded into splinters.

Bella dodged to the side, tripping over some small crate as the branch uncoiled in a swipe at her, slicing through the air where she'd been standing but a moment before. From her new position on the ground, she rolled to the side, narrowly avoiding a lash of the branch, which sliced right through the wooden floorboards she'd been laying on.

Hopping to her feet, Bella took a deep breath and choked on the thick dust in the air. She gagged at the sudden intrusion of dry mold and particles clogging the air around her, trying to force her words out but only managing to let out a harsh cough. As she pushed away from the hedge, the Beast Singer felt a wave of exhaustion roll over her as her Breakthrough Skill ended.

"She went quiet! Move faster, something must be terribly wrong!" The shouting was almost on her level, cutting through the tumult of the branches slapping furniture to and fro. Chairs and tables were tossed into the air, some of them impacting Bella as she rushed to stay out of range of the still-growing vines.

Skill increase! Serenade of the Swarm [Level 1 (Minimal) → Level 2 (Limited)]!
Requirement to advance to level 3: Create a swarm of no less than 1,000 creatures.

"By the system, what *is* that?" The question was followed by a metallic clunk, reminiscent of someone getting smacked for asking a foolish question.

"It's a Hedge Witch. That's a hedge. *Think* man!" Following the chastisement, there was a ringing sound of metal on wood. "Abyss, that's hard as steel! Get chopping; this is going to take a minute!"

Those words put a scowl on Bella's face. Going by how rapidly the vines were growing, at this point, she may not *have* a full minute. Glancing toward the doorway, she saw another branch starting to swing directly at her, barely allowing enough time to calculate her next movement. A duck and a sidestep allowed her to evade the dripping thorns, but only just.

Then a branch went under a table and flipped the entire thing, sending everything stacked on it flying around the room like shrapnel from an artillery spell. The huge oak swung up over her, then crashed down, driving her to the ground and only avoiding crushing her thanks to being caught by the larger furniture around her—which were reduced to splinters and remnants. Happily, the hedge seemed confused by the noise and vibration coming from different sections of the room at the same time and appeared to have lost its lock on her presence.

Thorns raked across the underside of the table above Bella, punching through slightly as they slithered overhead like a snake pursuing a frog. Doing her very best to barely even breathe, and certainly not make a sound, Bella held perfectly still as the contents of the attic were brutally shredded. Then a sound rang out, and the hedge went perfectly still.

It was a scream, this time from a much more mature throat. "You *killed* her!"

"Witch!" the authoritative voice bellowed in return. "Accept a quick death! For crimes against the kingdom, I hereby-"

"*Fool!*" Matringa's voice shook the very air, the pressure of her shout shattering the remainder of the windows in the manor. "Crimes against the kingdom? *I* am the only reason this kingdom yet stands! My sisters and I have weakened your enemies, brought a plague upon them to force them to kneel so you can sally forth to conquer them. My power has held the disease at bay, and I am repaid by being attacked in my own home? My oldest daughter put to the sword?"

"Her death was unfortunate, but perhaps she should not have cloaked herself in an illusion of *you* in order to give *you* a chance to escape!" The man, who must have been in charge of the royal guard, returned without a hint of pity in his voice. "Her death is on your head, and I refuse to accept that you did not order her to sacrifice herself so you could run. That's exactly what I would expect from a *Villain*."

"You want a Villain? You want to test your mettle against the Hedge Witch herself?" Matringa actually *cackled*, all of the dignity and decorum she'd always insisted were necessary at all times nowhere to be seen. "*Fine!*"

Bella let out a yelp as the hedge which had been seeking her out exploded upward, tearing the roof off the building as it answered Matringa's call.

FORTY-FIVE

"YOU SHOULD KNOW BETTER than to anger a *Witch*!" Matringa's howling voice convinced Bella to work harder to shift herself from under the table, but no matter how she pushed, she couldn't move the several hundred pounds of wood caging her in. "It can put you in a *prickly* situation!"

The house shook under Bella as the roof and mobile hedge slammed into the ground, damaging the walls of the main floor. Shredded and splintered items fell to the ground all around her, and the young woman let out a croaking shriek as the table ominously shifted closer to her.

"Over there!" a nearby voice called, and Bella weakly pounded on the table to show them where she was. Moments later, the obstacle between them was tossed out of the way as easily as the vile hedge had thrown it at her. Several hands reach down, scooping her off the floor and gently lifting her up and away.

In other circumstances, she may have been frustrated or embarrassed by being hauled around like a child, but between the wave of exhaustion from activating her Breakthrough Skill, the long sleepless night, and avoiding the searching thorns, she was more than ready to let someone else do the heavy lifting for a little while. "Isabella Vigatori, are you injured?"

"No," she managed to croak out, getting handed a water skin a moment later. She gratefully grabbed it, sprayed a bit of the liquid into her mouth, and spit out what felt like a mouthful of black dust. Bella tried again, this time managing to moisten her throat enough to have a short conversation. "What happened? Did my creatures help?"

"That was you?" The guards looked at each other then turned and started picking their way across the debris of the attic. "The birds managed to find the Witch, who was cloaked with an illusion, but it was an illusion within an illusion. The oldest daughter was cut down upon appearing; the youngest is bleeding heavily from scratches and pecking of various birds."

Bella woozily tried to make sense of what she was hearing. "How do you know? Weren't you in the house?"

"The Captain has a skill that keeps us apprised of the situation," the second guard told her shortly. "Where are you going to be safest? There's a full-on battle against a Witch going on out there, but the house might collapse during it."

"I need to see what's going on!" Bella demanded as she finally mustered enough energy to push herself away from the guard and onto her own feet. "All I need is a clear line of sight. I'll be fine now, go help the prince!"

The first guard ran off without another word, sprinting to the hole in the ceiling and throwing himself out into open air. Hesitating slightly, the second guard took a deep breath and shook his head. "The prince wants you safe, and he sent us to protect you. But I agree with you; he needs help. It's not like the queen would accept that I listened to his orders over hers, so… stay safe."

So saying, he followed his brother-in-arms through the opening, vanishing from sight a moment later. Bella ran after them, coming to a stop before going over the edge like the royal guardsman had, so she could have a clear view of the battle below.

And what a battle it was.

"Come now, surely you can do better than *that*!" Matringa, dressed in a voluminous, poofy, formal dress darted through the attacks raining down on her without allowing even one to *scrape* against the fabric of her gown. "What is this, Your Highness? First ever battle? *Adorable*."

Moving with supernatural speed, Matringa spun away and leapt high in the air, casually evading a catastrophic burst of flame. Mocking laughter rang out over the torrent of flame, and she spun in the air, pointing at a half-dozen places around the yard. The hedges fully surrounding the estate uprooted themselves, joining into the fray as they were *Masterfully* puppeteered by the Witch.

Prince Cinder did his best to anticipate her movements, a thick layer of flame swirling around him as he tracked her insectile movements across the yard. Each time she moved back to avoid a swing of a sword, a spinning fireball landed just far enough away to engulf her while leaving his soldiers unsinged. "Keep her in place! We cannot allow someone like her to escape into the kingdom!"

"I'm not trying to *escape*, Cinder!" Matringa responded in her usual sickly sweet voice. "I'm just trying to teach you a lesson. Don't worry, I'll ensure you learn it well. First, I'll break your toys-"

A huge wall of greenery crashed down onto a guard who was at the fringes of the fight, engulfing him for a long moment. There was a quickly cut-off scream before the hedges started moving forward again—leaving behind no sign of the man. Cinder let out a shout of grief then turned and amped up his flames.

His power lanced out, rushing into the greenery… and only ever so slowly beginning to char through it.

Matringa saw this and laughed. "You think your piddly

little skill would be enough to destroy *my* working? You might find my magic *overgrown* with surprises. What an adorable little temper tantrum. Don't worry... I've been practicing on how to fix that. As I was saying, once we're done playing with your toys, I'll introduce you to your new bride. It might take a few hours, maybe even a day or two, but eventually, you'll come to realize that Cattiva is your best option. A little music might even help to set the mood!"

Matringa was once more on the move, a blur of graceful violence. She grabbed the wrist of a guard as he swung his sword down at her, stopping him cold as though he'd punched a wall. Her other hand shot forward, catching the man around the neck. She twisted and turned, swinging the heavily armored guard through the air as easily as if she were shaking out a towel. He hit the ground and bounced, rolling for half a dozen feet before slowing.

The hedges had been edging closer, and a thick branch lashed out at the man. He got his bearings just in time, pulling his shield up and taking the blow on its surface—only to get tossed back the way he had come.

"Group together!" the captain of the guard shouted, positioning himself in front and just to the right of Cinder, so as to not block the powerful young man's line of sight. "Cinder, you were able to burn down a section of the hedges earlier; what's changed?"

"Her power must have a stabilizing influence!" Cinder shouted back, narrowing his eyes and focusing as sparks began dancing in the air around him. Each of them shot forward, transforming into a massive fireball and chasing Matringa across the lawn in a conflagratory barrage.

"Cinder, *Cinder*, you should really treat your future mother-in-law better!" Matringa called to him in a sing-song tone. "I'm going to have to take one of your fingers for that!"

Bella blanched at the memory of how her stepmother had been acting that morning and how close she'd come to losing her toes. Mustering her energy, she focused on the sprinting Witch and began to hum. She felt something burning deep inside her, like a muscle that had been worked too vigorously, but she pushed the sensation to the side and burst into song.

Serenade of the Swarm reactivated, and the sky above her began filling with birds. Once it had begun, it was easy to maintain, and Bella simply called as many creatures as her power would reach. For now, she didn't have them swoop at the deadly Witch far below, instead mustering them in one area. Birds began to circle in the sky, and small creatures began roiling over each other directly below them—all being pulled to one general location.

In the distance, Cinder raised his hands, his left reaching out toward Matringa as if in supplication, while the right went above his head as though he were asking a question in a class-room. Then he *twisted*, and the ground around the Witch in a wide circle burst into a roaring flame.

Matringa simply stepped through them, shaking her head as she slapped the flames clinging to her dress, instantly snuffing them out. "If that's the only thing you can do, I suppose it's a good thing you're a prince. Useless for every-thing but your bloodline. Really, your parents should have made you *branch* out more!"

She moved her arms in a mockery of his exaggerated motions, but to much greater effect. Thick branches erupted from the hedges, which had been tightening their encir-clement of the royal procession, slamming into the wagons and reducing them to splinters in mere moments. Most of the non-combatants had managed to flee by this point, but the soldiers were hard-pressed to maintain their formation.

Only the fact that they were wearing heavy armor instead of the ceremonial version at the insistence of the prince kept them standing as thorns scratched against their breastplates, and roots prodded at their boots and grieves, looking for weak points to push into.

"Command, *active blades!*" the captain suddenly called out, and the swords of the men around him began to shine with light. On their next swings, the weapons cut through the wooden defenses of the hedges as if they were mundane plants. "Your Highness, the magical weapons have been activated; we are *officially* on a time limit!"

In the attic, Bella was beginning to get light-headed as she sang out as long as she could. The swarm growing due to her power was becoming antsy, some of the larger creatures lashing out at the smaller ones. Even so, she knew it wasn't enough—not yet. She needed to wait to send them until they'd be able to do more than inconvenience her Witch of a stepmother.

"Oh, look, they brought out the *shiny* toys!" Matringa mocked the guards who were slashing and parrying the thick thorns. "I can just keep them growing and growing and growing... because this is *my* power. Using captured energy to keep you alive won't work for long. Unless...! Prince Cinder!"

"Hold your silence, Witch!" the captain replied on Cinder's behalf.

Matringa waved at the desperate guards casually, as if calling for silence. "Those magic swords, with their borrowed power, certainly look pretty as they shine like robin's eggs. I just have to ask, is that your something borrowed, something blue? Only two more little items, and we can have a proper wedding ceremony! Let me help by giving you something *old!*"

The hedges shifted to the side, rolling together and condensing. The wood latched onto itself, the thorns of one branch burrowing into the main trunk of another section. After only a few moments, hundreds upon hundreds of feet of hedges had condensed into a massive, writhing tumbleweed. It began rolling toward the group of guards protecting the prince, picking up speed *far* too quickly.

"Then allow me to contribute!" a new voice rang out, just

before a bolt of sparkling light arced through the air and sank into the hedge ball. "Something *new!*"

A detonation followed the proclamation, a soundless burst of energy that swept through the hedge and transformed a large chunk of it into hornets. With a threatening buzz, the newly created insects swarmed into the air and swept toward Matringa. For the first time in the battle, the Witch showed not only surprise but a hint of fear.

"You *dare* to interfere?" she howled, lifting her hands and releasing a thick plume of green spores, catching most of the insects and causing them to drop out of the air with loud thuds which belied their small size. Then, in a moment which caused Bella no small amount of concern, Matringa turned and glared at her. "I was saving that for *your* little pets, my pet!"

The tumbleweed had unraveled but was quickly reforming. But that wasn't the center of attention for the quickly tiring warriors; they were focused on the newcomer who was striding across the lawn with a stern expression on her face.

"Cinder, we may actually have a chance." The Captain of the Guard hadn't bothered to deactivate his skill, which made his voice reach everyone in range. He gestured wearily at the ageless woman who was approaching the seething Witch *far* too casually.

"That's the Great Fairy… Bibbidy the Evoker."

FORTY-SIX

"YOU HAVE NO POWER HERE, *FAIRY*!" Matringa screeched as she jabbed a finger at Bibbidy. "What are you going to do, *sell* me something? You're on my land, and I didn't start this fight! I haven't broken any of the accords, so you can't get involved."

"I'm here for Bella," the ageless woman sternly explained, remaining cautious but confident. Through her exhaustion, Bella felt a swell of love and gratitude for her godmother, finding the energy to hold on just a little bit longer. "I was given the right to protect her by her father, by her mother, and you have forfeited your control over her by trapping her in violation of a royal decree."

"You can't have her!" Matringa was practically foaming at the mouth as she screeched, "We determined she would be the perfect fuel *years* ago; why else would we have eliminated *both* obstacles to getting her under my thumb? Once she's eighteen, and without even an Advanced Class, I'll be taking her to the sea. After we extract her voice, we'll be able to control the spread of the plague, even in areas where it would otherwise be too extensive. Every kingdom on the planet will grovel or fall to the black death!"

"So, it *was* you who killed her parents? Or your kind, at

least?" Bibbidy shifted her stance, lifting her hands into the air. "Lucky me. I get to save my goddaughter, avenge Boppity and Boo, *and* stop you. It's shaping up to be a beautiful day."

Matringa let out a growling screech, and the much-diminished tumble-hedge began clattering across the lawn toward them. "I must thank you for improving my little garden so much... without all the dead weight of mundane wood and leaves, the bewitched sections are much easier to control. Let me *demonstrate!*"

Bella flinched as enormous spikes erupted from the rolling mass of vegetation striking at her godmother with cruel viciousness. But, instead of impaling the Fairy, a small panel of light appeared in the air and stopped the attacks dead each time they rained down on her.

"You were right about one thing, Matringa the Hedge Witch of the vile *Grimelias* Coven." Bibbidy's voice was raised, pitched to carry as far as possible. "I can't get directly involved; I can't attack you on your own land."

"How do you know that name?" Matringa raced forward, adding her own formidable strength to the brutal attacks coming at the ferry from all angles. "Who *broke*? We all swore an oath to take our secrets to the grave. *Name the oathbreaker!*"

"What I can do... is stay between you and everyone else while *they* fight." The Fairy's words were slightly strained, but their meaning was clear. The Royal Guard shifted into action, rushing forward with their gleaning swords to begin hacking away at the evil bush.

Matringa screeched and slapped at her neck, yanking away a hornet that had just jabbed down with its stinger.

Seeing that her evil stepmother had become decidedly distracted, Bella leaned forward and shifted the tone of her song. Immediately, hundreds of creatures began rushing across the yard. All manner of wild beasts snarled and snapped as the serenade pushed them into action. Her voice took on a rhythmic, chanting quality as her head swam, unused to the feeling of devoting so much of her energy to a skill for such a long period of time.

A handful of creatures on the ground made it through the thrashing vines, immediately working to savage Matringa's ankles. Their bites barely broke the skin, their claws scrabbling against her epidermis as though it were platemail. The birds had better luck, swooping in and spreading their wings wide to block her view as they lashed out with talon and beak, doing their best to force her eyes closed so the guards could cut through her.

The Witch was having none of it, and with each slap of her hands, dozens of birds were knocked from the air, never to flap again. She began moving back and forth, stomping down to *crunch* little creatures, refocusing her attacks on the Fairy who stubbornly placed herself between the elongated claws of the Witch and the guards.

Bella's perception of the fight began to waver, her vision tunneling as she pushed herself to keep her Breakthrough Skill active, targeting the person who had tormented her for most of her young adult life. She slipped, her mind turning off for a moment before restarting, and Bella found herself falling through the hole in the wall, the ground coming toward her as though in slow motion. "N-no, no, *no!*"

The animals attacking Matringa shifted immediately, winging and sprinting toward her in the same instant. By the time she'd fallen halfway to the ground, Bella was starting to slam into feathery bodies. When she'd reached the three quarters mark, scores of avians were flapping their wings, trying to slow her momentum. Only a few feet from the ground, a wave of flesh and fur rose up to meet her, all combining to slow her just enough to knock the wind out of her instead of pulverizing her bones.

"Bella!" Cinder called as he noticed the woman he'd followed home hit the ground.

"Bella?" Bibbidy's voice held a note of concern, and

Matringa used her moment of distraction to the utmost, slamming a hand into the Fairy's torso and sending her skipping across the ground.

Matringa turned slightly, facing the house where a pile of creatures were trying to untangle themselves. With a satisfied sigh, she leaned forward. *"Bella~a~a..."*

Her words drifted through the air like a long, drawn-out sigh. Then she was sprinting across the lawn, leaning forward and using the elongated claws which had pushed through her fingertips to stabilize herself when she would've otherwise fallen, in some moments running on all fours to maximize her speed. She slammed into the small creatures, who did their best to protect their friend but were overwhelmed in an instant by her strength and speed.

Matringa turned sharply, holding Bella by the back of her neck high above the ground. "Nobody come any closer! All of us want this child, but I bet I'm the only one willing to sacrifice her to get away."

"That's a clear violation of the accords!" Bibbidy shouted across the lawn as she rushed closer, only to come to a quick stop as Matringa lifted her off hand and trailed her claws across Bella's neck.

"Silly Fairy... I've already got *my* mark." Matringa cackled as she rubbed her wrist across her right cheek, causing a thick layer of makeup to be rubbed away and reveal a sickly looking black and green 'X'. "That's right, I've already maximized my negative reputation with the system. So tell me, *Great Fairy*, what's another little murder going to hurt?"

"Well, I admit this is a bad situation and not what I expected," Bibbidy stated with great discomfort, shifting back and forth in place and flexing her hands. "A Witch on the lawn, half through the day after dawn-"

"You can *finish* that evocation," Matringa's fingers were back at Bella's neck, and she started to slowly walk backward toward the edge of the estate's property. "Or... hear me out now, *or*… she can live a little bit longer. Up to you, really. Who knows? Maybe you'll even be able to rescue her someday. Isn't *that* a wonderful thought? You just keep thinking happy thoughts, and I'll fly away."

Bella was starting to get a bit sick to her stomach, being tossed back and forth in the air as she was. Between her exhaustion and the stress of the moment, she almost missed the feeling of tiny claws gripping her legs and scrabbling upward. Her eyes went wide; this was an all-too-familiar situation. She tried to choke out a demand for whatever small animal was moving on her to hold still, to keep themselves safe, but Matringa noticed her taking in a breath and lightly shook her.

"As for you, my pretty little child, *you're* coming with me." With the thick layer of makeup disturbed, Bella got a close-up view of her stepmother's true appearance. Just like the system marking on her right cheek, the rest of her flesh was aged and withering. As she looked on, the disguise melted away further, revealing deep wrinkles, warts, and pustules.

Bella tried to flinch away as the aura of evil energy around the woman merged with her true appearance, revealing them to be one and the same. Matringa cackled in Bella's face, sending a wash of rancid breath pouring over her. "Surprised by what you see? Imagine the sheer amount of effort I've had to go to over the years to keep you from catching me unawares. These masks aren't free, and your abyssal snooping nearly cost you your life on… oh, *so* many occasions. But finally…"

The Witch's eyes were wide, far too wide, showing how the whites of her eyes were actually bloodshot and jaundiced. "*Finally*… I get to hand you over and pay all debts. She'll be so pleased with me, how well I played my role. Maybe she'll even —*Ahh!*"

A bright light rippled in the air as Matringa tried to step

out into the road, only to be repelled by a barrier sparkling like starlight.

Bibbidy's voice floated across the lawn. "Did I *forget* to mention that I set up a small isolation area? Don't worry... too much. It'll come down when I deem Bella to be safe."

"*Safe*, you say? There's a plague out there, and I guarantee you it's about to get much, *much* worse around here." Matringa pulled Bella in close, and the young woman froze in terror even as a small lump wriggled higher under her dress. "I'm her *stepmother*. I'm her legal guardian! She's ever so safe with me... so long as you get this starlight barricade out of my way."

Bibbidy's eyes were wide, and she slowly raised her hands in the air. "You know that's not how it works, Witch. I can't take it down until the conditions are fulfilled."

"Conditions? Magic? Good, *good*... I'll add my own to the mix." The Witch dropped her hand to her side, pulling out a small orb which *exuded* evil to Bella's eyes. She held it to her mouth and whispered a word that cracked it and sent the energy flowing up and away. "*Pestice...*"

"It's done, Fairy. The curse is active, and even now, the populace is becoming infected." After Matringa's words, the tension mounted in the air as both groups stared at each other, each unwilling to budge in the slightest.

"Last. *Chance!*" Everyone flinched as spittle flew from Matringa's mouth when she shouted, shoving her clawed finger accusingly at the Fairy. "If I reach out and feel starlight between my fingers... *she dies!*"

"Then you'll be next." Cinder's shout coincided with the man erupting with intense flames. Glowing sparkles filled the air, circling around him as his eyes roiled with energy. "Put her *down!*"

"Humm...?" Matringa shook her head in amusement as she reached back, allowing herself to be wracked with pain as she drummed the fingers of her left hand on the barrier of solid starlight. "You didn't listen? Time to pay the price. I... warned... *you.*"

She'd barely finished her sing-song statement before her hand darted back to Bella's neck with inhuman swiftness, her claws tearing into flesh and sending a spray of blood into the air.

FORTY-SEVEN

"*BELLA*!" Bibbidy screamed in horror, only for Cinder's furious bellow to drown her out.

Sparks flew off of him, swirling through the air and bursting into massive explosions all over the area—everywhere except where the Witch stood, holding her dangling step-daughter. "Ahh, ha-ha-ha-*haaa*! Don't even want to char her *corpse*, prince of flames? Then I have an effective shield, don't I?"

Hiss. A black and white tail lifted threateningly, and Matringa managed only a single step forward before screaming as a spray of foul liquid shot into her face.

Stella the skunk had finally made an appearance on the battlefield.

Thanks to being momentarily blinded and in a state of sensory overload, a spark she hadn't noticed drifted around her... only to dive into the wound Bibbidy's magical hornet had dug through the nearly-impervious flesh of the Witch. She managed a second step before her eyes cleared, only to go wide...

...as her body was reduced to ash from the inside.

The process was nearly instantaneous, as Cinder had

packed a truly *immense* amount of magic into the spark. The girl dangling in the air fell to the ground, a light coating of soot settling on her, only to vanish as the wind picked up.

Bibbidy rushed forward, digging frantically through her pack as she ran. Cinder followed at a slower pace, stumbling from exhaustion as his adrenaline began to wear off. What remained of his Royal Guard moved with him as a unit, twitchy and overly aggressive, due to a sudden influx of noise from around the estate washing over them as the starlight barrier fell and allowed sound in once more.

Then everyone recoiled, Bibbidy even letting out a low shriek… when Bella sat bolt upright with a gasp, only to devolve into a horrible coughing fit.

With a shaking hand, she reached up to her neck and pulled away a small body, tears leaking from her eyes as she gently caressed the fallen mouse's head with one finger. "Mert the Third… you truly were the bravest of all mice. You saved me… I'll never forget you."

Then Bella was wrapped in a terribly tight hug as Bibbidy fell to her knees next to her, sobbing and babbling apologies. For leaving her alone for so long, with a *Witch*, how she just couldn't get back in time to warn the prince, all because she'd been kept waiting for an audience with the queen while— unbeknownst to her—the monarch was already sending out the procession.

Though she felt it a bit strange to need to be the one to comfort her Fairy godmother, Bella shifted in her grasp and pulled her tight with one arm, her other hand busy cradling the broken body of her savior. "It's… it's going to be *okay*, Bibbidy. She's gone, and I'm… I'm *free!*"

Both of them held each other for another long minute before the godmother gently reached out for Mert. "I have the perfect place to put him until we can have a ceremony. Let me carry this burden, as the death of this little one falls squarely on my shoulders. Also… I'm not the only one who wishes to speak to you."

After a moment of hesitation, Bella nodded and handed over the mouse, and Bibbidy carried him away with all the care and solemnity that *should* be afforded a hero who fell on the battlefield.

Cinder stood nearby rather awkwardly, uncertain where he fit into this display. Bella looked over at him, also unsure of how she should be acting in the presence of the prince. Finally, the captain let out an annoyed grumble and nudged his charge forward rather abruptly.

"*Williams!*"

"Your Highness, if you're just going to stand there silently, we might as well leave." The man's beautiful armor was covered in dirt and foul tiger blood, but he moved into a resting position with his eyes on the horizon. "Men, what lovely countryside there is to be seen over there. Don't you agree? You two, go gather the fallen."

There were general murmurs of assent, and the two young adults were given as much privacy as decorum would allow. Cinder still glared at Captain Williams for a long moment, but his expression softened as he returned his gaze to Bella, who was standing up and brushing herself off. "So… I must say, on behalf of the crown, if there is anything we can do to make up for the terrible life you must have led, being controlled by a Witch right under our noses… please name it."

"Yeah." Bella let out a long, drawn-out sigh. "You think your mother would be open to advancing my class? After being trapped here for so long, I'd like to travel. Anything to get away from… here."

Both of them glanced over to the estate, Cinder wincing as he saw the extensive damage to the structure, while Bella only looked on with a sad fondness. The prince began to nod. "That will be arranged, on my honor. But that's not enough, so… think about it?"

"We can start there, and I don't know if I'll need anything else." Bella stood up straight, looking the prince in the eye. "I'm used to hard work, and I think I'll be just fine, so long as I don't have someone locking me away and keeping me from learning and doing. For now... with all this... I'm just tired."

"Well, you can't sleep here." Cinder hesitated for a moment before allowing a weak smile to appear on his lips. "In fact, you can't stay here. Her Majesty the Queen has directly requested your presence, to explain your Breakthrough Skill and... I'm sure she'll also want to know what was going on here. Let's try to find a carriage that wasn't absolutely destroyed, and get you back to the Spring Palace. You can sleep there."

"Prince Cinder." Captain Williams leaned forward, appearing gravely concerned after one of his men had run over and whispered in his ear. "The youngest fledgling Witch, Cattiva... she's nowhere to be found."

"What?" Cinder waved at the surroundings. "Find her! She can't have gone far; there was Fairy magic keeping everyone in here."

"No... we found markings of someone escaping through what appears to be a tunnel under the lawn. When the hedges were ripped up, it was exposed. Here, we found this as well." The Captain handed over a sparkling glass slipper, which had a bloody handprint on it. "We think she grabbed this, and it cut her. There are droplets of blood leading into the tunnel."

"It comes out across the road." Bella pointed in the direction of the tunnel's exit. "I dug that. Look for the opening under a bush shaped like a brooding owl."

The motion caused the utterly exhausted young woman to stumble, and she nearly fell, only to be caught by Cinder before she could slump to the ground. "We need to get you some rest. Captain, send out a search party. She must be found. Bella... I'm not sure if you could ride a horse-"

"I'd be happy to offer you a ride." Bibbidy called as she

began walking over, an intricate jewelry box held between her hands. "First, Bella, where should we put your little friend to rest?"

"Not here," Bella stated firmly before she swallowed, hard. "I promised them I'd take them away from this place when I went."

"Perfectly understandable." Bibbidy turned to the prince, meeting his eyes steadily. "With her parents gone, and the Witch slain, as her Fairy Godmother, I assert my right to be the guardian of Isabella Vigatori. Until she is of age to unlock her Full Class, she is under my protection."

"So long as Bella is happy with that arrangement, I see no reason to complain." Cinder shrugged, uncertain why she was making such a big deal out of the situation. Captain Williams' annoyed grumble caused the prince to glance at his guard, only to find that there was a deeply annoyed expression on the man's face. Still, he didn't speak out.

"Good." Bibbidy wrapped an arm around Bella's shoulders and guided her to the carriage. Only after Bella had been seated and was comfortably resting did she motion for the prince and his retinue to follow. Captain Williams and Cinder stepped into the carriage, sitting on a comfortable bench as the other soldiers mounted their horses and provided an honor guard as they began their journey back to the palace.

For Bella, no time seemed to pass between getting into the carriage and being gently shaken awake to get out and enter the palace. Very groggy, she walked up the marble staircase she'd fled that very morning, though it seemed like ages ago. The beautiful decorations were ignored in favor of working hard to stay awake, but luckily, she wasn't led directly into the throne room. Instead, she was given a guest suite, and a bath was drawn for her.

Bella awoke once more, barely remembering the time spent cleaning up and getting dressed before collapsing into the softest bed she'd ever had the pleasure of sleeping in.

Bibbidy was waiting for her and joined the young woman in breaking her fast. Food was brought in, empty plates were taken away, and soon Bella was fidgeting restlessly, fighting the urge to do *something*. She looked at the last plate, wondering if she should take it somewhere or clean it herself, only to have a servant interpose and whisk it away, after quickly wiping down the small table.

"You seem distracted. Do you want to talk about it?" Her godmother offered a kindly smile, but Bella only shook her head.

"Just… ingrained work habits. Hard to get out of routine, you know?"

A gentle knock at the door halted their conversation, and a servant poked her head in to inform them to prepare themselves for their audience with the queen. Bella quickly dressed in a gown which had been laid out for her, while Bibbidy didn't bother changing out of the comfortable clothes she could usually be found lounging around in. Soon, the two of them were walking into the reception area of the throne room…

Then they were led in, to meet with the queen.

Bella bowed, and to her great concern, Bibbidy only gave the slightest of nods. "Liora, always a pleasure, dear."

"Great Fairy, the pleasure is all mine, as per usual." Though the tone the queen used was quite warm, her eyes were anything but. "I hear you have taken guardianship of Isabella Vigatori? I'm certain it will be a wonderful opportunity for her to learn from you."

"Indeed." Bibbidy's answer was nonchalant, and she simply remained in place, waiting with what appeared to be a patient expression.

Queen Liora shifted slightly uncomfortably. "Isabella, may I call you Bella? I need to know what has happened here, how a Witch gained so much power in my own kingdom. Amongst *my* nobility. Please… if you are willing, leave nothing out."

Slowly at first, but gaining confidence when she wasn't interrupted, Bella told her tale, starting from when her mother had died—apparently been *killed*, if the insinuation by Matringa held any weight—and ending with the walk up the marble steps of the Spring Palace only hours previous. The entire telling, very explicitly including the locations Matringa had visited to hand over what Bella recognized as cursed objects meant to induce the plague, took quite some time.

To her credit, the queen remained silent for the majority of Bella's speech, rarely interrupting, and even then only to ask clarifying questions. When the young woman had finished speaking, the queen leaned forward and examined Bella very carefully. "If I could be so bold, might I ask about the boons from the system you mentioned? It's very rare for someone to be given something like that, and... I would very much like to know."

The focus of the queen's questions was not at all what Bella had been expecting, so she took a moment to shoot a glance at Bibbidy before answering. "I... don't mind. The first is called the 'Gift of Patience' and apparently allows me to choose which class to unlock when I finally get a chance to do so. The second was 'Incorruptible Youth,' which allows me to see cursed energy and disperse it, so long as the source is destroyed or in contact with me. That's the last of the boons, but-"

The Queen grunted and waved at someone in the distance, nodding at them and making a strange hand sign. "Thank you, Bella. That'll be incredibly helpful if we're able to track down the cursed objects you had mentioned. Then, let's-"

"I'm so sorry to interrupt you, but I don't want to give an incomplete answer." Bella gulped as the queen's full attention returned to her. "The last gift from the system wasn't a boon, exactly. At least, it wasn't called a boon. It was a Unique merit, 'Apex of the Generation'. Apparently, my next skill will be upgraded to contain at minimum five modifiers."

There was a long moment of silence as Queen Liora looked between Bella and her godmother, who showed not a hint of surprise on her face. "Fairy, you knew this, didn't you?"

"I *suspected*." Bibbidy didn't sound *smug*, but her tone was right on the edge of it. "I was sure enough that, even if I wasn't her godmother, I would have stepped in to shield her from those who might try to use the situation to their benefit instead of hers."

"What are you talking about?" Bella's voice felt tiny in the massive room, as the two incredibly powerful women glared or serenely smiled at each other. "I know that's good, but it'll just be a Basic Skill in an Advanced Class. Is that really so important?"

Liora lifted her hands and smoothed her hair back over her ears before dropping her hands to the base of her chin, folded against each other as she stared into the distance.

"It is, Bella. That is an extremely notable achievement, and I'll explain in a moment. But first, while there is no *official* ranking of skills from the system, it is quite easy to see that the more modifiers a skill has, the more powerful the user can become. The kingdom's definition of skills starts at one modifier, which is the most common among skills. So, that became colloquially known as a 'common' skill."

"I see." Bella flushed as the memory of being taunted for being 'common' reappeared in her mind for a brief moment.

"Two modifiers is considered Uncommon, three, Rare, then Epic, with five being *Legendary*. We've never seen it, but there are rumors of a sixth modifier, a Mythical skill." The queen took a breath, adjusting herself to be staring into Bella's eyes once more. "For reference, Prince Cinder, an incredibly powerful fire mage, has an Epic skill for the control of his flames. As a note, we will be having another celebration in the near future for his achievement of level nine in his skill, *Mastery*, when he slew the Witch."

"Congratulations to him," Bella murmured, her thoughts not in the present at the moment. "You're saying that, when I get my next class, I'll be starting with a *Legendary* skill? A skill potentially even more powerful than the prince's?"

"That is correct... mostly." The queen steepled her fingers, taking in a deep breath and letting it out slowly. "Bella, the real answer is: that merit does not say your next *class* skill. It says your *next* skill. If you were to marry someone, you would gain a Legendary *Conjoined* Skill... and so would they."

CHAPTER
FORTY-EIGHT

Bella was rocked gently to and fro as Bibbidy's carriage clattered along the cobblestones. Her godmother looked at her, a small smile on her face, "That was quite shocking, wasn't it?"

"She bluntly proposed to me on behalf of her son." Bella shook her head ever so slowly. "That's not how it's supposed to work, is it? Marriage is supposed to be for love."

"Let's just say there are *many* reasons to get married, and some are certainly more valid than others," Bibbidy calmly stated, somewhat avoiding the question. "I will say, that's *not* the reason I took you under my protection immediately. It's because you're my goddaughter. Because I loved your parents and you. Now, it certainly doesn't hurt you to know that someone won't be hunting you down and forcing you into marriage."

"But wouldn't I just be cast to the side after the system validates our marriage? He'd have his skill; why would they need me anymore?"

"You see… bloodlines matter, my dear. If you have such a powerful skill, and so does your husband, there's a very, *very* good chance any children the two of you have will start out with at least a legendary version as well." Bibbidy looked out the window, trying to judge their position in the city. "The Royal Family is, as you might imagine, immensely invested in having the most powerful classes and skills possible. Beyond that, offending someone with a Legendary skill by treating them poorly or trying to cast them aside... I'm certain that wouldn't end well. Not for anyone."

"I see." Bella looked down at her feet, where her glass-slipper-encased feet were swinging just above the carriage floor. "Is that a good enough reason? For me? She wanted us to be married by the end of the month."

"It certainly doesn't have to be. Their desperate grasping for power absolutely is *not* your problem." Bibbidy reached over and firmly grasped Bella's hand. "Until your eighteenth birthday, your guardian needs to give permission for a system marriage to be validated. No matter *what* happens, you will be traveling with me, or I with you. I'll make sure you're learning and experiencing the world."

She paused for a moment, and Bella thought she might be done speaking, but the Fairy simply chuckled and spoke on. "If *you* decide to marry the prince, it will be a simple legal formality, then we'll be back in my carriage and roaming the countryside. Then, after your birthday, there can be a grand celebration to celebrate your nuptials. But, if you decide that's not what you want, believe *me* when I say they won't be able to say a word against your choice."

The carriage came to a halt, and the reality of their current situation hit Bella once more. "Are you sure about us doing this, Bibbidy?"

"It's the easiest way to stay in the kingdom's good graces while you're deciding on your future," Bibbidy explained as she opened the door. "Cursed objects are not so easy to handle or get rid of. The queen likely has access to a small few anti-magic artifacts, but once they are used, they're gone forever. Even more rare are the permanent Enchanted objects that can resist and redirect dark power. Now, to combine that with the ability to directly disperse cursed energy? Unheard of."

Bella took a deep breath and stepped out of the carriage, the glass covering her foot *chiming* as it came down firmly on the stone. "I'll admit, the rewards she promised for my service are more than tempting. If I can get rid of the first object, she'll transfer my father's title and holdings to me. When it's shown that this works, the next object's destruction will bring in enough gold to live on comfortably for... forever, if I invest it wisely."

"Yet you know there are at least *five*." Bibbidy chuckled softly. "By then, they'll *need* you to marry the prince, just so they don't have to empty their vault!"

The sudden joke startled a chuckle out of Bella, and she walked forward with more confidence. Several royal guardsmen were stationed outside the front door of the building, and Bella's smile faltered as she saw wisps of dark energy seeping through the cracks in the door frame. "You need to move farther away from the doors! It can reach you there."

None of the warriors hesitated, quickly stepping away until Bella nodded. "That's far enough; I'll... I'll take it from here."

Even her Fairy godmother didn't continue on with Bella as the young woman stepped forward and firmly grasped the doorknob. Tossing the door open released a foul stench of rot and mold, but she ventured forward without hesitation. At first, she was uncertain where to go, but step by step, the dense energy in the air either became darker or lighter.

She followed the darkest path forward, finally pushing through a door into a small closet, where a stone orb was resting gently in the beak of a waist-high statue of a raven. Double checking to ensure that the darkness wasn't pouring into her, Bella saw that the vast majority of the darkness touching her instantly flowed down to swirl around her feet, and the remnants were dissipated as they came in contact with her skin. "Okay... now to do this before I lose my nerve."

Reaching out, Bella directly grasped the orb and yanked it out of the bird's mouth. It was so lifelike that she was expecting the effigy to move or *caw* at her angrily, but... it really was just a sculpture. Not quite sure what to do next, Bella decided on the most direct course of action. "Matringa handed these off quite carefully. Let's hope it's because they were *fragile!*"

She whipped the orb at the ground, where it shattered like glass.

Immediately, the room was completely suffused with energy so dark that the light of day coming through the window couldn't penetrate. Bella let out a sharp gasp as she fell to the malicious, cloying energy trying to destroy her.

Chi~i~ime!

Her shoes began to ring as though someone were swirling their finger along the rim of a crystal wine glass. The roiling energy reacted instantly, dropping out of the air and becoming denser and denser around her legs. Seeing that things were once more going as expected, Bella took a deep breath and sat down in the darkness, which came up only to her chest, leaving her head and face clear of the foul miasma.

The thinnest of layers of clean air surrounded her skin, and for quite a while, it was difficult to see any progress in the purification. Yet, ever so slowly, the darkness at the edges of the room faded away, as the glass slippers pulled the energy in close, and her system boon purified it. Finally, the last of the ick vanished with a crackle like grease spattering from a hot pan, taking the foul odor in the air with it.

Hiss.

The sound came from the opposite side of the room, drawing Bella's attention to a large, sickly rat staring at her and bearing its teeth. Her eyes went wide as she saw wisps of dark energy collected on and in the creature, but as she reached forward to try and entice it closer, to cleanse the beast, it spun and fled into a hole in the wall.

"Plague rats." Bella shivered in disgust. "At least I know how the plague has been spreading so rapidly. And... and I can do something about it!"

Several things began falling into place quickly in her mind, and Bella felt her lips curl in a snarl. "That's how she was going to control the spread of the plague using my voice. Matringa was going to control the *rats*, not the disease. Well. If she believed she could use my skills to make people sick, I *know* I can use it to keep them from *getting* sick."

The immensity of the work ahead of her if she chose to directly scour the kingdom of plague rats fell over her, and Bella felt her shoulders slump. "I can't do this alone. Even just me and Bibbidy, Fairy and all, is just too few. I'm going to need help, resources, and... and... oh. Is this what she meant? That some reasons for marriage are more valid than others?"

"Becoming the person in charge means giving up doing only what *you* want to do or what's best for only yourself." Bibbidy's voice cut in as the Fairy walked down the hallway and offered her hand to Bella. "Good work destroying that curse, Bella. I knew you could do it."

"Thanks. I've gotten pretty good at cleaning over the years, and this was even easier. Just had to sit there." The young woman responded distractedly. "It's plague rats, Godmother. That's how this disease is being spread. Could I fix this problem by myself?"

"Potentially." The Fairy started to lead them out of the house, which was already smelling cleaner. "I admit having the resources and authority to make the necessary decisions would be quite beneficial, but you may be able to gain that simply by working in *conjunction* with the crown."

They stepped out of the building, pausing in surprise as a group of men on horses came to a stop, with one of them carefully hopping off and walking toward them. "Bella! I've been looking everywhere for you."

"Prince Cinder." Bella gave a polite curtsy. "What can I do for you today? I have good news; I was able to destroy the first cursed object."

"Oh! That's wonderful!" A bright smile appeared on his face, and his eyes began swirling with light. "I wanted to tell you in person, I managed to achieve Mastery with my skill, and the requirement to reach Perfection is practically laughable in comparison. I'd estimate two, maybe three years at the *maximum* before I have my own Breakthrough Skill!"

Bella waited for anything else, only politely nodding at his words. Cinder frowned, looking over his shoulder at his guards before returning his eyes to her, puzzlement clear on his face. "I'm sorry, I thought you would be more enthusiastic about this news. Our conversation at the ball... both of us are pursuing Perfection, are we not?"

"It's not that. Apologies, the queen had already told us about your skill increase." Bella smiled at him more sincerely. "Really, that's wonderful! Congratulations."

"What's going on here?" Cinder swallowed hard, seeming to be working against his instincts. "Why are you acting so... cold? I *hate* cold. I thought that after all we've been through in the last few days, we would at least be friends?"

"Friends?" Bella scoffed and chuckled. "Prince Cinder, is it possible you don't know that your mother asked me to marry you and is demanding an answer by the end of the week?"

"She *what?*" Cinder yelped and physically recoiled, managing to control himself after only a flinch of reaction. "I... I... Bella, it's not you, it's just that... I've been eighteen for less than half a week. I'm in no rush to wed."

Taking in a deep breath, Bella let it out in a long sigh of relief. "Thank goodness, I thought maybe you were putting her up to it."

"*No!*"

Bella cocked her head to the side slightly, her smile fading into a frown. "Do I disgust you so much that even the idea of marrying me is abhorrent?"

"No-*what*-you're... oh." Cinder sputtered to a stop as he saw the mischievous smile on her face. "You're teasing me! So we *are* friends?"

After a few more moments, Prince Cinder and one of his guards joined Bella and the Fairy in her carriage. Getting serious, the Beast Singer explained the interaction between the rats and the cursed objects, at the end of which, all parties lapsed into shocked silence.

"Rats..." Cinder shook his head in frustration. "They're so small, and they're *everywhere*. How can we possibly hope to destroy them in time to save the people of the kingdom? I hate to admit it, but the Witches chose their vector for disease well."

"There are a couple options to make it happen, actually..." Bella gulped as the Prince looked at her with eyes full of hope, and Bibbidy slowly turned with a raised eyebrow. "One of the options even offers excellent odds."

"Bella. Are you *sure* about this? Is this the choice *you* want to make?" Bibbidy interjected sharply.

"It's not only my choice to make, Godmother," Bella replied firmly. Steeling herself, she took a deep breath and explained to Cinder exactly *why* the Queen wanted the two of them to wed. The five-modifier skill each of them would gain, how the kingdom would become more powerful by having stronger heirs in the future, and how two people with a skill able to control enormous numbers of creatures *and* fire might tip the scales in favor of the kingdom's survival.

At first, Prince Cinder was shocked at the revelation, but as she finished her explanation and fell into silence, he slowly began to nod. "I see. That's... there are some very good reasons for her blatant actions. But... a system marriage is different from just being married. Beyond that, someday I will be king. You would be queen. Do you want that kind of responsibility? You want to travel, to see the world. And, *and*! You just got to safety. If you go out there, destroying curses and rats, the Witches might come after you."

"There has to be a world left to see, Prince Cinder," Bella calmly stated, all of her thoughts coming into alignment with each other. "If the Witches have their way, there won't be anywhere safe in the world... not for anyone. All of this to say... if you're willing to take the gamble that we might eventually be able to grow together and someday have a proper marriage, would you... Prince Cinder, I want to save everyone we can."

Licking her suddenly-dry lips, she met his eyes and flushed as she forced out her question.

"Would you please marry me?"

CHAPTER
FORTY-NINE

THE THRONE ROOM of the Spring Palace shimmered with a thousand hues as sunlight streamed through the stained glass windows far overhead. The marble floors had colorful patterns dancing across them, meticulously arranged decorations of flowers and silks coated the room and thousands of candles sparkling throughout the area.

Bella stood in front of the throne, heart fluttering as she tried to swallow down her nervousness. She shifted side to side, somewhat uncomfortable in the elegant dress she wore, coated with delicate lace and tiny pearls. The scholarly, powerful mage next to her looked every bit as regal as his parents… until he began fidgeting with his majestic attire.

He leaned toward Bella, rolling his eyes with annoyance as he whispered, "Flame won't harm me, yet someone figured out how to make an outfit trap heat so effectively that *I'm* sweating. Are we… we are doing the right thing, right?"

Oddly, his shifting and fidgeting calmed Bella down, and she reached out for his hand with a smile. "I think so. I guess we're going to have to find out together."

A slow, crooked grin appeared on Cinder's face, and tension noticeably left his shoulders. He let out a slow breath,

"That doesn't sound so bad. I'm even kind of looking forward to it."

"Kind of?" she teased him, squeezing his hand when he tensed back up. "I'm joking! You'll find I do that from time to time."

"Oh! Ha. *Ha!*" The awkward laugh cut off quickly after echoing around the room, and together, they turned their attention to the royals seated on their thrones. "Mother, Father. I think we are ready."

In the throne room were the few people who needed to be there to witness the system-official marriage. King Fella, Queen Liora, Bibbidy the Fairy, Captain Williams, Paca the puppy, and about thirty-seven mice. Suzy stood at the forefront of the latter group, cheerfully leading the others in a slow waltz around the marble floor.

King Fella raised his hand, and even the mice slowed and stopped, looking at him respectfully as a hush fell over the room. "We are gathered today, not just for the system to witness the union of two souls, but to honor the sacrifice these young people are making today. *Love...*"

He paused to allow the word to echo through the room. "All we have ever wanted for our son is to be able to marry in a way we were not able. To give him the option to marry for love instead of political machinations. But, like us, he's chosen to bind himself to another for a higher purpose—the well-being of our people, the future of this land. I can only hope that we set an example you can follow, where the duty we have taken on transforms into deep respect and an even deeper love."

"Cinder." The queen smoothly stepped into the silence. "You've always shown great promise as a leader. Your dedication to the kingdom, growing both your mentality and personal power to better protect the people, are qualities anyone would be proud of. But today, you have shown us that you have truly accepted what it means to be a prince."

Turning her eyes to Bella, Liora's gaze softened, and a gentle smile appeared on her face. "My daughter-to-be, your journey has not been easy, yet you have chosen the hardest road to continue walking. Your willingness to stand as a shield for people who have *failed* in their duty to shield you... I can think of nothing that would speak more toward your character and willingness to sacrifice for others. Someday, when I am no longer the queen, I know I will be able to trust you to take on the mantle."

Bibbidy stood forward, an extremely proud expression on her face as she took Bella's right hand and Cinder's left, looking between them as she spoke. "May your marriage be blessed with joy and the unwavering support of all those you are standing for. While circumstances may not show it, I believe the story of your eventual love will be sung for generations. May the stars of the system guide you into creating a kingdom filled with peace and prosperity."

The king and queen stood from their thrones as Bibbidy took the hands she was holding and placed them together before moving to stand on Bella's left. Though he needed the assistance of a cane, the king stepped forward and reached his hand out for the Fairy godmother's. His other hand took the queen's, and she joined hands with her son.

They held that pose for a long moment, then Bella and Cinder's right hands were pulled up to cross over each other, creating an 'X' that they held in midair.

Seeing that everyone was in position, the wounded monarch took a deep breath. "As the system-recognized king of this land, I call upon the system to make this marriage official, with the blessing of the mother and father of the groom and the blessing of the Great Fairy Bibbidy, guardian of the bride."

Immediately, time seemed to hold still as a wall of text appeared in Bella's mind.

Codex Arcane Ledger is responding to your request to become married to Crown Prince Cinder Fella!

Scanning…. Assessing… you are not being coerced or forced into making this choice.

*You are **not** at least at the age for marriage for your kingdom. Assessing… guardian override, birthdate is within the calendar year. Stipulation: 'legal marriage only', to be automatically upgraded into 'full marriage' upon the minimum age to accept a Full Class. Override accepted.
No skills or foreign substances are impairing your choices or altering your thoughts. Even so…*

Please think through this choice carefully. The effects of a system-witnessed marriage cannot be undone. Whom you marry matters greatly, as your highest unlocked skill in your most potent unlocked class will be combined with theirs to make a Conjoined Skill.

You may only ever have a single Conjoined Skill. It will increase in potency in a similar manner to your other skills, but will require the presence of your marriage partner to do so, unless they have died in a manner unrelated to you. Killing them or having them killed will forever halt the increase in skill level of your skill.

The system cannot be deceived.

If you choose not to continue this marriage witnessing and feel you may be in danger because of it, you will be instantly transported to a different Class Shrine with your safety guaranteed by the system for 24 hours.

With this knowledge, and with a clear understanding of your own thoughts, do you wish to marry Crown Prince Cinder Fella?

"I do," Bella stated at the same moment as Cinder, as if the system had aligned their thoughts and movements to be perfectly synchronized. They turned and smiled at each other, only for dozens more words to scrawl across their vision.

Marriage witnessed! Congratulations on this immensely important, <u>irreversible</u> choice! Generating Conjoined Skill.

System merit 'Apex of the Generation' has been applied. Skill modifiers modified!

*Special modifier applied: You have been granted a modifier '**Damsel of Distress**'.*

Against seemingly insurmountable odds, you transformed a set of skills or circumstances which nearly guaranteed failure or even death into a foundation for success with far-reaching and profound effects. By taking your fate into your own hands, you have broken free of the Codex Arcane Ledger's predicted outcome for your life.

Effect: When in the presence of another 'Damsel of Distress', you will be able to recognize each other as kindred spirits and [Minimally] share the benefits of your skills, if so desired, while in range. This will increase in potency with the skill it was acquired in tandem with.

Conjoined Skill: Cinder-Bella's Constant Companion. Level 1/10.

Having always been able to find companions when others would have been utterly alone, the system has fully recognized your deep desire for connection and community. While you have sacrificed much, you will forevermore have friendly fire by your side.

At any time, a familiar made of system-controlled flames, up to 1 x [1] meters in size can be sung into existence. The familiar will possess [Minimal] intelligence and will always follow your orders. If it is destroyed, it will explode violently, causing fire damage in the surrounding area. While your familiar is present, you gain a [Minimal] resistance to fire, as well as the ability to [Minimally] control fire, natural or otherwise, within your line of sight.

The form of your familiar grants an affinity to its kind, affording you [Minimal] control over any non-sentient creature of that specific type within line of sight, so long as it is smaller than the maximum size of the familiar you can create. You may change the form of your familiar by extinguishing it and singing it back into existence with a new body. Your familiar will retain its memories upon being resummoned.

When your Conjoined partner is within 1,000 meters of you, your familiar's size may increase up to the combined total size your skills allow. The control of flame and creatures will also increase by one rank, up to Perfect.

Requirement to advance to level 2: Summon your familiar for a total of 1,000 consecutive hours.

Bella and Cinder blinked and stepped away from each other, smiles rapidly appearing on both of their faces. Cinder broke the silence first. "Did you get a flame familiar?"

"I did! Did it give you fire resistance? I thought you might already have that," Bella excitedly replied as she stepped closer to hear the details of his new skill.

"So there *are* some differences!" Cinder stepped forward, clasping her hand with his. "I didn't get fire resistance; I got an affinity with animals. That's pretty helpful, as I can't currently send fire blasts from horseback without terrifying my poor stallion. Maybe I'll be able to keep him calm now… or at least calmer?"

"Nice! So that means you'll get a whole new way to practice your skills? I can't imagine riding and blasting will be the same as standing still and creating flames while intensely concentrating." Bella paused for a moment as her new husband went slack-jawed, his eyes going distant for a moment before sparkling with excitement. Seeing how he was lost in thought, she took a moment to decide the form she wanted her skill to manifest into.

With a blink, she realized the perfect design. Taking a deep breath, she sang her intent out to the system.

"With fur of flame and eyes so bright, I call upon my friend lost to the night. Mert the Third take this form. Bravest of mice, through fire reborn!"

As the last note of her short song rang out, a small explosion of flame detonated in the air above her, the quickly spreading flames pausing and yanking back in to collapse upon themselves. A moment later, a perfect replica of Mert the Third dropped to the ground, squeaking in confusion as it bounced.

"Oh, it's a mouse." Cinder let out an awkward chuckle as he stroked the head of a meter-long phoenix. "Turns out, you don't need to use mundane animals; it can be pretty much anything you think of. Hey... I wonder if I could make a tiny person, instead of an animal? There's so many things to test!"

King Fella cleared his throat loudly, breaking the two newlyweds out of their excited, skill-based chatter. "Welcome to the family, *Princess* Bella. How would you like to celebrate?"

"I've always wanted to see the world." Bella looked over at her new husband, shyly reaching out and taking his hand. "Perhaps we could start with a very thorough tour of the kingdom? I'm sure we can find things to do as we travel."

"Like controlling plague rats and *burning* them!" Cinder gasped with excitement.

Queen Liora slapped her hand to her forehead, letting out a long sigh and muttering. "I *tried* to tell him not to show overmuch his passion for pursuing skill gains-"

Bella didn't hear the queen, and her next words made the queen glance up in surprise, which quickly shifted to contemplation. "Think of the practice we're going to get! It'll be hard work, but at the end of the day, we'll be able to say we made a real difference. Plus, I can't think we'll finish before reaching at *least* Moderate rank!"

"It's a fantastic idea, Bella!" Cinder leaned in excitedly, the widening of his eyes showing the moment he realized they were practically nose to nose. He froze, then slowly leaned forward and placed his lips upon hers.

Their first kiss ended a moment later, and both of them smiled at each other.

Before the silence could stretch into the realm of uncomfortable for those around them, Cinder snapped his fingers. "After *this* kingdom, we could go and help our allies in the surrounding nations! Nothing would solidify our alliances and trade routes like stepping in and shutting down the plague in their kingdoms. Want to go see the world with me?"

"Yes!"

"Then let's *go*!"

Continue the Damsels of Distress series on Patreon.com/ DakotaKrout - or order on Amazon, geni.us/DamselsSeries.

Beauty X Beast
Rob X Punzel
Snow X Dwight
Red X Wolf

ABOUT DAKOTA KROUT

Good. Clean. Fun.

Dakota Krout is a celebrated author known for infusing fantasy novels with fun, punny, and clean humor. With multiple best-selling series—including "Divine Dungeon", "Completionist Chronicles", "Cooking With Disaster", and "Full Murderhobo"—he brings joy and laughter to readers. Dakota's work, renowned for its wit and creativity, earned a place as one of Audible's top 5 fantasy picks in 2017, a top 5 bestseller rank featured on the New York Times, and was chosen by Audible as among "the top 100 fantasy books of all time" in 2024.

Dakota's journey in publishing has been filled with gratefulness, and a deep desire to continue bringing smiles and laughter to the readers. "*I hope you Read Every Book With A Smile!*"

Connect with Dakota:
MountaindalePress.com
Patreon.com/DakotaKrout
Facebook.com/DakotaKrout
Instagram.com/DakotaKrout
Twitter.com/DakotaKrout
Discord.gg/mdp

ABOUT MOUNTAINDALE PRESS

Dakota and Danielle Krout, a husband and wife team, strive to create as well as publish excellent fantasy and science fiction novels. Self-publishing *The Divine Dungeon: Dungeon Born* in 2016 transformed their careers from Dakota's military and programming background and Danielle's Ph.D. in pharmacology to President and CEO, respectively, of a small press. Their goal is to share their success with other authors and provide captivating fiction to readers with the purpose of solidifying Mountaindale Press as the place 'Where Fantasy Transforms Reality.'

Connect with Mountaindale Press:
MountaindalePress.com
Facebook.com/MountaindalePress
Twitter.com/_Mountaindale
Instagram.com/MountaindalePress

MOUNTAINDALE PRESS TITLES
GAMELIT AND LITRPG

The Completionist Chronicles,
Cooking with Disaster,
The Divine Dungeon,
Full Murderhobo, and
Year of the Sword by Dakota Krout

Metier Apocalypse by Frank G. Albelo

A Touch of Power by Jay Boyce

Ether Collapse and
Ether Flows by Ryan DeBruyn

Unbound by Nicoli Gonnella

Lion's Lineage by Rohan Hublikar and Dakota Krout

Wolfman Warlock by James Hunter and Dakota Krout

Axe Druid,
Mephisto's Magic Online, and
High Table Hijinks by Christopher Johns

Tower of Jack by Sean Loomer

Dragon Core Chronicles by Lars Machmüller

Pixel Dust and
Necrotic Apocalypse by D. Petrie

Viceroy's Pride and
Tower of Somnus by Cale Plamann

Henchman by Carl Stubblefield

Artorian's Archives by Dennis Vanderkerken and Dakota
Krout